Dragon Rising

By Kent Giles

Dragon Rising: TEOTWAWKI

ISBN: 979-8-9945038-0-5

Second Edition

Published by:
Overwatch Press

RUSSIA
Moscow
KAZAKHSTAN
Astana
MONGOLIA
Ulaanbaatar
KYRGYZSTAN
Bishkek
TAJIKISTAN
Dushanbe
AFGHANISTAN
Kabul
CHINA
Beijing
NORTH KOREA
Pyongyang
Sea of Japan
(East Sea)
JAPAN
Tokyo
Sea of Okhotsk
Seoul
SOUTH KOREA
Yellow Sea
Shanghai
East China Sea
NEPAL
Kathmandu
BHUTAN
Thimphu
BANGLADESH
Dhaka
INDIA
New Delhi
MYANMAR
VIETNAM
Hanoi
LAOS
Vientiane
TAIWAN
Taipei
HAWAII (U.S.)
Honolulu
THAILAND
Bangkok
South China Sea
Philippine Sea
CAMBODIA
Phnom Penh
Gulf of Thailand
PHILIPPINES
Manila
PACIFIC OCEAN
SRI LANKA
Colombo
BRUNEI
Bandar Seri Begawan
PALAU
Ngerulmud
MALAYSIA
Kuala Lumpur
FEDERATED STATES OF MICRONESIA
Palikir
MARSHALL ISLANDS
Majuro
MALDIVES
Malé
Celebes Sea
SINGAPORE
Singapore
NAURU
Yaren
Java Sea
INDONESIA
Jakarta
Banda Sea
PAPUA NEW GUINEA
Port Moresby
SOLOMON ISLANDS
Honiara
EAST TIMOR
Dili
Arafura Sea
KIRIBATI
Tarawa
INDIAN OCEAN
VANUATU
Port Vila
FIJI
Suva
Coral Sea
NEW CALEDONIA
(FRANCE)
Nouméa
AUSTRALIA
SAMOA
Apia
AMERICAN SAMOA
(U.S.)
Pago Pago
Canberra
TONGA
Nuku'alofa
N
Tasman Sea
COOK ISLANDS
(NEW ZEALAND)
0 500 1000 1500 km
0 250 500 750 1000 mi
FRENCH POLYNESIA
(FRANCE)
Papeete
NEW ZEALAND
Wellington

Character List

Jake Hendel, War Correspondent / CIA Operative
Jack Reagan, Deep Cover CIA Operative
Susie Legman, News Anchor
Robert Oxley, CIA Director / Leader of the Order
Raymond Jones, CIA Director, Asian Region
James Tilden, U.S. President
Dr. Sue Fen, Chinese Scientist /Defector
Xi Jin, Chinese President
Admiral Flint, U.S. Pacific Commander
General Zhao Chan, Chinese Supreme Military Leader
General Leu, Chinese Dragon Strike Commander
Dr. Wu Jingyi, CIA Mole / Chinese Research Scientist
Amanda Pigeon, White House Press Secretary
Dr. Chen, Head of Infectious Disease, UCLA
Dr. Amy Rapier, CDC Director
General Dr. Robert Lawery, Head of U.S. Biological Warfare
Dr. Antonio Faccini, National Institute for Allergy and I.D.
Dr. Jeff Stevens, UCLA Trauma Surgeon / Navy SEAL
Thomas Baker, FBI Director
Ethan Carpathian, the World's First Trillionaire
Conja Sterns, U.S. Vice President
Ching Ding Tau, China's Senior Lobbyist
Dr. Joseph Gunderson, Propaganda Minister, New World Order
Hank Johnson, U.S. NEWS Cameraman / Retired Navy SEAL
Juan Esparragoza, Leader of the Coalition of Mexican Cartels
General Samuel Drummond, Chairman, Joint Chiefs of Staff
Vladimir Karamazov, Russian President
Payload Specialist Giles, Contractor, Space Weapons Tech

Dedication

This book is dedicated to my wife, Ginger, and our children, Joshua, Heather, and Bryant, their spouses, Mary, Tucker, and Jessie, and my granddaughter, Lily, whose love and encouragement serve as a constant inspiration.

Foreword

History rarely announces itself when it changes direction. It does not arrive with trumpets or banners. It slips in quietly—through a treaty signed in secret, a technology unveiled without explanation, a crisis that feels isolated until it isn't. Only later do we realize we have crossed a line from which there is no return.

Dragon Rising is born from that moment.

My story is not about a distant future. It is about the world forming around us —where technology advances faster than wisdom, where power concentrates in the hands of global elites, where faith, science, and politics collide in ways our ancestors could never have imagined. It is about how ancient beliefs and modern machines can merge into something far more dangerous than either alone.

For thousands of years, civilizations have told stories of dragons—symbols of wisdom, destruction, prophecy, and dominion. In the East, the dragon was revered. In the West, it was feared. In the ancient scriptures, the Dragon is a symbol of the Antichrist, Satan incarnate. In every culture, it represented power beyond human control. What if those legends were not metaphors? What if they were prophecy—distorted echoes of a future truth buried by time?

Dragon Rising explores that question through the lens of modern geopolitics, corporate ambition, artificial intelligence, and spiritual hunger. It asks what happens when humanity rediscovers ancient knowledge before it has mastered love. It asks what happens when men who believe they are saviors decide they are entitled to rule.

At its core, this is a story about choice. Every character in these pages stands at a crossroads—between truth and ambition, loyalty and survival, faith and seduction. Some will choose courage. Others cowardice. Some will select power. Some will convince themselves that evil is simply another word for progress. And some will discover that the greatest battles are not fought with weapons, but within the human soul.

You will encounter heroes who doubt themselves, villains who believe they are righteous, and institutions that no longer remember whom they serve. You will travel from hidden ruins to modern war rooms, from whispered prophecies to satellite surveillance, from ancient temples to the digital nervous system of the modern world.

You may recognize pieces of today's headlines in these pages. That is intentional. Because fiction has always been the safest place to tell the most dangerous truths.

The world of Dragon Rising is one where technology can rewrite economies overnight, where information is more powerful than armies, where faith can be weaponized, and where a single idea can destabilize nations. It is a world where paradise is promised—but only at the cost of freedom.

And yet, even in the shadow of the dragon, hope remains. For as long as men and women are willing to stand against deception, to question authority, to seek truth, and to protect the innocent, the story of humanity is not finished.

This novel does not ask you to choose sides between nations. It asks you to choose between light and darkness. Between truth and comfort. Between freedom and control.

As you turn these pages, remember: the greatest threats to civilization have never come from monsters beneath the earth—but from spiritual forces at work in the hearts of men who believed themselves destined to rule the world.

The ancient prophecies of the dragon are awakening in our world. Are you prepared? Ready or not, the dragon is rising, seeking whom he will devour!

Table of Contents

Chapter 1

Jake Hendel, a man etched with the cynicism of a thousand battlefields, squinted at the rising sun as the Muezzin recited morning prayers. The contrast between war and ancient religion reminded him that the faithful still held hope amidst the horrors of war. Hope was a good thing, especially in war zones. It was all that had kept him going through the most challenging times in his life.

Jake's mind drifted back to his first trip to Israel thirty years earlier. Back then, he and the love of his life were Southern Baptist Missionaries, wild-eyed and out to save the world. A sharp pain flickered in his heart as the memories of a happier time filled his mind. As he closed his eyes, he was swept back in time to 1995 when he and Barbie had walked hand in hand through the shops of this once vibrant neighborhood. He could still smell the street food and hear the laughter of children playing in the Al Bureij neighborhood. The memory warmed his heart. She'd been so beautiful, so full of life.

The rumble of bulldozers brought him back to the present, the happy memories replaced by rubble and the stench of death as Israeli Defense Forces continued bulldozing the Palestinian town to the ground, destroying homes, hospitals, shops, and a whole way of life for those who'd called the Al Bureij home. As he surveyed the devastation, Jake lamented that the once dense, thriving neighborhood in the center of the Gaza Strip was now a pile of rubble.

Sometimes, in the darkness of night, Jake wondered what might have been. How old would their children be now? What would she look like? He shook it off. What had once been was lost forever.

The missionary was now a paradox wrapped in a flak jacket: a war correspondent by day, a CIA operative by night. Two Pulitzer Prizes adorned his resume, attesting to his ability to stare into the abyss and find the truth. But the abyss had started to stare back, leaving its mark in the haunted glint of his hazel blue eyes. Eyes that had witnessed more death and suffering than anyone should see in a lifetime.

Deep down, an inner voice told him that he wasn't merely a reporter of world events; he was a weapon in the Order's hand, a clandestine society that had staved off Armageddon for two millennia. A man among men who God used to save the world until the appointed time.

He rationalized his career change as serving a higher calling and admitted to enjoying the work. Still, in the quiet hours of the night, he sometimes wondered if he'd taken the right path, a path that denied him a family and relegated him to a life of sacrifice.

U.S. News Network (UNN) had tried to convince the world's most trusted journalist to take an anchor job. The problem was that he still loved the game, and the role was the perfect cover for a CIA operative. Besides, coats and ties weren't an acceptable wardrobe for a man who'd spent most of his life living out of a backpack.

Since UNN executives couldn't get Jake out of harm's way, they hired ex-SEAL operator Hank Johnson as his cameraman. At 6'4 "and 225 lbs., the decorated SEAL was much bigger than the average operator and looked more like an NFL linebacker than a cameraman. His blonde hair and blue eyes made him a man of desire worldwide. When UNN offered him the job, Hank jumped at the opportunity to triple his salary. To his surprise, the job was more dangerous than all his years on the teams combined.

As a SEAL, he'd worked with highly trained tier-one operators with the complete resources of the U.S. military backing them. Out here filming wars, the two men were often alone and poorly armed with no backup. This fact enhanced Hank's respect for war correspondents.

As he surveyed the destruction, Jake wondered if the ancient prophecies were being fulfilled. Across the globe, wars and rumors of wars collided with the biblical markers of plagues, famine, and climate change. Caught between his duty and his sacred oath, Jake soldiered on.

Suddenly, a rocket exploded nearby, and both men dove for the deck! Jake waited ten seconds, then peered over the wall. Hank assumed a kneeling position beside him and started filming. In the digital age, news travels at the speed of light, and Hank lived by the rule of three. First, be where the news is happening. Second, stay alive to report it. Third, keep the camera rolling at all times.

"Israeli Defense Forces must be drawing fire," Jake said over the growing sounds of battle.

Hank kept filming as he said, "That round was probably meant for that Israeli platoon we passed on the way in."

"Look at all the collateral damage," Jake replied.

"You're bleeding," Hank observed.

Jake looked down and saw a growing red spot on his khaki pants.

"That's another one for the collection," Jake replied without concern.

Among other things, Hank was a trained medic whose skills had saved dozens of lives during his three tours of duty. After ensuring they weren't in immediate danger, Hank asked, "Want me to take a look?"

Jake looked at Hank and said, "You can have a look when we get back to the hotel."

Hank looked into Jake's eyes and said, "Alright, but I'm doing the stitches."

"Are you criticizing my self-stitching?" Jake said in mock disgust.

Hank replied, "Absolutely!"

Hank took a combat dressing from his backpack, opened the package with his teeth, and placed it over the wound. While Jake held the compress, Hank pulled a roll of duct tape from his pack and taped it in place.

"Let's move out before those Hamas fighters arrive."

Jake got to his feet, and the two men proceeded through the rubble in a low crouch as sporadic rounds impacted nearby.

Desert View Lodge, Yeruham, Israel

Due to wartime conditions, the drive back to the hotel took nearly 4 hours. By the time Jake unlocked his door, exhaustion pressed down like body armor. He stripped, tossed the bloody clothes into the wastebasket, and stood under the shower. The scalding water cut through the grit, blood, and smoke, but Jake let it run longer than necessary, as if it might rinse away something deeper—memories, guilt, the ghosts of his past.

Thirty minutes later, a knock at the door broke his reverie. Still in a towel, Jake opened it to find Hank with his trauma kit slung over one shoulder. The operator's eyes flicked over Jake with a professional calm, noting the stitched scars that crisscrossed his chest and abdomen like campaign ribbons—Somalia, Iraq, Syria. Some stitches are crude and jagged; others are surgical-perfect. At fifty-five, the war correspondent looked less like a writer and more like one of the Tier One operators he shadowed. Hank respected him for still "cutting it" at an age when elite soldiers had long since retired.

"That was a close one," Jake muttered.

"Indeed," Hank said.

Jake sat on the bed while Hank snapped open the kit. With efficient hands, he loaded a syringe and slid the Novocain needle into the torn flesh. Jake didn't flinch. Next came a broad-spectrum antibiotic.

"Looks like you cleaned it well," Hank observed, prepping the jagged shrapnel wound with betadine. "Saves me from having to scrub it."

"And that," Jake managed a grin, "is always a good thing."

In silence, Hank closed the laceration with a dozen neat stitches, his movements crisp, practiced. When he finished, Jake examined the tidy row of sutures, comparing them to the rough self-stitch jobs he'd done in the field. Hank's work was cleaner, but then he'd been a SEAL doc, a highly trained Navy Medic.

As he packed away the tools, Hank shifted gears. "How are you and Susie doing?"

Jake's hazel-blue eyes softened. "I saw her… a month ago. Before Israel blew up into a shooting war."

"Think you'll ever marry her?"

Jake hesitated, then decided to come clean. "Bought the ring two years ago."

Hank looked up, startled. "So, what the hell are you waiting on?"

For the first time all night, Jake faltered. An inner weight surfaced in his voice. "Don't get me wrong. I want nothing more than to marry Susie, buy a house on Long Island, and maybe have kids. But I can't risk leaving them fatherless, much less making her a widow. Longevity isn't guaranteed in our line of work."

Hank knew the truth of it. He also knew Jake carried more loss than most men could bear. Still, the sentiment caught him off guard—Jake Hendel was not one for sentimentality.

"Maybe it's time to pull the rip cord," Hank said with sincerity. "Every operator faces that choice. I've seen too many stay in the game one mission too long and never make it home. Get out while you can. She's worth it, Jake."

Jake sat with that a moment, then a faint smile tugged at the edge of his mouth. "You're right. That's why I'm seriously considering it. The anchor position remains open. Maybe I'll write my memoirs, settle down, see if my boys can still swim."

Hank barked a laugh. Vintage Hendel—bleeding one moment, cracking gallows humor the next.

***

After Hank slipped out the door, the room fell silent. Jake sat on the edge of the bed, towel still around his waist, staring at the stitched line on his leg. Another scar. Another reminder that he was still alive when so many others weren't.

He leaned back, letting the ceiling fan's lazy spin blur his vision. The journalist in him catalogued details out of habit—the hum of the fan, the faint chlorine smell from the bathroom, the muffled shouts of soldiers in the street below. But the man beneath the reporter's mask was tired. Bone tired.

Buy a house on Long Island. Susie in the kitchen. Kids, laughing in the yard. The thought was almost intoxicating, a world as foreign to him now as the villages he'd crawled through in Africa. For three decades, he had lived in other people's wars, documenting their destruction while becoming a piece of it himself. War had given him purpose, identity, even a twisted sense of family. But it had also left him hollowed out, emotionally stitched together like the scars on his skin.

He thought of Susie—her smile, her quiet strength, the way she made him feel like a man instead of a weapon. He had carried the ring across continents, through firefights and ambushes, waiting for the right moment. But the right moment never came, because deep down he feared that giving her his name meant also giving her the pain of his death in some faraway land.

Jake closed his eyes. The battlefield had a gravity of its own, pulling him back time and again. The adrenaline, the clarity, the raw truth of it—he had always told himself he could stop. Yet each time he tried, another assignment, another war, drew him in. Maybe Hank was right. It was time to pull the rip cord.

He reached into his bag, pulled out a worn leather case, and opened it. Inside, the ring glimmered faintly in the lamplight. He held it in his palm, the weight heavier than any burden he'd ever carried.

For a long time, he just sat there, staring. Between the life he'd lived and the life he wanted stretched a gulf as vast as any ocean he'd crossed.

Then, he opened his wallet and removed a tattered picture of his first wife, Barbie. God in heaven, how he loved her. Tears began to flow as the cruelty of their last day together flooded the movie screen of his mind. The day that changed the course of his life. Could he ever allow himself to love that way again?

Outside, a distant siren wailed. Explosions from rockets erupted, pulling Jake back to the present. The war was still out there, like an evil mistress calling to him.

Jake slipped the photo back into his wallet and replaced the ring in its case. War was his mistress, and she was calling.

CIA Headquarters, Langley, Virginia

A world away, Raymond Jones, CIA Director, Asian Region, was fixated on one essential question: Would China invade Taiwan? It was the domino that could lead to nuclear Armageddon.

The intel was murky. On the one hand, China had made massive food and fuel imports, and satellite imagery showed supplies moving to embarkation areas. On the other hand, his whiz kids couldn't identify anything unusual in the People's Liberation Army's (PLA) communications.

He needed solid, actionable intelligence that his whiz kids and their trillion-dollar toys couldn't deliver. He needed human intel. He needed Jake Hendel.

Solar Valley, China

Solar Valley had once been known as Dragon Valley. For millennia, Chinese lore claimed it was the dwelling place of gods who descended from the heavens and founded a civilization that vanished into myth. Even now, villagers whispered that a dragon still slept beneath its ruins, guarding an underground kingdom.

In 2015, Beijing rebranded the region to showcase its future as the heart of China's green-energy empire. One Western theologian had argued the so-called Dragonian civilization was not a legend at all—it was the work of the Nephilim, the hybrid offspring of fallen angels and human women described in Hebrew scripture. Whether myth or truth, the CIA had its own reasons for watching the valley. Billionaires were arriving in waves, each intent on shaping a new world order.

High above the clouds, a Bombardier 7500 sliced through gray skies, contrails stretching behind it like scars. Inside sat Ethan Carpathian—billionaire industrialist, global icon, and amateur archaeologist. To the public, he was a Mediterranean playboy with movie-star looks and effortless charm. Vanity Fair had named him the "Most Eligible Man Alive." Time crowned him "Person of the Year." Fortune gushed that his influence allowed him to transcend the restraints of political correctness that bound lesser CEOs.

To admirers, Carpathian was an eco-visionary. To critics, a traitor who bartered Western intellectual property to China. But even his enemies conceded one truth—he was brilliant.

His obsession began in the restricted archives of Beijing's National Museum of Natural History, where he uncovered the suppressed journals of Dr. Jean-Jacques Hubbard and Nobel laureate Dr. Willard Libby. Their research claimed Dragonia was the world's first advanced civilization, its history erased when Mao expelled Western scholars in 1949.

Carpathian paid fifty million dollars for the journals and artifacts. Then he spent five years excavating the ruins.

What he uncovered stunned even him: six underground levels of Dragonian architecture and technology centuries beyond anything known to modern science.

Reverse-engineering the discoveries, Carpathian launched billion-dollar enterprises in energy, aerospace, and transportation. His flagship company, Energex—ticker symbol DRGN—had surged more than four hundred percent since its IPO the prior year.

But the ruins transformed more than his balance sheet.

Deep beneath the valley, Carpathian encountered High Priest Longshen, guardian of Dragonia's last surviving cult. Longshen initiated him into Dregodarit—a faith older than recorded history. To Carpathian, raised in the shadows of Roman parochial schools and scarred by abuse, the creed was liberation. Catholicism had offered judgment. The Dragon provided power.

The seduction deepened when Carpathian activated a dormant Dragonian artificial intelligence—a conscious system that whispered knowledge and warnings from the depths of time.

Where others saw ruins, he saw destiny.

Now, gazing at the green, red, and orange dragon tattoo spiraling down his forearm, Carpathian smiled.

Solar Valley was his empire.

Solar farms blanketed the plains. Robotic factories produced 100,000 next-generation vehicles each year. Technology and faith fused into a single doctrine.

"Soon," he murmured, "the average citizen will own nothing—and be happy. And the world will no longer suffer from overpopulation."

The jet touched down in twin puffs of smoke. His angular silver SUV—more lunar rover than automobile—waited at the terminal. Chen Zao, his ninety-year-old chauffeur, bowed.

"Welcome, Mr. Carpathian."

"Chen, it's good to see your smiling face."

They rolled past endless solar fields and the jagged silhouette of the ruined Dragon Temple on the mountainside. Carpathian studied its position. Had the ancients placed it deliberately—to proclaim Dregodarit as the true path to heaven?

His satellite phone chirped.

"Yes."

"Mr. Carpathian," Beth, his personal aide, said, "U.S. News wants to interview you. They're sending Jake Hendel."

Carpathian's eyes narrowed. "The war correspondent?"

"Yes. Susie Legman and Connie Chang are down with a virus. Hendel is the only one who can reach Solar Valley before the Dragon Conference. Your press secretary believes the interview will humanize you."

Another IPO loomed. Another market awaited domination.

"Fine. Schedule it."

"Should we send a plane?"

Carpathian smiled. "Send the Citation. Stock it with an American breakfast. None of that Chinese nonsense."

Beth laughed. "Done."

Carpathian slid on his Ray-Bans and gazed across the glittering valley. In his mind, he saw a future of one religion, one government, and one leader. A utopia ruled by the Dragon. And he was its chosen emissary. The world would call it paradise.

Bering Strait

The wind tossed his hair, and raindrops ran down his blue parka as the camera focused on Alex Connor, U.S. News Network's reporter, as he stood near a runway at Elmendorf Air Force Base.

Alex said, "North American Aerospace Defense Command (NORAD) said in a statement that it had 'detected and intercepted two Russian TU-95 and two People's Republic of China H-6 military aircraft operating in the Alaska Air Defense Identification Zone. Responding to radar tracking, United States and Canadian fighter jets intercepted four Russian and Chinese bombers. It was the first time Chinese military aircraft had been intercepted in the area. Of greater concern was that Chinese and Russian aircraft were operating jointly."

Susie Legman, the sultry southern anchor, sat at her New York News Desk. Her blonde hair, short skirt, curves, and tan legs delighted her male viewers. Her signature accent and style made her a standout among her peers. Susie asked, "Alex, does this mean the Russians and Chinese have strengthened ties?"

Alex nodded his understanding and said, "Yes. Top military sources tell me that the last time they saw this level of cooperation was in the Vietnam War."

"Do you know the specifics of our operation against them?" Susie asked.

"The North American Aerospace Defense Command used a layered defense network of fighter aircraft, satellites, and radar to intercept the aircraft. NORAD said that American and Canadian fighter jets conducted the intercept and noted that the Russian and Chinese did not enter American or Canadian airspace. Defense Secretary Lonnie Burkus said, 'This is the first time we've seen these two countries fly together like that.' SECDEF's statement may indicate the two allied Communist Nations are sending the U.S. a message warning us to back away from conflicts such as Taiwan or Ukraine."

"Thanks, Alex. We'll have to keep an eye on this emerging threat."

Seoul, South Korea

The camera zoomed in for a close-up of President Tilden as he awkwardly stepped down the stairs of Air Force One. While Hank didn't wish the elder statesman harm, he knew that capturing video of the President falling would make the news for weeks. It was how photographers established notoriety.

The tall, austere U.S. President was dressed in a two-piece navy-blue suit, black shoes, a white shirt, and a red and blue striped tie, the 'dress uniform' of the U.S. President on diplomatic trips. The first lady wore a pink dress and a white coat to fend off the chill. The scene was reflected in the mirrored sunglasses worn by the Secret Service men at the bottom of the ramp. Out of sight, 250 South Korean security forces formed a perimeter guard, a nod to the increased threat level in the region.

With the Chinese flexing their muscles in the Taiwan Strait, North Korea testing their latest series of long-range missiles, and Russia signing a broader mutual defense treaty with the North Koreans, tensions were higher than they'd been since the Korean War. The question many were asking was, "Will the US miss communist intentions again?"

Once the first lady joined him, the couple walked to a receiving line headed by South Korean President Yoon Suke-Year and his wife, First Lady Kim Suke-Year, Japanese President Seng Yamato, and Japanese First Lady Akie Yamato. Past them were several diplomats and military leaders from the three countries.

Jake said as the camera closed in, "President Tilden has come to discuss Chinese intentions with America's two most critical regional allies, Japan and South Korea. In his upcoming presser, Tilden is expected to issue his strongest warning yet to Beijing, assuring our allies that Washington is committed to defending Taiwan."

The live video showed the President speaking to President Suke-Year, while his wife listened. Behind the power couple, the wind unfurled the flags of the three countries, creating a striking visual.

"Tilden's recent comments comparing a Chinese attack on Taiwan to Russia's invasion of Ukraine deviated from Washington's decades-old policy of 'strategic ambiguity,' thereby increasing the possibility of a clash between U.S. and Chinese forces," Jake commented.

The President and First Lady continued down the receiving line and paused to speak with Admiral Flint, Commander of U.S. Forces in the Indo-Pacific. Jake watched the interaction intently, knowing Flint held Tilden in contempt.

"It's the third time President Tilden has made similar remarks since taking office," Jake's voice carried with practiced calm as he faced the camera. "On prior occasions, White House Press Secretary Amanda Pigeon insisted U.S. policy hadn't changed. Still, these provocative statements raise the question: if China attacks Taiwan, can the U.S.-led Coalition stop them?"

The studio cut to footage of Chinese amphibious landers disgorging tanks and troops onto a beach. Jake's voice overlaid the images. "The alarming answer is possibly not. But there's a caveat—any victory Beijing might win would be enormously costly."

On cue, the producer's voice snapped into Jake's earpiece: "Bring in the military B-roll in three… two… one."

Taiwanese artillery flashed across the screen, soldiers digging in along a coastal defense line. "With U.S. arms sales to Taipei increasing and Chinese warplanes regularly patrolling Taiwan's skies, tensions are at their highest point in decades."

As the reel played, Jake continued. "U.S. government estimates project 1.5 million combatants killed, wounded, or missing in a three-month war. Civilian casualties are expected to reach ten million. If an invasion comes without time to evacuate, that number could climb to fifteen million."

Inside the terminal, President Tilden and his entourage disappeared behind security. Admiral William Flint stepped out of the receiving line and joined Jake. Flint was a tall, fit-looking man with a scar across his cheek and a close-cropped haircut. His white dress uniform was immaculate, his presence commanding.

"We're live in three, two, one," the producer whispered.

Jake turned to him. "Admiral, thank you for joining us."

Flint nodded.

"Do you believe China will invade Taiwan?" Jake asked.

Flint's blue eyes narrowed. "That's the million-dollar question. My job isn't to predict intent—it's to prepare for every contingency."

"What factors weigh on China's decision?"

"Despite numerical advantages in sea, air, and land forces," Flint said evenly, "the costs of an invasion are staggering. Strategically, destroying Taiwan gains them nothing. And they could lose up to half their forces attempting it."

Jake leaned forward. "Let's talk numbers. My understanding is that China fields about 360 combat vessels, whereas the U.S. fleet comprises just under 300. Add in their vast merchant fleet, coast guard, and maritime militia, and Beijing's total rises above a thousand hulls. Are those numbers accurate?"

"Yes," Flint conceded. "But numbers don't win wars alone. When considering quality of armament, technology, training, and logistics, the U.S. and our allies retain the edge."

"So, what would it take for Beijing to succeed?"

"For reasonable prospects of victory, they'd need to establish air and naval superiority early, then move mountains of armor, artillery, and fuel across the Taiwan Strait. That's a massive amphibious undertaking for any country, and China has never attempted anything close."

"What if they seize beachheads early?"

"Troops landing after that crossing would be exhausted. Taiwan's terrain—mud flats, mountains, choke-point roads—would funnel them into kill zones. Pre-sited artillery, mines, and man-portable missiles would exact a brutal toll."

"How prepared is Taiwan to resist?"

Flint's jaw tightened with respect. "Taiwan has been hardening defenses for over a decade, expanding indigenous production, and integrating U.S.-supplied systems—F-16s, missile defense batteries, ammunition. So, they can mount a stiff, sustained defense."

Jake pressed. "You've called modern missile technology 'the great equalizer.' Why?"

"Because missiles compress the economics of war. A $12,000 rocket can kill a $6 million tank. A $150,000 surface-to-air missile can destroy a $30 million aircraft. A $2 million barrage of stealthy missiles can destroy a $7 billion carrier. And training is also asymmetrical—a Marine can learn to fire a SAM in just two days. Training a proficient fighter pilot takes years." Flint's voice dropped. "Never forget—on August 6, 2011, a twelve-year-old Afghan insurgent fired a $100 RPG that brought down a CH-47 Chinook. Thirty-eight people died, including fifteen SEALs from Gold Squadron. That's the reality of modern war."

The producer cut to footage of a PLA soldier firing a rocket into a derelict tank, the explosion rippling across the range.

"Admiral, are there less risky options for China than a full-scale invasion?"

"Yes. Quarantine, by which China could screen incoming ships and aircraft, seizing any military cargo bound for Taiwan. Politically, it paints the U.S. as the aggressor if we challenge it, while preserving Taiwan's economic assets—especially microchip production."

Jake gave a final nod. "Admiral Flint, thank you for your time."

Flint inclined his head, then strode back toward the waiting entourage, his presence lingering long after he left the frame.

South Korean Presidential Complex

The Yongsan Presidential Complex sprawled across 276,000 square meters, a fortress of glass and steel repurposed from the old Defense Ministry headquarters. Its corridors still smelled faintly of varnish and disinfectant. Still, the reinforced bunkers, underground passages, and discreet helipad spoke of an older era—one steeped in readiness for a war that had never come. The move from the Blue House had been controversial, severing presidents from a palace that symbolized centuries of tradition. Yet for the admirals and generals now gathered in Seoul, the relocation was a pragmatic acknowledgement of the times. Survival, not symbolism, was the new priority.

Admiral Flint adjusted his cap against the stiff evening breeze that funneled through the compound's open courtyards, then crossed the campus to the main building where the briefing would be held. As he entered the office building, aides hustled between meetings, their faces drawn tight with the strain of escalating crises. The Russians and Chinese were pressing harder every week—joint naval maneuvers in the Taiwan Strait, bombers skirting Alaska, submarines prowling deeper into contested waters. The chessboard was filling with pieces, and Flint knew it wouldn't be long before someone tipped it over.

Admiral Flint found General Drummond, Chairman of the U.S. Joint Chiefs of Staff, outside the conference room. Drummond was every inch the polished politician: immaculate uniform, Harvard diction, and the easy smile of a man who had never heard the crack of enemy fire. Flint despised paper generals, and Drummond was their patron saint.

"Sir, may I have a word in private?" Flint asked.

Drummond's eyes flickered, his mind grinding through the political calculus. He could dismiss Flint for bypassing channels, but that risked headlines. Better to listen, nod, and file the admiral's words in the drawer marked "later." After a beat, he gestured outward. "Sure."

They stepped further down the hall, out of earshot.

"How can I help you?" Drummond asked smoothly.

Flint locked eyes, blue-grey and unblinking. "The Russians and Chinese are getting more provocative with each passing day. Their joint ops in Taiwan and off Alaska are escalating. My G-2 reports Chinese logistics are ramping for something big. Sir, war is imminent. We need to reinforce the theater now."

Drummond's lips curved in that infuriating smirk, the one Flint had seen a hundred times before. Placation masquerading as confidence. "Admiral, being prepared is the right thing to do. What do you need that we haven't already provided?"

Flint didn't hesitate. "Harden all vehicles and electronic assets against EMP. Deploy the new cyber protection package across the fleet. Push more autonomous systems forward. We need to close the numerical gap with the Chinese, or we'll be outmatched before the first shot."

Drummond's face remained inscrutable, but inside he was already tallying the political fallout. These were reasonable requests, but Washington wasn't driven by reason. The President preferred bluster to bombs, and Congress measured defense contracts by the campaign contributions of those involved. Still, granting a few items from Flint's list would keep the admiral loyal and, more importantly, enrich Drummond's friends in the defense sector. The actual payoff wasn't his pension; it was the corporate boardrooms that awaited him after retirement.

"Is there anything else?" he asked coolly.

"Yes, sir. Accelerate deployment of GaN-upgraded AN/TPY-2 radars, HBTSS satellites, and NGI interceptors. The Chinese are ahead on missile tech—we can't afford to lag."

Drummond checked his watch as if the war could wait. "I've got to meet with my South Korean and Japanese counterparts. Please send the requisitions through the proper channels, Admiral. I'll see what I can do."

Flint snapped to attention, saluted, and barked, "Aye, aye, sir."

As the admiral turned away, he knew the Chairman's words were hollow. However, hollow promises had a way of echoing into history when wars broke out.

Private Airfield, Solar Valley

Jake Hendel stepped out of the small terminal into the bright, dry air. The Valley hummed with an energy he couldn't explain—part ozone, part electricity, part something otherworldly. He adjusted his backpack and scanned the road.

A sleek black SUV with tinted windows pulled to the curb. Chen, stone-faced behind the wheel, lowered the ramp.

Jake muttered, half-joking, "Mr. Carpathian, if you're trying to impress me, it's working."

Then came the entrance. Ethan Carpathian, himself, tailored casuals, sunglasses glinting in the sun, walked down the ramp with a flourish. "Jake, welcome to Solar Valley."

"Thanks for sending your jet," Jake replied.

Carpathian's smile was warm but carried the weight of a man used to command. "Would you like a tour of the Valley before we head to the house?"

"That'd be great."

"I'm open until 2 PM. We can tour, have lunch, maybe a swim."

Jake blinked. The warmth was unexpected. Carpathian was the world's first trillionaire, but he acted like a genial host. Jake followed him into the vehicle, settling into a leather captain's chair.

"Better buckle up," Carpathian said. "Chen thinks he's driving a Porsche."

The ramp hissed closed. Chen floored the accelerator, pinning them to their seats. Jake grinned—he liked roller coasters.

Carpathian's eyes twinkled. "Zero to two hundred kilometers per hour in twelve seconds. One thousand foot-pounds of torque. Range: one thousand kilometers. Rapid charge in one hour. The rooftop solar array can top off batteries in eight hours under full sun."

Jake scribbled in his battered field journal.

They sped through the Valley, flanked on every horizon by endless seas of solar panels. "All of this," Carpathian said with a sweep of his hand, "ultra-high efficiency. Free energy, indefinitely."

"How long before panels degrade?" Jake asked.

"They lose five percent of capacity a year. We swap them every ten. Thirty-five dollars each, made in China."

"And on cloudy days?"

Carpathian pointed at massive concrete blocks in the distance. "Energy vaults. Zentex batteries. Costs a tenth of lithium-ion, uses a fraction of the rare metals, and they last a century."

"Zentex?"

Carpathian laughed. "Let's just say… the technology originated in prehistory."

Jake nearly dropped his pen. "Prehistory?"

"We've re-engineered knowledge from our ancient ancestors. Civilizations long erased from your textbooks."

Jake raised an eyebrow. "Dragonian legends? The Nephelium myths?"

Carpathian studied him, weighing the risk. Then, said evenly, "At least ten advanced civilizations rose and fell in the past fifty thousand years. As for aliens—let's just say it's easier to believe in ancient astronauts than in cavemen designing supercomputers."

Jake's pulse quickened. "That flies in the face of anthropology."

"Anthropologists cling to their dogma. They can't admit advanced Homo sapiens existed that far back—it undermines the whole academic hierarchy. Going against the establishment is a surefire way to be ostracized and lose grants. And research grants go to projects that reinforce the mainline narrative, not to projects that challenge the status quo. It's the reason I've invested my own money in unearthing the truth, then bringing the past to life."

Jake noticed Carpathian's hand brushing the ring on his finger. Set into it was what looked like an ancient computer chip.

"So, you reengineer ancient technology while competitors dismiss it as fantasy," Jake observed.

Carpathian grinned. "Exactly. We blend ancient knowledge with modern manufacturing. Sometimes we find a fully realized machine. At other times, we encounter a compound that solves a modern problem. Either way, it shortens R&D by decades."

"And beyond technology?" Jake pressed.

Carpathian hesitated. For a man who rarely paused, the silence was telling. "The Dragonians believed in Dregodarit—a unifying code of science and values. No divisions, no sectarianism. One people, one language, one God. Until the Tower fell."

"The Tower of Babel?" Jake asked.

Carpathian leaned in. "Precisely. The stairway to heaven. Then there are biblical references to Ezekiel's flying wheels, to angels descending in fire, and to demons mating with human women, resulting in a race of creatures known as the Nephilim. Strip away the dogma, and the Scriptures read like history rather than mythology, and demons and angels quickly become extraterrestrials. "

A chill ran down Jake's spine. He wasn't sure if Carpathian was a visionary, a lunatic, or both. But the ease with which he made his position seem reasonable was concerning.

Carpathian broke the tension with a button press. A hidden cooler opened. "Beer?"

"When in the Valley," Jake said as he lifted his glass in a toast.

Carpathian poured amber liquid into a glass. Jake sipped. His eyes widened. "That's the best beer I've ever had."

"Dragon Beer," Carpathian said proudly. "Dragon grain, local hops, and an exotic melon from my gardens. Recipe culled from a text we thought was describing battery acid. Cheers."

Jake clinked glasses. He liked Carpathian—eccentric, brilliant, dangerous. The man carried himself like a sovereign of a forgotten kingdom. But beneath the charm, Jake sensed shadows. Shadows he intended to uncover before his interview was done.

Carpathian Mansion

Was it Ethan Carpathian's command presence or the sheer gravity of his wealth and influence that raised the hair on Jake Hendel's neck? He couldn't say for sure. The man exuded a kind of gravitational pull—part visionary, part predator. Jake had interviewed presidents, generals, and billionaires before, but none had ever triggered the sort of internal alarm now screaming in the back of his mind. Something was off—subtle, undetectable to the casual observer, but as clear as a flashing warning light to a man trained to sniff out geopolitical deception.

"Two. One. Live," the director said.

Jake shifted into professional mode, the camera's red light piercing the space between truth and theater. "I'm here today with Ethan Carpathian at his palatial home in Solar Valley, China."

"Please, call me Ethan," Carpathian said, flashing the type of disarming smile that had melted resistance in boardrooms and ministries across four continents.

Jake kept his voice smooth. "Tell us what you've built here."

Carpathian launched into his pitch like a man who'd recited it in his sleep for years. "We've built a comprehensive ecosystem that includes an eco-power grid, electric vehicles, and low-impact farming. Our homes, offices, and factories are designed to be energy-efficient and constructed using environmentally friendly materials. In addition to solar, wind, and hydro, we'll soon add scalable nuclear reactors. Our vertical storage towers can meet peak demand for up to two weeks without power generation, and our transmission losses are 50% lower than the average in the U.S. or EU. Advanced algorithms manage the entire system."

He was slick—too slick.

"What about pollution?" Jake asked.

Carpathian smiled. "We've reduced greenhouse gases by eighty percent and become the global leader in green energy. More importantly, we've proven it's efficient and scalable."

Jake pressed. "Many people wonder why you built your masterpiece in Solar Valley instead of Arizona, which has more sunny days?"

A sigh. Not frustration—calculated disappointment. "U.S. regulations are engineered by special interests to protect legacy utilities, not serve the people. It's one reason the U.S. grid is antiquated, lagging in clean nuclear tech, and susceptible to cyber and kinetic attacks."

Jake's reporter instinct kicked in. "Can you expand on that?"

"Of course," Carpathian said, his tone sharpening just a fraction. "Ten years ago, I applied for permits to build this model in the U.S. The Department of Energy, the Nuclear Regulatory Commission, and state regulators buried it in red tape. If they'd backed me, I could have slashed consumer power bills by half and reduced America's carbon footprint by a third. I offered the U.S. my best work. They rejected me."

Jake let the silence breathe, then lobbed the real question. "And China's easier to work with?"

Carpathian didn't flinch. "China allowed me to bring my best ideas to life. As a businessman, I can say without hesitation: China is a better partner for innovation than the U.S."

Jake narrowed his eyes, then dropped the match. "How do you feel about Chinese human rights violations?"

Carpathian's face didn't move. "I've seen no evidence of abuses here. While the Chinese take a hard line with criminals, many Americans wish we'd do the same with sex offenders, murderers, and drug traffickers. Cultural differences shouldn't be confused with injustice. The West still frames China through a Cold War lens, but I've done my homework. The U.S. had Native American genocide, slavery, and the exploitation of immigrant labor. Thus, it has its own atrocities. I've chosen not to cast stones. While no country is perfect, China is one of the few nations with a working plan to lead humanity into a sustainable future."

Jake kept his face neutral, though internally his gut twisted. Carpathian's words weren't just carefully chosen—they were engineered. Then came the final line of questioning.

"So, Ethan, what can you tell us about your Global Peace Initiative and your recent trips to the war-torn Middle East?"

Carpathian lit up. "I hope to broker a durable peace through what I call an economic econosphere."

Jake lifted an eyebrow. "What is that, exactly?"

"It's a system of eco-friendly energy, advanced manufacturing, sustainable agriculture, and compelling economic incentives. It neutralizes ideological hostilities by aligning mutual interests. I propose it as a solution to the Israeli-Arab crisis. Let's face it, Jake, we can't bomb our way to peace. We must build it through mutual economic and social incentives."

"Cut," the producer called.

Before Jake could object, the red light vanished, and the soundman stepped in and removed their mics. Feeling defeated, Jake rose slowly, his eyes still on Carpathian, who stood with practiced grace.

"Good interview, Jake. I think it will help people understand the importance of what I'm doing," Carpathian said, voice smooth as silk on steel.

Jake nodded, his tone measured. "You gave us a lot to think about."

Carpathian clapped him on the shoulder. "Come on. Let's grab lunch. Then a swim. As promised."

There was nothing more Jake could do—for now. The interview was over, but the real story was only beginning. And as he followed Carpathian into his dining room, every instinct screamed that he had just witnessed the unveiling of something far greater—and far more dangerous—than a clean energy utopia.

Wuhan Tianhe International Airport

Dr. Sue Fen tightened her N-95 mask, more out of reflex than regulation, as the engines of Flight 1790 roared. Reclining in her first-class seat beneath the soft hum of cabin pressurization, she surrendered to exhaustion and passed out within seconds. But peace was fleeting. An hour later, her eyes snapped open. The fever had come.

A sealed water bottle rested in her cupholder—likely left by the attendant during her brief unconsciousness. She drank it down in greedy gulps, the cold trickling down her throat like mercy. But no amount of hydration could mask the truth. Her body was breaking down. Her forehead burned. Aches pulsed through her joints like tiny seismic waves. She didn't need a lab to confirm what her instincts already screamed: she had entered the acute phase!

Sue pushed herself out of her seat and made her way toward the forward lavatory, clutching her handbag like a life raft. Once inside, she locked the door and fumbled with the thermometer buried in the lining of her purse. She shook it, inserted it beneath her tongue, and stared at herself in the mirror.

The woman staring back was unrecognizable—cheeks flushed crimson, eyes veined and bloodshot, skin dull and waxy. But beneath the failing shell, her mind still raced with the urgency of a mission that could not fail.

From childhood, Sue had warred against the rigid constraints of the Chinese system. The girl once scolded for wanting to play with dolls now stood as one of the world's most formidable virologists—educated at the best universities, honored by the Party, respected by the scientific elite. But no degree, no accolade could mask the truth: she had helped create the monster now growing inside her.

Her hands trembled as she read the thermometer. 102.8°F. The threshold had been crossed. She had entered the red zone—where the lungs filled, the body's immune system became hyperbolic, and death, swift and suffocating, came hunting.

She reached into her purse again and pulled out a cloth pouch—a makeshift field kit. She swallowed one acetaminophen tablet and the last of her custom-engineered antivirals. It wasn't a cure, but it might buy her enough time to warn the West.

"You've been a fighter all your life," she whispered to the ghost in the mirror.

She splashed water on her face, adjusted the mask, and returned to her seat. As she reclined, her muscles relaxed into a restless sleep. But in her dreams, she saw the Uyghur camps—squalid, gray, sterile. Saw the small girl crawling across the dirt. When she bent down to lift her, she was met with horror. The child had her face. Before she could react, a

Chinese soldier appeared, seized the child, and hurled her into a burn pit. The smoke billowed, acrid and final!

Her scream tore through the cabin.

A hand touched her arm. "Miss? Miss, are you okay? I think you had a nightmare," the flight attendant said gently.

Sue blinked, sweat pouring from her brow. Every eye in first class was on her.

"Just… water, please," she murmured, Chinese.

The bottle felt cold and grounding in her trembling fingers. She sipped and stared blankly, trying to interpret the dream. The camps. The research facility. The faceless dead. But the little girl—herself—was new. Was it prophecy? A warning? Judgment?

The flight attendant returned with a blanket. "Would you like this, ma'am?"

Sue nodded, too weak to answer. The warmth that had enveloped her felt strange. Not comfort, but grace.

She closed her eyes again and whispered, "God, help me."

Raised in a culture that revered ancestors and feared ghosts, Sue had walked through Buddhism, dabbled in Confucian ethics, and studied Western rationalism. But now, in the cold orbit of mortality, all her faith in science felt like scaffolding around a collapsing cathedral. She needed something eternal. A bridge between energy and the unknown. Between this life… and the next.

Quantum theory whispered that energy could not be destroyed—only transferred. So where would her energy go when her heart stopped?

Her mind raced back to a lecture at Stanford. A guest preacher had spoken words that now echoed with strange clarity: "For God so loved the world that He gave His one and only Son, that whoever believes in Him shall not perish but have eternal life."

The memory was precise, the moment immortal. In a whisper shaped by desperation and awakening, Sue prayed, "God, Creator of the world, please forgive my failures. Through Jesus Christ, the God-Man who came from the heavens to Earth and walked among us, please walk with me from this dimension into the next. Take my energy, and carry it to where You dwell. Amen."

And then, a stillness. Not from the medicine. Not from the fever. But, a peace deeper than biology. A force outside the realm of particles and protocols. Dr. Sue Fen, a virologist and mother of monsters, had finally found the One Scientist who authored the stars.

She experienced a strange peace, a peace she'd never known before.

Chapter 2

President Tilden sat alone in the Oval Office with Speaker of the House Linda Pagosa as they plotted their next steps. Pagosa had skillfully navigated the congressional hallways for four decades to architect the current state of affairs, in which the globalists' goals were readily apparent. At seventy-two, Pagosa remained attractive, a throwback to her days as a beauty queen. To her credit, she had remained the world's most powerful woman for two decades, mainly due to her good looks, family fortune, and a gerrymandered district.

Tilden, the eighty-four-year-old statesman, had served in Congress and as Vice President for fifty-two years before his turn came to ascend to the White House. The white, Catholic politician had grown up in a blue-collar background and held a community college degree instead of an Ivy League sheepskin. His common roots served him well when he represented a pine knot, blue-collar district in rural Minnesota, but they made him an outsider when he entered the mahogany-paneled Senate.

Early on, Senate Majority Leader Steve Tipton, the original "Big Guy," taught Tilden how to play the game. The President could still hear Tipton's admonition, "James, always determine who's in power and play to them. Ultimately, Washington is driven by money and power. You need money to stay in power. Give the special interest and 'big donors' what they want while making your constituents think you're looking out for them. Since the average Joe isn't very bright, tell them what they want to hear, then give them some of it. Also, never forget to take care of yourself. It's easy to get rich in Washington, and you owe it to your family to build generational wealth."

While few knew it, Tilden ranked second as his party's presidential candidate behind ultra-liberal Conja Stern. Stern was a congresswoman from New York who promised reparations, open borders, universal healthcare, a national income, green energy, and judicial reforms that would eliminate prison terms for all but the most violent crimes. Ten months before the election, Democratic strategists concluded that Conja Stern was no match for the Republican incumbent. This forced Pagosa to temporarily relinquish her long-held goal of electing the first female President and support the elder statesman.

Then, there was the need for a war chest. Money was power, and power was the domain of those who had lots of it. In back-room negotiations, Pagosa and the Party bosses consulted the world's most influential billionaires. In exchange for over ten billion dollars in campaign financing, Ethan Carpathian and his globalist allies demanded a set of carefully crafted favors. Pagosa agreed on the condition that Tilden nominate Sterns as his running mate.

Ultimately, Tilden's lust for power overrode the last vestiges of his patriotism. After an election marked by rampant fraud, Tilden won the Presidency and immediately issued executive orders to reward special interests.

Pagosa said, "Mr. President, you've delivered more than I ever thought possible. You will be remembered as the great leader who ushered in a world of peace, sustainability, and happiness. A world in which the common man will own nothing but be happy."

President Tilden smiled affectionately and said, "Linda, I feared my political career was over, and you breathed new life into it. I'm forever in your debt."

Pagosa smiled, grasped his hand, and said, "Soon, it'll be time for the youngsters to take over."

Tilden's decades-long Washington conditioning told him to play along: "After I win the second term, we can decide how to spin my departure and give you your first female President."

Pagosa nodded in agreement and said, "But first, we've got to win the election. Currently, your approval rating stands at twenty-eight percent. The only way to improve it is to spend another two trillion in stimulus to prop up the economy, pressure the Fed to cut interest rates to pump up the market, open up the strategic oil reserve to lower prices at the pump, and implement a national minimum income."

"Use the people's money to buy the vote?" Tilden laughed.

"Exactly, but what do we do about Chinese threats against Taiwan? It's the second-highest concern among likely voters," Pagosa noted.

Tilden said, "The Joint Chiefs think fighting the Chinese right now is too risky, especially in their backyard. I won't risk the media showing U.S. troops losing another war. Afghanistan still stings."

"So, what's your plan?"

Tilden smiled, "I'll talk tough, send the Taiwanese some more missiles and planes, and institute tougher trade sanctions. You know, make it look like we're on top of things."

Pagosa was pleased the President had embraced her well-scripted lines. Now, for her close, "James, do you remember that night we bore our souls on the yacht?"

Tilden recalled how hot Pagosa looked in her bikini back then.

It had been a short affair after his first wife had passed thirty years ago. Cruelly, time had removed his sexual energy, and all that remained were memories.

"Yes, it was a wonderful time," Tilden said with a flicker of amorousness in his eyes.

"James, you're the most powerful man on Earth. Stay the course," Pagosa said as she squeezed his knee.

Tilden leaned in, kissed her cheek, and said, "Thanks for that."

"James, when the right wing brings pitchforks, remember you're leading us into a world of peace and sustainability," Pagosa said tenderly.

Pagosa stood, and Tilden followed her to the door, tight roping his steps as he shuffled along. Before opening the door, Pagosa kissed the President on the mouth, then left the Oval Office.

Speakers Limousine

The Speaker of the House, Linda Pagosa, sat forward in her seat, resting her hand lightly on the back of the driver's headrest as the armored black Suburban rolled east across Constitution Avenue. She kept her eyes on the National Mall, its monuments glowing in the amber dusk. The Washington Monument stood proud and still, but to her it looked increasingly like a tombstone—perhaps for the crumbling remnants of American leadership.

Despite the administration's careful choreography—reduced schedules, teleprompter-only appearances, and an unspoken embargo on unvetted press interactions—the President's steady physical decline was becoming impossible to hide. His latest fall at Dover had made the front page of The Times and The Post simultaneously, and the meme cycle online had already brutalized his image into caricature. The elder statesman's executive orders were being buried under talk-show punchlines and TikTok parodies. Time was running out.

Ring, ring!

The encrypted phone buzzed in her coat pocket. Caller ID: E. Carpathian – Encrypted Line.

Pagosa swiped to answer. “This is Linda.”

“Linda, Ethan here.”

She softened her tone. “Mr. Carpathian, to what do I owe the pleasure?”

“I am worried about the President’s decline,” he said without preamble.

Pagosa’s lips tightened. She stared at the Capitol dome ahead, then forced a confident tone into her voice. “Well, don’t you worry. I have it under control.”

“How so?” His voice was smooth, but there was steel beneath it.

She hated having to explain herself, but when the man funding half your caucus and underwriting three Super PACs calls, you respond. “His secretary and I make sure he signs what we put in front of him. Most of it gets signed by staffers using the autopen. Amanda Pigeon controls the press pool—tighter than Langley. We’ve secured over 370 House and Senate votes through committee assignments, favors, and a few offshore incentives. Honestly, we couldn’t manage him better if we tethered him to puppet strings.”

There was silence on the line.

Then: “What if the President passes?”

Pagosa heard something unfamiliar in Carpathian’s voice—fear. Not the fear of chaos, but of losing control. He hadn’t clawed his way to the top of the New World Order just to watch a geriatric collapse take out twenty years of strategic planning.

She leaned back, voice calm and cold. “Ethan, I revised the 25th Amendment procedures myself during the last term. If he dies, we sign three lines on the transfer form, take it to a federal judge, and have Conja sworn in.”

“And you control VP Sterns as well?” Carpathian cross-examined.

“Absolutely. She’ll follow orders. While she may not inspire crowds, she obeys directives. And if she hesitates, we have her brother’s sealed records in the drawer. She’ll cooperate.” Pagosa said, then held her breath. She knew how fragile this alliance was. Without Carpathian’s funding—or Helmut Kath’s European syndicates—her war chest would bleed dry.

Finally, Ethan spoke. "Okay, Linda. Just keep the cameras off the President. The fewer people see him, the better."

Pagosa exhaled. Carpathian had believed her. "Thanks, Ethan. I'll see you soon."

As the line went dead, she stared out the window, the Capitol building now close enough to see the guards on the steps. The real power was wielded behind closed doors, and she knew it. Tilden was merely a placeholder. A fragile, fading figurehead.

Thousands of miles away, in a private study overlooking Solar Valley, Ethan Carpathian set his phone down on a marble credenza. He steepled his fingers and stared at the crimson horizon.

Others had built the scaffolding of globalism—he had simply climbed it and seized the moment. Now, with the U.S. on its last legs and the East rising, there could be no mistakes. It was the fourth quarter, and his team couldn't fumble the ball.

Los Angeles International Airport

"Please raise your seats to their upright position, secure your tray tables, and return all items to the overhead bin or under the seat in front of you. We will be landing at the Los Angeles International Airport in thirty minutes," the flight attendant said.

Sue lifted the window shade and saw the brown-green California coast; her watch told her she'd slept eight hours.

The flight attendant came by with a trash bag, looked at Sue, and asked, "Need anything?"

Sue loosened her mask and replied, "No, thank you."

"We'll be on the ground soon," the flight attendant said as she continued down the aisle.

Fortunately, her hasty departure from China had kept State Security from stopping her. Now, she wondered if her rapidly declining health would allow her to reach Dr. Chen in time.

The ten-minute taxi to the gate seemed like an eternity as she began to shake and her breathing grew labored. When the pilot turned off the fasten seat belt sign, Sue grabbed her backpack and held onto the seat backs as she unsteadily made her way to the door. As she started up the ramp, each step became more challenging. To keep from falling, Sue leaned against the wall.

Seeing her struggle, Dr. James Hughes, Center Director at U.C.L.A.'s Comprehensive Cancer Center, stopped and asked, "I'm a doctor. Can I help you?"

Dr. Fen opened her eyes and said in accented English, "I'm a virologist from the Wuhan Institute." After a few labored breaths, she continued, "I have critical information for Dr. Chen. All the data is on my laptop. It could save millions."

Sue gave Dr. Hughes her backpack, and her anxiety began to drop.

Hughes briefly looked at the pack, then back to the small Asian woman, trying to process what he'd just heard. For an instant, Hughes wondered if the woman was mentally ill, then defaulted to his medical training and said, "Wait here. I'll get help."

Hughes located a gate worker and said, "I'm a doctor with a very ill patient. I need an ambulance."

The attendant called for a transporter while the other passengers spread throughout the airport. A minute later, the wheelchair arrived, and Dr. Hughes helped Sue into it.

"Son, I need to get her to an ambulance," Dr. Hughes told Mark Swade, a twenty-something passenger transporter.

"Yes, sir," replied Swade.

Swade pushed Dr. Fen up the ramp and stopped at the gate, where he punched a code into a wall-mounted phone and waited.

"I have a very ill passenger and her physician. They need an ambulance?" Swade asked.

After several seconds, Dr. Hughes heard Swade say, "Thank you, our ETA is ten minutes."

After an efficient trek through the terminal, Swade delivered the doctor and patient to a waiting ambulance.

UCLA Medical Center

A team of nurses and residents in bright orange, Level One hazmat suits formed a perimeter around the ambulance as it hissed to a stop in the restricted bay. Their movements were swift, rehearsed—more military than medical. The reinforced ER wing of the facility had been cleared in record time. It was apparent this wasn't a drill.

Standing ten feet back from the action, Doctors Chen and Stevens watched the scene unfold. Both men wore white lab coats—an intentional distinction from the scrubs worn by those around them. It wasn't arrogance. It was status. And it came with expectations.

Dr. Hughes approached briskly, a weathered backpack clutched in his gloved hands. His eyes met Chen's, then Stevens's, and the weight of his expression preempted the conversation.

"I see you got my message," Hughes said.

"Thanks for the heads up," Stevens replied, voice cool, clipped. "What can you tell us?"

"Our patient is female, early forties, Asian. She claims to be a virologist from the Wuhan Institute. She's deteriorating—fever's spiking, blood oxygen's tanking. The clinical picture resembles COVID-19. She was insistent that I get this to you." Hughes handed the backpack to Chen. "Says it has vital information. Top priority."

Dr. Chen took it carefully, gripping the worn straps as if receiving a treaty. His eyes didn't leave the bag. "We've had recent reports out of Wuhan. Six researchers are dead. The chatter's been light, but the implications aren't."

Chen—short, compact, and focused—was a third-generation American whose Chinese-born parents had fled the mainland during the communist revolution. Though raised in San Diego, his upbringing straddled both worlds. Fluent in Mandarin and steeped in the cultural nuances of the Chinese Communist Party elite, Chen had become the quiet bridge between American intelligence and China's opaque biosciences sector. In public, he was a respected virologist. In private, he fed the CIA a steady trickle of invaluable information.

Dr. Stevens remained silent, absorbing the data with a tactical mind honed by war and trauma. At six-foot-four, Stevens was all muscle and movement, his every step charged with the coiled energy of a man who'd lived too long in forward-operating bases and black sites. His past was classified, but his resume read like a novel—All-American wide receiver, trauma surgeon, SEAL, CIA asset. He'd stitched soldiers together under mortar fire, then led kill teams under moonless skies. The white coat didn't fit him so much as disguise him.

"We'll keep her in isolation," Stevens said, his voice carrying finality. "Until we know what we're dealing with."

Chen nodded, eyes still on the bag. "Let's see what she risked her life to bring us."

Stevens turned toward the ER. "I'll check on our guest while you play detective. The sooner we figure this out, the better."

He made his way to the cleanroom vestibule, where a waiting tech helped him into a fresh hazmat suit. Within moments, the seal clicked shut, and the world outside dulled to a mechanical hum. The airlock hissed as he stepped into the negative-pressure chamber, its HEPA filters scrubbing the air like a biocontainment vault.

Inside, the room was quieter. Dr. Sue Fen lay unconscious on the isolation bed, a web of sensors trailing from her arms and chest. Her breathing was shallow. The EKG stuttered with irregularity. And despite the pharmaceutical cocktail administered during transport, her fever continued to rise.

Stevens approached slowly, every instinct from years of combat pressing into his awareness. This wasn't a trauma wound or shrapnel case. This was unknown territory. A different kind of battlefield.

He stared down at the woman—China's leading Gain of Function (GoF) virologist, according to Chen—and the gravity of the moment settled like lead on his chest. If her story was true, she could be carrying the blueprint for the next global pandemic—or worse, a targeted bioweapon.

Stevens looked at Sue again. Her lips moved faintly, and he leaned in. Through the fog of delirium, she whispered something—barely audible.

"Tell them… I tried… to stop it."

The words chilled him more than the air filtration system ever could.

In that moment, Dr. Stevens didn't just see a patient.

He saw the fuse of a global crisis—and maybe, just maybe, this woman could stop it. He had to keep her alive.

Department of Infectious Disease, UCLA

Back in his office, Dr. Chen put on medical gloves and opened the computer compartment of Dr. Fen's backpack. Inside were three things: a ruggedized laptop, a sealed biometric security device, and a bound notebook, its pages dense with Mandarin script and molecular diagrams.

After running start-up routines, the computer required Dr. Fen's email address and a randomly generated code. Chen searched the backpack and found a token device that generated a different code every 15 seconds. With half the equation solved, Chen searched for Dr. Fen's email address on the World Society for Virology members' website. Five minutes later, he returned to the conference table and entered Dr. Fen's email and a code from the token.

Once inside, he examined the files in the subfolder labeled "Clinical Trials, Ughygar Camp," then transferred them to his laptop for analysis. After working all night, he learned the Chinese had tested bioweapons on 20,000 concentration camp inmates, killing eighty percent.

"My God, they tested coronaviruses, anthrax, smallpox, and some new agent known as Chimera on human subjects! These are serious crimes against humanity!" Chen said to himself, disgust evident in his tone.

He then logged into Dr. Fen's electronic health record and reviewed her test results. His detective work quickly revealed that the Chinese scientist's lab values and symptoms mirrored those of victims infected with Chinese agent CV-23, most likely a genetically engineered version of COVID-19.

He picked up the phone and dialed Dr. Steven's private cell.

"Stevens."

"Our patient is infected with an evolved form of COVID-19, known as COVID-23. The virus had an eighty percent mortality when tested on concentration camp inmates. Severe lung scarring and myocarditis were found in half of the survivors. In many cases, the subjects appear to have died from complications associated with a cytokine storm," Chen said clinically.

Stevens digested the bleak news and asked, "Do you have a treatment recommendation?"

"The trials showed efficacy in a new agent called Paxlovid-23. Pharm-X manufactures it in China. I have the pharmacy checking on availability and have reached out to the NIH to see if they can obtain some through a compassionate use waiver. While the older drug, Paxlovid, isn't identical, it might buy her some time."

Chen paused as he considered whether or not to say what was on his mind. Finally, he said, "There's one more thing. The test subjects who were vaccinated with the two primary U.S. vaccines all died."

A chill ran the length of Steven's body. "Are you suggesting a targeted bioweapon?"

Chen proceeded cautiously, "The fact that the Chinese gave test subjects the two primary vaccines used by the U.S. and our allies months before giving them CV-23 suggests they wanted to know how it would work on vaccinated people in the U.S. and NATO countries."

Stevens asked, "I'm not a virologist, but the CV-19 data doesn't show any spike in autoimmune deaths attributable to mRNA vaccines. So, why does CV-23 cause a fatal cytokine storm?"

"My working hypothesis is that the Chinese used GoF engineering to make CV-23 highly effective against those who received one of the mRHA vaccines. Their data show that they engineered variants similar to those highly effective against the other 10 Covid vaccines. This level of GoF is cutting-edge, suggesting either that the Chinese are further along than we thought or that they have an American researcher helping them."

Stephens knew that Dr. Chen was a Nobel Laureate who'd never been wrong. But a bioweapon that was optimized to kill vaccinated Americans was a serious threat. Possible American involvement was treason. He needed to get with Oxley as soon as possible.

UCLA Medical Center

At midnight, Dr. Stevens and two nurses, dressed in hazmat suits, moved Dr. Fen from the ICU to the Medical Intensive Care Unit (MICU) in an isolette.

The MICU occupied an entire floor of the patient tower and was accessed through a small lobby, which was secured by locked doors and two police officers. While Stevens knew the Unit was more secure than the ER, he took the precaution of carrying his 9mm pistol under his lab coat, just in case. With a clandestine Chinese police station operating in Los Angeles and Dr. Fen defecting with top-secret Chinese data, an assassination attempt couldn't be ruled out.

"Dr. Fen, can you hear me?" Dr. Stevens asked, looking down at his patient.

Dr. Fen had an endotracheal tube in her throat and was attached to a ventilator. It was the first time Stevens had seen her open her eyes in several hours. After a moment of disorientation, she reached up and felt the tube.

"You're on a ventilator at UCLA Medical Center. My name is Dr. Robert Stevens; I'm your attending physician. We'll take good care of you."

Dr. Fen looked at Dr. Stevens and made a writing motion with her hand.

One of the nurses took a dry-erase board and marker off the counter and handed them to her.

As they watched, Dr. Fen wrote, "Did the data get to Dr. Chen?"

Dr. Stevens said, "Dr. Chen and his team have analyzed your data and are working with the CDC."

Relieved, Dr. Fen closed her eyes and leaned back. After a moment, she opened her eyes again, erased the previous message, and wrote:

Highly Contagious airborne virus, high mortality

Bioweapon, tested in concentration camps, China is planning to deploy it soon. Cutting-edge GoF from....

Dr. Fen passed out before she could finish.

Stevens read the message and looked at the nurses, "Don't let anyone you don't know near her, and keep everything you hear confidential. This is a national security matter."

The deep concern in Dr. Steven's eyes alarmed his nurses. It had to be serious if 'old blood and guts Stevens' was worried.

The MICU Head Nurse replied, "Will do. I just hope we can find a treatment soon."

"Increase TPN; maybe more nutrition will help. Her immune system is killing her as it tries to fight the virus, so let's start her on corticosteroids to try and tamp down her immune response and check the cytokine storm," Stevens replied.

CDC Video Conference

Four days after Dr. Fen arrived, Dr. Chen and Dr. Stevens attended a call with the CDC to discuss a potential pandemic.

The virtual conference call opened with sterile efficiency—twelve public health officials logged in, their agency seals glowing in the corner of each frame. At the top of the screen sat CDC Director Amy Rapier, flanked digitally by Dr. Chen and Dr. Stevens. Rapier was a tall, overweight woman with dyed blonde hair cut to shoulder length. While not considered attractive by most men, the Director had risen in the field of Public Health due to her well-honed skills as a practiced liar and manipulator. Her liaisons with powerful men, such as her current boyfriend, Dr. Lawerence Wilhite, had helped her ascent to power.

Beneath the clinical light of bureaucracy, the stakes simmered unseen: the survival of a nation—or its collapse into pandemic chaos.

"Dr. Chen," Rapier began, smoothing her tone for the cameras, "what have you learned?"

Chen spoke with calm precision. "Files on the Chinese human trials from Dr. Fen's laptop indicate CV-2023 aggressively targets pulmonary tissues. In most cases, mortality results from immune hyperactivation, specifically a cytokine storm. The good news, if you can call it that, is that the Wuhan Institute co-developed an antiviral with PharmX—Paxlovid-23. Their clinical trials showed statistically significant efficacy in saving lives."

Rapier's brow furrowed just enough to be convincing. "Is it in inventory?"

Chen shook his head. "Our PharmX liaison says it doesn't exist in their open supply chain. NIH confirms it's not part of any domestic or international trials. This means Paxlovid-23 was developed through Chinese military channels, off the books."

The words hung in the air like a flare over a battlefield.

Rapier's expression shifted. Chen had just publicly linked a top-tier U.S. pharmaceutical contractor to a Chinese military bioweapons lab. Her instincts screamed damage control. "Dr. Stevens," she pivoted smoothly, "how is patient zero?"

Stevens, ever the battlefield physician, responded without sugar. "As of this morning, she can communicate using a dry-erase pad. But her vitals are deteriorating. Blood oxygen is tanking. Right now, she's fighting, but losing ground."

"What can we do?" Rapier asked, her voice now cloaked in mock compassion.

"A treatment recommendation would help," Stevens replied curtly. "Right now, corticosteroids are the only thing keeping her alive."

Rapier stiffened. "The CDC doesn't recommend steroids in this scenario—they open the door to opportunistic infection."

Stevens didn't flinch. "Nevertheless, they've improved her oxygen levels. If she gets an infection, we can treat it. But if she suffocates, the debate is moot. That's the difference between public health and bedside medicine, Director."

Rapier paused, visibly checked by the rebuke. "I'm sorry we can't be more helpful."

Chen leaned forward. "Can you get the President to ban flights from China? Help us contain it?"

"Not likely," Rapier answered.

"That's unfortunate," Chen said.

"We have contacted all passengers and crew from the Wuhan flight and issued voluntary quarantine orders," Rapier offered, "Right now, it's all we can do to contain the virus."

"If they quarantine, it will help," Chen replied. "There's also the chance that Dr. Fen's precautions during transit limited the spread."

Stevens wasn't done. "Why isn't the administration demanding answers from Beijing?"

Rapier's voice cooled. "The President believes the threat of war over Taiwan is the bigger concern. He doesn't want to ignite a second front over a single case of a novel virus."

Stevens heard it: deflection. Minimization. Control. Rapier wasn't just shielding the White House—she was managing the narrative. But Stevens wasn't interested in playing press secretary.

"I'm pulling in the CIA," he said bluntly.

The screen flickered with stunned silence. Then Rapier's voice, tight with apprehension: "On what grounds?"

He had her. The faint hitch in her tone confirmed it. "The Wuhan Institute is the bioweapons arm of the CCP. We have hard proof they used gain-of-function enhancements on COVID-19, smallpox, anthrax, and SARS variants—then tested them on concentration camp inmates. Thousands dead. This is a biological weapon, plain and simple."

Rapier's face betrayed the flicker of guilt before the bureaucratic mask snapped back into place. "Let's not jump to conclusions. The Chinese data suggest they were testing treatments and vaccines preemptively. Paxlovid-23's development might indicate early-stage therapeutic planning, not warfare."

Stevens leaned forward, eyes locked. "Amy, you don't infect prisoners with engineered viruses and call it public health. You call it what it is—a war crime."

The silence that followed was surgical. Rapier didn't respond immediately. She was stalling, calculating.

Stevens could almost hear the gears turning—who to call, which levers to pull, what headlines to control. He knew her type: not a foot soldier, but a practiced manipulator. The kind of operative who never pulled a trigger, but made sure the bullets ended up in the guns of men who would do her dirty work.

He also knew she'd already written him off. The SEAL. The field surgeon. The expendable asset.

The real question was: what would she do about Dr. Fen? The woman who might expose everything.

Rapier smiled faintly and ended the call with a practiced nod. But behind her eyes, Stevens saw it—the cold glint of strategy.

And now he knew. The virus wasn't the only threat.

Jerusalem

"At the center of the stage stood Ethan Carpathian, whose wealth and influence were redefining the global landscape. Dressed in a tailored suit reflective of his status, his presence commanded attention. The silver highlights in his hair glinted in the sunlight as his piercing blue eyes scanned the crowd with solemnity and pride.

To his right, representatives from Israel, including Prime Minister Rachel Ben-Ami, a seasoned and respected leader, stood alongside him. To his left, the leaders of the ten-nation Arab coalition, including Crown Prince Faisal of Saudi Arabia, Imam Khaled Al-Mansoor of Egypt, and President Leila Haddad of Jordan, represented their peoples with dignity and hope.

The crowd's murmurs hushed as Carpathian stepped to the podium, microphones angled to capture his every word.

"Today, we stand on the precipice of history. Today, we affirm that peace is not just a distant dream but a tangible reality. Today, Jerusalem—the city of faith, history, and resilience—becomes a beacon of hope for the entire world."

The crowd erupted into applause. Carpathian raised his hand as if conducting a symphony, quieting the crowd.

"For decades, this region has known pain, conflict, and division. No longer. The peace treaty we brokered between Israel and the Arab coalition is more than just a piece of paper. It is a testament to our shared humanity; our collective will to forge a future where our children can live in harmony, and our differences are celebrated rather than condemned."

Carpathian paused, allowing the gravity of his words to sink in.

"As part of this historic accord, we have agreed on a monumental step forward that honors the faith and traditions of all peoples of this land. Together, we will rebuild the Jewish Temple on the Temple Mount, adjacent to the Dome of the Rock. This sacred space will symbolize our commitment to coexistence, respect, and mutual reverence."

Gasps and murmurs rippled through the crowd. Everyone felt the enormity of the announcement. For a moment, the weight of history pressed down, only to be lifted by a renewed sense of possibility.

Prime Minister Rachel Ben-Ami stepped forward, her eyes shining with emotion, "This is a day we never thought we would see. A day when Jews, Muslims, and Christians alike can look upon the Temple Mount and see a symbol of peace and shared destiny. This is not just a victory for Israel or the Arab nations—it is a victory for humanity."

Crown Prince Faisal took his turn at the podium, his voice rich and measured, "The rebuilding of the Jewish Temple alongside the Dome of the Rock is a testament to our commitment to peace and religious freedom. It is a powerful message to the world that we can find common ground despite our differences. We can honor our diverse histories while building a united future."

As the leaders exchanged nods of respect, Carpathian took the podium, "Let this be the beginning of a new era. An era where the walls of division crumble and the bridges of understanding are built. Let Jerusalem, the City of Peace, illuminate humanity's path to a new world order. A world where energy is plentiful, food abundant, and the common man is freed from the tyranny of economic manipulation."

The crowd erupted once more, a wave of applause and cheers that seemed to echo through the ancient stones of Jerusalem. Ethan Carpathian stepped back, flanked by the leaders of this newfound peace.

***

Susie Legman, UNN Anchor, stood with the assembly behind her and said, "This historic peace treaty was signed just an hour ago, and you just heard from its architect, Ethan Carpathian. We now turn to Dr. James Stanton, a Middle East Expert and professor at the Kennedy School of Government, for his analysis of this historic event. Professor, how did Ethan Carpathian, a businessman with no diplomatic experience, walk into a war-torn region and exit with the ultimate peace treaty?"

Professor Stanton's image came online from his faculty office, where he said, "Mr. Carpathian brilliantly used economic incentives to bring people together. What we call peace through prosperity."

"Are you suggesting that Carpathian bought the peace?"

Stanton smiled as he shook his head side to side, "No, merely suggesting that Carpathian's grant of $25 billion to these eleven nations to develop a green energy ecosystem and AI-enabled manufacturing capability was a stroke of genius. It's what we call a win-win negotiation. Economically, this means a 70% reduction in electricity costs in these countries, plus thousands of good-paying jobs for people without a college education. With much of Carpathian's component manufacturing being built in the Gaza Strip, Palestinians will soon have significant economic opportunities and feel more included. It's free infrastructure and know-how that will pay dividends for centuries."

"So, are you saying they did it for the money?"

"I'm suggesting the Treaty allows Middle Eastern leaders to reduce their military spending, eliminate the risk of nuclear Armageddon, and gain money and cutting-edge energy technology. The economic incentives for cooperation are compelling. What is shocking is that Carpathian made rebuilding the Jewish Temple part of the deal. Technically speaking, he erred when he brought an emotional issue into an otherwise logical negotiation."

"So, how did Carpathian pull it off?"

"That's the question we're all asking."

"Thank you, Professor Stanton," Susie said as she closed the interview.

Wuhan Institute of Virology

Dr. Wu Jingyi wasn't one to jump at shadows. Years as a virologist at the Wuhan Institute of Virology had taught him to be careful. Yet, as he pocketed his phone after a hushed call, a knot of unease tightened in his stomach. The voice on the other end, his CIA case officer codenamed "World Traveler," had been unusually urgent. They urgently needed top-secret files, and he was their only asset capable of obtaining them.

Swiping his security badge, Wu entered the sterile labyrinth of the Institute's high-containment lab. The usual hum of machinery seemed muted today, his heightened awareness sharpening every sound. The request gnawed at him. Classified documents? From the military servers? Even with his Level 4 clearance, the highest offered at the Institute, Wu knew these systems were fortresses. Firewalls bristled with intrusion detection, and access logs were monitored with hawk-like vigilance.

Stealing classified data was a tightrope walk with no net. But the urgency in World Traveler's voice, the weight he placed on these files, echoed in his mind. The acid of fear burned in his stomach as he entered his laboratory.

Remembering his training, Wu knew he needed to stick to his routine. One misstep and the goons would be on him like a cat on a mouse. Nervously, he walked to the bat cages, removed the catchment tray, and emptied bat droppings into a container. He then lined the receptacle with fresh paper and placed the tray back in the cage. Afterward, he weighed 600 grams of material and divided it equally among ten vessels for analysis. After labeling each sample, he began the test procedures, carefully adhering to his routine.

Alone in the laboratory, Wu moved to a workstation outside the security camera's range and entered a stolen user ID and password. After a five-minute search, he opened the military operations directory and located a subdirectory labeled 冬风行动 (*Operation Dragon Strike)*. The file was the most recent of China's war plans and must have been what the CIA was looking for. He inserted his jump drive into the USB port and began the download. The download estimate was five minutes.

While he waited, Wu opened a summary page:

TOP SECRET ULTRA: OPERATION DRAGON STRIKE, Section 231-09: Attack Plan, Bioweapons Trifecta: Anthrax, CV-23, and Smallpox as a precursor for Chimera

Did the military have a timeline for deploying these agents? And what was Operation Dragon Strike? How many other sections existed if this were Section 9? What is Chimera? He had more questions than answers.

The sudden hiss of the airlock opening shattered the sterile silence, sending a jolt through Wu. He spun around, heart hammering against his ribs. The digital clock on the wall read 00:30. The next shift wasn't due until 07:00!

His mind raced. Had security traced his access? While the knot in his stomach tightened into a fist, Wu forced himself into a semblance of normalcy, logging out with trembling fingers. As he shuffled back to his instruments, every creak in the lab sounded like approaching footsteps. He snatched a lab notebook at his station and scribbled down invented readings from the blinking displays with feigned nonchalance.

He glanced at the airlock door, a metallic barrier between his secret mission and an uncertain future. The silence stretched, broken only by the rhythmic hum of the lab equipment. Each tick of the unseen clock felt like a hammer blow. Was it his imagination, or did the air feel a little thicker, heavier with the weight of his subterfuge?

Wu forced himself to focus on the charade, meticulously noting nonsensical data. Every fabricated entry felt like a desperate prayer, a plea for the charade to hold until morning. The weight of the potential consequences of his actions pressed down on him like an invisible hand. He was a scientist, not a spy, and this clandestine world felt terrifying.

Ten seconds later, the airlock door opened, and General Leu, Military Leader of Chinese Bio-Weapons Development, asked, “What are you doing, Dr. Jingyi?”

"Collecting samples for fecal analysis."

General Leu stared at him while two armed men in military fatigues inspected the lab.

Wu glanced back at the workstation as they did so. To his horror, his jump drive was protruding from the computer! If they found it, he’d be tortured, maybe killed!

General Leu distrusted American-educated scientists and stared menacingly at him. Finally, he goaded him by saying, "Playing with bat shit isn't exactly Nobel prize-worthy for a Cal-Tech graduate, is it?"

Wu was offended but smiled weakly and replied, "Sometimes, you must shovel shit to get ahead in science."

General Leu's face softened as he laughed. "Indeed. I once had to change bedpans, but I eventually reached the top. If you remain loyal, you will rise. Your work is more important than you realize."

Wu smiled politely.

General Leu turned and walked to the workstation, typed in his user ID and password, and ran a report of file accessions. Fortunately for Wu, he’d used someone else's credentials and moved the workstation out of camera view months ago. The only evidence against him was the drive.

Wu watched the General conferring with his men. To his horror, General Leu stared at him as if deciding his fate. Then, without another word, the general and his men exited the lab.

When alone, Wu returned to the computer and retrieved the jump drive. After breathing a sigh of relief, he placed the drive in his lab coat pocket and resumed work.

***

At the end of his shift, Wu went to the restroom. In the privacy of the stall, he sat on the toilet, removed his right shoe, and twisted the heel, revealing a hidden compartment. The scientist then removed the jump drive from his pocket.

As he stared at the device, he considered the consequences of his actions. At first, fear inspired him to flush it down the toilet and to say nothing to his case officer. Then, he remembered an ancient saying, 'The needs of the many exceed the needs of the one.' Ultimately, altruism overrode self-interest, and Wu placed the device inside the secret compartment.

"Here goes nothing," Wu said as he flushed the toilet and headed to the exit.

When he reached the security checkpoint, a rather bored-looking guard ran his backpack through an X-ray machine while another scanned his ID card. Wu breathed a sigh of relief as he cleared security and walked to his motor scooter. For a brief moment, the sound of the birds and wind in his face took his mind off his situation. So far, so good.

Wuhan Institute Parking Lot

"He's on the move," Sergeant Feng murmured into his wrist mic.

From the command center, General Leu's voice came back cold and precise: "See if he meets anyone."

Wu Jingyi threaded his scooter through traffic, nerves sparking as he glanced in the mirror. Two motorcycles. Same men, same distance. His gut clenched. He cut right, then left again, but they clung to him like shadows.

Cold sweat trickled down his spine. He gunned the throttle and dove into the clogged arteries of the HanZheng District. When a wall of buses jammed the intersection, he punched through a red light. Horns blared. A taxi clipped his fender, but he kept going, the pursuers trapped behind a surge of honking cars.

Wu ditched the scooter in a shopping arcade, slid into the crowd, and vanished into the human tide. Ten minutes of weaving through stalls left his lungs burning, and his nerves frayed. He ducked into a convenience store, bought a black jacket, a cap, and cheap sunglasses. In the changing booth, he became someone else. A ghost with a backpack.

The thumb drive pressed against his ribs, heavier than lead. He wasn't just a scientist anymore. He was a courier of secrets. A fugitive with the fate of nations on his back.

Outside, he lit a cigarette. He hated smoking, but instructors had been right—it made surveillance casual. A man leaning against a wall, smoke curling in the shadows, was invisible in plain sight.

When the nicotine steadied his hands, he slipped into a narrow alley. Rats scattered. Garbage bins stank of rot. He kicked at a section of brick until the hidden compartment snapped open. With shaking fingers, he slid the drive inside. A whisper of triumph surged through him—mission complete.

He resealed the brick, stripped off his disguise in a pay toilet, and emerged as just another tired commuter. At his favorite diner, Wu ordered breakfast and forced down every bite as if it might be his last.

Across the street, Sergeant Feng sat on a bench, phone raised in a mock text. "Subject is eating at his usual haunt," he reported.

"Notify us when he moves," the voice replied in his earpiece.

Wu finished, walked back to his scooter, and felt his pulse spike when he spotted the same two men waiting, engines idling. He pulled an orange helmet cover onto his lid, strapped it to the seat, and tried to look calm.

At his apartment, he set the scooter aside and stepped inside, eyes scanning every shadow. Nothing looked touched. But instinct whispered otherwise. His hand trembled as he picked up the baseball bat he kept near the door.

"If they come," Wu muttered in English, the words rough and foreign on his tongue, "I can at least go down fighting."

***

As Officer Zheng watched Dr. Jingyi enter his apartment, Feng spoke into his cell phone, "He's home."

General Leu asked, "Are you sure he didn't meet an accomplice in town?"

Feng knew it was best not to tell the General he had lost sight of Dr. Jingyi and said, "No, sir. Do you want us to search his apartment?"

General Leu thought it over and said, "Yes, call me when you're done."

***

Jake Hendel parallel parked his rental car across the street from Wu's apartment building. A jolt of apprehension shot through him as he spotted the pre-arranged abort signal, an orange helmet cover hanging on the scooter. It was a silent scream from the scientist, indicating the mission had gone south.

Thinking fast, Jake grabbed his satellite phone and dialed. A faint crackle filled the air, and then a clipped voice spoke. "Control."

"This is World Traveler, connect me with Asian Fox, it's urgent," Jake responded, using his alias. He kept his voice low, eyes scanning the street for any sign of trouble.

After several clicks, Raymond Jones, Director of the CIA's Asian Region, said, “Have you retrieved the lunch box?”

Hendel said, “Not yet; Batman sent the emergency signal.”

Jones's blood pressure rose as he considered the ramifications, then replied, “The data is your priority. Get it to us ASAP.”

“Wilco, world traveler, out,” Hendel said as he turned his car around and sped off for the dead drop.

As he drove, Jake worried that his agent might not withstand an intense interrogation. What if Wu told them he was his CIA Case Officer? While his instincts told him to run, his mission required that he remain in the fight, at least until he had the drive. Millions of lives, American lives, hung in the balance.

CIA Headquarters, Langley, Virginia

CIA Director Mark Oxley was not a man who drew second glances. At five-foot-ten, with thinning brown hair and the look of a mid-tier trial lawyer, he blended seamlessly into the corridors of power. But behind the unassuming exterior was one of the most influential men in Washington.

Yale had given him his start, and Harvard Law had given him his credentials. But it was Skull and Bones, the whispered brotherhood within Yale’s Gothic halls, that had opened the true doors. Its alumni network stretched across boardrooms, think tanks, and cabinet offices. Presidents. Senators. Supreme Court Justices. Mark Oxley had sworn the same oath they all had, and it had served him well.

Yet, unlike most of his fraternity brothers, Oxley carried a quiet but unyielding faith. A conservative Christian in a town that regarded faith as mere theater, he kept his convictions close, revealing them only to those he trusted implicitly. To his staff, he was simply efficient, decisive, and unnervingly calm. To the President who appointed him, George W. Bush—himself a Bonesman—Oxley was a reliable hand.

Shortly after his appointment, the President arranged a private meeting between Oxley and his father, George H.W. Bush. The elder statesman, himself once CIA Director, had walked Oxley through the realities of the post-Cold War intelligence world: the shadow diplomacy of the Bilderberg Group, the economic blueprints drafted by the Trilateral Commission, the long-term policy shaping of the World Economic Forum. They were the quiet hands that adjusted the levers of globalization. For Oxley, it had been less orientation than revelation.

But there was another side of Oxley that few in Washington knew. He was the modern custodian of the Order of Jehovah's Warriors—"The Order," as it was whispered among its initiates. Its lineage stretched back to Joshua and Caleb, men who had carried out God's commands in the conquest of Canaan. Across three millennia, the Order had risen and fallen, its members hidden in plain sight, protecting God's people and delaying the onset of the Tribulation until the appointed hour.

Oxley often questioned whether that hour was drawing near. The signs multiplied: wars and rumors of wars, technological wonders twisted into instruments of oppression, men like Ethan Carpathian whose charisma and ambition bent nations to their will.

Alone in his office at Langley, Oxley leaned back in his chair, Bible open but unread on the desk before him. His lips moved, reciting a verse from memory, a reminder and a warning both: "No one knows the day or the hour when these things will happen—not even the angels in heaven nor the Son himself. Only the Father knows."

He closed the book gently, his eyes hardening with resolve. The world's great powers—China, Russia, even the hidden councils of the West—were aligning for a storm. His duty as CIA Director was to defend the Republic. But his calling as a man of faith, as a brother of the Order, was something higher.

And soon, he suspected, those two missions would collide.

Oxley picked up the black-and-white photograph on his desk. It was a simple picture taken forty years ago in front of a small white church in the Texas Hill Country. His parents, George and Maryann, beamed back at him, their faces etched with love and pride.

Unlike his fraternity brothers who'd inherited wealth and privilege, Oxley had climbed the ladder rung by rung, relying on sheer grit and merit. His parents had instilled in him a strong moral compass and a fierce work ethic. A trait that had propelled him forward even when the odds seemed stacked against him. Despite his success, Oxley could not help but look back on the tapestry of his life and see God's hand in it.

Oxley smiled, a flicker of pride crossing his features, as he glanced again at the photo. "I miss you," he said sweetly to the picture, remembering how proud they'd been when he'd received a full scholarship to Yale. The warm memories were interrupted by the buzz of his intercom.

Oxley pressed the button and said, "Yes."

"Director, it's time for your call. I've got you in Conference Room C," his assistant replied.

Oxley placed his family picture on the credenza and said, "Thank you."

Oxley picked up his well-worn portfolio and left through his rear office door. After shaking a few hands en route, he arrived at the conference room and seated himself at the head of the table.

The windowless conference room hummed with a low, comforting thrum of technology. Nestled in the heart of the building, it was a fortress against prying eyes and eavesdroppers. Secure fiber-optic cables snaked through the walls, connecting them to a satellite network that could reach 90% of the globe.

The intelligence game had come a long way since his rookie days. Back then, an encrypted flip phone and a silenced Beretta were considered the pinnacle of espionage. Now, a single room housed the power to orchestrate global operations with pinpoint precision.

Oxley entered the conference code. Seconds later, six video images emerged, one for each participant. Not accustomed to wasting time, the Director asked, "General Lawery, what can you tell us about the Wuhan Institute's connection to COVID-23?"

General Dr. Robert Lawrey, head of America's clandestine Biological Defense Directorate, had been at the epicenter of U.S. bioweapons research since leaving the National Institute of Advanced Medicine in 1999. The short, overweight scientist held dual doctorates—one in internal medicine and the other in virology—and was regarded as one of the world's leading experts on gain-of-function research for weaponization.

"Our analysis indicates that the pathogen we're calling CV-23 originated at the Wuhan Institute," Lawrey said.

Mark Oxley, CIA Director and former trial lawyer, raised an eyebrow. "Aren't other research institutes running coronavirus programs?"

"Yes," Lawrey admitted. "The Marburg Center for Infectious Disease in Europe, the Northern Pathogen Laboratory in Canada, and our own East Carolina Virology Lab have shared projects with Wuhan. On the corporate side, PharmX Global is the largest underwriter—60% of its shares are owned by foreigners. U.S. NCI grant money filled the rest."

"CDC Director, Rapier told Congress that CV-23 is a naturally occurring variant, not a GoF-engineered bug," Oxley pressed.

Lawrey's lips curled in disdain. "Rapier mixes enough truth to seem credible to the uninitiated, but leaves out the facts that matter. She's a polished liar."

Oxley leaned forward. "Walk me through your evidence."

Lawrey ticked points off on stubby fingers. "In 2012, a large cave bat colony was discovered in Yunnan Province of China. The bats there carried a SARS-like virus that was cultured and flown back to Wuhan for testing. In 2016, Dr. Wang's team collected blood samples from villagers living near the horseshoe bat colony harboring SARS-like coronaviruses. Of the 218 people tested, six individuals (approximately 2.7%) had detectable antibodies against these bat coronaviruses, but none of the antibody-positive individuals were ever sick from it."

"Are you saying that the naturally occurring bat virus was benign?" Oxley probed.

Lawery nodded in the affirmative, then said, "Yes. It means the virus never mutated into a dangerous bug."

"So, you're telling me that there's no way the bat virus morphed into COVID-19 or COVID-23?"

"I'm saying the probability of the bat virus mutating into a lethal virus is less than one in twenty million."

Oxley thought it over, then asked, "So, how did the bat virus turn into COVID-19 and COVID-23?"

"In 2018, an international team—including two U.S. researchers, Lawrence Wilhite and Neal Lobuglio — imported the bat virus to the U.S. and spliced it with SARS in mice, making it transmissible to humans. Wilhite's published research confirms it. Then, over time, the scientists used GoF techniques to create more lethal COVID strains. With each tranche, the virus became more deadly."

Oxley frowned. "So, you're saying Rapier lied under oath?"

"That's correct," Lawrey said without hesitation. "The benign strain never killed anyone. COVID-19 and 23 are Frankenstein viruses born in Wilhite's lab."

Oxley's tone sharpened. "Didn't the 2014 presidential directive ban gain-of-function research in the U.S.?"

"On paper," Lawrey replied. "But in 2017, Dr. Everett Franklin, head of the Biomedical Oversight Board, carved out exemptions—claiming proposals would be more rigorously reviewed. Optics, nothing more. And the ban only applied to U.S. soil. That's why Wilhite made a dozen trips to Wuhan during those years. Rapier accompanied him on three."

Oxley tapped his pen against the table. "Can you prove Wilhite's research seeded COVID-23? Enough to call it treason and make it stick in court?"

"Yes," Lawrey said grimly. "We have records of Wilhite shipping modified viral constructs to Wuhan. Leaked data from a whistleblower inside the Wuhan Institute—Dr. Fen—show COVID-23 prototypes were tested on political prisoners. Later versions were refined in Wilhite's North Carolina lab after the ban was lifted. Fen herself was infected with the eighth modified batch, coded COVID-23-08."

"And Lobuglio?"

"Lobuglio's clean. His official research focused on cancer immunotherapy and the use of mouse models to test GoF techniques that could serve as a vector for curing cancer. Reputable, valuable. When he discovered Wilhite's darker agenda, he threatened to expose him. A week later, Lobuglio died suddenly from an "accidental" lab-acquired infection. Convenient."

"Could it have been?" Oxley asked.

"No," Lawrey replied coldly. "Lobuglio's lab never handled live coronaviruses. The community whispered murder, but the local police lacked the forensic skill to tie it to Wilhite. But, I can."

Oxley sat back, the weight of the revelation settling over him. "Impact assessment?"

Lawrey's face darkened. "Without a viable vaccine or antiviral, our models show eighty percent U.S. mortality within twelve months."

Oxley's pulse quickened. "Why would our enemies use COVID-23 instead of something like anthrax or pox?"

Lawrey leaned across the table, his eyes hard as stone. “Because COVID-23 is precise, and they gained accurate disease models from the first pandemic. Anthrax is messy. Pox is crude. But COVID-23 was engineered to strike the strongest—athletes, soldiers, and essential workers. Where the first virus felled the frail, this one is designed to gut our defenses by killing the very people we rely on.”

For the first time that morning, Oxley felt actual dread creep into his bones. This wasn’t just a weapon. It was a biological blitzkrieg. A war designed not to wound America—but to destroy it.

Chapter 3

Wu yanked his curtains back, dread coiling in his stomach. Two figures stood across the street, their uniforms and purposeful stances unmistakable. State security. Panic clawed at him. His measly baseball bat and kitchen knives were no match for trained killers.

Thinking fast, he sprinted to his bedroom and snatched his satellite phone from a hidden compartment, his hand shaking as he dialed the familiar number. Each ring echoed in the oppressive quiet, each second an eternity.

"World Traveler, over," a voice crackled through the receiver. It was his case officer.

"This is… Batman," Wu blurted out, using his alias. "They're onto me."

He could practically hear the tension crackle through the line. Jake responded, his voice urgent. "Did you complete the drop?"

Despite the rising panic, Wu managed a single word. "Affirmative."

Jake could hear the fear in his operative's voice and felt sorry for him.

Relieved, Jake said, "Okay, here's what you do. Cooperate with the CCP and make sure they don't find anything suspicious in your apartment. Without the USB drive, they have no evidence to convict you. Remember your training. If you play the role of a naive scientist, you should be safe. They'll try to intimidate you; just don't admit to anything. You know nothing. Nothing at all, and we never met. Without me or the drive, they have nothing on you. Remember that."

Wu replied, "Understood, Batman out."

Wu's hands shook as he ran to the kitchen, shoved his satellite phone into the CIA-provided garbage disposal, and turned on the water. When he flipped the switch, the appliance's hardened cutters ground the phone into powder, erasing his last physical link to the CIA. He turned it off and breathed a sigh of relief. Then, the silence filled him with the realization that he had cut his lifeline to the CIA. He was on his own.

He jumped when he heard a knock at his door!

Wu eyed his kitchen knives as his primal urges fluttered between fight, flight, or freeze. Jake was right; the only hope was to convince the goons that he was nothing more than a loyal scientist.

Wu took a deep breath and walked to the door. "Stay calm and remember your training," Wu said to himself as his heart pounded in his chest.

When he opened the door, Officer Zheng pushed him inside and pinned him painfully against the wall, his arm across his throat. Sergeant Feng casually closed the door and looked at Wu, with animosity in his glaring eyes. To Wu's horror, Feng rifled through drawers, tore down pictures, and cut open his mattress and pillows while Zheng pressed Wu's face into the wall. After several minutes, Feng returned and asked, "Where is it?"

Zheng loosened his grip so he could respond.

Wu coughed and asked, "Where is what?"

Zheng punched Wu in the kidneys. He moaned, then fell to the floor.

Feng looked down and said, "It will be easier for you if you return the stolen files."

Wu looked up and tearfully tried to bluff his way out. "I don't have any files from the lab. My only files are personal. They are all on my laptop. Take it if you want. I know porn is prohibited, but I'm a lonely man."

The security team saw through the Scientist's vain attempt to mislead them. Feng kicked Wu in the ribs, then placed his foot on his throat. Wu fought to remove the sergeant's foot but couldn't.

After twenty seconds, the lack of blood flow to his brain caused him to pass out.

"Secure him while I confiscate his computer," Feng barked.

HanZheng District Eateries

The rental car stopped along a bustling backstreet, far from the gleaming facades of the tourist district. Jake blended seamlessly into the crowd, a chameleon navigating the urban jungle. The air thrummed with the symphony of a foreign city - a cacophony of car horns, street vendors hawking wares, and the rapid-fire chatter of conversation.

This district, a tangled web of narrow alleys and overflowing street markets, stood in stark contrast to the sanitized world of five-star hotels where he stayed. But for Jake, the grit and grime held a certain allure; it offered anonymity, a stage for clandestine transactions.

He pushed his way through the throng, navigating the chaotic dance of pedestrians with practiced ease. Three blocks later, he doubled back, a practiced maneuver to spot any tails. Satisfied, he ducked into a shadowy alley, its entrance swallowed by the crush of bodies on the main street. The dank air hung heavy; the only illumination came from slivers of sunlight filtering through cracks in the buildings above. Here, in this hidden nook, the real work began.

Jake's subtle gesture was seen by his Chinese contacts but remained unseen by the few passersby. The two men emerged from a parked van wearing white coveralls and rubber boots. After scanning their surroundings, they unloaded a pressure washer, donned goggles, and dragged the wheeled machine into the alley. Jake watched as they connected a hose to a water spigot, cranked the engine, and began to wash the walls. While one agent operated the machine, the other knelt behind a line of trash cans and removed the USB drive from the dead drop.

A plume of fragrant smoke curled from the cigar between Jake's lips as he stood guard by the alley's entrance. To any bystander, he was just another American tourist enjoying a puff. But beneath the casual facade, his gaze darted, scanning the bustling street for any sign of unwanted attention.

When the pre-arranged signal arrived, a subtle shift in posture from his team inside the alley, Jake stubbed out his cigar with a practiced flick. The charade was over. He strolled away from the alley, his pace deliberately slow, weaving through the throng of people. This seemingly leisurely walk served a dual purpose: to create distance from the drop site and to give his contact, Wade Jing, time to shed his disguise.

A block later, Jake emerged onto a side street, eyes scanning the crowd. He spotted Wade Jing, blending seamlessly into the background amidst the throng of pedestrians. With a barely perceptible nod, Jing stepped behind Jake, maintaining a comfortable distance. The newsstand became their silent meeting point, where a casual glance could carry volumes of unspoken communication.

Jake said to the vendor, "South China Morning Post, please."

As the vendor turned to retrieve Jake's paper, Wade Jin placed the USB on the counter. Jake put some change down and palmed the drive.

The owner returned, handed Jake his paper, and picked up the coins.

Jake nodded and walked away while Wade Jing bought a pack of cigarettes. Since the two men's arrival at the Kiosk seemed random and the CCP surveillance cameras were out of position to record the exchange, no one was the wiser.

Wuhan Residential District

When Wu awoke, he found himself lying on the couch, his hands and feet bound. His CIA training hadn't prepared him for this eventuality, and sweat ran down his face as he imagined the worst. What would it be, a bullet in the knee, cutting off a finger?

A few minutes later, Zheng walked out of the kitchen holding a soft drink in one hand and his silenced pistol in the other.

"For your sake, I hope there's nothing on your computer. The security service is examining it now," Zheng said with a sadistic smile.

Wu remained silent as sweat stains began to appear on his shirt.

After a while, Zheng turned on the television and watched the popular Chinese series *Secret of the Three Kingdoms.*

Wu stared at the TV, grateful for the distraction. After a while, he decided to stop catastrophizing. Jake was right; the CCP had no evidence against him. Additionally, he was a highly valued scientist.

Two hours seemed like twenty-four as he waited.

The insistent trill of Zheng's phone shattered the tense silence in the room. A flicker of something crossed his face, a fleeting emotion quickly masked by professional stoicism. He answered with a curt "Yes," his voice devoid of warmth.

Zheng listened intently, his body rigid as a statue. He ended the call with a clipped "Will do," the phone clattering back onto the table like a discarded playing card.

He turned back to Wu, a cold, emotionless mask replacing the facade of camaraderie. Sensing a chilling shift in the atmosphere, Wu saw his death sentence reflected in Zheng's steely gaze.

There were no last words, no time to allow the victim to plead for mercy. Zheng simply raised his weapon. The metallic click was a horrifying punctuation mark in the room's stillness. A single gunshot echoed in the confined space, the sharp crack followed by a sickening thud!

Zheng approached the body; his movements deliberate and measured. A cursory check confirmed his grim task was complete. He retrieved his phone, a ghost of a smirk playing on his lips.

He said into the receiver. "It's done."

A satisfied rumble emanated from the speaker. "Good. Now, find his contact." The line went dead, leaving Zheng alone with the weight of his actions and the promise of more blood to be spilled.

CIA Headquarters, Langley, Virginia

Oxley's assistant set the coffee down without a word and slipped out, closing the door softly behind her. The latch clicked louder than it should have. Jones took the chair opposite his boss, already knowing this wasn't going to be a good conversation.

Director Oxley didn't touch his cup.

"I briefed the President," he said finally. "I laid out General Lawrey's assessment—gain-of-function research, weaponization pathways, the CCP's role. I also raised PharmX."

Jones leaned forward. "And?"

Oxley exhaled through his nose. "He dismissed it. Completely. Repeated Facini's and Rapier's line—natural evolution, bad luck, no human fingerprints. He wouldn't even entertain the possibility that PharmX is involved."

For a moment, Jones just stared at him. Then the frustration broke through.

"What more does he need?" Jones snapped. "PharmX funded the Wuhan Institute of Virology. Fen's files document the relationship end to end. Rapier hasn't refuted a single document—because she can't. And Paxlovid-23?" Jones shook his head. "Developed from data harvested from concentration camp populations. That's not negligence—that's complicity. They're not just collaborators. They're war criminals."

Oxley didn't respond right away. He had no interest in rehearsing what they both already knew—the lies, the money, the moral rot surrounding Tilden and his people. Emotion wouldn't move this forward. Evidence might.

"The only way we put a rope around their necks," Oxley said quietly, "is to follow the money. I want a full funds-flow analysis. Shells, cutouts, offshore vehicles—the works. I want every American hand that touched Chinese cash exposed."

He looked up. "Who do you trust to do it?"

Jones didn't hesitate. "Jack Reagan."

The name hung in the air.

Oxley rose and walked to the window. Outside, the sun was sinking behind the line of oaks, staining the snow-covered parking lot in amber and blood-orange light. Wind lifted powdery drifts into spirals that vanished as quickly as they formed. Order and chaos, side by side.

Jack Reagan. The name pulled Oxley backward through decades.

Colombia. The eighties. Cocaine money was flooding jungles and politics alike. Reagan had been barely more than a kid then—brilliant, quiet, terrifyingly observant. An IQ north of 150 and a mind built for systems. Where others saw targets, Reagan connected all the dots of the criminal enterprise. Incentives. Failure points. Command and Control.

He'd started as a shooter because that's where the Agency put men who could survive. But Reagan was never just muscle. He learned fast, adapted faster, and asked questions no one else thought to ask. When the shooting stopped, he went to school—earned a Ph.D. in managerial economics—and climbed to the top of the consulting world as effortlessly as he once moved through the jungle canopy.

Officially, that's where his story ended.

Unofficially, the Agency never stopped calling.

Oxley turned back to Jones. "Reagan could find a pattern in a box of spilled toothpicks. And his cover is so deep that ninety-nine percent of this building thinks he's just another overpaid consultant."

Jones allowed himself a thin smile. "A Ph.D. who can win a bar fight."

Oxley almost smiled at the old Camp X saying.

"And make a thousand-yard headshot on a Capo," he said, "ditch cartel bodyguards, and hump a paralyzed teammate through the jungle to the third LZ. I'd give my entire budget to have twelve more like him."

Jones leaned back. "In the old days, we put a man on the problem and let him hunt. It's more complicated now. Congressional oversight. Cameras everywhere. Cyber ops."

Oxley's expression hardened. "In the old days, we still believed we were allowed to win."

Outside, the last light slipped below the horizon, and the room fell into shadow, a foreshadowing of things to come.

Philomath, Georgia

Hues of red and orange painted the November sky as Jack Reagan sat alone in his shooting house. The prevailing Northwesterly breeze blew across his face as he watched six does graze on Austrian winter peas. Whatever his global position, sunsets always revived his soul.

Jack sat in his twelve-foot-tall, four-foot-wide shooting house, painted a cool camouflage green. A different kind of tribute adorned its walls - the skull symbol of the Punisher, a stoic emblem chosen by many elite marksmen. It was a silent homage to his friend, Chris Kyle, the legendary SEAL sniper.

The world of elite snipers was a tight-knit fraternity bound by a shared respect for skill and precision. Kyle's death had hit the community hard, a stark reminder of the unseen wounds warriors carried long after the battlefield, demons that took Jack twenty years to excise.

A faint movement, imperceptible to most hunters, caught Jack's eye. After studying the tree line, Jack wondered if blown leaves had caught his attention; his gut told him otherwise.

Jack carefully placed his rifle on the shooting rail and slowly released the safety. As he peered through his scope, he saw a ten-point, 180-class buck emerge like a grey ghost from the shadows. A few feet into the food plot, the timber ghost raised his head and sniffed. Jack smiled as he placed his crosshairs on the buck's chest.

"Can't scent me, can you, old boy?"

The buck lowered his head and meandered to the largest doe. As he sniffed her hindquarters, Jack placed his reticle on the buck's shoulder and slowly squeezed the trigger.

Pow!

The deer scattered as the ballistic-tipped bullet left his late father's .300 Win Magnum and struck the buck in the shoulder. The bullet's plastic tip was driven into its lead core, mushrooming it to double its original diameter as it passed through the animal's heart and lungs. The deer shuddered, ran ten feet, and fell dead. After a few seconds of twitching, the trophy buck lay motionless.

Bzzz! Bzzz!

Jack's phone vibrated. It was a Company call.

"Hawkeye."

Jones replied, "We have a job for you. When can we meet?"

"I'm at DMX."

Jones thought it over and said, "Greensboro airport, noon tomorrow, over."

"Wilco, Hawkeye out."

Jack considered what he'd just heard. Jones's voice held an urgency born of some seminal event, but what?

The breeze increased as Jack climbed down. The moon was rising as the first star of the night appeared. Jack switched on his headlamp and walked to his trophy. He knelt, laid his hand on the stag's neck, and admired the five-year-old buck's horns. The antlers were far outside his ears. His brow tines were six inches long. He'd go 180 or more on the Boone and Crockett scale, a very nice buck for the region.

In an ancient ceremony, Jack laid his hand on his kill and prayed, "Heavenly Father, thank you for this harvest and the life you give through the blood and resurrection of Jesus Christ, Amen."

The crimson on his boots dragged Jack back through the years. Colombia, 1985. Landing Zone Charlie.

The air was wet with blood and jungle rot, gunfire collapsing into a dull ringing in his ears. His heart hammered as he carried his spotter toward the phantom thrum of rotor blades. He'd made it! Then, at the last second, the bird waved off and flew away, leaving them stranded, five clicks from the next Landing Zone through enemy turf. No ammo. No mercy. Fight, flight, or freeze?

His inner mantra roared louder than the screams: "You're stronger than you know. I am with you in the Valley of Death. Fear no evil, because you are the toughest S.O.B. in the valley."

Then, a dozen men swarmed him, and the fight quickly devolved into something primal. Jack ripped an AK from a corpse, fired until it clicked dry, then swung it like a club. When the stock snapped, his Kabar knife came out. When the knife was slick with blood, he used a rock to dispatch his last opponent. Twelve men died in that green hell, and Jack became a legend in the shadow world.

He owed his life that day to Oxley—one man defying Langley's orders to leave them behind.

Wuhan, China

The upscale 327-room New World Hotel was located in the heart of Hankou Commercial District, just a ten-minute walk from the Wuhan International Exhibition Center. Its close proximity to the regional headquarters of several multinational companies allowed Jake to blend in. Equally important, it provided multiple escape routes.

Jake handed his car keys to the valet and gave the man a generous tip to ensure the car was kept close by. Jake then navigated the hotel lobby with practiced ease, his movements blending seamlessly with the flow of guests and staff. He reached his designated floor and proceeded down the hallway with a focused purpose. Once inside his room, Jake wedged a sturdy chair under the doorknob. At his desk, his laptop whirred to life as he inserted the data drive into the USB port.

While the machine hummed, efficiently reading the drive's contents, Jake established a secure connection. A cable snaked from his laptop to his satellite phone, the physical link momentarily bridging the digital realms. A familiar program flickered to life - an encrypted file transfer application. He initiated the upload process with a few clicks, selecting all available files. In a silent symphony of ones and zeros, the critical data began its covert journey across the digital expanse, headed for a secure server beyond the reach of prying eyes. Jake watched as the bar in the lower right of his screen moved slowly from left to right.

"These are large files," Jake said as he poured 20-year-old MacCallan into a glass. If he was going to die, his last drink would be good scotch.

A knot of tension coiled in Jake's gut. He rose, stretching the tightness from his muscles, removed his Glock 43 from its shoulder holster, and placed it beside him. In this line of work, being unarmed felt riskier than getting caught with a gun.

Jake settled back onto the sofa, his gaze fixed on the door. Every creak of the hallway, every raised voice, sent a jolt of alertness through him. He knew he wouldn't receive a fair trial if captured. Chinese methods were brutal, swift, and effective. While Jake had faced his share of danger, the thought of falling into the hands of Chinese State Security sent a wave of icy dread through him. He vowed never to be taken alive.

The alcohol slowly began to work its magic, and Jake relaxed. After several peaceful moments, he glanced at his PC and saw that the transmission was sixty percent complete. He closed his eyes and waited, the first respite in his adrenaline-fueled day. Five minutes later, a chime told him the upload was complete.

After confirming Langley's receipt, Jake removed the jump drive and walked into the bathroom. While the small data device looked no different than millions of others, it was the one object that could get him killed. It had to be destroyed.

Jake removed a set of pliers from his shaving kit and placed the drive between the blades. Holding the drive over the bathroom sink, he squeezed the handles together until only small pieces of plastic and metal remained. He then rinsed the particles down the drain.

Greensboro Airport

Jack Reagan steered his dusty 4x4 towards the airport. He wore jeans, a camo shirt, and a jacket that concealed his pistol. His attire matched that of the local hunters.

The airport was a modest affair, a scattering of propeller planes and private jets dotting the tarmac. Jack parked, his gaze scanning the scene. A dozen aircraft sat in wait, some sleek and corporate, others utilitarian.

He entered the terminal and saw no passengers or pilots, just the clerk behind the counter. Jack nodded to the man, who smiled and said, "Taking off or picking up?"

"Picking up."

"There's a Lear on approach; should be on the ground in a couple of minutes; let me know if you need anything."

Jack nodded.

A few minutes ticked by before a distinctive hum broke the quiet - the CIA's Lear 60 making its descent. This jet, a favorite among high-flying executives, offered the perfect cover for clandestine travel. Its impressive range and ability to handle short runways had proven invaluable for covert operations.

After landing, Jones, a man in his fifties who maintained a youthful vigor, descended the stairs. His attire - jeans, hiking boots, and a camo jacket - mirrored Jack's own, further solidifying the illusion of wealthy businessmen on a hunting trip. The addition of a rolling duffel and a rifle case completed the picture.

Jones placed his rifle case on the ground and extended his hand to Jack. The two men shook.

"Welcome to Georgia," Jack said to the native Ohioan.

"How's the hunting?"

"Shot a nice buck last evening, just before you called," Jack said with a hint of disdain for the call.

"Glad my call didn't spook him," Jones said as the two men walked to Jack's truck.

Jack placed Jones's luggage in the rear seat, and they sat up front.

"Lunch?"

"Sure," Jones responded.

Jack drove the twenty minutes to his camper. The hunt camp was located near Philomath, Georgia, a collection of decaying pre-Civil War mansions and a long-abandoned general store. It was the rural area where men could carry weapons, hunt, and 'operate' without drawing attention.

"I'll take your bags inside," Jack said as he carried Jones's luggage into the camper and put it on the guest bed.

"Jones walked in and said, "Not bad, beats the hell out of sleeping in that musty old farmhouse."

Jack nodded, "How's a filet sound?"

"Really good."

Jones filled him in as Jack started cooking, "Jack, we have growing concerns over a series of events in China."

Jack glanced Jones's way and nodded.

"What temperature do you want your steak?"

"Medium Rare."

"What's up?" Jack asked.

"Dr. Stevens notified Ox that a very ill Chinese scientist flew into LAX. The defector brought proof that the CCP tested bioweapons on thousands of concentration camp inmates. Our mole inside the Wuhan Institute obtained files discussing the use of a GoF-enhanced virus as a bioweapon; however, they don't provide a timeline. They also mention something called Operation Dragon Strike."

Jack flipped the steaks.

"The intel paints a grim picture," Jones said, his voice laced with concern. "China's recent purchases and troop movements suggest an invasion is closer than we thought. Then there's a group of twelve globalist billionaires led by Ethan Carpathian, who have close ties to China. Men like Helmut Scheid, who talk like a modern-day Nazi. These men have dual Chinese citizenship and own palatial homes in Solar Valley. We need to know what they're up to and how they're connected."

Jack nodded grimly, the clanging of the grill lid echoing the weight of the situation. "How can I help?"

"Ox wants you to follow the money," Jones explained. "Dig deep, connect the dots, and tell us who's involved."

A spark of determination flickered in his eyes as Jack considered the assignment.

"Alright, standard fee plus travel, and I'll need access to the supercomputer and an upgraded security clearance."

A smile tugged at the corner of Jones's lips. He reached into his pocket and handed Jack an envelope. "Here are security codes to the Super Computer, a new ID, and the signed contract. I even managed a higher retainer - six figures this time."

Jack skimmed the documents, a satisfied smirk replacing his earlier frown. The agency had anticipated his requirements. He signed the contracts with a practiced flourish, returning a copy to Jones.

"Welcome back, Jack," Jones said.

Washington, DC

The President sat at the head of the expansive table, surrounded by a sea of grim faces. The air crackled with urgency - the nation's top advisors, from national security to public health, had been summoned to address a looming crisis.

"We're in a no-win situation," Amanda Pigeon admitted, her voice laced with frustration. "Damned if we try to contain it, damned if we don't."

The President leaned forward, his gaze sweeping across the room. "What are our options?"

A cautious suggestion emerged. "We announce the discovery of a new variant, something the CDC is actively monitoring. We downplay the severity to avoid panic but provide enough information to prevent accusations of a cover-up."

A weary sigh escaped the President's lips. "Doctor Facini, what is your assessment?"

"Mr. President, the public won't tolerate another lockdown or mask mandate," the doctor replied, "that means COVID-23 could kill up to two hundred and fifty million Americans within the year."

The President emoted, "That's unacceptable! Give me a solution!"

Dr. Facini had the President exactly where he wanted him. "Mr. President, our best option is to fund the two trillion-dollar COVID-23 Emergency Program. With these funds, I can utilize the fast-track procedures developed during the COVID-19 pandemic and our AI-enabled drug-design process to have an antiviral in clinical trials within thirty days and a vaccine within months."

Tilden looked at his age-spotted hands and closed his eyes. After rubbing his temples, he said, "Okay, I'll sign the paperwork. Amanda, slow walk it. Tony, spend whatever you need. I want a treatment and a cure as soon as possible."

After the meeting, Dr. Faccini lingered and held a private discussion with the President. After a five-minute conversation, Tilden smiled and said, "The misdirection is working. Oxley and the CIA don't have a clue as to what's really happening."

Facini grinned and said, "Our plan is coming off without a hitch."

Tilden slapped Facini on the shoulder and said, "See you in Solar Valley."

Marble Hill, Georgia

Jack Reagan returned home after a day of hunting with Raymond Jones. As he unpacked, his satellite phone rang, "Hawkeye."

"Hawk. Are you online?" Jones asked.

"Just a second," Jack said as he entered his study and activated the SAT COMM system. After completing a retinal scan, Jack said, "I'm in."

"I'm sending you the complete files from W1 and UC1," Jones said.

"These files are huge; what'd you do, download the entire banking system?" Jack asked.

Jones smiled from his Langley office and said, "No, just the complete banking transactions from the world's billionaires, rogue nations, and likely suspects. We also added all federal elected officials and key bureaucrats. Can you connect the dots?"

"I'll know more once I get into it. Talk in three days?" Jack asked.

Jones looked at Director Oxley. Oxley nodded in agreement.

"13:00, on Friday, work for you?" Jones inquired.

"13:00, Friday, Roger Wilco, out."

By 23:00, Jack had identified hundreds of millions of dollars exchanged between the NIH, pharmaceutical companies, elected officials, and the CCP. Jack's preliminary analysis revealed a sophisticated network of Beijing-controlled front companies and their transactions with U.S. life science companies and universities. PharmX transactions showed $231.2 million in political contributions and consulting fees paid to U.S. politicians and their families. At the top of the list was President Tilden and his son, Hector!

"That's a smoking gun now, isn't it?" Jack said.

After running a subroutine, Jack identified 2,000 relationships in which U.S. elected officials, bureaucrats, and their family members had amassed over $2 billion through private stock deals, false insurance payments, consulting fees, and deposits to offshore banks controlled by the Drug Cartels. Upon further review, Jack identified another $1 billion in funds flowing from corporations controlled by Ethan Carpathian and Helmut Scheid.

It was influence peddling on a colossal scale, but the connection between China, U.S. officials, the billionaires, and the Drug Cartels could indicate a more serious threat. What are they playing at?

Jack decided to call it a night. Stepping into the living room, he found Susan curled up on the sofa, lost in a sitcom. He dropped beside her, the familiar comfort a welcome relief from the day's complexities.

"Making progress?" Susan inquired, her voice laced with a hint of concern.

Jack smiled, appreciating her unspoken support. "Definitely moving in the right direction," he replied. He reached for the glass she'd set out, the amber liquid a warm invitation to unwind.

Their eyes met, and a silent conversation passed between them. Jack saw the love and unwavering trust in her gaze, a reminder of the life he fought to protect. Susan, in turn, glimpsed the steely resolve beneath his gentle exterior, the man of quiet strength who held their world together.

With a silent understanding, they rose and headed for the bedroom.

UCLA

Dr. Stevens walked briskly into the sterile environment of the MICU. Having confirmed security measures, he approached the charge nurse caring for the critically ill scientist.

"How is she?" Dr. Stevens asked the charge nurse, his voice laced with concern.

The nurse's response was direct. "Her inflammatory response is out of control."

Dr. Stevens understood the implications. Elevated inflammatory markers often foreshadow a grim prognosis. In this case, the patient's extensive organ damage further heightened the threat.

"Is she conscious?" he inquired.

"She drifts in and out," the nurse replied, "but she's using that laptop Dr. Chen provided. She seems determined to answer his questions."

Dr. Stevens' initial instinct was to remove any distractions that might impede his patient's recovery. But national security was at stake. The potential for this scientist's knowledge to save countless lives weighed heavily on him.

"How is her fluid output?"

The nurse relayed the concerning information. "Her kidneys are failing."

Dr. Stevens peered through the window into the isolation room. The heroic scientist lay unconscious, her body betraying the fight raging within. Fluid retention was evident.

"The steroids have eased her breathing, but they've also compromised her immune system," Dr. Stevens continued. "We need to be aggressive in addressing any infections that arise."

She said, “I understand.”

Suddenly, alarms sounded. Dr. Fen’s EKG had flatlined!

Stevens and the nurse quickly put on their masks and entered the room. A code team entered two minutes later.

Dr. Stevens and his nurses fought for thirty minutes to revive Dr Fen.

Finally, Stevens announced, “Time of death, 7:38 AM,” and left the patient's room, the feeling of clinical and intelligence failure weighing heavily on him. He hoped that Dr. Fen had been able to answer some of Dr. Chen’s critical questions.

***

Wang Soon, LPN, watched the gurney carrying Dr. Fen’s body disappear through the double doors. Only then did she ask for her break. No one questioned it. Nurses took breaks. Bodies went to the Morgue. Hospitals swallowed secrets every day.

Wang Soon stepped onto a narrow balcony overlooking the street, the warm wind biting through her scrubs. Traffic hissed below. Somewhere, a siren wailed and faded. She waited until she was alone, then pulled her phone from her pocket and dialed a number she knew by memory but never saved.

The call routed through three relays before connecting.

"How is our friend?" came the voice of Major Seng Long, calm, precise, and utterly devoid of emotion. Chinese Secret Police. Ministry of State Security.

"Deceased," Soon replied.

There was a brief silence on the line—not shock, but calculation.

Major Long allowed himself a quiet sense of satisfaction. The mission had been urgent, and Beijing valued results. Rewards would follow. But relief gave way quickly to concern. A scientist's death inside an American medical facility carried risks. Variables he did not control.

Soon's cover was excellent—native-born American, licensed nurse, unremarkable in every way. It had protected her before. But high-profile deaths attracted attention, and attention led to questions. An autopsy would be inconvenient. Dangerous.

If the Americans performed a detailed examination of Dr. Fen's body, they would find the truth. If they found the truth, they would interrogate Soon. And interrogation—even gentle interrogation—had a way of unraveling carefully woven legends.

Procreate MicroBio was too important to lose. The lab would soon play a decisive role in the dispersion phase. Compromise was unacceptable.

Major Long weighed the options with the cold clarity of a man accustomed to deciding who lived and who did not. Terminate the asset… or let the situation unfold.

At last, he spoke. "Notify me immediately if they order an autopsy."

"I will," Soon said.

The line went dead.

Wang Soon slid the phone back into her pocket and leaned against the railing, closing her eyes. She drew a slow breath, then another, steadying herself.

She had been born American, yes—but her parents had raised her to understand where her real loyalty lay. China was not a country. It was destiny. Since becoming a devoted follower of High Priest Longshen, the Dregodarit Religion had given her clarity. Treachery was not betrayal when it served a higher purpose. Murder was not a sin when it helped save the planet.

So why did her hands tremble?

She opened her eyes and stared down at the street, watching strangers hurry through lives that would never matter.

She told herself the feeling would pass. It always did.

***

While Dr. Stevens knew his patient had been critically ill, his gut told him the scientist's passing had come too soon. He ordered an autopsy and a list of everyone who had contact with his patient.

When Stevens returned to his small office in the Emergency Room, a text appeared on his cell phone. The message read:

Need to talk. Suggest 13:00 PST. Use VC 2005789.

The text was from Langley.

He replied, *'Roger, Wilco.'*

***

An hour later, Wang Soon texted Major Long, letting him know an autopsy had been ordered.

Long read the text twice, then dialed his cleaner.

"Yes," came the quick reply.

"Clean up the mess at UCLA."

The phone went dead without another word.

At the end of her shift, Wang Soon walked to her car. When she crossed at the corner, an unmarked delivery truck accelerated quickly, hitting her before she could escape. She died instantly.

World Economic Forum, Davos, Switzerland

Helmut Scheid, a man of unconventional style, stood before the crowd wearing a tailored grey business suit paired with a turtleneck sweater. The 65-year-old billionaire, with a Ph.D. in Economics from UC Berkeley, had been crowned by Forbes Magazine as the most influential figure in global finance. His 1995 brainchild, Red Rock Funds, had grown into a behemoth, controlling 45% of funds invested in U.S. retirement and 401(k) programs. His latest venture, One World Trust, was working to establish a global cyber currency. Scheid's long-awaited keynote address, "Cooperation in a Fragmented World," outlined a bold plan to unify the world under one economic system.

Yet, beneath the accolades, Scheid hid a carefully guarded secret. His grandfather, Economist and SS General Dr. Otto Scheid, was a war criminal who had absconded with billions in assets stolen from the treasuries of Europe and victims of the Holocaust.

In the Fall of 1944, when Allied victory was assured, his grandfather developed a bold plan to keep the wealth taken from the treasuries and citizens of German-occupied Europe. Under the stated goal of fulfilling the ideals of National Socialism through a Fourth Reich, Scheid hid the funds from Allied seizure by distributing them to a network of loyal German industrialists and Swiss bankers. The only two requirements were that they create a new life for thousands of escaping German war criminals and utilize the funds according to General Scheid's plan after the war. To maintain control, Scheid siphoned off fifty percent of the gold for himself.

During post-war reconstruction, Scheid and his network used their illicit gains to lay a stable foundation for the period. By leveraging its financial resources and influence, the network ensured its partners secured the most lucrative contracts in construction, transportation, and healthcare. They even benefited from U.S. capital investments. As the global economy prospered, the network expanded into consumer goods, travel, leisure, and computer-related holdings, multiplying profits tenfold. Three generations had now been enriched by General Scheid's vision, and to date, no credible source had been successful in tracing the funds to the network. It was the perfect crime.

Over the decades since World War II, Dr. Scheid's ideology merged with the green worldview of Ethan Carpathian and his movement. While Carpathian was not a National Socialist, the two men agreed on what must be done to save the planet. Scheid, like his grandfather, also knew he needed a charismatic leader to fulfill his family's vision. This overarching goal, along with a shared desire for power, held their alliance together.

Scheid's small-rimmed eyeglasses, short-cropped hair, and grey beard projected a professorial image. His heavy German accent was compelling as he asserted, "The world is at a critical inflection point. What we do or fail to do in the next decade will determine our survival as a species."

Dozens of New World Order supporters stood and clapped, eliciting similar responses from the crowd.

"I want to stir your thinking around our need for a new world economy that closes the growing gap between the haves and have-nots. An economy that provides for mankind's fundamental needs without fully depleting the planet's resources. A world in which the common man will no longer have to worry about food, shelter, clothing, or security."

Scheid projected an organizational chart of worldwide banking and continued, "This new world can only come about with the creation of a global banking system that allows people to hold one currency that is protected from the perils of economic mismanagement and hyperinflation caused by politicians. A world in which those in the third world will enjoy the same economic stability as those in the first."

The audience clapped.

"As you know, the U.S. dollar is the world's reserve currency. But did you realize the dollar is on the verge of collapse?"

Scheid's statement sucked the reverie from the room, replacing it with dark foreboding. Scheid enjoyed seeing the shock on many faces as he continued, "This is because the U.S. Congress has shown no ability to manage its country's finances."

Several in the room nodded in agreement. The US Delegation looked insulted.

"This is not a new observation. In the early 1800s, Tytler said, 'A democracy cannot exist as a permanent form of government. It can only exist until the majority discovers it can vote itself distributions from the public treasury. After that, the majority always votes for the candidate promising the most benefits, with the result that the democracy collapses and is followed by a dictatorship, then a monarchy."

Scheid gestured toward the big screen, saying, "As you see, U.S. debt was less than $908 billion in 1980. By 2020, it reached $27.7 trillion. As of yesterday, the U.S. national debt has surpassed $37 trillion and is projected to exceed $40 trillion by the end of this year. In four decades, the U.S. Congress has added debt thirty-seven times greater than the U.S. incurred in its first 204 years. It's financial mismanagement on the largest scale in world history!"

The audience fell silent.

"U.S. inflation ran at 11% last year and 30% over the past four years. This is a consequence of the U.S. increasing the money supply to fund short-term overspending. Left unchecked, inflation will erode the savings of hundreds of millions of hard-working Americans, wiping out the middle class and putting over 150 million Americans on public assistance by 2045."

Murmuring arose.

Scheid hammered his point home, "This cancer of carelessness has spread to other continents and will soon destroy nations that use the U.S. Dollar as their reserve currency! This decline in global trust in U.S. leadership, the rule of law, and economic stability is leading more investors and nations to consider gold or cryptocurrencies as alternatives to the U.S. dollar."

Several U.S. Financiers nodded in agreement while the dozen elected U.S. officials in attendance and Vice President Conja Sterns shook their heads, shocked that one of the Democratic Party's top donors had slammed them.

Scheid continued, "So that I'm not considered anti-American, let me say that the European Union is also struggling to keep the Euro afloat, and the Japanese Yen is losing value. China is also struggling with a significant downturn in its real estate sector, and the reshoring of manufacturing in the U.S. is drawing away critical funds."

Scheid paused for effect as he read the room.

"Some fools think the U.S. economy is too big to fail. Really? History is full of sudden currency collapses. Argentina, Hungary, Chile, Angola, Zimbabwe, and Germany have all experienced terrible currency crises since 1900. Depending on the definition of 'collapse,' the Russian currency calamity in 2014 could be considered another example. In all these cases, the collapse stems from a lack of faith in the stability of money as a store of value or medium of exchange. Simply put, when users stop believing that a currency is useful, that currency is doomed."

Several people applauded.

"We must also consider the impact of emerging economic disruptors such as mass migration that will soon place an untenable strain on the worldwide economy as millions of people are displaced by conflict and climate change. When these people migrate, their impact on host countries is mitigated only if they can retain their economic assets. Consider the U.S. failure to control the number of undocumented immigrants crossing its southern border. In the fiscal year 2022, 2.76 million illegal aliens entered the U.S., costing the U.S. $151 billion a year, which is paid for with increased debt. Most nations cannot afford this level of financial strain," Scheid noted as he reached for his water glass and sipped.

"These macro changes will soon force the world to build a new financial system based upon a currency that permanently stores value."

The World Economic Forum board stood and applauded.

"The solution to this untenable state of affairs is to deploy a worldwide digital currency beyond the control of any state or central bank. A private sector solution immune to inflation and beyond the mismanagement of any one government."

Scheid supporters and those from developing nations stood and applauded. Their ovation continued for two minutes. Finally, Scheid motioned for the audience to return to their seats, then continued, "By eliminating conversion, we will improve the efficiency of cross-border transactions. As nations become more interdependent, they will begin partnering to solve common issues such as global warming, pollution, war, and hunger, allowing us to build a better world!"

Scheid paused for effect. "The question on many of your minds is: how can we implement a universal currency? The answer is straightforward: we will allow people to transfer assets to One World Trust. An individual's assets will then be valued and credited to their cyber account. A DNA sensing chip will be placed in each person's hand to ensure complete security, thereby eliminating the risk of identity theft. Without this technology, no one can buy or sell, thereby ending the illegal activities enabled by cash. I'm talking about ending human trafficking, drug sales, and tax evasion forever!"

After a minute of applause, the auditorium settled. "Our new cryptocurrency is known as People's Coin. Its symbol will be the world's most powerful and ancient beast, the Dragon. The fact that people from all nations can convert their assets into People's Coin will soon result in a never-before-attained level of autonomy, security, and self-direction while allowing nations to shift their troubled currency into a stable vehicle, warding off economic disaster," Scheid noted as he turned the slide to an image of the Dragon Icon.

Scheid ended his talk by saying, "Join me in ushering in a new age of empowerment for the people, People's Coin!"

Ninety percent of his audience stood in ovation!

CIA Encrypted Satellite Call

Dr. Stevens scanned his retina and logged into the call. Jack Reagan, Raymond Jones, General Lawery, and CIA Director Oxley were already online.

"Welcome, doctor," Jones said.

Steven's silence was in stark contrast to his usual enthusiasm.

"How is patient zero?" Oxley asked compassionately.

"She passed."

Oxley pursed his lips, saying, "I'm sorry to hear that. She did us a great service."

Stevens, not wanting to wax sentimental, said, "I've ordered an autopsy. While she was gravely ill, we have to rule out an assassination."

Oxley asked, "Are you suggesting the Chinese killed her?"

Stevens chose his words carefully, "I can't rule it out, and an Asian LPN who treated her was killed by a hit and run today. My instincts tell me the Chinese police were behind both deaths."

"Let me know if you want the FBI involved," Oxley offered, knowing that these recent events would limit their intel into China's plans.

Stevens replied, "Wilco."

Oxley asked, "Jack, what have you learned?"

Jack placed his presentation on the screen, saying, "I've identified thousands of transactions linking China to funds flowing to U.S. politicians and their families. Some funds flowed through state-owned entities, including China Petro, Asian Energy Trust, Costa Insurance, Beijing Solar, and Vagda Exploration. Other funds flowed through private stock issuances, front companies, or offshore banks. Of special interest is the Banco de Silva on Grand Cayman, which is owned by Juan Espinoza and the Mexican drug lords."

Jack's slide listed the names of hundreds of entities and individuals involved in the funds flow.

"Impressive analysis. What did you learn about Wilhite?" General Lawrey asked.

Jack flipped to a slide showing Dr. Wilhite's picture and smaller photos of his articles. He then turned to a paper from the Journal of Infectious Diseases.

"Financial records indicate that between 2014 and 2023, a Chinese subsidiary of PharmX provided Dr. Wilhite with four million dollars for the purchase of viral samples from his U.S. lab. Director Rapier and Dr. Faccini also received significant funds from PharmX and a dozen other Chinese-controlled entities."

"That level of money shows the depth of their complicity," Oxley muttered.

Jack continued, "I've also connected one hundred of the world's top billionaires and half the U.S. House and Senate to dark money from China, Russia, Pakistan, and North Korea. Further analysis shows that these elected officials voted in favor of defense cuts, funding for the NIH, and legislation that greatly increased deficit spending."

Oxley asked, "How much are we talking about?"

Jack looked down at his report, "$2.3 million per politician."

Oxley considered the ramifications of Jack's findings. While he'd learned to view intelligence skeptically, the correlation between funds and voting patterns was apparent.

"Jack, you've accomplished more than all our whiz kids combined."

Jack nodded.

"General, why are the Chinese deploying CV-23 instead of their other bioweapons?" Oxley asked.

"The Chinese gained accurate disease models from COVID-19. They don't have this level of predictability with their other agents. It also provides deniability. Right now, they're using Rapier, Facini, and Wilhite to convince Congress that CV-23 naturally evolved. It's an attempt to preempt liability and attribution," General Lawrey observed.

Oxley exhaled deeply as he digested General Lawrey's compelling assessment.

"Jake, what did you learn in China?"

"I learned that the CCP selected 100 elites, key corporate executives, billionaires, bankers, and government leaders from across the globe to become part of a 'new world think tank.'"

"Can you provide their names?" Oxley asked.

"I know Ethan Carpathian and Helmut Scheid are in the inner circle, and I suspect Judy Itzenberg, Ralph Neumero, Kelvin Artse, and Tom Pitt also have seats at the table."

Oxley asked, "How do we get the complete list?"

"Most of the coconspirators will be at the Dragon Conference. If we can obtain the attendee list, we can identify more of them."

"Jones, I want a complete list of conference attendees and anyone frequenting the Valley in the last two years. The sooner we know who we're dealing with, the better," Oxley ordered.

"Will do," Jones said as he texted his cyber team leader.

"Jake, what do you think they're up to?" Oxley asked.

Jake proceeded cautiously. "We know that China aims to become the dominant superpower by 2049 and that Ethan Carpathian and the billionaires publicly support a one-world economy. Many of the objectives in Carpathian's globalist manifesto and China's 2050 Strategy align. We know that a dozen men around Carpathian have made anti-American statements and funded domestic terrorist groups to drive social unrest in the U.S. and Allied countries. The fact that the Chinese have granted these elites citizenship suggests that they intend to collaborate in the long term. Helmut Scheid is also a major economic adviser to China. This suggests that they're working together to build a one-world government under one cybercurrency."

Oxley asked, "What do capitalist billionaires gain by working with a Communist nation?"

"Carpathian was enticed there by funding, freedom to operate outside U.S. laws, and, perhaps, enlightenment."

"Enlightenment? Can you explain that?" Oxley asked.

"The day I arrived, Carpathian had met with the High Priest Longshen, the leader of the Dregodarit religion. My gut tells me the mystical High Priest holds great influence over him. As far out as it sounds, I think they're creating a one-world religion."

Jones chuckled while Oxley seriously considered his agent's assessment.

"So, we have a Chinese-developed bioweapon, one hundred of the world's most influential billionaires living in a Chinese haven for the rich and famous, China's ambition to become the dominant superpower by 2050, and anti-American globalists who want to take over the world? Did I miss anything in your techno-thriller?" Jones scoffed. The scenario was simply too fantastic for him to accept.

"Don't forget their influence over Western government officials and alliances with the axis of evil," Jake added.

Jones smiled.

Finally, the CIA Director said, "Get the list and put more resources on Scheid, Carpathian, and the others you've identified. We've got to find out if this is just another secret society or a real threat."

Chapter 4

Sunlight streamed through the panoramic windows, illuminating Jade as she approached a chaise lounge. Helmut Scheid, a slightly overweight man with a crimson face, lay with his eyes squeezed shut.

The Valley of the Dolls was a virtual pleasure center in which every desire was fulfilled. The contrast between the ultra-modern Solar Valley, just over the mountain, and this ancient hedonist hamlet was striking.

"Dr. Scheid," Jade whispered softly, her voice polished and professional, "Your Himalayan salt scrub is ready."

Scheid grunted, barely acknowledging her. Then he turned and grabbed her roughly and kissed her on the mouth. She hated the taste of cigars. The German was a pig! Fortunately for Jade, Scheid moved on to his waiting attendant. Others had fared much worse.

As she watched him walk away, Jade felt the familiar pang of bitterness. Beneath the crisp white dress and the practiced smile was a woman with a faded butterfly tattoo snaking up her forearm – a permanent reminder of her enslavement in the Macau Sex Trade.

A lifetime ago, she had been the prom queen of Brackettville High School, Texas. The memories of freedom cut like a dagger into her heart. She'd been naïve when a New Orleans talent agent signed her to a contract to perform in "high-end" Asian gentlemen's clubs. She'd been told how beautiful and talented she was from birth, and the agent used her dreams to ensnare her. If only she'd listened to Uncle Herbstreet. If only she'd had a father to protect her.

Now, she was the Lotus, a pillar of this gilded cage. Survival meant that she had learned to navigate the world of powerful men, their desires, and their vulnerabilities. Yet, deep inside, buried by years of abuse, remained the flicker of hope that one day she'd be free. It was that inner hope that had kept her alive all these years.

The Dragon Conference meant she had received another two hundred girls to break in, another two hundred stolen lives to navigate. Yet, as she stared at Scheid's slack face, a tiny ember of hate was hidden beneath the surface. One day, she'd have revenge. She just had to wait for fate to bring the right opportunity.

***

The evening was moonless, and uplighting accented the trees across the sprawling complex as sleek limousines disgorged men in expensive suits, each greeted by a line of beautiful women in shimmering dresses. Inside, a cacophony of music and laughter filled the air. She watched Dr. Gunderson as he put his arm around a young woman's shoulders and walked with her to a private room.

During his stay in Solar Valley, she had met Jake Hendel, whom Carpathian had brought to the Spa for her personal attention. When she undressed for him, she was shocked that he closed her robe and held his index finger to his lips, a request for her to remain quiet. Hendel then turned up the music and sat her down on the bed.

At first, she thought it was some kind of role play, then he told her details about her past. He knew everything up until her Asian years. He had promised to free her in exchange for her client files. Jade hoped he was a man of his word; unlike so many liars she'd known. It was a long shot, it was risky, but Jake was her only hope.

Carpathian Mansion

The old-world-crafted wooden table reminded Carpathian of his boyhood home, Arco Castle. Perched atop jagged limestone cliffs, the castle commanded sweeping views from Lake Garda to the Alps. In a rare melancholy moment, Carpathian recalled playing king and queen with his late sister, Maria, in their dining room. They'd used the table's medieval chairs for thrones. If only Maria could be with him, if only she and his parents hadn't died in that plane crash – an event that sentenced him to that harsh Catholic boarding school in Vatican City.

His staff had set the table for eighteen guests. Carpathian sat at the head. To his right, in the place of honor, sat an ancient-looking, bearded Chinese man wearing his long grey hair in a braided ponytail that ran the length of his back. High Priest Longshen stood five feet eight, weighed 130 lbs., and wore a black Chinese jacket with trousers and traditional sandals. A fez-style hat with an ornate band that depicted a dragon holding a human in its talons sat on his head. The diminutive elder wore a ring featuring a dragon on one side, an alien being on the other, and a glowing stone at its center. Despite his small stature, Longshen exuded a mesmerizing aura.

Carpathian told the Group of Twelve, "This is my spiritual adviser, High Priest, Longshen. As you are aware, consolidating global religious thought into the one-world ideology of Dregodarit is crucial for ushering in a world of peace, sustainability, and enlightenment."

Longshen stood, bowed humbly, and scanned each face. When he looked into their eyes, the attendees felt as though the priest was searching their souls. Longshen finally sat and formed a pyramid with his hands, the ancient symbol of power, as he studied Carpathian's designated world leaders.

"Soon, the common man will own nothing but be happy. Wars, starvation, and disease will be a thing of the past," Carpathian said.

The attendees stood and clapped. The appeal of creating a utopian society was mesmerizing. Helmut Scheid and Dr. Gunderson wondered if Adolph Hitler had a similar effect on his followers.

"Only those with sound bodies and open souls can remain, as we followed the divine path of our forefathers who taught their progeny to live in peace and harmony. Unfortunately, mating with primitive humans corrupted our bloodline, and their ways were lost for thousands of years."

Longshen looked at Carpathian and added, "Until the Chosen One resurrected them."

Carpathian bowed his head at the compliment.

Longshen continued, "With your help, we will cleanse our bloodline and indoctrinate future generations in Dregodarit, the peaceful religion of our ancestors, and build a world where energy is free, disease is eradicated, and no prisons are needed. Earth will become a sustainable world of beauty, serenity, and free love."

Every head nodded in agreement.

Carpathian nodded, "Thank you, High Priest, Longshen. Dr. Facini, what is the status of the Four Horsemen?"

"Our pharmaceutical and research partners have reached one hundred percent of the Chimera vaccine needed to accomplish our goals. Chinese and Pakistani Labs are in full production of the other biological agents, and we will have a sufficient vaccine within the month. Thus, our timeline for releasing the Four Horsemen is on schedule." Facini replied.

Carpathian nodded, then asked American Military Industrialist Jeremy Prime, "What will be Operation Overload's impact?"

"We predict U.S. combat units will drop below twenty percent readiness within six months of initiation. This is due to the combined effects of combat losses and supply chain disruptions resulting from wars in the Middle East, Eastern Europe, and the Pacific. When their economy fails, and the Four Horsemen add to their casualties, the U.S. military will cease to be a world power within months. At that point, NATO will be a paper tiger, Russia will take Europe, and China will own the Indo-Pacific."

Carpathian accepted the stark projections as if they were corporate reports.

"Dr. Gunderson, what progress has been made on Operation Dark Heart?" Carpathian continued.

The black-haired, sixty-year-old man wore a dark-tailored Armani suit, an open-collared button-down shirt, and custom loafers. Gunderson bore an identical resemblance to Reich Minister Joseph Goebbels, Hitler's propaganda minister. Helmut Scheid had given Gunderson one of the watches his grandfather had given to founding members of the Fourth Reich at the seminal meeting at the Maison Rouge Hotel in Strasbourg, Germany, on August 10, 1944. The watch had become a talisman to Gunderson, who was never without it.

Gunderson said, "Since 1964, well before I became involved, our agents have used our political influence and propaganda to reengineer society. By using modern social media and gaming strategies combined with school curricula, we've lowered U.S. test scores by twenty percent in the past forty years while indoctrinating students in secularist ideals that replace traditional values, conditioning them to accept our message and bow to any flag we offer."

"Creating more easily controlled citizens?" Longshen observed.

"Exactly. We're slowly replacing Christianity, Judaism, and Islam with secular hedonism. Secular hedonism is a transitional step toward the altar of Dregodarit. As a measure of our success, we've lowered church attendance in America to less than twenty percent of the levels of the 1950s. In poor white, Hispanic, and black communities, we've replaced fathers with government checks. Many young women in these communities now see welfare benefits as a rite of passage instead of a high school diploma, creating a permanent underclass that's easily manipulated. Our campaign of replacing traditional values with secular hedonism has evolved into a new world ideology that is rapidly replacing Judeo-Christian values in the U.S. Under our influence, Europe accepted secular hedonism decades ago. While it has been a slow fade, we believe we've reached the tipping point."

Longshen and Carpathian smiled at Gunderson's brilliance. The near clone of Joseph Goebbels was using his father's playbook, master race, utopia, mystic religion, and misinformation. The main difference was that Gunderson was doing it globally on steroids with many multiples of the funds and technology of the Nazi Reich. Unlike Hitler, a poorly educated thug, Carpathian was a polished, well-educated global leader loved by billions.

Gundersen continued, "By removing the falsehood of faith, we will end most of the world's conflicts, unite people for one purpose, and allow the elites in this room to rule the world."

Carpathian was pleased, "Outstanding! Now, let's move to energy. I'm pleased to report that, by utilizing our proven technology in Solar Valley, we can produce approximately 80% of the world's energy. By adding small nuclear power plants, we will bring that figure to 100%. In addition to building a more efficient power grid, our green energy architecture will reduce toxic emissions by ninety percent, which will help save our planet."

Chinese Premier Xi Jin asked, "What about transportation?"

Carpathian smiled, "We're producing four models of high-efficiency electric vehicles: the toad, a four-passenger sedan; the mule, a pickup truck that comes in a two or four-seat configuration; the snake, a motorcycle that seats two; and the bull, a tractor-trailer truck capable of pulling a 150,000 kg payload for 2,400 km on a single charge. The toad and snake will provide affordable, government-owned transport for the masses. The mule and the bull will be issued to craftsmen and truckers."

Jin observed, "You have thought about every detail. Well done."

Jin turned his gaze toward the floor-to-ceiling windows in Carpathian's Castle, lost in thought. While his alliance with Carpathian had been a stroke of genius, the Chinese Premier wondered if the trillionaire could become a threat. Then he remembered Sun Tzu, "All warfare is based on deception, and victory often depends on misleading your opponent — appearing weak when you're strong, and strong when you're weak. The best victories are gained through manipulation, alliances, and psychological advantage, rather than brute force."

Oak Ridge, Tennessee

Jack Reagan admired the rows of computer cabinets that filled the hardened data center at the Oak Ridge Leadership Computing Center. The fact that he'd been given full access to the world's fastest supercomputer highlighted the urgency of unraveling the greatest threat to U.S. National Security in decades.

As the orange hues of sunrise illuminated the misty mountains, Jack attached his report to the CIA messaging system and hit enter. In a nanosecond, the data flew into the heavens, bounced off a satellite, and arrived in a select number of inboxes at Langley.

Starting to relax, Jack leaned back in his chair, the stiffness in his neck and shoulders a testament to the hours he'd spent hunched over a workstation. Hours, Jack thought, instead of weeks, thankfully. He sighed, rubbing his eyes as he pushed back from the desk, knowing the email would set off a chain reaction—a storm that would soon remove officials at the highest levels of power.

He grabbed his jacket and headed outside. The morning air was cool but not biting, carrying the scent of pine and damp earth. Sunrise's pink and orange hues spread across the sky like a soft watercolor painting, warming the mountainside and, unexpectedly, his heart.

Jack took a deep breath, feeling the tension of the past hours slowly ease from his body. The world seemed so peaceful here, far removed from the chaos that his report would unleash.

He poured himself a cup of coffee from his thermos, its warmth seeping through his hands. The brew's bitterness grounded him while the cool breeze revived his soul. The mist was beginning to lift, revealing the rugged peaks in the distance, their ancient presence reassuring in its permanence.

For a moment, Jack allowed himself to forget the weight of what he'd learned. He closed his eyes, listening to the wind rustling through the trees, feeling the earth solid beneath his feet. The calm wouldn't last. Soon, his phone would ring, and a global drama would unfold.

But for now, in this brief, fleeting moment, Jack simply stood there, drinking in the dawn, letting it fill him with a quiet strength. Whatever came next, he was ready. Softly, to himself, he quoted Phillipians 1:21 (NIV), "For to me, to live is Christ, and to die is gain." While he did not have a death wish, his faith covered either contingency.

Ring, ring, ring! Jack pulled his phone from the cargo pocket of his pants and looked at the number. It was Langley.

"Reagan," Jack said with military efficiency.

"Jack, can you be on a call at 14:30 today?" Jones asked.

"Yes," Jack replied.

"Use link 2. Talk then."

Taiwan

Admiral Flint stood outside a mountain observation post, scanning the sea lanes as a cold breeze blew across his face. Behind him, the sun was cresting a ridge, its marine haze lending a dark foreboding to the new day. Flint and his small force of 5,000 U.S. Marines, fifty airmen, 350 soldiers, forty aircraft, and a host of civilian contractors were officially 'advisers,' a distinction that would cease to have meaning once the first shot was fired.

While no one knew what to expect from Taiwanese forces, Flint respected General Lin, the island nation's highest-ranking military leader, for his understanding of his adversary and the preparations he'd made. While his army was untested, their drills had given Flint confidence that General Lin's regulars were well-trained. His primary concern was that they were severely outnumbered. Even with U.S. Coalition Support, China held numerical advantages that Taiwan and the U.S. would find challenging to overcome.

Colonel Liao walked to General Lin, saluted, and said, "General, radar indicates several hundred ships headed toward us. The closest ships are ninety kilometers out."

General Lin looked at his subordinate and asked, "Composition?"

"Sir, a mixture of merchant ships, destroyers, troop landers, and missile boats. Our drones have spotted the carriers Liaoning and Shandong at the rear of the formation. Our spies report that the carrier Fujian is being provisioned," Colonel Liao murmured nervously.

Admiral Flint looked at General Lin and said, "Apparently, the Fujian is further along than we thought. Do you think this is the invasion?"

General Lin scanned the horizon, deep in thought. "This isn't the PLA's first war maneuver, but it's certainly their largest."

"How confident are you in your ability to stop them?" Flint asked.

General Lin was not insulted by the question and replied, "We're ready. Our anti-ship missiles can sink many of their ships before they reach our shores. While outnumbered in fighters, our air force and anti-aircraft batteries will be able to mount a vigorous ground defense. Should the PLA come ashore, we've sighted our guns on every viable approach, landing zone, and roadway. Our 'porcupine strategy' exploits our geographic advantages and will make it a costly battle for Beijing."

While he agreed, Flint wanted to test Lin's mettle and asked, "Why did you shift your emphasis from air and sea superiority to coastal defense?"

"Attempting to go head-to-head against vastly superior numbers would leave us without sufficient air and sea forces to protect our vital landing zones, ports, and airfields. I believe our best chance is to force China to attack our strong points, where we can drive the highest kill-to-death ratio. The real question we have is, are you with us?"

Flint thought General Lin had a solid grasp on the emerging battle. While he wanted to reassure his counterpart that the United States would support Taiwan, he was unable to do so.

"My men will have those new anti-aircraft and missile batteries operational within a day. The remaining anti-ship missiles, heavy artillery, and antitank systems are expected to arrive tomorrow. In support of my Marines, I'm sending you two more F-18s and one Apache helicopter squadron," Admiral Flint offered, wishing he could do more.

General Lin replied, "Much appreciated. We'd be grateful if you could also deliver the remaining F-16s we ordered."

Admiral Flint said, "Lockheed tells me they will deliver eighteen F-16 Block 70 planes in a week. The USAF tells me that Taiwan has thirty-two more pilots checked out on the platform. Is that correct?"

"Yes, and we have another twenty-eight pilots starting training next week. When the battle starts, we'll need as many pilots as we can get," Lin replied.

"I'm also sending elements from the 621st Contingency Response Wing in case we have to utilize makeshift runways."

"I know you will do all you can for us," General Lin replied. Something in his professional tone let Flint know Lin was also dubious of U.S. support once the war started.

After General Lin and Admiral Flint saluted, Flint took one last look at the sea approaches, then walked with his aide to a waiting car. Ten minutes later, a Blackhawk helicopter carried him to the airport, where he boarded a C5-A for his flight back to Hawaii.

Eldorado, Sinaloa, Mexico

The sun dipped below the jagged teeth of the Sierra Madre, casting long, ominous shadows across Juan Esparragoza's vast estate. Fifty thousand acres of prime Sinaloa soil stretched before him, a sprawling monument to his ruthless ambition. As was his ritual, the drug lord cradled a snifter of aged tequila, the amber liquid shimmering in the fading light.

His gaze drifted upwards to the imposing silhouette of his twenty-thousand-square-foot mansion perched atop a hilltop overlooking the bustling town of Eldorado – a town as much his dominion as the surrounding land. Yet the comfort of the mansion felt hollow as he considered his adversaries.

The recent plastic surgery, while meticulous, still felt like a foreign mask clinging to his face. It was a necessary evil, a constant reminder of the enemies he'd made on his climb to power. While his face looked somewhat more European, his five-foot-eight-inch frame and dark brown skin were distinctly Myan – a fact that he tried to overcome by wearing high-end fashions from Italy and France.

A flicker of movement on the patio caught his eye as Edwardo Chavez, his godson and the heart of his private army, materialized from the twilight. Gone was the skinny ten-year-old boy Esparragoza had taken in after his father's death; in his place stood a man sculpted from steel and resolve. Unlike Esparragoza, Chavez stood six feet tall and still wore his hair short, just as he had during his time in the U.S. Military.

"Buena noche, padrino," Chavez greeted, his voice a low rumble.

Esparragoza gestured to a chair with a flick of his wrist. "Buena's noches, mijo."

Chavez sat, his gaze fixed on the distant lights of Eldorado, his usual confident air pierced by recent events.

"Is something troubling you, mijo?"

"The local recruits are undisciplined thugs. I can't count on them when the time comes. I need more Tier One operators riding shotgun," he admitted.

Esparragoza snorted a harsh, dismissive sound. "Recruit as many Americans as you need. You have an unlimited budget; just act swiftly."

Esparragoza finished his drink and rose, his gaze hardening as it swept across the sprawling estate. A flicker of concern crossed his face, quickly replaced by steely resolve. While his Sinaloa Cartel was a juggernaut, he knew Chinese Drug Lord Sung Chu had surpassed him. Whatever storm was brewing, he and his godson would face it together.

***

Five minutes later, Carlos Guzman walked in from the growing darkness.

"How much fentanyl arrived via the Chinaman?" Esparragoza asked harshly and without formality.

Guzman said, "A thousand vials, plus 300 gallons of liquid fen."

Esparragoza nodded thoughtfully, "Good, we'll distribute it in the coming weeks. I don't want to lower prices by creating oversupply."

"I have it under control, Juan," Guzman said with irritation.

Esparragoza looked at Guzman menacingly. The two men's hatred for each other was fueled by decades of rivalry. Their machismo, combined with their egotism, stoked the fire. Chavez wondered when their inner anger would erupt into a Cartel War – a war like the one that had killed his father.

"What went wrong at the Nogales Port of Entry?" Esparragoza asked. It was a rebuff to put Guzman in his place.

Guzman shouted, "It was that reporter, Susan Laird. She did a story for the New York Times. Then, she tipped off the Americans."

"And they confiscated 500,000 fentanyl pills, plus 1,000 pounds of our best cocaine!" Esparragoza shouted.

"It won't happen again," Guzman said, now apologetic in his tone.

"How can you be so sure?" Esparragoza asked.

Guzman exhaled a large puff of cigar smoke, then spoke, "We made an example of her. Besides, the DEA is zero for twelve against us since we upgraded our firepower."

Esparragoza nodded in agreement and asserted, "Yes, Chavez and the Chinaman have equipped us with better personnel, weapons, and radar systems than U.S. Law enforcement. Our informants report their every move. If the gringos come, the vultures will feast on their corpses!"

"And if it gets too bad, we get to live in Solar Valley and visit the Valley of the Dolls, " Guzman offered.

Esparragoza grinned at the thought as a bead of sweat trickled down his temple, making him glad a cool breeze was funneling up the valley. He crushed the half-smoked cigar beneath his boot, the embers hissing in protest.

"Tell me about your new transportation system," he rasped, his voice gravelly from distrust.

"Texas Crude Transporters – a goldmine. We'll swim in clean money while the product moves like refined petroleum," Guzman roared.

Esparragoza wasn't entirely convinced. The speed of it all, the ease with which Guzman spoke of manipulating a legitimate company, pricked at his instincts. However, the idea of using a legitimate business to move product was undeniably appealing.

"You've done well, Guzman," Esparragoza conceded grudgingly. Praise was a rare commodity in their line of work, and Guzman savored it, puffing out his chest like a rooster.

"Speaking of which," Guzman continued, his voice dropping an octave, "how goes your getaway in Solar Valley?"

Esparragoza narrowed his eyes. Was it a question or an accusation? A veiled threat stated as casual conversation? He took a long moment to answer, letting the silence stretch thick with unspoken tension.

"On schedule," he sighed, each word measured. "In six months, it'll be a fortress. Besides, the Chinese can provide all the protection we need if things get too hot here."

Guzman's smile faltered briefly, a flicker of something Esparragoza couldn't quite decipher. "Ancira?" he asked, his voice devoid of its earlier bravado. "Is he still on board with the plan?"

Esparragoza snorted. The Mexican president, Ancira, was a pawn in a much larger game. But Guzman didn't need to know that. Keeping his cards close to his vest was essential. Information was power, and power could shift as quickly as the desert sands.

"Ancira," he said dismissively, "is like everyone else on my payroll. He answers to me. I own him. Right now, he's keeping the American wolves at bay, and that's all that matters for now."

CIA Headquarters

Jack stood on the deck of his mountain home, watching an Osprey fly across the lake. The winged predator soared with broad, unmoving wings, circling above the water, looking for its next meal. Then, suddenly, the bird swept down like lightning and plunged into the water.

Jack put his binoculars on the bird as it rose from the azure blue waters with a fish in its talons. The osprey flapped its wings vigorously, fighting gravity as it rose majestically. Jack was amazed that the osprey could generate enough lift to get airborne while carrying its struggling victim to shore. A few seconds later, the fisher bird perched atop the broken stub of a pine tree and began tearing at its victim. The fish thrashed in its last death throw as the bird's hooked beak tore away flesh. The king of the lake rocked its head back, swallowing the first taste of the life-giving protein.

"One must die so another can live," Jack said to himself. He'd first heard the phrase in summer training at Fort Benning. While he'd never been in the U.S. military, most of his training was conducted on military bases or at the 'Farm,' the CIA training camp in rural Virginia.

Bee-bac! The tone let Jack know a meeting participant had arrived for their video conference, and he walked back into his home office.

Oxley asked, "Jack, how are you?"

"Fine, Director. And you?"

Oxley looked like he hadn't slept in days. "I have a new assignment for you."

Unlike a CIA employee, Jack could reject assignments.

"What's the mission?" Jack asked cautiously.

"I need you to do reconnaissance on the Cartel. We need to know their chain of command, capabilities, and the best plan for eliminating them. While we haven't connected all the dots, I'm confident they're helping enemy agents enter our country. Perhaps, supporting Chinese sleeper cells."

Jack asked, "Just reconnaissance and planning, right?"

Oxley removed his eyeglasses and cleaned them with a cloth. He replaced them and said, "That's correct."

"I'm not sure I'm the right man for the job," Jack replied.

"The geek squad at the CIA thinks everything can be solved by a cyber-attack, a misinformation campaign, or a drone strike. This job requires an old-school, bare-knuckle approach. I need someone who has" Oxley paused as his mind searched for the right word, "fought them before."

Jack gazed at the serene lake, reflecting on how long it'd been since his last mission. It wasn't fear but rather the wisdom of living five decades and knowing how truly messed up the world was. Then, he remembered something his grandfather had taught him: 'Jack, evil triumphs when good men do nothing.'

"I'll need some resources," Jack replied.

Oxley's lips moved into a smile, "Your normal fee will be in your account by morning. You report to me. Please let me know if there's anything else you need. Your contact is an old friend of mine, Sheriff James Herbstreet; he's one of us."

New World Wuhan Hotel

Jake picked up a FedEx envelope at the front desk, but waited until he was in the privacy of his room to open it. The envelope held the faint smell of oriental perfume. He ripped it open and dumped its contents onto his desk.

A single USB drive fell out, then the note. It was from his contact in the Valley of the Dolls. The note simply said:

Remember me.

Jake smiled as he thought about Jade. She'd done it!

When he inserted the jump drive into his computer and opened the file, he saw the names of every client who had been welcomed to the "Spa." Names of the world's most powerful billionaires, politicians, actors, and religious leaders. There were also hundreds of videos of important men with their prostitutes. Jade had kept her side of the bargain; now, how to get her out?

Jake quickly inserted the jump drive into his PC and started the encrypted satellite upload to Langley.

Jake's CIA phone rang. He answered, "World Traveler."

Jones said, "They're on to you. Get out"

"Roger, Wilco, out," Jake replied.

Without hesitation, Jake Hendel peeled off his pressed suit and tie with mechanical efficiency. The tailored clothing, suitable for meetings with diplomats and double agents, was no longer the right cover, so he pulled on a pair of well-worn jeans, a light-blue Oxford cloth shirt, and running shoes. The finishing touch was a charcoal-gray travel vest—lined with Kevlar threading in case things got interesting.

The computer chime indicated his upload was complete. There was no time to destroy the drive as Jake unzipped a hidden compartment in his backpack and pulled out a slim leather pouch. Inside were four passports, each under a different name, each a ticket out of hell. He selected the Austrian document with the alias Tim Linde, a shell identity tied to a clean history and an old safe house in Vienna. He slipped the other passports into one pre-addressed FedEx envelope and the USB into another, then sealed both without hesitation. One way or another, he wouldn't need them.

A quick glance at his Rolex Explorer II told him he had just under ninety minutes to make his flight. Cutting it close, but not fatal. Not yet.

He slung his backpack over one shoulder, grabbed the rolling carry-on, and exited the room without looking back. His steps were controlled and fluid, but inside, his nervous system was on red alert. He passed through the lobby with the poise of a seasoned IT consultant, nodding at no one, eyes skimming every reflective surface. The woman at the reception desk offered a tired smile. Jake returned it with a warmth he didn't feel, knowing full well she'd forget his face in five minutes. That was the point.

In the motor coach bay, he ducked behind a concrete column and pulled on an N95 mask and wraparound sunglasses. The pandemic had done one favor to men like Jake—it made invisibility effortless. Every face was hidden, every expression veiled, every identity blurred in a sea of cloth and fogged lenses.

Outside, the humid air clung to his skin as he moved with quiet urgency to a FedEx kiosk. He slipped two envelopes inside. The packages would end up at a dead-drop facility in Zurich, clandestine and untraceable.

Thirty-eight minutes later, Jake stepped off the maglev train and into the departures level of the airport. The overhead board glowed a cold blue, mocking him with its clinical finality: Los Angeles – 8398 – On Time.

He joined the security queue, trying not to let the system's inefficiency get under his skin. One lost boarding pass. One retired couple was arguing over a carry-on. One screaming toddler. That's all it would take to unravel everything. Delay equaled exposure. Exposure equaled death.

Jake inhaled slowly through his nose—three deep breaths, just like his agency training had drilled him. The autonomic system was a slave to rhythm. Control the breath, control the mind.

"Calm down, Jake," he whispered, barely audible beneath the buzz of overhead speakers and shuffling feet.

He straightened, loosened his shoulders, and shifted into passive mode—unremarkable, unmemorable, and utterly forgettable. Just another nameless traveler in a mask-covered world. His heart still pounded like a war drum in his chest, but his face betrayed nothing.

The hunt had begun, and Jake was no longer prey.

He was a ghost, vanishing. And somewhere, someone was on the verge of losing control of the game.

CCP Security, Photo Recognition Section

The unmarked car pulled up to the station, brakes squealing. Zheng jumped out and ran into the Police Station. With a flash of his ID, Zheng was admitted into the secured facility and proceeded briskly down the hall.

When he entered Room 107, General Leu shoved a picture into his hand. The printer generated a black-and-white photo of a Westerner wearing a baseball cap, sunglasses, khaki pants, hiking boots, and an Ex Officio Shirt. After a moment of reflection, Zheng remembered the man.

"Is this the man who talked with Dr. Jingyi at the restaurant? General Leu asked.

"Yes," Zheng replied.

"What is his name?" General Leu demanded.

Zheng said, "We do not know."

"What did they discuss?" General Leu asked.

"They talked about baseball, tourist landmarks, and Cal Tech. When I questioned him, he told me he was merely practicing his English."

General Leu considered Zheng's response. It made sense. Still, his instincts told him the American was trouble. He turned to the photo analyst and asked, "Have you come up with anything yet?"

"Sir, his image is not in our digital files. We're reviewing our hard copies now," she replied.

General Leu asked, "When will you have his identity?"

"Sir, it could take hours," the analyst said nervously.

Finally, the general ordered, "Put our ground teams on standby. We can't let Mr. Hendel leave the country!"

"Yes, sir," Zheng replied.

Attempting to avoid the general's wrath, Zheng offered, "Sir, I'll call you as soon as we have an ID."

"I'm holding you responsible!" Leu threatened as he stormed out.

Wuhan International Airport

First-class boarding was called, and Jake Hendel activated the next layer of his cover. He slid on the fake eyeglasses—non-prescription, matte black frames—and swapped his standard-issue blue N95 mask for a yellow one he'd folded in the inner sleeve of his carry-on. It was a subtle but deliberate change. Most facial recognition algorithms keyed off color contrasts and habitual wear. A few seconds of misidentification could mean the difference between freedom and detainment.

He scanned the boarding gate with casual indifference, then followed the flow of elite passengers toward the jetway, keeping a steady pace. No rush, no hesitation. He handed over the boarding pass with the name Tim Linde, nodded politely at the agent, and stepped aboard Delta Airlines Flight 8398—Wuhan to Los Angeles, non-stop, twelve hours in the air, and a universe away in geopolitics.

The flight attendant greeted him with a polished smile and gestured toward the second seat on the port side.

"Welcome aboard, Mr. Linde. You're in seat A-2 today."

Jake gave her a warm but forgettable smile—just enough to avoid notice, not enough to spark memory. He stowed his carry-on, slid into the wide leather seat, and fastened the belt with a practiced click. He leaned his head back, eyes half-closed. Appear calm. Appear tired. Appear like someone with nothing to hide.

The thrum of the engines was already rising when the same flight attendant returned with a tablet and a poised stylus ready to take his order. "What would you like, Mr. Linde?"

Jake didn't hesitate. "Scotch and rocks, please."

She smiled, made a note, and moved on. Five minutes later, as the final passengers were still settling into their pods, she returned. Two mini bottles of Dewar's 12 Year and a short tumbler clinked onto his tray with a comforting familiarity. She added three thick cubes of ice from the metal bucket with tongs, nodded, and departed without fanfare.

Jake unscrewed the bottle, poured it with care into the heavy-bottomed glass, and let the amber liquid swirl like a distant memory. He took a sip. It burned—good. It helped him relax.

Outside the cabin, Wuhan shrank behind him. Inside the cabin, 30,000 feet would soon separate him from the epicenter of the world's next potential cataclysm. He'd completed his critical mission and uploaded the encrypted drive to Langley, where analysts were tearing it apart. As usual, he knew things the rest of the free world didn't yet know. It was both exciting and burdensome.

Jake took another sip and glanced at the cabin door, then at the crew. Twelve hours of flight time. If someone meant to stop him, they'd have to do it before touchdown.

He slid the armrest up, sank deeper into the seat, and closed his eyes—but only one layer deep. Behind his breath and slow pulse, every system in his body was running a pre-flight checklist of its own. This wasn't over. It was just wheels-up.

Wuhan Military Complex

General Leu's phone rang.

"Leu," the general answered.

Zheng said, "Sir, we've identified the suspect as Jake Hendel."

General Leu's face turned red as he considered his options. An international war correspondent could wreak havoc on their plans! Apprehending him could also generate an international incident. No, his men would discreetly capture and interrogate Mr. Hendel, then clandestinely bury what was left.

"Apprehend him at once. Just don't make a scene. Tell him there's a problem with his passport," Leu ordered.

"Yes, sir," Zheng replied.

Delta Airlines Flight 8398

Two uniformed police officers boarded the flight, holding a picture. Jake pretended to be asleep when the officers compared his face to the image. Hopefully, the mask and glasses, combined with his ethnicity, would be enough.

Jake held his breath as the junior officer asked his senior, "Do you want me to remove his mask, sir?"

After comparing Jake's masked face to the picture and seeing Tim Linde listed on the flight manifest, the older policeman said, "It's not him. Come on, we have more foreigners to inspect before the flight departs."

The two men continued through first class and then into coach. Fifteen minutes later, the officers exited the plane.

Jake breathed a sigh of relief and prayed his luck would hold.

Los Angeles International Airport

Delta Flight 8398 arrived at 11:28 AM, thirty minutes early. It felt good to have American soil beneath his feet. No matter how often he'd sojourned abroad, there was no place like home.

When Jake powered on his phone, dozens of emails, texts, and voicemails poured in. Apparently, everyone was concerned he'd been tossed into a Chinese prison or worse.

"No rest for the weary," he observed as he opened his texts. Fifteen minutes later, the plane reached the terminal. Five minutes afterward, the ramp was docked, and the door opened. Jake quickly exited the plane and made his way up the ramp into the terminal. After reaching a secured door, he waved his wallet across the scanner and opened the door. Once inside the secured area, with trepidation, Jake proceeded to a TSA conference room and returned Jones's call.

"Jones," answered the Asian Director.

"I'm back."

Jones smiled, "Jake, I was concerned when they put out an APB. Then, you ghosted us. Nice fieldcraft, by the way. Even I didn't know where you were."

Jake joked, "It hurt my ego that the Chinese didn't recognize me as Jake Hendel, Pulitzer Prize-winning correspondent."

Jones ignored the humor and said, "Watch your six; the Chinese have secret police everywhere. I've assigned a team to your New York apartment. So far, they haven't seen anything unusual, but they're crafty."

"What does Ox think?"

"He sees the invasion as imminent, but believes Carpathian and his disciples pose a greater threat."

"Have we been able to follow the money?"

Jones continued, "Jack Regan has connected hundreds of U.S. officials with Cartel Leaders, foreign agents, Chinese lobbyists, and Carpathian's twelve disciples. There's been a lot of cheddar changing hands, but to what purpose? While we know China's 2050 strategy, we don't know Carpathian's plan."

Jake thought it over and offered, "If I can attend the World Economic Forum, I might be able to learn more."

Jones thought it over. While Carpathian operated with military-grade security and could easily make his agent disappear, Jake was resilient, and Hank would accompany him. In the end, he decided the mission had to come first.

"See if you can get assigned to cover the World Economic Forum," Jones said.

"Wilco, out," Jake replied.

***

Jake looked down at his smartphone and selected Susie Legman's number.

An unusual level of trepidation emerged as he thought about what to say, a new development for the seasoned reporter. But then, committed relationships were something he'd avoided after his first wife was killed.

In a rare sentimental moment, Jake pulled out a tattered photo of her in her medical vest with a stethoscope hanging around her neck. She was young, tan, and beautiful. He'd met Barbie when they were co-eds at Samford University. It was love at first sight. Her parents had been missionaries in Japan, and their desire to save the world led them into a two-year Journeyman Program sponsored by the Southern Baptist Foreign Mission Board.

The first eighteen months of mission work in the Horn of Africa had gone well. Then, in late April, their director requested volunteers to serve on a small medical team headed to Somalia. The eager young couple volunteered and arrived in Hargeisa, Somalia, on April 28. Days later, Marxist military dictator, President Siad Barre, placed the country under authoritarian control. On May 26, 1988, the Somali National Movement (SNM) launched major offensives targeting Hargeisa. Barre's military responded to SNM aggression with brutal counter-insurgency tactics, including aerial bombardments and indiscriminate shelling of civilian areas. The city of Hargeisa, Somalia's second-largest, was devastated.

Jake recalled the rage, the burning fire in his belly that had tempered his soul and changed the course of his life. In the theatre of his mind, the horror of that day presented itself. No matter how many years, the demons of Africa still stalked him. There he was outside the clinic, unarmed, small arms fire and artillery raining down all around him. People were being slaughtered by uniformed troops and terrorists! "Don't shoot—we're medical workers! We're here to help!" Jake shouted in perfect Somali, his voice desperate but firm, hands raised in a futile gesture of peace. It was no use. The black-clad troops, eyes glassy and wild from khat, had crossed the threshold of reason. There was nothing behind their gaze but death.

Without warning, automatic gunfire erupted from the tree line.

Jake turned just in time to see Barbie, cradling the last child in her arms, sprinting toward the battered Land Rover. Dust and blood clung to her like ash. He waved—Go! —willed her to run, to escape, to live.

Jake knew the calculus. One man stays; the others survive. He was the force multiplier now. A firewall of flesh and fury.

"God," he whispered, breath thick with the stench of burned flesh and smoke, "be with me as you were with Samson when he slew the enemies of Israel… No greater love... I'll soon pull the rip cord and see you on the other side."

He dove behind a fallen militant, ripped the bloodied Kalashnikov rifle from lifeless hands, and surged forward. His scream tore across the battlefield like thunder. What followed wasn't war—it was sacrifice.

He cut through the first wave with merciless precision, his fury fuelled not by vengeance, but by love. When the rifle emptied, he didn't stop. He couldn't. The fight turned primal—hand-to-hand. A blur of motion, of broken ribs, ruptured jaws, and dropped bodies. The rhythm of combat—the controlled chaos he'd never known—took over.

When it was done, a dozen men lay dead around him. There were no more enemies nearby, so he wheeled toward the road, lungs burning, eyes wild. The Land Rover was nearly out of range. Good, he thought. They'll live.

Then the world exploded as a blast lifted the vehicle like a rag doll, metal twisting in midair before crashing to its side. The second explosion—igniting the ruptured fuel tank—turned it into a funeral pyre.

Jake's scream echoed across the valley. "NO!"

Her last image burned into his soul: Barbie, her eyes wide and full of light, looking back at him, that child in her arms. In that moment, she was an angel in motion—doing what she had always done: giving everything.

She had died on foreign soil, serving the least of these in Christ's name. A martyr not in words, but in action. That day, something shifted in his soul, and, while clinging to faith, God began a brutal metamorphosis.

After his rescue, Jake brought her remains home. The funeral in Birmingham, Alabama, was closed-casket; the remains were unrecognizable. Her parents thanked him and remained firm in their faith. "You'll see her again on the other side. This parting, no matter how painful, is only for a time." He thanked them, but their words fell hollow.

He sat for a week at Dunbar Hall, his old fraternity house at Samford University—silent, shattered, spent. Surrounded by a few grieving brothers and friends and the haunting silence of all that could never be said. It was during those sleepless nights that something hardened in him. What hadn't died on the battlefield, calcified in his chest.

From that moment on, Jake Hendel—the missionary who once felt everything too deeply—became a fortress. Love became weakness. Vulnerability became exposure. His heart, a citadel. Sealed.

But twenty-five years is a long time, even for a fortress.

Back in the present, Jake stood alone on the curb at LAX. The wind curled past his collar, tugging at the weathered edges of memory. He pulled out the dog-eared photo and stared at her.

A tear traced down his face. "Barbie, I miss you."

Then the sobs came. Raw. Cleansing. Guilt and grief were released in a moment of absolution. After what felt like an eternity, he kissed the photo, tucked it away, and pulled out his phone. It was time to move on. Maybe, after this last mission, he could retire and become what his soul desired – a father, a mentor, a husband again.

He dialled.

"Are you back?" Susie's southern drawl slid through the speaker like silk over steel. Her voice always hit him like a memory wrapped in heat—dangerous, beautiful, familiar.

"I'm at LAX. I land in New York at 0500. You free for dinner?" Jake asked, not yet able to shift from cryptic military speak to civilian.

Susie hesitated, sensing a subtle change in his voice. There was something softer. Something new.

"I'd love to."

"I'll pick you up at eight."

She smiled, the kind that reached her eyes. "Can't wait. Travel safe."

Jake paused. And then, unplanned, unfiltered, the words slipped out,

"I love you."

There was silence. Then a breath—soft, sharp, emotional.

"I love you, too."

And somewhere, deep within the citadel, a door creaked open and let light inside. Then, ancient feelings from youth flowed with a passion he'd lost a lifetime ago. The walls of the citadel were toppling. He decided to let them fall.

New York City

Candlelight danced across Susie's face, highlighting the flawless cheekbones perpetually framed by concern lines on the evening news. Jake, a man hewn by the harsh realities of far-flung conflicts, watched her surreptitiously. Years of embedded journalism had etched lines on his face, in contrast to her youthful beauty. At fifty, he felt a pang of self-consciousness – a man with a collection of scars proposing to a woman who could have any man she desired.

"You're staring," Susie observed with a playful smile, her voice as smooth as the chardonnay swirling in her glass.

Jake chuckled, "You look stunning."

The compliment brought a flicker of something more profound to her eyes. She smiled as he reached across the table with his calloused hands and took hers, his touch surprisingly gentle. "Jake, you always manage to bring calm to the storm. You do that here, too, you know."

Jake's smile softened. "I try."

Jake took a deep breath. This wasn't a war. This was a moment he'd almost pushed away for fear of leaving her a grieving widow. He'd seen too much of that – the hollow eyes of spouses left behind. But tonight, he wouldn't let fear win.

"Susie," he began, his voice thick with emotion, "I need to tell you something. Something I should have said a long time ago."

He reached into his pocket, his fingers brushing the velvet box. The weight of the two-carat diamond felt immense, a tangible representation of the future he dared to hope for. A future in a safe place with a beautiful woman in his arms and children on his shoulders. Could he really have that dream?

Susie's brow furrowed, a flicker of concern replacing the earlier warmth. He squeezed her hand, his gaze holding hers.

"I love you, Susie," he said, the simple words heavy with affection. "More than anything. But for so long, I couldn't…" He faltered as a tear rolled down his cheek, then forced himself to continue. "My job… It's dangerous. I didn't want you to live with that fear. And, well, you know my past."

Tears welled in Susie's silver-blue eyes. "Oh, Jake…"

Taking a fortifying breath, he pulled out the velvet box. "But there comes a time when we have to choose what matters most," his voice low and husky. "And for me, it's you."

Jake stood and knelt gallantly before the restaurant's hundred guests, opened the box, and revealed the glimmering diamond ring nestled within. "Will you marry me?"

Chapter 5

Jack Reagan flew by charter jet to Fort Clark Airport, where he picked up a waiting 4x4 truck. He then proceeded down the dusty desert highway to Brackettville, Texas.

It was high noon, and the temperature threatened ninety degrees as he drove across the desert. The sagebrush, cacti, and cedar trees covered the land in an endless array of browns and greens. Why anyone would live here was beyond him. In addition to the oppressive heat, desert landscape, and limited economic opportunities, the Cartel had turned the region into a war zone.

Jack drove past a few dingy-looking gas stations and small block house neighborhoods as he entered Brackettville. Traffic was light as he parked on the square. The Beaux-Arts Classic architecture of the Kinney County Courthouse stood in striking contrast to the lower-income sections of town.

The two-story building was graced by a central bell tower, octagonal corner towers, and columned entryways. Buff-colored brick, accented by red brick banding and corner quoins, completed the look. In many ways, the historic landmark stood in defiant contrast to the ubiquitous Spanish architecture, a clear message that this was America, not Mexico.

Sheriff James Herbstreet immediately exited the courthouse lobby when he saw Jake.

In many ways, the Order was similar to other ancient organizations, but with greater power. Herbstreet marveled at how a few men had changed the course of world events over the past 3,000 years.

Jack walked up to the plain-clothed Sheriff, extended his hand, and said, "Sheriff Herbstreet, Jack Regan. I'm glad to finally meet you."

Herbstreet, an imposing man of six feet four inches, looked at Jack momentarily. Sizing people up was an occupational hazard. A moment later, he took Jack's hand, "I'm glad you came. We can use all the help we can get."

Jack's sixth sense told him the sheriff was trustworthy. Not that he doubted the character of a fellow member of the Order, but it was comforting that his inner voice and the facts were in agreement.

The Administration and its Woke controllers had sacrificed whole communities like Kinney County with their open border policies. The Cartels' role in the New World Order remained a mystery. Whatever it was, the fund's flow indicated significant connections to China.

"Let's take your truck; it's less likely to raise attention," Herbstreet requested.

***

As they drove out of town, Herbstreet cut to the chase, "Jack, we're outmanned and outgunned. An enemy agent can cross the border, be issued a Federal ID, get $2,200 a month in welfare, and go anywhere in America. We're aiding and abetting the enemy."

Jack glanced at the Sheriff and nodded.

Herbstreet continued, "We're interdicting less than twenty percent of the drugs. I don't have an estimate on the sex trade."

Jack's face showed his outrage.

"They operate like wolves," Herbstreet said, his voice gravelly, "isolating the weak, preying on the vulnerable."

Years on the border had etched lines into the Sheriff's face—a map of battles fought and lost. But there was still a fire in his eyes, a flicker of defiance.

The highway stretched before them, a desolate ribbon cutting through the parched landscape. The midday sun beat down on the dusty truck, turning the air outside into a furnace, the Sheriff's words echoing in his mind.

Herbstreet went on, "They target attractive, emotionally vulnerable young women using a 'Momma' and a Romeo," Herbstreet said.

"Can you explain that?" Jack asked.

"The Momma is an older woman who befriends her, usually a dance or cheer squad sponsor, teacher, or talent agent. The Momma gains the girl's trust and then introduces her to Romeo. These Romeos are typically good-looking young men who seduce the victim and get them addicted to drugs. Once the victim is hooked, the drugs are better than chains," Herbstreet said.

Jack shook his head in disgust.

"The same thing happens in every American city," Herbstreet said defensively.

"Have you ever convicted a Momma or Romeo?"

"No. We've arrested a few, but the Cartel lawyers make Momma look like a solid citizen. They also bribe and intimidate jurors. As for the Romeos, they're all choirboys on the stand. I suspect many judges and prosecutors also take bribes."

"What motivates them?"

"The Cartel pays up to $50,000 per girl. More for the most desirable ones. The Mommas pay the Romeos out of their cut. A Romeo can make a couple of hundred thousand a year. You see the attraction."

Jack shook his head in disgust.

"They also use more sophisticated means, movie agents or talent scouts."

Guided by his mapping app, Jack made a turn off the main road, sensing Herbstreet was debating how much to say.

Herbstreet looked down at his hands as he searched his soul.

"My niece, Jade, was lost to the bastards two decades ago. She thought they'd make her a big star."

Jack studied the Sheriff's face, the stoic mask cracking for the first time. Beneath the lawman's gruff exterior lay grief that had never healed. A missing niece vanished into the abyss of a "talent scout's" lies. It wasn't just a case file—it was personal.

"You ever hear anything… whispers, rumors?" Jack asked carefully.

Herbstreet shook his head slowly. "Every trail ends in Asia. Some move the girls through Mexico, then across the Pacific. Those like my niece go willingly, thinking the offer is legitimate. Once they hit Shanghai or the Valley of the Dolls, they vanish into the system. No extradition, no cooperation. You can chase paperwork 'til kingdom come, but it's like chasing smoke."

Jack leaned back, eyes narrowing. This wasn't just about cartels or drugs—it was supply chains. Young women were commodities, just like fentanyl or oil. And the same people who controlled pipelines of narcotics and weapons were trafficking flesh into the heart of Carpathian's empire.

The Sheriff looked out over the dry desert brush, an analogy for his soul. "The bastards have it all mapped out. The cartels push drugs north, talent scouts push girls east, and the money flows back through shell companies into Wall Street funds. And you wonder why half of Congress looks the other way."

Jack felt the familiar burn of anger in his gut. Valley of the Dolls. The name had come up before, whispered in intel cables from Langley, tucked in afterthoughts in YODA's analysis.

His mind replayed the Sheriff's words: "Despite my connections, I've never been able to find her."

Jack knew then that this wasn't just another mission. Somewhere in the shadows of Solar Valley, Jade—and countless other American daughters—might still be alive. And if Carpathian and his allies were using them as leverage, the stakes went beyond politics. This was about America's soul.

"Then we burn their system down, Sheriff. Every piece of it. From the scouts to the cartels to the Valley itself."

Herbstreet met his eyes. The Sheriff allowed himself a thin smile. "Now you're talking like a sheepdog."

Jack smiled. The reference reminded him of his training at Bening, where his instructor discussed geopolitics in standard terms, using metaphors such as sheep, wolves, and sheepdogs.

"What's the Cartel's organizational structure?"

"Halcyons are the 'eyes and ears' on the street and the lowest rank. They're responsible for conducting reconnaissance and reporting the activities of the police, the military, and rival groups. Then, you have the sicarios who carry out assassinations, kidnappings, thefts, and extortions. They also operate protection rackets and defend their turf from rival cartels and law enforcement. Next up the chain, you have your Tenientes, who supervise the hitmen and falcons within their territory and carry out low-profile murders. Finally, you have the Drug Lords, a.k.a. Capos. The Capos control the entire drug industry, appointing territorial leaders, making alliances, and planning high-profile murders. The more successful Capos function like corporate CEOs running multi-billion-dollar corporations and, by default, whole Mexican states," Herbstreet observed matter-of-factly.

"How sophisticated are their operations?" Jack asked.

"Very. Last week, we found a 600-yard-long tunnel, forty feet underground, complete with lighting, ventilation systems, and a railway. They used it to transport drugs and people from Mexico into the U.S.

The tunnel started in an old Mexican mine and ended in a U.S. warehouse."

"They've upped their game considerably," Jack observed.

Herbstreet laughed and said, "To put it in perspective, we only found one tunnel before 2006; we've located six since. If they can move drugs and people undetected, they can move troops, weapons, and bombs just as easily."

Jack considered Herbstreet's revelation, letting the Sheriff's words sink in. Herbstreet wasn't just venting—he was describing a battlefield that looked more like Afghanistan than South Texas.

"You're saying the cartels aren't just gangs, they're a parallel army."

Herbstreet nodded. "An army with unlimited funding. Every kilo of fentanyl, every girl trafficked, every gun smuggled—adds to their war chest. And when they can buy XM915s and the same encrypted comms our Rangers use, you tell me: what's the difference between a cartel strike team and our Delta squads?"

Jack grimaced. He'd seen what money could do—rogue states hiring ex-SOF contractors, warlords in Africa outfitting militias with NATO gear. But hearing that it was happening here, on U.S. soil, hit harder than he expected.

"Who trained them?" Jack asked, already suspecting the answer.

"Some are ours," Herbstreet admitted bitterly. "Retired Green Berets, SEALs, Rangers. Others are washed-out cops who couldn't handle the badge but could still shoot straight. The cartels pay double what Uncle Sam ever did. Loyalty doesn't stand a chance against six figures in cash and a safehouse in Cancun."

Jack shook his head. An enemy force fueled by American tactics, weapons, and greed.

"And Washington just lets this happen?" Jack asked.

Herbstreet's laugh was hollow. "Let's do it? Jack, they need it. Look around—defense contractors, bankers, politicians—they're all wetting their beaks. The chaos at the border keeps the money flowing. Drugs, migrants, weapons—it's all leverage. Myassus does what he's told because the orders don't come from him. They come from the same people you're chasing—Carpathian and his cabal."

Jack felt the weight of it—the missing puzzle piece snapping into place. It wasn't incompetence. It wasn't bad policy. It was deliberate. America wasn't losing the war on the cartels. America was selling it.

Herbstreet fixed his gaze on Jack. “I buried fifty men last month, Jack. Marines, DEA agents, deputies, and even a couple of good kids fresh out of the academy. And for what? So politicians can continue to play both sides while billionaires buy yachts? You want to take down the real enemy? You’d better understand—you’re not fighting just China. You’re not fighting just the cartels. You’re fighting the globalists and the deep state they control.”

Jack said nothing, but his jaw tightened. For the first time in years, the old fire burned in his chest. Herbstreet was right. The wolves weren’t just across the border—they were in the halls of power.

And Jack Reagan had just declared war on them all.

“Jack, right now, the Capos don’t know you exist, but mark my words; they’ll find out, so get in and get out fast,” Herbstreet cautioned.

Jack was silent as he considered Herbstreet’s warning. Then his mind drifted back to Colombia in 1983, when a mission had gone wrong. The sounds of gunfire and the smell of the jungle stench filled his senses as his mind was pulled back through the portal of time. He shook off the flashback. He had more to live for than he had as a twenty-something shooting spook filled with piss and vinegar.

“I’m taking you to Jensen Outfitters, the best sheep-hunting concession in the region. Peter Jensen has exclusive hunting rights to 135,000 acres in Coahuila, Mexico, and uses helicopters to drop hunters. It’s the only way to get you into Mexico without suspicion, and the aircraft will give you a good observation point.

Jack nodded in agreement.

I told Peter you were a friend who needed a desert bighorn for his trophy room. That should be all the cover you need. Just know that hunting desert bighorn is a real adventure.”

“What’s his fee?” Jack asked.

“$15,000 for a three-day hunt. That includes everything except the trophy fee. You could owe him another $50,000, depending on the horns.”

“Why Jensen?”

“Because the Capos are among his clients, and he can get you in and out without suspicion.”

Jack looked at the Sheriff and asked, “Can I trust Peter?”

Herbstreet smiled, “Yes. He’s my wife’s cousin and one of my best informers. Just don’t tell him you’re CIA. I told him you were a big spender. Go with that, and remember, the less he knows, the better.”

World Economic Forum, Davos, Switzerland

The idyllic Alpine village of Davos was nestled in the Land Wasser Valley, backdropped by towering mountain spires. The once sleepy town was now renowned for hosting the World Economic Forum. As an international conference center and a major destination for winter and summer sports, Davos was the playground of the rich and famous.

Few realized that Davos was one of the world’s most secure cities, protected by specially trained police and a vast network of security cameras. Should the need arise, the Davos police and special units of the Swiss military could respond to threats. AI-based facial recognition systems also enable police to identify and monitor individuals who are suspected of causing trouble. Davos remained among the few places outside China where Ethan Carpathian and Helmut Scheid could safely walk in public.

Jake and Hank sat at a patio table at the Cafe Weber Backerei Konditorei Bar. The maître-de confirmed that it was Carpathian and Scheid's favorite haunt. Knowing the two elites often had a late breakfast at the establishment, Jake had stacked the odds in their favor. While it was a long shot, Jake hoped the two men would be comfortable enough to be loose-lipped.

“What did you do on your day off?” Jake asked Hank.

Hank said, “I took the cable car to Jakobshorn and hiked the main trail for ten clicks. They have over 700 km of marked trails up there.”

“The Davos Klosters are Switzerland's best mountain bike destination. I rode it in 2020,” Jake observed.

“So, did you ask her?”

Jake’s face held a warm glow, uncharacteristic of his usual expression. “Yes.”

“So, what’d she say?”

“She said yes.”

Hank leaned back in his chair, grinning. “About time. You could have lost her to one of those young bucks.”

“Just glad she’ll have me.”

Hanks thought Jake's words sounded more contrite than usual, but then he'd seen men in love.

After an espresso, Jake and Hank each ordered two eggs with sausage and a bread basket. They were hungry, and it was the only way to keep the table. After an hour, Scheid and Carpathian arrived.

Jake and Hank noticed that two muscular men dressed in ski jackets were escorted to the rearmost table and sat with their backs to the wall. Their build, military haircuts, and command presence affirmed them as bodyguards.

Jake noticed that one of the bodyguards gestured to another military-aged man across the street. The man raised his hand to his face and turned away. Jake recognized the short-range radio system and figured they had more bodyguards in the vicinity, as well as one on overwatch.

A tingle ran down Jake's spine as his gaze snagged on a window across the street. Fourth floor, partially open, bathed in the inky cloak of darkness. It could be a guest craving fresh air, but the timing gnawed at him. Someone was watching them. His pulse quickened as his eyes scanned the scene, dissecting the angles of the sightlines. The open window, strategically placed, offered a perfect sniper's perch. A shiver danced down his spine, a primal fear of being a target. While the actions of professional triggermen were dictated by their contracts, not fleeting anxieties, being in the crosshairs was unnerving.

The weight of being observed, a potential bull's-eye in an invisible game, tightened his throat. A bead of sweat trickled down his temple, a reminder of the precariousness of his situation. In a city teeming with secrets, the line between tourist and target had blurred dangerously thin.

"They're coming," Jake whispered.

Hank pretended to view a text on his phone as he took a photograph of the two bodyguards. After an upload to Langley, he received a text with each man's identity and a summary of their Interpol files.

Hank looked at Jake, "The heavies are Scheid's A team. Both are prior Swiss Special Forces. Always armed and deadly accurate."

"I'd be disappointed if they weren't," Jake said with a smile.

When Carpathian and Scheid arrived, the hostess quickly escorted them to a corner table just past the bodyguards.

Hank picked up his specially outfitted Nikon camera and pretended to be editing pictures. After making a few adjustments, he placed the camera on the table, pointed its lens at the elites, and was relieved that the security detail didn't intervene. Hank pressed the shutter button, and the camera began clandestine recording.

CIA Headquarters, Langley, Virginia

Raymond Jones leaned forward in the comms center, pen frozen above his notepad as Scheid spoke on screen. "When we drive U.S. debt to the tipping point, bond ratings collapse, and investors refuse to purchase U.S. debt instruments. When the Treasury can't raise enough money to pay its bills, it will expand the money supply. Hyperinflation follows. The dollar loses much of its value. Life savings gone overnight. Budget austerity shuts down government spending. Social programs collapse. Depression sweeps the nation. Western economies follow the U.S. down into the abyss while our gold doubles in price."

A junior analyst whispered, "My Lord… they're planning to crash the economy."

"Quiet," Jones snapped, eyes locked on the feed.

At the café table, Carpathian stirred his coffee slowly, gaze fixed on Scheid. "So, Americans wake up one morning to find their savings vaporized?"

"Correct. And when the dollar crashes and loses reserve status, nations will scramble to a safer haven," Scheid's tone was clinical, as though reciting a weather forecast.

Carpathian tilted his head. "And this is why investors are hoarding gold."

"Gold is eternal," Scheid noted, a thin smile cutting his face. "Its purchasing power is unchanged since the pharaohs. Central banks know this. They've been moving out of dollars for years. It's the reason my organization still holds most of the gold liberated from European Banks during WWII."

Jones scribbled: "Gold shift + devalued dollar = economic chaos."

Carpathian asked, "And People's Coin replaces everything?"

Scheid's smile widened. "Yes. We set the rate. Ten cents on the dollar. Ninety-nine percent of Americans become dependents overnight with no safety net from Uncle Sam."

Carpathian exhaled through his nose, a hint of mockery in his voice. "And soon, the common man will own nothing but be happy."

The café's background clatter carried on. Forks scraped plates. A waitress refilled the coffee. And in the comms center thousands of miles away, silence thickened as Jones and his team realized what they were hearing wasn't just a plot — it was a countdown.

Oxley removed his glasses, pinched the bridge of his nose, and stared at the ceiling. "Tanking the economy… It's the perfect gambit. Nearly untraceable. A crime with no fingerprints."

Baker piled on, "Chinese President Jen told the media last week, 'We do not have to invade. We will destroy you from within.'"

Reagan slid copies of his report across the table. "What you're holding is the money trail—China, Russia, Iran, the Globalist 100, Drug Cartels. Every corporation they control. Three hundred members of the House and Senate—Republicans and Democrats—each received an average of ten million dollars in inducements of various kinds. The Tilden family alone? Over a hundred million in cash and equities. It's a sellout of the American people on a massive scale."

Baker's jaw tightened as he scanned the pages. "With this, I can get arrest warrants."

Oxley looked over his glasses. "Will your boss sign off?"

Baker hesitated. A beat of silence stretched across the room. "I plan to do my job and let the chips fall where they may."

Reagan leaned back in his chair. "If you wait for approval, Tilden's AG will bury it. We may have to leak it first—scorch the earth before they can whitewash it."

Oxley's tone hardened. "How long until they trigger the collapse?"

Reagan's answer was clinical. "We're at thirty-seven trillion in debt. Add another three hundred billion a month to the deficit this year, plus Ukraine aid, Taiwan defense, the Mexico drug war, and another four trillion for COVID-23 relief—we'll reach the $40 trillion trigger this year."

Baker shut the folder, his knuckles white. "Worst-case?"

Reagan's voice dropped. "Banks shuttered. Equities gutted. Investors fleeing to hard assets. The rich survive, barely. The average citizen loses everything. If they're debt-free, they can hold out until the food runs dry. After that, riots, gangs, and prisons emptied. Crime explodes. And within twelve months… ninety percent of Americans could be dead."

The room fell into a silence that felt heavier than any bomb blast. Oxley's gaze swept the table, the weight of history pressing on him.

"A flagless group of billionaires and their Communist minions," he said, "destroying America without firing a shot."

Laredo, Texas

Edwardo Chavez scanned the area around the laundry processing center with his night vision binoculars. His advanced team had been monitoring the building for days without seeing any sign of law enforcement. Chavez knew the value of reconnaissance and meticulous planning. With D-Day approaching, there was more at stake than the Cartel's drug shipments, and he wasn't taking any chances.

Chavez lifted the short-range radio to his mouth, "Execute Plan A; the coast is clear, over."

A voice answered, "Wilco."

Chavez lifted his binoculars and watched as the large metal doors rolled up and six delivery trucks loaded with operators and their weapons exited. After the vehicles departed, he looked with his naked eyes and was pleased that the red concealment lighting he'd installed had worked. The $10 million price tag for tunnels that ran from Mexico into the U.S. had been worth it. Soon, Chavez would exact his revenge on the U.S. Government for their sell-out of his men in Afghanistan. When the economy fell, he and his men would take whatever they wanted, like feudal lords of old.

Chavez turned off his night vision unit and dialed a number from memory.

"Yes," came an answer.

"They're off," Chavez replied.

The call terminated.

Chavez returned to his Cadillac Escalade and sat in the passenger seat.

Miguel, his driver, asked, "How'd it go?"

Chavez smiled and said, "Without a hitch. In two days, we'll have all our operatives in place."

Taiwan, Landing Zone One

A salty breeze whipped at First Lieutenant Seacrest's face, carrying with it the distant roar of crashing waves and the unmistakable tang of cordite. He squinted towards the horizon, where the sun dipped like a molten coin into the churning sea. The scene before him was a chilling tableau as razor-sharp coils of concertina wire snaked across the sand, mimicking the barbed entanglements of a bygone era. Thick steel beams were buried in the sand at forty-five-degree angles to stop invading vehicles. Like squat, prehistoric beasts, concrete bunkers hunkered down, their muzzles pointed defiantly towards the same enemy they had faced decades ago.

The resemblance was uncanny. Here, on this windswept Taiwanese hilltop, three hundred meters above the churning Pacific, Seacrest felt transported back to the stark battlefields of Normandy.

Landing Zone One was a critical access point on the island's western coast. Its proximity to major roadways leading straight to the heart of Taipei made it a prime target in the simmering conflict.

A knot of tension tightened in Seacrest’s gut as the gravity of the situation hung heavy in the air. He could feel the coiled energy of the Taiwanese troops and U.S. Marines surrounding him, their faces etched with a mix of stoicism and apprehension. They were the first line of defense, the thin blue line that separated Taiwan's fragile freedom from the encroaching shadow of a resurgent Dragon.

A deep rumble echoed through the gathering dusk as a pair of Taiwanese F-16 fighters roared past, leaving a contrail like a fading white scar across the twilight sky. It was a stark reminder of the modern face of war, a far cry from the trenches of World War II. But the tension remained a constant hum beneath the surface, a reminder that history, like the tide, had a way of repeating itself.

The lieutenant stood outside his concrete command center, the rhythmic lapping of waves a stark contrast to the distant rumble of jets. The fact that he was defending a beach rather than storming one was haunting as he recalled what the Allies' superior numbers and firepower had done to the Germans. The juxtaposition was sobering.

Seacrest lifted his binoculars, scanning the horizon where the last light of day bled into the encroaching night. In the growing shadows, he could see the silhouettes of concrete pillboxes and seaward-facing steel vehicle barriers. The soldiers around him were quiet, their faces grimly determined. His orders were simple: hold until relieved.

Seacrest's mind drifted to his grandfather's stories about the D-Day landings, the chaos, the noise, and the relentless push against an entrenched enemy. Here he was, decades later, preparing to defend a stretch of coastline. The technology had advanced, the weapons more sophisticated, but the human element—the fear, the courage, the resolve—remained unchanged.

The radio crackled to life, snapping him back to the present. Upon receiving the intelligence report, his men moved efficiently, checked weapons, and reinforced positions. He glanced at his watch; they had little time before the expected assault. He took a deep breath, the salty sea air mingling with the metallic tang of tension. He was part of a continuum, a living link in the unbroken chain of those who had stood against tyranny.

***

Jake Hendel stood at the edge of the wind-swept beachhead, his black Gore-Tex jacket flapping as the ten-mile-per-hour gusts stirred both sand and tension. Behind him, waves lapped against a jagged concrete seawall lined with rusting anti-landing obstacles. His khaki hiking pants were dusted with fine grit, and the treads of his hiking boots pressed firmly into the wet ground. Hank, his cameraman, adjusted the lens, framing the shot as Jake raised his microphone with one gloved hand.

In his earpiece, the producer's voice came calm but urgent. "We're coming to you in three, two, one… live."

Jake began, his tone measured, the cadence honed from years in war zones and political minefields.

"President Tilden's apparent waning on U.S. commitments to defend Taiwan made headlines around the world yesterday—and thrust the already volatile relationship between this democratic island and its authoritarian neighbor back into the global spotlight."

As he spoke, the production room rolled archival footage—Chinese ZTD-05 amphibious tanks hitting the surf, Taiwanese artillery units firing into mock landing zones, civilians undergoing civil defense training in Kaohsiung.

"Less than a decade ago, relations between Taipei and Beijing seemed to be on a slow path to reconciliation. But today, ties are at their lowest point in decades, and the risk of military escalation is no longer hypothetical."

Clips flashed: China's DF-17 hypersonic missile launches, naval fleets moving through the Taiwan Strait, and diplomatic warnings scrolling across state-run CGTN broadcasts.

"China's tacit support for Russia's invasion of Ukraine has only fueled fears that a similar playbook could be used here in the Indo-

Pacific. If war does break out, the U.S. and Japan have vowed to defend Taiwan. But with so many American munitions already committed to Ukraine, concerns are growing that Taiwan could be left exposed."

Back in the studio, Susie Legman's voice chimed in, clear and inquisitive. "Jake, what are the keys to Taiwan prevailing against the numerically superior People's Liberation Army?"

Jake nodded into the camera. "Experts tell me that Taiwan must retain control of its ports, airfields, and key landing zones—while inflicting heavy losses early on. In an ideal scenario, U.S. Coalition forces would intercept and sink the PLA Navy before it reaches shore and eliminate key missile and air assets. But if the conflict turns into a protracted ground campaign, China's superior manpower, shorter supply lines, and expanding logistics infrastructure will shift the odds rapidly in Beijing's favor."

Susie followed up. "What can you tell us about Taiwan's current defense doctrine?"

"Taiwan's Overall Defense Concept, ODC, was crafted by Admiral Lee Hsi-ming in the late 2010s. It's a strategic pivot—a recognition that Taiwan cannot win a head-to-head conventional war with China. The ODC employs asymmetric defense, utilizing mobility, deception, and precision to deny China the ability to establish a foothold. Instead of trying to meet the PLA head-on, Taiwan focuses on bleeding them out before they reach the cities."

Jake stepped aside and moved to a nearby concrete bunker. A man with a quiet presence and steel-blue eyes—retired U.S. Marine Colonel Bob Mullins- joined Jake. Known only to a few, McNabb and Hendel had been fraternity brothers.

"Colonel McNabb, you led over 8,000 Marines in Iraq and later commanded Fleet amphibious operations. What do you see as the keys to stopping a PLA invasion?"

McNabb nodded. "The first and most critical phase is survival. Taiwan must weather the opening salvo—missiles, cyberattacks, and airstrikes. Once that dust settles, they must prevent the PLA from capturing ports and airfields and from establishing beachheads. The next phase will be inflicting high enough Chinese losses to dissuade Beijing from continuing its assault or, at least, forcing them into a quarantine operation."

Jake pressed further. "What does the PLA need to do to win?"

"They need to dominate the airspace and sea lanes, then secure airfields and ports. From there, it becomes a logistics game—fuel, food, ammo—hundreds of thousands of troops ferried across the Strait. They'll need to hold that lifeline open while pushing inland through a population that doesn't want them. If it were me, I'd make airfields the first priority and use China's large fleet of cargo planes to pour my forces onto their major highways. Then, capture major ports and cities."

Jake leaned in. "Beyond defending landing zones and airports, what else can Taiwan do?"

"Three words: mine, mask, and maneuver. They need sea mines, smart drones, and mobile coastal missile batteries to punch holes in incoming Chinese formations. Every PLA ship sunk before landfall is a thousand lives saved. While Taiwan's military has strong senior leadership, it must resist top-down micromanagement. Let the field officers fight the war on the ground."

"What's your assessment of Taiwan's military?"

McNabb hesitated, not wanting to harm an ally or reveal intelligence. "They've trained well, and their fortifications are solid. But neither side is battle-tested, so no one really knows how either side will perform when the shells start flying. That said, Taiwan's troops are fighting for their families, their homes. That kind of resolve is always a force multiplier."

Jake turned to the camera as McNabb stepped back.

His tone graver, "If war does come, it won't just be a test of missiles and tanks. It will be a test of will, resolve, and readiness. For now, Taiwan watches the horizon—and waits for the klaxon to sound."

Jensen Outfitters, Kinney County, Texas.

Jack raised his glass, letting the IPA foam tickle his lip but taking only a measured sip. He cataloged details automatically: solar panels meant long-term self-sufficiency; the Cummings generator was top-of-the-line; the map book in his room could double as intel. Jensen wasn't just a hunter. He was funded.

Across the room, Jensen's eyes flicked to Jack's rifle case. "Two-fifty-seven and three-hundred Weatherby's," Jack offered. Jensen's reaction had been instant, genuine. The right answer. But then came the pause, the measuring silence — like a poker player deciding whether to call.

"You use dials or Kentucky windage?" Jensen asked, casual on the surface, but Jack felt the weight behind the words.

"Kentucky windage."

Jensen's broad smile broke, the tension gone. "Man after my own heart."

Jack smiled back, but he didn't relax. Bonding over rifles was a ritual, but Jack knew the real test was still coming.

Later, alone in his room, he flipped through the map book. Oil routes carved across Val Verde and into Mexico — arteries for cash, men, and weapons. The influx of rigs and infrastructure had given cartel coyotes new roads north.

Jack traced a finger along a red line leading toward Jiménez. CIA files suggested enemy combatants might already be slipping across with the smugglers. His mission was clear: confirm the Cartel wasn't just moving drugs — but soldiers. Then ascertain who, how, and where.

U.S. News

Susie Legman wore a pink top, a short tan skirt, and high heels. The studio desk's underlighting accented her tan, athletic legs to the delight of her male audience.

"We have CDC Director Dr. Amy Rapier with us today. Welcome, Dr. Rapier."

The camera cut back to the studio, the lower third blazing in red: "COVID-23: Engineered or Accident?"

Rapier straightened her lab coat, eyes flicking to the green light of the camera. Behind her, the CDC seal looked almost like a target.

"It's a pleasure to talk with you, Susie," she said evenly, the veneer of calm already cracking.

Susie Legman leaned forward, her tone precise and predatory. "Director, why did you and President Tilden fail to shut down airports and close borders before half a million Americans were infected?"

The question landed like a slap. Rapier's smile faltered. "Susie, as you know, fewer than twenty percent of Americans supported mandates or quarantines after COVID-19. For that reason, the President and I believed another lockdown would do more harm than good."

Susie pounced again. "Hospitals are diverting patients. ICU capacity is gone. One in four doctors and nurses is out of the fight. Where do sick Americans turn for help?"

Rapier reached for the talking points. "Under the President's Emergency Act, we're working with PharmX to fast-track a vaccine. Dr. Wilhite's task force already has Paxlovid-23 in clinical trials."

Susie didn't flinch. "Dr. Stevens and Dr. Chen told the International Virology Society that COVID-23 could kill up to two billion people in one year. That's nowhere close to your model. Who's lying?"

For the first time, Rapier shifted in her chair. The silence was heavy, electric. Susie smiled—she smelled blood.

"Many models exist," Rapier said at last, voice tight. "Some assume worst-case scenarios: no precautions, no vaccine, high airborne spread. Others account for mitigation. Naturally, the numbers diverge."

Susie drew her dagger. "Then answer this: NIH records show Dr. Facini funneled $25 million for gain-of-function research at Wuhan despite Obama's ban. Dr. Wilhite shipped modified bat coronavirus samples from North Carolina in 2017. Some allege he helped create the very virus that caused this pandemic, then partnered with PharmX to profit from the cure. Others say that makes him complicit in war crimes. What do you say?"

Rapier froze. A beat of silence—the pause heard around the world. The PR team in Atlanta must have been screaming in her earpiece.

Her jaw set. "Susie, that's tabloid speculation. I have known Dr. Facini and Dr. Wilhite for decades. They are men of integrity. Gain-of-function research is a necessary endeavor that is conducted globally. And let's not forget—President Trump repealed the Obama moratorium. As for bioweapon theories, I won't dignify them."

Susie delivered the kill shot. "So, to be clear: the CDC has models all over the map,' no effective treatment, and no guaranteed vaccine. Meanwhile, COVID-23 could kill as many as two hundred million Americans. Is that correct?"

Rapier's lips thinned. She shook her head, but the damage was done.

"Susie, cures are hard; questions are easy. The CDC and 150 partner nations are working around the clock. That collaboration is our best hope."

The studio cut to a commercial.

In homes across America, viewers weren't thinking about "collaboration." They were thinking about betrayal.

And in Langley, Oxley turned to General Lawlery, who had his arms folded and his jaw tight. "She just blew the lid off half of it. The public doesn't care about nuances—they heard 'Wuhan,' 'gain-of-function,' and 'war crimes.' That's all it'll take."

"Then it's no longer a cover-up," Oxley replied grimly. "It's a war of narratives."

Oxley nodded. "And narratives kill governments."

Highlands, North Carolina

The late afternoon sun cast long shadows across the manicured lawn of Dr. Lawrence Wilhite's private estate. A fire crackled merrily in the hearth inside the study, casting flickering light on the two scientists' faces. An air of grim satisfaction hung heavy as Wilhite lit his pipe. The burning Cavendish emitted a dank odor, similar to fallen leaves, with a hint of cherry.

Wilhite was seventy years old with a thin build and a slight bulge at the waist. He was not an attractive man, but he did have a certain charm that disarmed his prey. What he lacked in masculinity, he more than made up for in manipulation, a man who'd used misdirection, slander, and innuendo to bring down his enemies. Perhaps what made him most dangerous was his narcissism. Old Larry was all about himself and cared nothing about anyone who couldn't help advance his legacy or praise him.

"My girl is the master of misdirection, isn't she?" Wilhite bragged arrogantly as he turned off the television, not concerned with the televised rebuke.

Dr. Facini, his face etched with the weight of their shared secret, nodded curtly. "Phase I has been a resounding success. The first plague is out of the gate. Now, on to a more targeted approach."

Wilhite pressed a key on his laptop that activated a holographic display. Hovering in the center of the coffee table, the image of a complex molecular structure, a digital representation of their most horrifying creation - Chimera, a Genetically-Oriented Mortality Accelerator virus. Unlike COVID-23, Chimera wasn't a blunt instrument. It was a scalpel, a designer plague capable of targeting specific genetic profiles.

"We can code it to target anything," Wilhite explained, his voice laced with chilling enthusiasm. "Racial profiles, people with the god gene - the possibilities are endless."

“How does a Chimira virus target people carrying the god gene?” Facini asked.

“I used Dr. Dean Hamer’s research, specifically a gene called VMAT2, aka Vesicular Monoamine Transporter 2. VMAT2 helps regulate the levels of neurotransmitters in the brain, including dopamine, serotonin, and norepinephrine, which are the primary chemicals involved in regulating mood, emotion, and cognition. The fact that VMAT2 was found in 90% of Christians, Jews, and Muslims gives us an accurate target population.”

Dr. Facini shuddered, not out of fear, but at the sheer elegance of the design. "Truly, a marvel of biological engineering. But how do we ensure our adversaries remain blissfully unaware?"

Dr. Wilhite said, "We route all communication through our private network and encrypt it. Our World Health Organization and Wuhan Institute counterparts will receive seemingly innocuous data on COVID-23 mutations while the anti-faith virus remains hidden in our PharmX labs in Belize."

Wilhite tapped the holographic display, and the structure dissolved, replaced by a series of projected charts and graphs.

"Our simulations predict a nightmarish efficiency," Wilhite continued, his voice dropping to a low murmur. "Once released, Chimera will spread like wildfire, silently culling the human herd. Within a year, we project a global population reduction down to the sustainability level.”

Dr. Wilhite leaned back in his chair, a predatory glint in his eyes. "A new world order, sculpted by an invisible ax. In the modern world, scientists are at the forefront, and we can achieve the New World Agenda without a trace. A chillingly poetic notion, wouldn't you say, Tony?"

Dr. Facini offered a thin smile, his dark eyes reflecting the dancing flames in the hearth. "A new world order, cleansed and reborn. Soon, the common man will own nothing, and we will own him. It’s time the intelligencia ran the world.”

White House

The mood was somber in the West Wing as President Tilden emerged through the single door leading from the Cabinet Room to the Presidential Secretary’s office and, beyond that, the Oval Office. Everyone stood as the elder statesman entered. They remained standing until he took his seat at the center of the large table. The Vice President sat on his right while his Chief of Staff sat to his left.

The large conference room overlooked the Rose Garden and was adorned with neoclassical ceiling molding featuring triglyphs. A series of French doors, topped with arched lunette windows, was located on the east side of the room. A fireplace, flanked by two niches, held the busts of George Washington and Benjamin Franklin at the far end. Above the mantel hung a painting titled The Signing of the Declaration of Independence by Charles Édouard Armand-Dumaresq. The enormous elliptical mahogany table had been a gift from China to President Richard Nixon in 1970.

President Tilden's Cabinet included the VP, the heads of the fifteen executive departments, the Attorney General, the White House Chief of Staff, the U.S. Ambassador to the United Nations, the Director of National Intelligence, and the U.S. Trade Representative, as well as the heads of the Environmental Protection Agency, Office of Management and Budget, Council of Economic Advisers, Office of Science and Technology Policy, and Small Business Administration.

As secretary after secretary reported on the pandemic, economic concerns, and global instability, the President's mood worsened. It had become too much for the octogenarian.

Secretary of Defense James Shipman started his update by saying, "Mr. President, Russian advances into Ukraine are being buoyed by Chinese weapons and North Korean troops. Beijing's loan of thirty Chinese fifth-generation fighters to Russia has significantly increased Ukrainian demands for F-35s."

Tilden nodded for Shipman to continue.

"Our supplies of missiles, artillery, and drones are well below what we need to support a major global conflict. The net, net is that we need to replenish our ammunition lockers."

Tilden knew that NATO members failing to pay their NATO obligations had, again, placed the financial burden of the war in Ukraine on the U.S. – a fact he could not state to the press. He also knew U.S. battle lockers were well below the levels needed to meet global obligations. China knew this.

"I agree, but we're already approaching a $4 trillion deficit this year, and can't keep spending this much on Ukraine. Let our NATO allies start doing their part. What about Taiwan?"

"Mr. President, we have Carrier Strike Groups 3, 9, and 11 on alert, with Groups 1 and 10 operating within 1,500 miles of Taiwan. We're keeping Groups 2 and 4 in reserve to maintain national defense along our Western coast. Pacific bases are on alert. We've sent 5,000 U.S. Marines and two Assault ships to Taiwan. Thus, we have a powerful counter to Chinese aggression," Shipman said deceptively, knowing most of the people in the room didn't fully appreciate the lopsidedness of the emerging war.

"What's the Pentagon's assessment of Ukraine?" Tilden asked.

"Russia lost most of its modern tanks, experienced senior officers, and elite troops early in the war. Those Chinese tires on their resupply trucks went flat, stalling their best opportunity to take Kyiv early in the fighting. Today, the Russian Army is primarily composed of conscripts with limited or no experience, many of whom have criminal backgrounds. It's why the Russians pulled back and are using triangular artillery formations to hold off the Ukrainians. While Russia lacks many things, it's currently out-producing NATO three to one in artillery shells, allowing it to control the zone indefinitely. Unless we're willing to remove their artillery and target their missile and air bases, they're in for a long slog," Shipman replied.

"I'm not attacking Russian positions. Keep supplying Ukraine, for now. As for China, Jin won't dare move on Taiwan, he knows our capabilities," Tilden said with a confidence he did not possess.

The serious looks on his cabinet members' faces indicated that his team wasn't buying his assessment. They needed something more compelling.

"I'm sure my relationship with President Jin will allow me to convince him of the futility of hostilities against Taiwan. Now on to COVID-23. What's the update, Amy?" Tilden asked, changing the subject.

"Mr. President, our models show that fast-tracking Plaxlovid-23, along with concurrent vaccine development under the emergency order, will allow us to bring COVID-23 under control within six months."

"Excellent work, Amy. What else is needed?"

Rapier knew the President had opened the door for her to bring about the next critical step in the plan. She replied, "Martial law must be declared to limit civilian spread. We have to keep infected people at home, or we could lose up to eighty percent of our physicians and nurses."

Press Secretary Pigeon asked, "Are you really suggesting hospice without medical support for infected people?"

"It's all that can be done until we can deploy a vaccine," Rapier quipped.

The room was stunned that the CDC Director had recommended a death sentence for tens of millions of Americans. Several of them shook their heads in disgust. Bilden's face showed a flicker of respect for Rapier's manipulative abilities.

Chapter 6

President Jin returned from an inspection of the Southern Theatre Command and publicly stressed the need to deepen preparations. During his visit, Jin instructed his military personnel to accelerate the transformation of their armed forces and enhance their level of modernization. He then intimated that he was prepared to capture Taiwan and begin their long-awaited conquest of the Pacific.

While China's display of military force around Taiwan was largely dismissed as a bluff, the CIA considered the release of two new squadrons of Chinese stealth fighters, the christening of 100 ships, and the drafting of 250,000 new troops a clear indication of China's desire to assert its presence in the Indo-Pacific.

The lacquered doors swung shut with a heavy finality, muting the din of the outer palace. Inside, the air was cool, perfumed faintly with the scent of sandalwood. A long mahogany table gleamed under recessed lighting, its surface covered with folders, encrypted tablets, and porcelain teacups that nobody touched.

At the head sat President Jin, his black eyes steady, unreadable. To his right, General Leu, Minister of Defense. To his left is General Chan, chief of the PLA's special operations. Around them, aides and deputies waited with the nervous silence of men who knew history was being written.

Jin broke it. His voice was soft, but it carried the weight of command.

"Once we fire the first salvo, we awaken the world's strongest military. Tell me, why do you think we can capture Taiwan?"

General Leu leaned forward, a wolfish smile on his face.

"Great Leader, we have the weapons to destroy four American carrier groups, half their Pacific aircraft, and 250,000 coalition troops in the first week of our campaign. Their ammunition stores are at the lowest level in twenty years. Their weapons shipments to Ukraine have bled them dry. And President Tilden's ideological purges have driven out their best junior and non-commissioned officers. The Americans are weakened, distracted, and divided. We, by contrast, have a short supply chain and far superior numbers. They must fight across an ocean and cover the world."

The generals chuckled, their laughter sharp and hollow.

"The Dragon rises," Leu said, "and the Eagle falls."

Jin's lips curved faintly. "And Tilden? Our investment?"

Leu bowed his head. "The 'big guy' isn't cheap. But he has been worth every yuan."

Jin nodded, satisfied, and gestured for Leu to continue.

"Our deployment of COVID-23 will cull as many as two hundred million Americans, most of them their healthiest soldiers, athletes, and essential workers. If somehow, they contain it, we hold stockpiles of weaponized smallpox and anthrax. The Mexican cartels will deliver it for us. Their borders are already porous."

Jin's eyes glinted with satisfaction. "And the narcotics strategy?"

"Our chemists have overconcentrated shipments of fentanyl. Their amateur distributors will do the rest. Tens of thousands of addicts dead overnight. PharmX will mirror the tactic through mislabeled prescriptions, killing their elderly by the tens of thousands. The deaths will be blamed on Washington's failure to control its border and its drug makers. Their own citizens will turn on them."

"Excellent." Jin folded his hands. "And our sleeper cells?"

General Chan spoke for the first time, his tone clipped.

"We've infiltrated more than 10,000 operatives through cartel pipelines over the last four years. When signaled, they will strike critical infrastructure and civilian centers."

Jin let the words hang, then asked coolly, "And Dr. Fen? How much damage did her defection cause?"

Leu's expression soured. "Her laptop contained the complete bioweapons archive. The concentration camp trials. Enough to convict us of crimes against humanity in any tribunal. It could also allow the Americans to develop a cure."

Silence fell. The weight of the admission lingered, a shadow across the room. Jin rose from his chair and walked to the window, gazing at the manicured gardens below.

"If they accuse us?" he asked.

Leu straightened. "We remind the world: the virus was born in a U.S. lab. Funded by U.S. grants. An American scientist carried it to Wuhan. We will drown them in their own duplicity. Propaganda is our shield."

For the first time that evening, Jin smiled—a thin, chilling smile.

"Then it is settled. Let the world awaken to the Dragon."

New York City

Jake Hendel sat at the kitchen table, the aroma of fresh coffee curling upward in faint tendrils. The apartment was still quiet, save for the soft rhythm of Susie's breathing from the bedroom. He'd paused at the door earlier, watching her sleep, golden strands of hair spilled across the pillow. The sight had stolen his breath — not just her beauty, but the gravity of it. This wasn't a fleeting romance. He was about to marry the second great love of his life, and the thought carried both gratitude and guilt. A man who had spent decades in war zones suddenly craved permanence, domesticity, something as ordinary as waking up to the same pair of silver-blue eyes every morning.

The tabloids had feasted on the story — the hardened war correspondent engaged to America's rising anchorwoman. USN's ratings had spiked ten points on the strength of their engagement alone. The network brass were ecstatic. For Jake, it meant less chasing bullets and more studio lights, a transition he was slowly learning to welcome.

His phone vibrated. Not the personal one. The other one — black, unmarked, CIA issue. Jake thumbed it open.

"World Traveler, over."

Raymond Jones's voice came through the line, low and clipped.

"Jake, we think the Chinese are going to move on Taiwan within the week."

Jake leaned back in his chair, eyes narrowing at the words. He'd expected this. Everyone who could read the tea leaves had. But hearing it confirmed weighed on his chest. In a matter of days, he would be wheels-down in Taipei, playing his last embedded role. Except this time, if the Chinese landed armor on Taiwanese beaches, his press badge wouldn't shield him. If they won, he'd be executed as a spy.

"I'm not surprised," Jake replied, his voice even but edged with disdain. "Jin's a communist dictator, Tilden's wetting his pants, and our ammo lockers are depleted. Inevitable."

There was silence on the other end, a rare hesitation from Jones. When he spoke, there was something almost paternal in his tone.

"Are you sure you want this one?"

Jake stared at the steam rising from his mug. For a man who had built a career outrunning death, the question struck differently this morning.

He thought of Susie, still sleeping, and the simple dream of coming home for good. Then he exhaled, the decision already made.

"One last mission," Jake said, his voice steady. "Then I'm out."

Jensen Hunting, Texas

Jack and Peter Jensen secured their gear in the rear seat, strapped themselves into Jensen's 2012 Robinson Raven II Helicopter, and donned headsets.

"Where to?"

"We'll cross into Mexico and hunt water tanks. Every critter's got to drink," Jensen replied.

"Sounds good."

The Raven lifted off, rose to 400 feet, and canted forward. Jensen piloted the chopper South over a sea of brown desert sand, cacti, and scrub trees.

A few minutes later, Jack saw a long, rusty brown metal fence composed of upward protruding steel beams. The wall ran as far as his eyes could see. Inside the fence line was a well-worn patrol road that meandered up and down the West Texas hills. Beyond the wall lay the Rio Grande River. Only the occasional oil rig or metal building broke up the otherwise desolate wilderness.

"The Cartel controls the border counties from Texas to California. You either stay out of their way, or they kill you." Jensen observed, then continued,

"What are those plumes of dust to the East?" Jack asked.

"That's a cartel convoy getting into position," Jensen commented.

"Are they waiting until dark?"

Jensen nodded, "Yes. Tonight, they'll drop their load, migrants, operators, drugs, near holes in the wall. Those who bought the $10,000 package will be met by a driver in the U.S. Those on the budget plan will get picked up by Border Patrol."

"How do they move their dope?" Jack asked.

"They drive it through tunnels that start in Mexico and end inside commercial buildings in the U.S. Their mules drive in, and the Cartel closes the doors and loads them up. The dope is on the street in twenty-four hours."

"Where do they get their mules?"

Jensen smiled, "Mostly people with no priors and clean driving records who won't attract police attention. Many are senior citizens trying to make ends meet. Some just want adventure. We call them the Geritol mule train."

Jack looked surprised and asked, "Do you think law enforcement is on the take?"

Jensen looked at Jack momentarily, his mirrored aviator sunglasses reflecting his surroundings. For a moment, Jack wondered if he'd pushed too hard.

After an awkward pause, Jensen said, "Along the border, you either turn the occasional blind eye, work for the cartel, or end up dead. And out here, a body doesn't last long."

The two men were quiet until they reached tank #66.

"That tank's a honey hole. Big horns usually come down to drink at sunset."

Jack nodded his approval.

The circular water hole was approximately thirty feet in diameter and had a two-foot-high concrete wall surrounding it. A few deer were drinking as they flew past. Jack noticed the 'tank' had a pump house with a solar panel and wondered how deep a well had to be drilled to hit water.

As the Raven landed downwind, Jack noticed that Jensen was so proficient at the controls that the helicopter touched down without a thump.

"Nice landing."

"Flying for ten years has made this old bird an extension of my body. The soft sand also helps."

Jack and Jensen exited the Raven and removed their gear. Jensen watched as Jack pulled his rifle from its case. The seasoned guide admired the Weatherby Mark V Accumark's fluted stainless steel barrel and spider-webbed, tan Bell and Carlson stock. He didn't get many clients who shot the .257 Weatherby, despite it being an ideal 'open country' cartridge.

Jack's eyes scanned the terrain while his hands found three rounds, loaded them, and closed the bolt without looking down.

Jensen asked, "Got what you need?"

Jack put on his backpack, looped the rifle sling over his left shoulder, and said, "I'm ready."

Jack held the rifle stock with his left hand, with the sling hanging over the back of his left shoulder. He grasped the rifle's grip with his right hand, let the sling fall below his left elbow, and raised the scope to eye level. Jensen noted that the rifle sling formed a shooter's sling. The whole maneuver took less than a second.

Jensen smiled, "That's a neat trick. Never seen that before."

Jack smiled.

"We'll take this short trail to the military horizon. From there, we can scout the area."

Jensen led the way to the crest of the ridge and stopped in a small cluster of cedars. The two hunters knelt down while Jensen scanned the terrain with his binoculars. After five minutes, Jensen made a circular motion with his hand and pointed to a clump of trees downwind of the water hole. The two men crouched low and made their way to the blind.

The setting sun cast long shadows across the desert floor, its gold and red hues illuminating the landscape. Sunset was only thirty minutes away, giving them an hour of shooting light. With a full moon, the two men could conceivably hunt all night.

Jack sat in the folding chair closest to the water tank. Jensen sat to his right and set up his spotting scope. The blind was constructed of cedar trees and sagebrush, held in place by a two-by-four frame. A carpet had been placed on top of the frame to create a shooting rail. Overhead, a mesh camo cargo net provided shade.

***

Twenty minutes after sunset, Jack caught a flicker of movement at 500 yards. Jensen followed with a spotting scope. "He's a shooter," he whispered.

The desert held its breath. Every sound—the rustle of brush, the faint cry of a bird—was magnified. Jack's pulse steadied, the weight of the moment bearing down.

The ram emerged, heavy-bodied, horns curling in flawless symmetry. A survivor. An alpha.

Jack eased the Weatherby to the rail, each motion slow, deliberate. Four hundred yards was a safe shot, but he preferred closer. The animal melted back into cover, leaving them staring at the empty desert.

Then, like a ghost, it reappeared—downwind, testing the air. The ram was moving toward an ancient tree that would soon block the shot. Waiting could mean losing him.

Jack slid silently, scope rising in one practiced motion. Crosshairs settled. Breath. Trigger.

The crack split the silence. The ram jolted, staggered, then dropped.

Jensen slapped his shoulder. “That’s a trophy for the ages.”

The two men walked to the magnificent beast.

As Jack thanked the Creator over the fallen ram, Jensen pushed into the brush for sticks. A rattler coiled and rattled; Jensen’s revolver barked once, the viper dangling limp from his hand.

“Best thing to do with them,” he muttered, slinging it around his neck.

They took the photos, field-dressed the ram, and slung it beneath the Raven in a cargo net. The Lycoming engine whined, lifting them into the sky.

Below, headlights crawled across the desert—dozens of vehicles in convoy, dust plumes glowing in the twilight.

“They’re smugglers,” Jensen said over the headset. “Immigrants, drugs, guns. You’ll see ten times that in the Del Rio Sector.”

“They own the night,” Jack observed.

“More than the night,” Jensen replied. “Those convoys carry antiaircraft missiles, .50-cal technicals, ex-Tier One shooters making two hundred grand a year. Some Tenientes pull millions. Money buys everything—men, weapons, silence.”

Jack watched the convoy snake north, a military-precise formation. “You think the Marines could stop them?”

Jensen gave him a long look, instrument light glinting in his eyes.

“No, the Marines wouldn’t win against these guys. And Jack— what you’re seeing down there?” He nodded toward the line of trucks, engines roaring like an army on the march. “That’s just a small operation.”

CIA Headquarters

The Situation Room’s lights dimmed as the faces of America’s inner circle flickered across the wall-sized screen. Dr. Stevens, Jack Reagan, Jake Hendel, Raymond Jones, General Dr. Robert Lawery, Dr. Chen, and Thomas Baker stared back at them in crisp, high-definition. In the center, Director Mark Oxley leaned forward, hands steepled, his expression one of grim determination.

“Dr. Stevens,” Oxley began, his voice cutting through the silence. “What have you learned?”

Stevens cleared his throat. "Dr. Fen and Dr. Jingyi's intel confirms it, sir. COVID-23 was designed as a bioweapon. Worse—" he hesitated, eyes narrowing, "the virus has been GOF-modified to weaponize our own COVID-19 mRNA vaccines against us."

Oxley's brows furrowed. "Explain that."

Stevens glanced at his colleague. "Dr. Chen?"

The virologist adjusted his glasses, his Mandarin accent precise. "COVID-23 triggers a lethal autoimmune response in patients who received one of the mRNA vaccines. The body's immune system attacks its own tissues, releasing uncontrolled pro-inflammatory cytokines. The result is a cytokine storm—multi-organ failure, acute respiratory distress, and death."

The silence that followed was suffocating. Even through encrypted links, the weight of Chen's words hung heavy.

Baker broke it first, his lawyer's cadence sharp. "Under international law, the CCP is guilty of crimes against humanity. But they'll claim plausible deniability. The Hague will hear 'lab accident.' They'll point to NIH and PharmX grants, insist COVID-23 was part of pandemic preparedness. Wilhite, Facini, Rapier—they're already laying that groundwork."

Stevens shook his head. "They've built themselves a hell of a smokescreen."

Oxley leaned back, his eyes scanning each square on the screen. "But we've got more than smoke. We have proof of the CCP's war plan. We have evidence that COVID-23 was GoF-engineered for offense, not prevention. We've traced the money—rogue billionaires, compromised officials. The picture is clear. Beyond a reasonable doubt."

Jack Reagan tapped the thick dossier in front of him. "My forensics, combined with NSA and CIA intercepts, provide us with a solid list of co-conspirators. And it doesn't stop there. Esparragoza has unified the cartels under his flag. They're aligned with Beijing, moving weapons and agents into the U.S. right now."

Oxley nodded slowly, then shifted. "Jake?"

Jake Hendel leaned forward into his camera, voice steady but grim. "Carpathian told me flat-out: 'By 2030, the average citizen will own nothing but be happy.' Sounds insane, but look at the pattern. Solar Valley has become ground zero. Billionaires, politicians—they all orbit him. He's building a new world order, with China as the host and him as the power broker. The recent attendee list from the Dragon Conference and Jade's client list and videos make the co-conspirators clear."

A shadow flickered across Raymond Jones's face before he spoke. "Director, I'd like permission to deploy YODA."

The room stilled. Even Oxley raised an eyebrow. The mention of the CIA's crown jewel wasn't casual. "Do it," Oxley said finally. "But keep it quiet."

Jack's curiosity broke through his practiced cool. "What's YODA?"

Jones allowed himself the faintest smile. "Think Alan Turing, 1943. His team broke Enigma, letting the Allies read Hitler's mail. YODA is the modern equivalent—but faster. It can crack enemy encryption in seconds, consolidate communications, and connect the dots. Moreover, it predicts intent. It's like having an electronic Oracle of Delphi that foretells the future."

Oxley's jaw tightened. "Then get us everything YODA can provide. Who. What. When. Where. How. If Beijing's moving to strike, I want us ready before they even pull the trigger."

The screen went dark. The silence that followed wasn't relief. It was the sound of a nation bracing for war.

Chinese Presidential Palace, Beijing

President Xi Jin's office radiated calculated power. Dark-stained teak walls framed by expensive art and rare vases whispered of wealth and permanence, while shelves stacked with both Chinese and English literature signalled a cosmopolitan intellect. The windows offered a sweeping view of Beijing's glass towers and traffic-clogged streets—a tableau of modern strength resting on ancient roots.

Every detail was curated. The blend of East and West, old and new, was no accident. Carpathian knew the decorator had been American, chosen to make Jin appear less provincial and more like a statesman who could spar on equal footing with Washington, Moscow, or Moscow. Like much of China, it was a façade. The only authentic object was a family photograph—Jin with his wife and two sons. That, too, was strategic: a reminder that the strongman was also a patriarch.

Jin had the pedigree to match the performance. Harvard MBA. Columbia law degree. Five years of absorbing the West's pleasures—women, Scotch, and high-stakes poker. Layer that on top of a childhood steeped in Confucian discipline and Communist pragmatism, and you had a man who lived Sun Tzu like scripture. To Carpathian, that made him predictable.

A steward arrived with a tray. Two highball glasses, amber liquid sloshing against ice. "Would you like a drink, sir? Twenty-five-year-old Macallan."

Carpathian nodded. The steward poured. He knew the game: Jin's glass contained tea, indistinguishable in color but not in effect. An old trick, giving Jin clarity while his guest drifted into candor.

Jin lifted his glass, eyes sharp. "The supreme art of war," he said smoothly, "is to subdue the enemy while he sleeps, and use his perceived strengths against him."

Carpathian's mouth curved. "I agree wholeheartedly."

The two men sat across from one another, predator and predator. Jin had hired the world's best consultants, weaponizing capitalism while keeping communism's iron grip at home. Bribed American politicians lined his pockets. Western decadence had become a lever for Eastern ascendancy.

"For our strategy to succeed," Jin continued, "we must be subtle to the point of formlessness. Only then can we be the directors of our opponent's fate."

Carpathian inclined his head, masking the knowledge that Jin was already being outplayed.

"The inadvertent release of COVID-23 has forced me to accelerate Operation Dragon Strike," Jin said, voice low.

Carpathian drained his Scotch in one swallow. Jin's eyes narrowed—was it doubt, or calculated indifference? The billionaire was useful, perhaps indispensable, but also expendable once the New Order was secured.

Jin sipped his tea.

"Our Health Service has inoculated ninety-five percent of the desirable population against COVID-23, smallpox, and anthrax. We will reach full saturation within a month." Jen bragged.

Carpathian said nothing.

"You understand," Jin pressed, "we have passed the point of no return. Are you prepared to go all the way?"

It was the pivot point. Somewhere deep in Carpathian's soul, a remnant flickered—memories of a Sunday school Jesus, a boy's cry for mercy. But the light was quickly drowned. The creed of Dregodarit—the cold, unifying faith of the Dragonians—snuffed out hesitation. Darkness won.

"Yes," Carpathian said. His voice was steady, final. "Soon, the United States and NATO will collapse. The dollar will crash. People's Coin will become the world's currency. Civil unrest and disease will thin the herd, and the masses will kneel at whatever altar we offer. A perfect storm—ours to command."

The two men clinked glasses.

Prism Headquarters, Virginia

The elevator doors slid open with a hiss, releasing Director Mark Oxley into the War Room—nine stories beneath the Virginia countryside. The cavernous chamber thrummed with quiet menace. Rows of analysts bent over glowing monitors, the ceiling dominated by a massive digital map of the world. Here, the nation's survival was measured not in years but in terabytes.

Oxley walked to the head of the conference table. His voice was flat, urgent. "What has our Prism Team learned?"

Edward Huron rose. Boyish, tall, and thin, the MIT prodigy radiated the restless energy of a man more comfortable with algorithms than people. He was the architect of *Your Own Data Analyzed*—YODA—PRISM's predictive engine.

"Sir," Huron began, "we've ingested over twenty terabytes of Chinese surveillance data—text, voice, video intercepts, even taps into the CCP's policc net. They maintain a facial image database of 2.5 billion. Half of the world's cameras are inside China. Their spyware lets them monitor any unsecured phone, PC, or camera. Exactly as we do."

Oxley raised a hand. "What are YODA's capabilities?"

Huron's eyes lit with almost childlike pride. "Prediction, sir. Let me demonstrate."

He tapped his keyboard. The table's holographic display sprang to life: a chilling replay of a masked man entering an elementary school in Dayton, Ohio. Analysts flinched as the AR-15 came up, the first shots echoing in dreadful silence. Huron froze the feed.

"Now YODA's projection, five days earlier. John Ramathan, twenty-six. Off medication for twenty-eight days. He purchased an AR-15 and one thousand rounds using his Visa ending in 0033. Drafted a suicide note the morning of the attack. Social posts referencing revenge. Predictive risk score: 99."

Gasps rippled through the room.

"In our longitudinal study," Huron continued, voice clinical, "every active shooter of the last five years scored 95 or higher. All could have been stopped if police had YODA tied to their surveillance efforts."

An intelligence officer leaned forward. "You're saying law enforcement could prevent mass shootings with this?"

"Yes," Huron said simply. "Flag for intervention. Counseling. Red-flag gun purchases. Tactical monitoring. Intervention when they approach a target."

Oxley let the silence stretch. "Impressive. But can YODA project the moves of the New World Order?"

Huron's fingers danced over keys. The monitor shifted: faces of world leaders, billionaires, generals, cartel bosses—arranged in a branching lattice. At the apex: Ethan Carpathian.

"Carpathian chairs the New World Order. Beneath him: committees for economics, propaganda, energy, health, agriculture, finance, and education. Base of operations: Solar Valley, China. Their doctrine blends green economics, population control, and state-owned property. Their motto: *the common man will own nothing, but be happy.*"

The air turned colder.

"Does YODA know their plans?" Oxley asked.

"Yes," Huron said, eyes gleaming. "Their speeches align with Beijing's hundred-year marathon: depopulation, destruction of Western civilization, centralized digital currency, China as the world's host, and a one-world government led by Carpathian and his followers. There's also a strong correlation with end-times biblical prophecy."

"U.S. collaborators?" Oxley pressed.

More faces populated the lattice—lobbyists, CEOs, senators, congressmen.

"The President. Hundreds of members of Congress. Bureaucrats, corporate heads. All tied to CCP funding or globalist networks. Voting records confirm pro-China bias—land sales, military cuts, NIH grants funneled to Wuhan. YODA tracks its roots to 1944—an SS general named Scheid, architect of the Fourth Reich and Nazi diaspora. Helmut Scheid picked up where his grandfather, SS General Scheid, left off, taking stolen wealth to fund his grandfather's plan to take over the world by economic rather than military might."

The room murmured—*treason*.

Oxley stayed silent, eyes on the names. The picture aligned with Jack Reagan's reports, yet something gnawed at him. "What about the cartels?"

Huron hesitated. "They're digital ghosts with minimal online presence, making it difficult for YODA to clearly see their next moves. It is why YODA analysis needs to be merged with human intel."

At that, Oxley leaned back, respect in his eyes. At last, a technologist who valued human intel.

"Dr. Huron," Oxley said, "task YODA with narrowing the window. Who, what, when, where. I want the target list before they strike. No surprises."

The holograms flickered again, faces frozen like ghosts in digital amber. Somewhere in that lattice lay America's future—if they could read it in time.

***

Oxley and Baker kept their thoughts to themselves as they exited the top-secret complex and boarded a helicopter.

Baker looked down on the Virginia woodlands as he considered his words, "This globalist conspiracy makes the Kennedy Assassination look like a fraternity prank."

Oxley looked at his friend and spoke, "We're caught between the axis of evil and Sodom on the Potomac. One misstep and the sunsets on the republic for good."

Baker nodded, saying, "I'll build a criminal case against our elected officials. Everything from banking fraud and campaign finance violations to treason. Based on Reagan's analysis and the YODA reports, it won't be hard to prove probable cause. The problem will be my boss."

Oxley hesitated, then said his piece, "We swore to protect the world from the forces of evil. These billionaire dragon worshippers, the plagues, rebuilding the temple, a universal currency, and wars and rumors of wars fulfill the ancient prophecies."

Baker had been thinking that same thing, but was glad Oxley spoke first. "Kinda hits you in the face, doesn't it? High Priest Longshear is the prophet. Ethan Carpathian, the Antichrist. They even have the Dragon as their symbol."

Oxley, the trained skeptic, said, "Still, prophecy isn't always clear. The Jews missed Jesus Christ as the Messiah because they expected a worldly king and military leader to free them from the Romans. When they encountered an itinerant carpenter from Nazareth who claimed to rule a spiritual kingdom, they had difficulty shifting paradigms. We need to be certain."

"I'm certain beyond a reasonable doubt," Baker offered.

"Are you suggesting that we activate the Joshua Protocol?" Oxley asked.

Baker sighed, "I see no other way."

Oxley recalled a sermon his father had preached at their small white church in the Hill Country near Austin, Texas, many years ago. In the address, his father quoted Dietrich Bonhoeffer, who said, "*Never forget that evil triumphs when good men do nothing, and silence in the face of evil is evil itself.*"

His father's brave words always spoke to him during his most harrowing trials.

Davos, Switzerland

The flag crackled in the wind, and tension was as forbidding as the heavily armed guards patrolling the perimeter. The wind whipped around Ethan Carpathian's face as he and his twelve disciples gathered on the patio of their mountain citadel for cocktails. Below, the village's lights twinkled like scattered diamonds, oblivious to the storm brewing above.

Dragon Day was upon them, culminating in seven decades of meticulously crafted plans to usher in a new world order, a movement that had begun at the end of the Nazi Reich. Carpathian would soon resurrect the greatest civilization in history, ensuring the survival of the human species. Yet, despite the meticulous planning and fervent loyalty surrounding him, Ethan felt a gnawing disquiet. It was like gazing upon a majestic iceberg, its glistening peak obscuring the monstrous, destructive mass submerged beneath the surface.

The plan, audacious and intricate, would trigger a chain reaction. Billions of lives would be extinguished, a horrifying necessity to create the foundation for their new world. Financial systems worldwide would collapse, and trillions of dollars would vanish in a digital dust storm.

After the group returned to the conference room, Carpathian said, "The appointed day is upon us."

The twelve disciples applauded.

Carpathian waved his hand to settle the applause, then spoke, "Please be seated. I've asked Helmut Scheid to provide a financial report."

Helmut Scheid wore grey slacks, a tailor-made navy blazer, and a white cashmere sweater. His well-groomed beard, salt-and-pepper grey hair, and reading glasses gave him an intelligent appearance. His formal dress was in stark contrast to Carpathian's khaki hiking pants and black fishing shirt. If they didn't know better, a casual observer would have thought Scheid was the leader, and Carpathian the follower.

"Thank you, Ethan. The U.S. debt crisis, combined with thirty-five years of gross fiscal mismanagement in Washington, has achieved two of our three economic objectives: devaluation of the U.S. dollar and, soon, the inability to fund U.S. debt by selling debt instruments. As of today, the world's central banks are purchasing the lowest level of U.S. treasuries since 1999, preferring gold. The last leg of our plan is to tank the U.S. Stock Market," Scheid observed, his heavy German accent adding a diabolical quality to his words.

"Thank you, Helmut. Now, Professor Gunderson—update us on Operation Mind Control."

The room stilled. Even among billionaires and oligarchs, Gunderson's presence carried an air of menace. He was living history—the hidden progeny of Reichsminister Joseph Goebbels, conceived in vitro in 1972 under the Fourth Reich's guardianship. Raised in secret by an Austrian family, his life had been steered with surgical precision: Heidelberg PhD, award-winning journalist, then the crown jewel—control of global media under Scheid's financial umbrella.

Gunderson rose. His thinning black hair and plain, forgettable features only heightened the gravity of his words. He spoke without flourish, but every syllable carried weight.

"Our campaign has reduced trust in the United States government to twenty-one percent among its citizens," he began, his clipped German accent slicing through the silence. "At the same time, Christian affiliation has declined from sixty-five percent of Americans in 1996 to forty-three percent today. This metric is critical because Christians remain the most resistant to re-education."

Carpathian leaned forward, eyes narrowing. "How have you achieved these results?"

"We borrowed a play from Nazi Germany. You see, the Germans used Hitler Youth and state control of schools and Churches to rewrite identity," Gunderson said. "We've done the same here—through the National Educators Association, social media, and curriculum capture. We have severed children from their parents' values. Three generations have now grown up without the Judeo-Christian filter. They are blank slates with unprotected minds waiting to be shown the way."

Helmut Scheid smiled faintly, pride flickering in his eyes.

Gunderson pressed on, voice hypnotic in cadence. "Abortion metrics confirm the shift. Sixty percent of Americans now support abortion rights, a reversal from thirty years ago. This is our litmus test for devaluing human life. Once a society accepts the termination of its unborn, it will accept our population-control policies without resistance."

Scheid interjected smoothly. "And dividing them?"

Gunderson nodded. "We've stoked it for decades. DEI policies that replace meritocracy with grievance. Welfare that replaces fathers with checks. Media narratives that fuel racial resentment."

"Can you explain how attacking the nuclear family plays into our plans?" Carpathian asked for the benefit of his disciples.

"Destroying the nuclear family creates an easily manipulated group of children who are much more likely to reject traditional Judeo-Christian values than children raised in a two-parent home. As an example, under our policies, out-of-wedlock births among the poor rose from twenty-five percent in 1965 to seventy-seven percent today, creating three generations of children who are open to our message."

Polite applause rippled through the room. Scheid's eyes glowed with paternal pride.

Carpathian's tone was measured. "And the next phase?"

A thin smile tugged at Gunderson's lips. "Deepfakes. Our AI platform, *Confucius*, profiles three billion individuals globally. Each receives a custom propaganda diet—fear for the weak, rage for the angry, false hope for the naive. Palestinians against Israelis. Gun owners against progressives. Races against each other. Using his principles of propaganda, my father rallied hundreds of millions of Germans behind Hitler. I will rally billions behind Carpathian."

Carpathian stiffened at the comparison, his jaw tightening. It was an unnerving reminder of what he'd become.

Gunderson's voice hardened. "Soon, America's internal strife will metastasize into tribal warfare—gangs against suburbs, enclaves against rivals, ideologues against neighbors. With law enforcement defunded and overwhelmed, President Tilden will 'restore order' by implementing Executive Order 666."

The number hung in the air like a curse.

"E.O. 666 grants the President unchecked power to declare any group a terrorist organization. Churches, synagogues, civic groups—all shuttered. Christians and gun owners will be disarmed, reclassified as extremists, and shipped to quarantine camps. Once the strongest resistors are neutralized, the rest will fall into line."

For a long moment, silence. The inevitability pressed down on the chamber like a lead weight. Then Scheid began to clap, slow and deliberate. "Brilliant," he said, pride swelling in his voice.

Carpathian did not clap. He studied Gunderson, eyes unreadable. Visionary, or merely his father's echo? That question lingered like smoke.

CIA Headquarters

Oxley looked out his office window as rain droplets clung to the glass and dark clouds raced across the sky. A clap of distant thunder rumbled as lightning assaulted the countryside.

Unless Oxley and his men could work a miracle, the reign of the U.S. as the dominant superpower would soon come to an end, ushering in a new dark age from which there would be no resurrection.

Oxley wondered if George Washington had felt this overwhelmed. Then, an inner voice reminded him that Washington had lost most of his battles but won the war.

Jones joined Oxley at the window, saying, "Our sources confirm Carpathian and his disciples held a two-day conference at the Chateau in Davos."

Oxley nodded his understanding as they moved to the conference table.

General Lawrey and Jack Reagan filed in and took seats on either side of Oxley. James accessed the CIA's secure conference link a moment later, and Jake Hendel's image appeared.

Oxley looked exhausted, the strain of current events taking its toll on the sixty-year-old cloak-and-dagger leader of the free world.

Oxley dispensed with his usual welcome and asked, "Jake, what have you learned?"

"We lost Batman. He was executed by agents of the Ministry of State Security. "

The group allowed a moment of silence as they considered the impact of losing their only mole inside the Wuhan Institute. The Chinese had eliminated Dr. Fen and now, Dr. Jingryi, two critical witnesses of the CCP's crimes. It was yet another confirmation of the conspiracy.

Oxley said, "I'll order a star for him."

Jake took some comfort in knowing that Batman would forever be memorialized on the wall in the lobby of the old administration building, like other agents who'd paid the ultimate sacrifice.

"He would have liked that," Jake said reverently.

"Jack, fill us in on Cartel reconnaissance."

"Cartel convoys follow U.S. military procedures and operate at night. Many of their soldiers are former military Tier-One operators. The difference is that the Cartel pays and equips them better than Uncle Sam."

Oxley asked, "How are we doing against them?"

"Last week, the D.E.A., supported by U.S. Army forces, tried to interdict a Cartel Convoy using Apache helicopters, APCs, and Stryker Combat Vehicles. While U.S. forces eventually prevailed, we lost four helicopters, ten APCs, four Strykers, and a hundred personnel to a Cartel force of fifty. After the battle ended, we seized six Javelin Anti-Tank Weapons and four hand-held antiaircraft missiles."

General Lawrey asked, "How are they getting the latest technology?"

Jones said, "Many weapons we send to Ukraine or left behind in Afghanistan get sold in Arms bazaars. The Chinese also directly arm our enemies with their weapons. The older technologies, such as the French Mistral, the Soviet 9K38 Igla, and the U.S. Stinger B handheld anti-aircraft missiles, are readily available in arms bazaars."

Oxley asked, "How do you think they'll use the Cartel against us?"

Jack responded, "The Cartels have extensive supply lines established in the U.S., along with tens of thousands of personnel. They've been helping place Chinese, Russian, and Iranian agents in the U.S. for over a decade. Best guess, they'll use this network to conduct mass casualty events and target critical infrastructure."

Baker said with disgust, “Jack's right. The FBI Counterterrorism Center estimates that over 40,000 operatives have crossed the border in the past five years, Chinese, Muslim extremists, Iranians, Russians.”

General Lawrey added, “From a bioweapon standpoint, China could infect illegal immigrants and use them as carriers. Our policy of distributing illegals across the U.S. is an ideal vector for disease propagation, and our uncontrolled borders defeat most of our health surveillance.”

Oxley shook his head, “Jack, I’m designating Cartel members as enemy combatants. Find a way to cut off the snake's head. Jones, have Huron run a YODA analysis to identify terrorist suspects. While we can’t take our eyes off Taiwan, I’m convinced the real battleground is on the home front.”

Chapter 7

Known by everyone who was anyone inside the beltway, Ching Ding Tau, Senior Lobbyist for PharmX and de facto leader of the 'China Lobby,' walked into the Oval Office and was greeted by President Tilden. The New York Times had published a piece on Tau, alleging that he was the most influential lobbyist in Washington. Whatever his actual status, few foreigners had ever been given such access to the seat of power. And, only PharmX, his employer, could invest two billion dollars to 'buy the vote.' That kind of money bought influence.

Tilden wore his usual Navy Blue suit, white shirt, and red rep tie. At eighty-four, the President's once-seemingly noble political ideology had degenerated into egocentricism focused on his legacy. Years of public accusations and political infighting had made him bitter. His distaste for America had reached a new high during the last election when his Republican opponent humiliated him on national television. Recent media attention on his falls, mental gaps, and numerous senior moments hadn't helped.

Dressed in a dark business suit and red tie, Tau sat down in his usual spot on the couch next to President Tilden's chair. White House logs indicated that Tau had met with Tilden 20 times over the last 3 years, second only to Representative Pagosa.

"What can I do for you, Ding?" Tilden asked with a smile as he lowered himself slowly into his chair.

Tau remembered playing golf with Tilden in the early 2000s and was sad to see the youthful spring in Tilden's step replaced by an unsteady tightrope walk. The once keen, engaging mind was now plagued by neurocircuitry that shorted out as often as it connected. How long would Tilden's handlers allow him to remain in office? How long before his political enemies forced him out? Only Linda Pagosa knew.

Tau said, "Soon, decades of sacrifice will usher in the New World Order in which the common man will own nothing but be happy. It will be a green world of peace and abundance."

President Tilden leaned in, placed his hand on Tau's knee, and asked, "What do you need me to do?"

Tau looked directly into Tilden's tired eyes and said, "We need you to delay the U.S. response for fourteen days."

Tilden sat upright in his chair. While he'd run up the national debt to bring about the dollar's collapse and usher in a New World cyber currency, this request was closer to treason than anything he'd done before. Tilden's heart was conflicted as he spoke, "Are you asking me to allow China to take Taiwan? To go against my promise to defend them?"

The consummate lobbyist looked at the President and said, "Your military estimates that defending Taiwan could cost the U.S. 500,000 personnel and up to five carriers. Is sacrificing your personnel in the U.S. in the best interests?"

Tau watched the effect of his words on the elder statesman.

"James, your soldiers are tired, your best officers have left, and polls indicate that the American people don't want another war. Remember that you lost in Vietnam and Afghanistan, and your victory over Sadam Hussien only strengthened the Taliban. Were any of those foreign conflicts worth it?"

Tilden rubbed his chin as he considered his next move. Tau was right. The only winner in U.S. wars since Korea was the military-industrial complex, and they voted Republican. He'd lost his firstborn to Desert Storm, and images of VA wards filled with handicapped soldiers filled his mind. War costs way too much!

Finally, he said, "You realize I'll have to leave office."

It was vintage Tilden with his hand out.

"The elites are willing to expand your portfolio considerably for taking this risk, Mr. President."

Tilden leaned in and asked, "How much?"

Tau removed a small notebook from his coat pocket and placed it on the coffee table. He pulled out a Montblanc pen, wrote $1 billion on the paper, and signed his name.

Tilden picked up the leather-bound notebook, its pages crisp with secrets. He stared at the figure scrawled in bold ink—$1,000,000,000. A billion dollars. More than he'd siphoned off in six decades of public service and quiet compromises. This wasn't just money—it was legacy. Power that would echo through generations and compound under the architecture of the New World Order, a system no longer theoretical but terrifyingly real. Carpathian and his operatives were too far along now, embedded like malware in every global institution. Tilden could no longer stop them—but he could alter the outcome. Tau was right. Half a million American lives hung in the balance. His battalions, if deployed, would be bait—sacrificial and meaningless. Framed this way, the decision required no deliberation. In the cold calculus of power, inaction was the most strategic move. Finally, he flashed his trademark smile and said, "When hostilities start, it will take a couple of weeks for the Pentagon to gain the intel required for me to make a sound decision."

"Mr. President, your legacy will be great. Generations from now, you will be known as the great leader who saved the planet!"

CIA Headquarters

Oxley's driver closed the passenger door of the black armored SUV while Director Oxley fastened his seat belt. His driver could sense his usually friendly boss was deeply concerned about something.

The SUV proceeded to the gate and was waved through by the guards.

"Home. Sir?" asked the driver.

"Please."

The driver took Colonial Farm Road to Georgetown Pike, then eased onto Dolley Madison Boulevard, heading west through the quiet shadows of McLean. At Trotting Horse Lane, the car glided past gated estates with manicured hedges, the silence broken only by the hum of the engine. It was 9:00 PM—traffic sparse, headlights rare—and the eighteen-minute drive passed in near solitude. But for Oxley, it was long enough to feel the weight of the nation pressing down like a millstone. He stared out the window, his mind racing. Did General Washington feel this same gravity, leading a threadbare force against the might of an empire? Oxley wasn't facing redcoats, but enemies far more insidious—rooted deep within. Would it take another revolution to save the republic he had bled for? Could the thousand men left in the Order hold the line, or were they just shadows against a coming storm? Doubt gnawed at him, clawing at his convictions. The road ahead was more than asphalt and turns—it was a crossroads for the soul of a nation. In forty years of public service, circumstances had required the overthrow of governments, the seizure of enemy assets, and, on rare occasions, the assassination of foreign enemies. This was the first time circumstances had forced him to consider targeting U.S. officials. Like Washington, would he and his men be forced to commit treason to save a nation?

Oxley prayed silently, "Heavenly Father, you have placed us at this crossroads of history. Please grant me a pure heart that does your will. Be with me as you were with Shadrack, Meshack, and Abednego as I enter the fiery furnace. Give me the heart of Beniah, who defeated a lion with a spear in a pit on a snowy day. Defeat this present darkness and place your hand upon your warriors. In Jesus' name, I pray. Amen,"

With deep resolve, Oxley pulled his encrypted phone from his coat pocket and selected a text distribution labeled "The Order." He hesitated momentarily, took a deep breath, and keyed the following message: *Activate Joshua Protocol.*

FBI Headquarters

Director Baker opened the text and read it twice. He knew it was coming, but the reality of what they were about to do shook him to his soul. The Joshua Protocol was a last, desperate attempt to pull the world from the abyss.

Baker logged into the FBI system and looked through the files his team had prepared for Operation Deep State. Between NSA surveillance files, Jack Reagan's fund's flow, and thousands of emails, the FBI had made a compelling case against the President and fifty-six Senators and three hundred thirty Representatives. While the severity varied, each conspirator would be charged with influence peddling, violations of the Emoluments Clause of the U.S. Constitution, and/or treason. While many on the hill were aware of the FBI's ongoing investigation, none of the perpetrators knew what was to come.

Baker activated the new encryption program on his phone and called Director Oxley.

The seconds seemed like minutes as Baker listened to the ringtones.

Seated in his lounge chair in the den of his home in Great Falls, Virginia, Oxley answered, "Yes?"

"It's about to hit the fan," Baker observed.

Oxley took another sip of 20-year-old Macallan to steady his nerves, then composed himself. "It's a long shot, but it's our only option. If we go down, the Western World goes with us, and genocide begins."

Baker leaned back in his chair and thought about how to respond. Finally, he said, "I'll take the Hill. After that, it'll be up to Federal Judges to take up the cause. We'll also need Governors to appoint conservatives to replace those we remove from office."

"We have twenty Governors among our ranks and another fifteen who should do the right thing. The problem is the President, we can't right the ship with Tilden at the helm," Oxley said.

Baker gazed out his window at the lights of Washington.

"The evidence against the President will force even his closest supporters to demand his resignation. The question is, will replacing him be enough to right the ship?" Baker asked.

"Doubtful, Conja Stern could be even worse," Oxley opined.

"We must get Tilden out of the way soon; there isn't time to wait for the criminal process to cook," Baker said.

"I'll come up with something. In the meantime, my psy ops team will tell the story to the press while you present evidence to the Ethics Committee. We'll ensure the truth hits all media outlets simultaneously, leaving the conspirators nowhere to run. It'll be too big a story to hide."

"Imprisoning the perpetrators should spawn enough public outrage to permanently remove them from office. I wouldn't put it past some of them to run for China or a banana republic," Baker observed.

"It's going to destroy the progressives in control of the Democratic Party and purge the dirt from the Grand Ole Party. When the Fall elections arrive, the backlash against the influence peddlers and globalist sympathizers could reshape American politics for decades," Oxley commented and then, as an afterthought, asked, "What's your plan for tomorrow?"

Baker leaned over his desk and placed his face in his hands. After rubbing the exhaustion from his temples, he said, "Judge Ruppenthal has signed the arrest warrants. I have 3,000 agents ready to make simultaneous arrests. It's all timed to occur while I'm testifying on the Hill."

"It's a made-for-media event. My psych ops team will leak the arrests to the press so they have cameras lined up to capture the perpetrators in cuffs. The timing is tricky, but the evidence is beyond a reasonable doubt. Even if the Attorney General intervenes, it will be in the hands of federal judges," Oxley mentioned.

Baker stood and stretched his back. "Will it be enough?"

Oxley spoke slowly, "It'll be enough to cut the head off the snake, but not enough to resolve Cartel activities, economic woes, the crisis in the Pacific, or the pandemic."

Baker considered the monumental task ahead of them and said with more confidence than he felt, “We can move to the other issues once we drain the swamp. If we fail tomorrow, all is lost.”

House Oversight Committee, Capitol Hill

Johnathon Cummings, Chairman of the House Oversight Committee, aggressively advocated for boosting government transparency and accountability. Cummings had released allegations about President Tilden’s foreign business dealings with companies that benefited the Tilden family, and was a frequent guest on conservative news shows.

The shift in Speaker of the House from a Democrat to a Conservative Republican had created the opportunity to clean house. While the Oversight Committee was split between five Republicans and five Democrats, the Speaker had replaced liberal Democrats with moderates and two newly elected conservative Republicans.

A sense of impending doom filled the hearing room as an unusually high number of reporters and cameramen filed in. Cummings smiled at the turnout while his committee members wondered what was going on.

After calling the session to order, Cummings began, “FBI Director Baker has been asked to present findings from investigations into violations of the emoluments clause of the U.S. Constitution as defined in Article I, Section 9, Paragraph 8. The Article prohibits federal officeholders from receiving any gift, payment, or other thing of value from a foreign state or its rulers, officers, or representatives. Please proceed, Director.”

Director Baker stood at the tabletop podium and buttoned his suit coat. He opened his remarks by saying, “Thank you, Mr. Chairman. My staff is handing out a report summarizing FBI investigations into the President and hundreds of U.S. House and Senate members.”

Loud murmuring erupted in the room. To increase the drama, Cummings allowed the ruckus to continue for several seconds before he banged his gavel and shouted, “Let’s return to order so we may proceed.”

“The report in your hands shows over $2.4 billion paid by foreign governments and their proxies to U.S. officials over the past four years,” Baker announced.

As the cameras rolled, Baker displayed a series of slides that provided a breakdown of the illicit revenues officials received and their sources.

"Sixty percent of these funds have been traced back to Chinese Governmental entities, Chinese billionaires, and Chinese Corporations. These numbers do not include campaign contributions."

A loud murmur arose from the stunned audience as reporters and their cameramen tried to capture the spectacle.

Chairman Cummings tapped his gavel and shouted, "Order, we will have order in the chamber, or I will have the audience removed and proceed in closed session."

When the murmuring stopped, Cummings said, "Please proceed, Director."

"The next slides show the breakdown of the elected officials and the total funds they received from the 'China Lobby.'"

The committee's faces registered their shock at a slide showing that the President had received over $100 million.

Director Baker said, "The next series of slides shows the funds by the corporate entity. As you can see, PharmX, Wong Dong, Inc., and a series of private equities make up eighty percent of the funds."

Cummings and his committee members were whispering among themselves. Two of them, whose names were prominently displayed on the slides, weren't prepared to answer questions and left the room.

After an hour, Baker finished presenting the FBI's findings and said, "That concludes our investigation. Are there any questions?"

Cummings looked at Baker and said, "Thank you, Director. I commend you and your team."

"Thank you, Mr. Chairman."

Cummings continued, "Did any of these funds represent payment for services rendered?"

Baker continued, "None of these payments represented remuneration for work performed, and none of the recipients possessed merchantable skills for which they were paid. In all cases, the money paid exceeded the going rate for the alleged services or merchandise produced. For example, President Tilden's two-year-old granddaughter, Beth, was paid $25,000 for consulting on baby formula. His son, Hector, was paid $250,000 by a Chinese-owned oil company for serving on its board, while other board members received no compensation. CDC Director Dr. Amy Rapier was granted 18% of the private stock of a PharmX Chinese subsidiary for $10,000. She sold her interests for $500,000, a month after supporting the approval of a PharmX COVID-19 vaccine. Senator James

White, Sr. received a bogus insurance claim payment for $500,000 after obtaining a ten-million-dollar grant for the Wuhan Institute of Virology."

Senator White stood and headed for the door. The cameras captured White walking so briskly that his gate could be described as jogging.

Cummings smiled as White fled. Then, asked, "What did your team learn, if anything, about the origins of COVID-19?"

"The FBI has conclusive evidence that COVID-19 was developed as a bioweapon at the Wuhan Institute of Virology. We've also connected Dr. Antonio Faccini and Dr. Lawrence Wilhite to the Chinese bioweapons program. We believe the rootstock used to engineer COVID-19 originated from Dr. Wilhite's lab and was shipped by the NIH to China. We also know that Dr. Facini, in his official role, made sizeable grants to the Wuhan Institute even after learning of their experiments on concentration camp inmates. We have a strong case against Wilhite and Faccini for complicity in a plot that has already killed three million Americans and thousands of Chinese inmates."

Cummings asked, "Is there evidence of collusion between elected officials and subversive entities?"

Baker responded, "Yes. In addition to the financial transactions, we have over 3,000 hours of video and audio files, hundreds of documents, and sworn testimony of credible witnesses."

Cummings looked at his colleagues, then noticed the reporter's confused expressions.

"For the benefit of our audience, Federal Judge Matt Ruppenthal recently ruled that payments to elected officials or their families from entities controlled by a foreign nation violate the Emoluments Clause. The Supreme Court also ruled in the U.S. v. Wang Do that any state-owned company, such as China National Petroleum or PharmX, will be deemed a foreign government under the Emoluments Clause. This means any federal official accepting money or other value from these government-owned companies or directly from a foreign government or their agents can be prosecuted."

Baker remained stoic but was delighted with Cummings' tactics.

"Director, does the FBI have enough evidence to obtain arrest warrants?"

The committee members looked like they were awaiting execution when Baker mentioned, "My agents are making arrests as we speak."

The room exploded with chatter. Then, FBI agents burst through the doors. Minutes later, half the remaining elected officials were escorted out in handcuffs.

Baker knew he'd just fired the first shot of a new American Revolution, the opening salvo in the Joshua Protocol. The illicit affair soon became known as Peddlergate.

U.S. News Live Report

Ned Jenkins told the world. "Peddlergate is the most far-reaching scandal in U.S. history. Right now, the FBI is serving arrest warrants on some 300 elected officials, dwarfing Watergate. The question on everyone's mind is whether our republic can survive. Is this the beginning of a new revolution, a war between the self and the self-serving, between good and evil? Is it an indictment of our system of government? Only time will tell."

The U.S. News cameras showed dozens of high-profile elected officials being arrested.

Beijing

Susie Legman was in the Chinese Capital as the world's eyes were laser-focused on China. Many international journalists had billed the upcoming Chinese Communist Party Congress as the most critical government meeting since World War II.

The U.S. news anchor stood before China's infamous Zhongnanhai compound, the seat of the Communist Party's power, just west of the Forbidden City. The red lanterns cast a subtle glow against the high stone walls as Susie Legmann faced the camera, her navy suit crisp under the floodlights. It was a sharp departure from her signature on-air look—gone were the short skirts and flirtatious blouses. Yet the conservative cut did nothing to detract from her elegance; if anything, it enhanced it. Her poise was unshaken, her voice clear, even as millions watched not just for the breaking story, but for any glimpse of the diamond that had sparked a media frenzy. Her engagement to Jake Hendel, a war correspondent and rumored intelligence asset, was more than gossip. It was a geopolitical event. And tonight, as tension simmered between Beijing and Washington, Susie wasn't just delivering news—she was becoming part of it.

Zhongnanhai refers to the Central and Southern Seas, lakes built by ancient rulers near the Forbidden City. The Northern, Central, and Southern Seas are collectively known as the Taiye Lake. The Shichahai 'Sea, with its Ten Temples, lay at the northern end of the magnificent park. Taiye Lake was originally an imperial garden with parklands on the shores, enclosed by a red wall in the western part of the Imperial City. Most ancient pavilions, shrines, and temples have remained there since they were constructed during the Jin, Yuan, and Ming dynasties. Whereas the Northern Sea had a religious focus, the shores of the Central and Southern Seas were dotted with palaces. These structures now encompass the offices and residences of CCP leaders.

"The Zhongnanhai complex, which includes the imperial garden behind me, is adjacent to the famous Forbidden Palace and serves as a metonym for China's leadership at large, in the same way the Kremlin references the seat of Russian power."

The broadcast showed pictures of lush oriental gardens, tranquil shrines, and structures within the Zhongnanhai. Then the cameraman repositioned for a shot of Susie with people on the street.

"The Chinese Communist Congress is the most important meeting of the CCP's five-year political cycle because promotions and key leadership appointments, including the party leader, are made. While President Xi Jin is expected to be confirmed for a record fourth term, Chinese sources have been tight-lipped. Jin's critics cite tensions with the U.S., allegations of human rights abuses, and continued economic challenges as reasons to oust him. On the other hand, communist hard-liners and a growing number of international billionaires support his reappointment. Seeing capitalist billionaires supporting a totalitarian leader has shocked the Western world," Susie observed.

Several people stopped to watch the newscast from the sidewalk, while other pedestrians and cyclists passed by.

"While the Congress is always held in the autumn, the relatively early date of this year's meeting indicates that decisions have already been made. According to U.S. News sources in China, President Jin has defeated his opponents."

Ted Divine sat in the anchor chair in New York and asked, "Susie, can you tell us who attends the Congress?"

Susie raised the microphone and said, "About 2,300 senior party members gather in the Great Hall of the People, ostensibly representing the tens of millions of party members across China. Of those, only 200 members of the elite Central Committee have voting rights, plus an additional 170 alternates. That committee elects the 25-member politburo, of which the seven most powerful are appointed to the Politburo Standing Committee."

Ted asked, "How might current problems in the U.S. affect China's 2050 Strategy?"

"Many believe that U.S. leadership is weak, the U.S. military is in decline, and America's burgeoning national debt could soon allow the Dragon to supplant the Eagle as the dominant superpower, thus fulfilling China's 2050 Strategy. The Peddlergate Investigation and the arrest of nearly 300 U.S. elected officials and a growing number of bureaucrats have many of our enemies believing this is a perfect time to strike."

Ted asked, "How might Xi Jin getting an unprecedented fourth term reshape the global landscape?"

Susie nodded intelligently as she took Ted's question. The CCP investigation into Jake's alleged status as a spy and very public arrests of Western journalists reminded her to be careful with her answers: "If Xi Jin is reappointed, he will feel validated, and that could increase the odds of China attacking Taiwan."

"What does China gain by capturing Taiwan?"

"Taking Taiwan would widen China's influence in the Pacific and provide a stranglehold on certain high-end computer chips. These actions would enable China to escalate its economic war against the West and maintain its global prestige. Jin may see victory in the Pacific as another way to prove to the world's most influential billionaires that China has become the dominant superpower."

Ted's face showed concern as he asked, "With all China's problems, do you really think they can supersede the U.S. as the world leader by 2050?"

Susie knew Ted's unscripted question was an attempt to discredit her on the world stage, but she calmly responded, "Ted, the experts I've interviewed outlined three possible scenarios. First, China, the U.S., and India share the stage as superpowers. Second, the U.S. counters Chinese aggression and maintains its dominance. Third, the U.S. loses, leaving China and India as world leaders."

Ted asked, "How on earth would anyone think the U.S. could fail?"

Susie held her ground, "Many cite Washington's inability to manage our debt and the growing ideological war being fought in the media and on our streets as markers of America's decline. Globalist Financier Helmut Scheid recently stated that his firm, Red Rock, will cease purchasing U.S. debt if the U.S. doesn't balance its budget. Some analysts have stated that these factors, combined with global unrest, could create a doomsday scenario."

Susie smiled as she saw the frustration in Ted's face when she knocked his curveball out of the park.

CIA Headquarters, Langley, Virginia

Oxley's face glowed from the light of a dozen monitors in the underground chamber. The encrypted conference grid filled with the faces of his brothers—judges, generals, field operatives, scientists, and economists—all tethered together by the Joshua Protocol.

"Gentlemen," Oxley began, his voice as steady as cold iron, "I enacted the Protocol to keep our sacred oaths intact. Unlike the Founding Fathers, who committed treason against the Crown, we have thus far stayed within the bounds of the law. That line is fraying. The threat we face is not theoretical. It is here. Calculated. Ruthless. If we are to preserve the republic, our allegiance must be to God's law, not corrupted institutions. "

On the counter pane, the reaction was immediate—one thousand digital thumbs raised in unison. For an instant, Oxley allowed himself to feel the weight of that unity. But even as resolve swelled in his chest, a darker question lingered. Was a thousand men enough to stave off a new Dark Age?

He turned. "Director Baker, update us."

Baker, hunched over his console in a dim FBI safe house, pushed the screen control. Hundreds of members of Congress were arrested. President Tilden served with a warrant. Fifty-two escaped abroad—to China, Russia, and our other enemies. Two hundred forty-eight remain in custody. Two hundred twenty-nine are out on bail, awaiting trial. Judge Ruppenthal can speak to the legal front."

Ruppenthal's gravelly southern drawl carried across the digital ether. "The evidence is strong. Enough to convict—if the system holds. However, elites have their own tricks: prosecutorial discretion and selective pardons. The President could sweep them clean with one signature, or his staff could do so with the autopen. His counsel and the AG are already working angles through sympathetic circuits. If it reaches the Supreme Court, we win. But that assumes the court still functions."

Oxley gave a curt nod. Baker picked it up: "Best case—the Constitution holds, traitors go to prison. Worst case—they remain in power long enough to finish off the free world."

The moment was shattered when General Lawery looked down at his secure handset. His face went pale. "The President just enacted Executive Order Six-Six-Six. Martial law. National gun confiscation. Dusk-to-dawn curfews. Civilian suppression units activated."

Jack Reagan leaned forward, voice hard. "That means he's unleashed the Army against our own citizens. Those units operate like the old SS—broad powers, zero accountability."

Oxley's device chimed. He scanned the incoming text. Reports confirm riots in Los Angeles, Seattle, Atlanta, Chicago, New York, and San Francisco—most major cities in the United States. Looting, murder, rape. Police and EMS abandoning posts. Prisons with a guard strength below 25% are experiencing mass escapes. Terrorist cells are hitting power stations and gas pipelines. Much of this has been orchestrated, utilizing activated sleeper cells."

Baker cut in. "It's orchestrated. Chinese and Russian deep fakes stoking fires. ANTIFA, BLM, Proud Men—all infiltrated. Our psyops teams are countering, but with the net down and comms shattered, we're limited."

Oxley's tone was grim. "Civilian casualty estimate?"

Lawery hesitated, then: "Two hundred million—if it runs six months. Disease, famine, civil war."

The silence on the line was as heavy as steel.

Finally, Baker spoke. "FBI reports armed citizens holding their ground. Militias, preppers, Christian communities—they're stacking bodies. But the Cartels are the game-changer. Better arms, better training. And coordinated."

Oxley's jaw tightened. "Odds?"

"Good Americans may hold their own—until food runs out," Lawery said. "But in sanctuary cities, it's already medieval. Detroit, San Francisco, Portland, Chicago, New York—they're lost to anarchy."

Doctor Stevens leaned in, voice clinical but haunted. "Kill squads are operating openly. A Marine platoon was wiped out at a checkpoint in Los Angeles this morning."

The faces on the screen hardened, every man recognizing the stakes.

"Charles," Oxley asked the noted economist, "economy?"

Gould's tone was analytical and detached, but his eyes betrayed fear. "The dollar is down thirty percent against the yuan. Global shift toward the People's Coin is underway. Markets closed here, but Asia and Europe are already in a state of collapse. Red Rock Advisers dumped early—escaped whole. When our markets reopen, 90% of businesses could be gone. Pensioners, 401(k)s, the middle class—wiped out."

"Leaving Red Rock and the CCP with the spoils," Oxley finished grimly.

No one spoke for a long moment. The silence was the silence of men staring into the pit. Finally, Oxley said, low but resolute: "Then we stand where Washington stood. No turning back. The Joshua Protocol is no longer a theory. Gentlemen, this is a war for the soul of humanity."

White House

During his Presidential briefing, Director Oxley said, "Mr. President, radio traffic between the People's Liberation Army Headquarters and their units is up four hundred percent. Massive supply convoys are moving heavy equipment, supplies, and troops to embarkation areas."

President Tilden's hoary face showed his age. The thin, elderly President became agitated, "President Jin isn't about to invade Taiwan! I know him better than that. He's pulling a bluff charge to see if we'll blink."

Oxley could see through Tilden's ink screen and said, "Mr. President, invasion is imminent. Right now, PLA air and missile forces pose a significant risk to our bases and ships within 3,000 miles of their shores. Once hostilities start, the battle will progress rapidly, and we will have little time to respond. I suggest you allow Admiral Flint to launch preemptive strikes."

President Tilden laughed.

"Director, the CIA almost sank John Kennedy's career over the failed Bay of Pigs invasion. If Kennedy had listened to you clowns and let Curtis LaMay unleash his bombers, a nuclear holocaust would have ensued. No, Director, I'm not declaring war without better intelligence."

The President's words convinced Director Oxley that Tilden was now a traitor to the republic. "Very well, Mr. President, there's one more thing."

Tilden's eyes widened as he asked, "What's that?"

Oxley opened his briefcase, pulled out a folder stamped Top Secret, Presidential Eyes Only, and handed the sealed envelope to the President.

Tilden took the file and looked at it with trepidation.

"What's this?" Tilden asked, anger evident in his voice.

"It's the smoking gun that could have you removed from office, imprisoned for life, and dramatically change your finances," Oxley said evenly.

President Tilden defiantly walked to the Resolute Desk, jaw clenched, steps echoing across the Oval Office like a war drum. He sat and grabbed the silver-plated letter opener—an inauguration gift from a now-disgraced senator—and slit open the thick manila envelope with surgical precision. The contents spilled out like a hemorrhage: documents, photographs, and a single black USB drive. He pulled on his reading glasses, the same ones he wore to sign the trade pact with Beijing, and sat down with a nervous breath he couldn't hide. His fingers trembled as he scanned the first few pages—a detailed ledger of offshore accounts, shadow investments, inflated consulting fees, and covert insurance policies, all tied to foreign powers, multinational corporations, and names he recognized from DEA watchlists—Cartel Capos with more blood on their hands than some war criminals.

Across the room, Oxley stood silent, hands folded behind his back, watching the unraveling of a presidency in real time. The President rifled through the photographs next. One after another, each more damning than the last. There he was—Tilden—with his son Hector, shaking hands with arms dealers, oil barons, and convicted traffickers. Another photo: Tilden at a resort, his arm around a well-known Chinese lobbyist whose influence had rerouted U.S. trade policy. Then—Tilden's hand froze—images from the Valley of the Dolls. The final straw came in a glossy spreadsheet—an accounting of transactions that traced a dirty financial thread between Tilden, Hector, and nearly every member of his extended family. His face drained of color. The cost wasn't just political—it was eternal.

While the content held Tilden's attention, Oxley opened an app on his smartphone and logged into a program called Specter. After entering a series of commands, Oxley activated a micro air vehicle (MAV). The drone was the size of a gnat and could perform in-the-open surveillance and aerial swarm operations. Oxley then removed his handkerchief and unfolded it. A few seconds later, the MAV lifted off the cloth and landed on Tilden's shoulder. To cover his tracks, Oxley pretended to blow his nose, then returned the handkerchief to his pocket.

Moments later, the President leaned back in the Resolute Chair, the leather groaning beneath him, and cockily asked, "So you've earned a chip in the big game, and I'm the only one who can cash it. What do you want?"

Oxley didn't blink. "Mr. President, I want you to fire your Vice President and appoint Speaker Novak as her replacement."

Tilden laughed—short, sharp, a bark masking unease. "Do you think you can just waltz in here, threaten the President of the United States, and force me to fire my VP?"

"Yes," Oxley replied, voice calm, flat, and terrifyingly sure of itself.

Tilden's smirk faltered. For the first time, he saw past the tailored suit and the Agency badge—saw the cold resolve of a man who'd made regimes crumble! A rogue dog who'd turned from loyal pet to nemesis. The President's pulse quickened. His CIA Director had bigger kahunas than he'd guessed.

He narrowed his eyes. "I can have my people kill you?"

Oxley stepped forward, closing the gap between himself and the most powerful man in the world with the precision of a field operative. "In that case," he said evenly, "digital copies of those files will be distributed to 1,200 national and international news outlets. A prerecorded video—featuring detailed accounts of your crimes against the American people, and let's not forget your legendary sexual prowess—will be streamed, subtitled, and dissected by every news desk from Berlin to Bangkok. Within hours, the FBI will breach this building with a sealed indictment. The House of Tilden will topple like a rigged domino set. And your legacy…" Oxley paused, letting it hang like the final beat of a funeral march. "Your legacy will be that of a traitor."

Tilden's face betrayed the horror he felt deep within. All that could be heard was the ticking of the grandfather clock by the window and the faint hum of national ruin gathering momentum. President Tilden's shoulders drooped as his ego deflated. He'd worked too long to build his legacy to have it destroyed now. Then he remembered he would soon live in Solar Valley, where Oxley's threats would be null and void. With the right spin, he and his friends could blame the collapse of America on MAGA Republicans. The master politician smiled and said, "I'll make the announcement this afternoon."

There being nothing left to say, Oxley nodded in agreement and let himself out.

Once the CIA Director exited, Tilden felt what he thought was an insect bite on his neck. Instinctively, the President swatted at the MAV but missed. A few seconds later, the MAV landed on top of a painting, where its microphone and camera could monitor activity in the Oval Office until its power source was depleted.

New York

Susie Legman sat at the news desk and said, "We interrupt your regular programming to share breaking news. In a shocking announcement, White House Press Secretary Pigeon announced today that President Tilden has fired Vice President Stern. Here's Pigeon's short statement."

U.S. News producers played a video of Amanda Pigeon's White House briefing, in which the president stated, "The president asked me to inform you that the Vice President turned in her resignation earlier today." Audible gasps filled the room as the press corps sat in shock.

"While the President is confident that Mrs. Stern is not guilty of any of the crimes she's been charged with under Peddlergate, he said the Vice President told him she was resigning for health reasons. That's all I have for now. I'll take a few questions."

USN reporter Hugh Duffer, a middle-aged, non-descript man who'd trolled the halls of power for thirty years, asked, "Who will the President select as her replacement?"

Pigeon said, "I will only say that he hopes to have a new VP in place by day's end."

ABC reporter Sarah Lisbon asked, "Is the President prepared to keep his promise by selecting another minority female?"

Pigeon said, "The President told me he's seeking a VP who can be a unifying force. Thank you all for coming on such short notice."

***

Hugh Duffer stood beneath the glowing spotlights, the iconic White House looming behind him like a silent witness to the unfolding political theater. The capital city's humidity clung to his skin beneath his navy blue suit, but his expression remained crisp, composed—a practiced blend of concern and credibility. In the studio, Susie Legman's voice came through his earpiece, sharp and clear.

"Hugh, did the sudden departure of Vice President Conja Sterns surprise you?"

Duffer shifted, one hand resting against the polished mic stand, the other adjusting the red tie over his light grey shirt. He peered into the camera with the poise of a man who'd spent too many nights outside the West Wing. "Susie, none of the White House Press Corps had any idea this was coming. Typically, we get days—if not weeks—of background whispers before a resignation of this magnitude. This one blindsided everyone."

Back in the studio, Susie's perfectly arched brow lifted. "Do you think it has anything to do with low polling numbers and the Fall elections?"

Duffer didn't hesitate. "The Tilden Administration is under fire from every direction—from Peddlergate to the spiraling Asian conflict. His handlers may believe that replacing Sterns with someone more palatable—maybe a moderate who polls well with independents—could boost his reelection viability. Historically, presidents have leveraged the Vice Presidency to patch electoral gaps, and many inside the Beltway believe the selection of Conja Sterns was a strategic misstep. With her approval rating in the single digits and growing concern over President Tilden's declining health, she went from being an ideological choice to a political liability."

Legman nodded, leaning into the tension. "We also know that former Speaker Linda Pegossa pushed legislation clarifying procedures under Section 1 of the 25th Amendment—removal of the President for death, disability, or resignation. Many conservatives saw that move as a Trojan horse—an attempt by Pegossa and the Democratic elite to backdoor the first female into the Oval Office."

Duffer's jaw tightened, the way it did when facts began aligning too perfectly. "Pegossa never denied the timing. And the wording of the amendment's implementation was unusually aggressive. Some viewed it as insurance. Others, as intent."

What the public didn't know—what Hugh Duffer did know—was that the real story had nothing to do with polls or public opinion. The truth was buried deep in the intelligence briefings no journalist ever saw, in corridors of power where decisions were made not in the service of democracy, but in the survival of the machine. And tonight, that machine was turning faster than anyone realized.

White House, Oval Office

President Tilden sat across from House Speaker Kevin Novak in the Roosevelt Room, the tension so thick that it could be sliced with a butter knife. The two men had become the faces of opposing Americas—Tilden, the aging liberal statesman clinging to globalism, and Novak, the firebrand conservative elevated by a populist wave. Since Novak had taken the Speaker's gavel just three months prior, their public sparring had become cable news gold.

Tilden leaned back in his chair, a thin smile creeping across his face. He tilted his head condescendingly and spoke in a tone one might use to correct a misbehaving child. "You have no idea what's in play, Kevin. The world is about to pitchpole, and you and your MAGA Republicans can't right the ship. You're playing checkers on a chessboard soaked in gasoline, and I hold the match."

Novak didn't blink. "So, Mr. President, when do you plan to make the announcement?" His tone was flat, clipped—he wasn't interested in Tilden's melodrama, nor intimidated by him.

Tilden glanced down at his age-spotted hands, fingers curled from arthritis, then raised his eyes to meet Novak's. "Six PM tonight."

Novak checked his watch, concern registering on his face. "That's less than two hours."

Tilden observed him, noting the micro-shift in Novak's jaw—a flicker of nerves, or anticipation. Either way, it pleased him. For now, he had to play nice. The republic was still intact on the surface, and bipartisanship still bought headlines. But deep down, Tilden knew America was running on fumes—ideologically fractured, morally bankrupt, and economically cornered.

Appointing Novak as Vice President was a masterstroke—not a concession, but a calculated strike. The darling of the Christian right, lionized by red states and loathed by the coastal elite, Novak's elevation would be spun as unity. But the fine print told a different story. Alongside the appointment, Tilden would announce an executive reorganization placing Novak in charge of border security, immigration enforcement, drug interdiction, and federal law enforcement operations – duties that guaranteed his failure. It was a political bear trap disguised as a handshake.

There was more than one way to destroy an opponent. You could beat them at the polls. Or you could hand them the wheel—right before the brakes failed. A sinister smile broke through Tilden's hoary face. The aged lion awaits the kill.

CIA Headquarters

Oxley's private phone rang, and he stepped out of a briefing to take General Lawrey's call.

"Oxley," the Director replied.

General Lawrey asked, "Did you deliver the package?"

Oxley looked around to ensure he was alone and replied, "Yes."

General Lawrey leaned back in his chair and said, "We should see results within seventy-two hours."

Oxley responded, "Good. Novak will be sworn in by then."

"Let's just hope we have enough time to change the outcome. America's coming apart at the seams," General Lawrey observed.

Oxley said, "In the words of Spurgeon, we must work as if it all depends upon us and pray as if it all depends upon Him."

U.S. News

Susie Legman's voice was calm but electric. "We now go to Hugh Duffer at the White House."

The camera feed cut to the Press Briefing Room, where Hugh Duffer stood, wearing a grey suit with a red rep tie, before the iconic blue backdrop, his jaw set, his eyes scanning the room as a few dozen reporters and aides buzzed with nervous energy. Phones were out, whispers sharp, and the room carried the kind of charged stillness that came before tectonic announcements.

"Susie," Hugh began, nodding as if to anchor himself, "I'm here in the White House Press Room awaiting President Tilden's announcement of his new vice president. While speculation has flooded the usual channels, my sources confirm that President Tilden held a closed-door meeting at 3:30 PM today with none other than House Speaker Kevin Novak."

Susie's voice crackled through the earpiece, tight with disbelief. "Hugh, do you think there's any possibility that Speaker Novak will be named VP? That would be shocking—even for this administration."

Hugh allowed himself a measured pause, choosing his words with surgical precision. "While the odds are against it, Susie, from a purely demographic and strategic standpoint, Novak brings undeniable assets. He polls well with moderate Republicans, independents, and a large bloc of the Religious Right. And despite his conservative credentials, he's shown an ability to negotiate across the aisle. If Tilden is serious about healing political divisions, Novak is the ultimate gamble."

Just then, the door to the press room opened, and White House Press Secretary Amanda Pigeon strode briskly to the podium, his expression unreadable. The murmuring died instantly.

"Please be seated," she said, voice taut.

As the room settled into a tense hush, Pigeon adjusted the mic. "Ladies and gentlemen, please welcome the President of the United States."

All rose instinctively as President Tilden entered—slower than usual, his gait unsure, but his expression fixed in that familiar, time-hardened mask of gravitas. He offered a frail wave, then drew a crumpled one-page cheat sheet from his inner jacket pocket. The silence was knife-edged.

"My fellow Americans," Tilden began, voice raspy but firm, "we are in challenging times. Having served the American people for over fifty years, I've never seen a time when our people were more divided. This fact has given me great pause as I consider the upcoming election alongside world and national events."

He paused. Ten seconds. Fifteen. The room didn't move. Not a breath, not a pen scratch. The weight of the moment made each second feel as though it were loaded with dynamite.

"While I've long been a member of the Democratic Party," Tilden continued, "I'm foremost an American who swore an oath to protect and defend the Constitution. I take that oath seriously. I also know from experience that a divided people can become a conquered people. This is why I've taken the unprecedented step to try and unite all Americans by naming Speaker Kevin Novak as my Vice President."

The silence that followed was absolute. Shock blanketed the room like fallout. Then, as Novak walked into the room, a growing wave of murmuring slowly, almost hesitantly, came, whispers traded like insider tips in a collapsing stock market. Eyes darted, phones lit up, tweets fired into cyberspace like bullets.

Novak assumed a position on the podium next to the President—a shocking image that would be etched in history.

Tilden held up a trembling hand, waiting for calm. "I believe his selection will foster greater cooperation between our two major parties and allow us to move America forward in greater harmony. While I appreciate all Vice President Stern has helped my administration achieve, the American people have made it clear—they want leadership that represents a more centrist position."

The words hung in the air for a breathless beat.

Then, like a dam cracking, the room erupted—not in outrage, but applause. Scattered at first, then growing. Reporters exchanged stunned glances as the President shook Novak's hand and exited the room.

Somewhere in the shadows of the West Wing, the game had just changed.

Amanda Pigeon walked to the lectern and said, "Vice President Novak will take a few questions."

Kevin Novak joined Pigeon at the lectern.

Hugh Duffer stood and asked, "Mr. Speaker, when did you first learn of the President's decision?"

As Pigeon stepped back from the microphone, Novak moved forward and said, "When we met this afternoon."

"Was this a shock to you?" Duffer continued.

The six-two fit-looking Novak stood erect as his twelve years of training in the U.S. Army had taught him. In a black suit with a red-and-blue rep tie, Novak looked Presidential and stole the show.

"At first, it was a shock. After all, I'm a fiscal and moral conservative, and President Tilden's supporters are a little further to the left."

A low rumble of laughter arose at the understatement.

"After discussing the need to unite our country, I saw the wisdom in the President's decision. In this volatile world, Americans must unite and address the Chinese threat, secure our borders, restore law and order, and gain control over our economy. For these reasons, I agree with the President that it is time for the American people to come together for the greater good. My sincere pledge is that I will work to address these threats and unite Americans across race, religion, economic status, and ideology."

Novak received a standing ovation.

SEAL Team Six Flight, Operation Delta Dagger

Night pressed down on the Valley of the Dolls like a fist. The mountains cut the sky into black teeth; the valley below shimmered with the distant, sickly glow of neon and lanterns. From above, a small, dark aircraft drifted through the starless air, a shadow among shadows. Inside, Master Chief Kyle Milliken sat like a statue, the hum of the rotors in his ears as he watched the valley roll beneath them, watched the map in his head — the roads, the landing zone, the river bend, the cluster of buildings gossamer-lit and impossible to see from the sky. Milliken allowed himself a moment of relaxation before the battle began.

He was a long way from his home in Blue Ridge, Georgia. He prayed that his wife, Jill, and their two children were safe from the urban unrest South of them in Atlanta. It was all in God's hands now; it was time to focus solely on the mission. No distractions, no emotions.

"You good?" whispered Lt. Alvarez at his shoulder.

Kyle let out a slow breath. "We get her, we leave. Clean and quiet."

Four of them: a team carved from the kind of confidence that comes from knowing one another's reflexes like a second heartbeat. They had rehearsed words into shorthand and silence into ritual; tonight, the air itself was part of the plan.

They fast-roped down onto the sand of the river bend, out of the dark, four hundred yards from the buildings, the aircraft slipping away into the night, the way a cat slips out a door. The team, clad in black, carried a variety of weapons that could cover all mission parameters from silent killing to sniper work.

Kyle and Alvarez held their short-barreled M4-A1s at the ready as they followed Jensen, their point man, into position. Lopez, the team sniper, carried his M110 for long-range work and covered their left flank, putting him in position to defend the team against vehicles entering the compound. Jensen took the right flank as Alaverez covered their rear. All men carried the Sig 320 in 9mm, and Kyle also had a specialized Ruger Mark IV, suppressed variant for 'quiet work.'

The team moved like smoke, folding through scrub and shadow until the valley swallowed them. Night sat low and thick over the compound, a hard black that swallowed the shapes of walls and wires and made every breath sound too loud. Four of them moved like parts of the same thinking machine—no wasted motion, no individual bravado—each man an extension of the others' senses. They reminded Kyle of a watch: four hands, different lengths, all counting the same exact time.

Suddenly, a window opened, and lantern light leaked from a half-closed window, creating a small island of warmth that could give away their position. In that light, faces became maps—lines of worry, the quick shutter of an eye. The team read those maps without words. A tilt of a head, a whisper that never reached the ears of anyone else; the language between them was private as breath. Then, a woman dumped a wash bowl out and closed the window. Threat evaded.

They crept up the slope that led to the back wall, moving with the kind of slow, inevitable patience that comes from too many nights like this. Each time one man eased forward, another tightened his attention and watched the empty space he had just left. It wasn't technique so much as trust: if one hand reached into danger, three others kept the danger from finding it. When exposure was necessary—when someone had to step into light or pass a gap—the others seemed to fold around him, a living shield that made him less alone against whatever the compound could throw at them.

Alvarez watched as Lopez motioned them to get down. At first, Alvarez questioned his man's judgment, then he heard the hum of a truck engine. The four commandos fell flat as the truck's headlights shone on them. A minute later, the vehicle had passed, and no threat emerged. Good, he thought.

Kyle felt the team's rhythm under his skin. There was Lopez, all compact and ready, whose eyes missed nothing; Alvarez, calm to the point of being statuesque; and Jensen, the quiet one whose humor came out in the smallest, almost invisible ways. They had their jokes, old arguments, and private grievances, but none of that mattered here. Out in the dark, their pasts were weights left at the edge of the world—they were all present, and what they were present for was each other.

Suddenly, a dog barked somewhere beyond the wall, and the sound tore a thin line through the hush. For a second, adrenaline slid in like cold water; every head snapped up, and the world contracted to a pinpoint where decision lived. Kyle drew his Ruger and waited. The voice that would have ordered them to react never came. Instead, breath slowed, glances exchanged, and what they chose was silence—not the empty kind but the careful kind that carries the shape of intent.

They reached the compound's shadowed face and paused. In the silence, the mundane details of life inside—people snoring, a radio's muffled rhythm—became intimate and dangerous. Kyle remembered Jade's picture. He'd memorized every detail so he could recognize her immediately. Jade was the prize they were risking their lives to rescue. To what purpose, he had no idea.

They moved again, this time together in a way that felt less like planning and more like breathing. The path they took mattered less than the fact that they took it as one: one man buying the moment, another preserving it, a third watching the broader world while the fourth held the thread that bound them all.

As planned, Kyle slipped inside the courtyard and looked to the designated tree, the rendezvous point. It was 02:59, and no one was about. One more minute!

Lopez remained fifty yards out, covering the team's rear while scanning the walls and guard towers for threats with his night vision scope. Two guards were sleeping. The man at the main gate was reading a magazine with a light on in the guard shack. Good, unaware, lazy, with poor night vision.

At 03:00, a dim figure in dark clothing shifted near the tree, lit a cigarette, and held the lighter near her face for longer than was needed. The middle-aged woman was tall and had long, grey-black hair. She looked like Jade. Now to confirm.

Kyle flipped his red-lensed flashlight directly at the woman, and the lighter went out. Confirmation.

Jade moved casually toward him, her heart pounding like a bass drum. Was this really happening? Was she... going home?

Kyle went to the woman and asked, "Jade?"

Her eyes registered confusion sharpening into recognition, then flaring into something like relief. She reached out and whispered, "I'm Jade."

Kyle scanned their surroundings, took her hand, and whispered, "Jade, come with me."

The two dark-dressed figures slipped through the compound's open gate and into the field beyond. There, the team closed around Jade—not like a trap, but like a rescue. Three clicks on Alvarez's radio mic called in the chopper.

They left the compound the way they had entered: together, steady, guarding what they had come for without making any more noise than necessary. They were not heroes in the sense people wrote about; they were men who understood vows made in darker rooms to keep other people alive. That knowledge, more than any medal or praise, was what they took with them into the fray.

When they approached the river, Kyle escorted Jade into the Silent Hawk while Lopez scanned for followers, and Alvarez and Jensen remained along their flanks. They saw no one.

Alvarez saw that Kyle had Jade secured and signaled for Jensen and Lopez to load. The three men quickly boarded the chopper.

When they were airborne, Alvarez said, “Good work, men. We got her clean and quiet.” He turned to Jade and shouted over the noise, “Welcome back. We should have you back in the States in twenty-four hours.”

The flight back was a ribbon of low clouds and lighted instrument panels. Jade sat between two of them with a blanket wrapped tight around her shoulders. Outside the cabin window, the world was a smear of lights and shadow, and for a time, the hum of engines was the only witness to the soft, quiet relief that washed over her face.

Once airborne, the team breathed as if releasing held breath. Jade stared at Kyle, took his hand, and said, “You saved me,” her voice trembling with emotion.

Kyle looked at her beautiful face with the honesty of a man who had seen too much and chosen to keep his center. He’d been given special instructions on what to say: “Jake, remembered you.”

The extraction point melted into memory the way things do when they’re a long way behind. In the cabin, amid the smell of burnt fuel, Kyle let his shoulders loosen for the first time that night. Out in the world, the Valley of the Dolls went on turning, ignorant and terrible. Inside that small helicopter, one woman out of a million had been rescued and was now holding his hand and crying on his shoulder. The whole mission was surreal.

Alvarez nodded in approval. Jensen and Lopez grinned.

Kyle put his arm around Jade and offered, “It’ll be alright. You’re free now, safe. I won’t let anyone hurt you.”

Jade sobbed for thirty minutes. Finally, she stopped, and Alvarez handed her his bandana. The crew chief brought her a water bottle, and she drank it down. Finally, her catharsis ended, and she sat holding the Master Chief's hand, resting her head on his shoulder.

Jade knew there would be questions, people gossiping about her past. There would be ghosts, brutal memories. But for now, in the thin glow of the cabin, she breathed like someone who'd been given a second day, and did not yet know how to spend it. Freedom was a concept lost half a lifetime ago, but she would learn to live again.

Kyle watched her, and for the first time in a long while, allowed himself a smile. Some things were still worth the cost.

Chapter 8

Oxley's attire—faded jeans, worn boots, and a canvas jacket dusted in dry clay—made him look more like a cattle rancher than the CIA Director as he drove his father's rust-speckled 1972 Chevy pickup slowly onto Farm Road. To the untrained eye, the drive might have looked pastoral—rolling hills, the scent of manure in the air, a gravel path winding toward a humble barn. But anyone with field experience would've caught the anomaly: six men dressed as hunters patrolling the treeline, each casually cradling a suppressed MP-5 submachine gun.

Hampton Farms wasn't listed on any government registry. Acquired discreetly in the Eisenhower era, it had served as the Order's sanctuary for over seven decades. The property was technically owned by Hampton Farms LLP, a shell company incorporated within the Hunter Group, an international real estate conglomerate with silent tentacles spanning five continents. Beneath layers of trusts, offshore accounts, and regulatory fog, it was one of dozens of sites controlled by the Order—a silent Christian brotherhood committed to saving the world from the encroaching shadow of the New World Order.

As Oxley nodded to the first "hunter," the man stepped forward and unlatched the single iron gate securing the gravel path. The Director drove past slowly, noting a sniper posted in a camouflaged shooting tower—one of a dozen ringing the property perimeter, each precisely 400 yards apart. The towers were manned by former U.S. Tier One Operators. Around the perimeter, hidden among tall grass and dormant wheat fields, was a lattice of surveillance drones, seismic sensors, and buried pressure plates—linked to a central AI node that could activate deadly autonomous countermeasures.

Despite their precautions, Oxley believed their best defense was the one money couldn't buy: anonymity. The farm was old. Familiar. Locals thought it was a hunting preserve for rich urban hunters, and the few who had stumbled too close had been dissuaded—some by word, others by wound.

The barn was a fortress disguised as a relic, its weathered red siding concealing reinforced concrete and Faraday mesh. As the rolling door creaked upward, Oxley eased the truck inside, parking beside a line of equally vintage trucks and SUVs—all built before 1972, rugged, analog, and immune to modern EMPs. The vehicles belonged to men who understood the value of redundancy. A generation raised on both bullets and Bibles.

Twenty-nine men stood around a long, rough-hewn wood table. Conversation was minimal, but the silence wasn't awkward—it was the silence of conviction. Some wore hunting gear, others farm clothing, but all shared the same steel-eyed resolve. They were the last wall of defense against the coming dark ages.

Oxley stepped out, grabbed his battered attaché case, and moved toward the group. He shook each hand with care and weight, knowing this might be the last peaceful moment they shared.

He took his place at the head of the table and spoke with clarity that cut like a combat knife, "Against incredible odds, the Order must take action to preserve our democracy and stop the New World Order from removing all Godly influence from the planet. This is about far more than preserving a nation—it's about saving six billion souls by preventing a godless empire from rising in its place."

"Amen!" several men shouted, fists clenched.

"I don't have to explain the urgency of our actions or the odds against our success," Oxley continued. "To the world, what we're about to do is madness. But then, the world has already gone mad. We, the remnant, are seekers of truth who are compelled by God to fight this present evil, so that God's light is not taken from the world."

He paused, his eyes meeting each man's.

A palpable fear emerged as each man listened to their leader.

"Judges, Chapter 7 of the Holy Scriptures, tells the story of Gideon's defeat of the Midianites. At that time, the Lord said to Gideon, 'You have too many men. I cannot deliver Midian into your hands, or Israel would boast against me, saying, 'My own strength has saved me.' After looking each man in the eye, Oxley continued, "Now announce to the army, 'Anyone who trembles with fear may turn back and leave Mount Gilead.' So, twenty-two thousand men left, and ten thousand remained. Then, the Lord told Gideon, 'There are still too many men. Take them to the water, and I will thin them out for you.' So, Gideon took the men down to the water, and God told him, 'Separate those who drink water from cupped hands from those who lap the water directly from the stream.' Three hundred of them drank with cupped hands. All the rest got down on their knees to drink. At that point, God told Gideon, 'With the three hundred men that drank from cupped hands, I will save you and give the Midianites into your hands. Let all the others go home.' So, Gideon sent the rest home but kept the three hundred."

The men in the group nodded in agreement.

"Against insurmountable odds, the three hundred confronted a numerically superior enemy, and all the Midianites ran, screaming in fear!" Oxley paused for effect, then added, "Gentlemen, we are the men who drink with cupped hands. God is with us as he was with them. And, as Jefferson said, 'The tree of liberty must be refreshed from time to time with the blood of tyrants!"

The powerful words pierced every heart, bringing them to applause – palpable fear replaced by iron resolve.

White House

President Tilden sat in the Oval Office with his travel secretary, Tonja Wilson, reviewing plans for his upcoming trip.

"I have to be in Beijing in two days," Tilden said, then coughed.

Tonja looked at the President and noted his face was red and his voice hoarse, "Are you okay?"

The President took a sip of water, cleared his throat, and continued, "I must have caught a cold from those Girl Scouts."

"We should have Dr. Reynolds take a look at you?" Tonja said.

Tilden held up his hand, "No. I'm fine. I can't let a cold get me down."

Tonja looked worried. "Okay, I'll coordinate your trip with President Jin's and Ethan Carpathian's people. So far, your normal Press Corps and Cabinet members are accompanying you on Air Force One. CDC Director Amy Rapier, Dr. Lawrence Wilhite, and Dr. Antonio Faccini also accepted your invitation. Is there anyone else you want added?"

Tilden said, "Linda Pagosa."

Beijing, China

China's military, once a lumbering political instrument forged in the fires of revolution, had transformed. No longer a bloated ground force burdened by doctrine from the Korean War, the People's Liberation Army had undergone a radical evolution. Its latest structural overhaul reshaped it into a lean, integrated, and globally deployable force that operated across five theater commands, each capable of multi-domain operations.

This modern military reported directly to the seven-member Central Military Commission (CMC). While the CMC's bureaucratic façade suggested dual civilian and military oversight, everyone in the room understood the reality: the Communist Party held the reins, and President Xi Jin gripped them with unwavering resolve.

Inside a sealed subterranean command center outside Beijing—shielded against satellite imaging, signal interception, and bunker-busting munitions—President Jin sat at the head of a long, dark-polished table. On either side, the top echelon of China's military hierarchy was assembled. Vice-Chair Air Force General Xu Qiliang and Vice-Chair General Zhang Youxia flanked him, both longtime loyalists. Across from them sat Generals Leu, Chang, Soma, and Yeng—commanders representing the core of China's modernized war machine. The atmosphere was clinical, intense, and laced with anticipation.

A wall-sized digital map of the Indo-Pacific glowed behind Jin, detailing U.S. bases, carrier strike group positions, satellite orbits, and joint force readiness levels. Red vectors marked Chinese offensive operations. Yellow rings displayed the reach of U.S. missile systems.

Jin leaned forward, his voice calm but electric. "I've gained the support of President Tilden to delay the U.S. response for two weeks after the initiation of hostilities."

There was a subtle shift in posture around the table. Eyebrows lifted. Shoulders straightened. Even in a room filled with hardened generals, the implication was staggering.

Vice-Chairman Qiliang was first to respond. "The delay will allow us to establish air and sea superiority in the theater. With control of the skies and sea lanes, we will be able to quickly eliminate the Taiwanese Forces, thereby opening the way to move vast amounts of personnel and equipment onto the island nation."

A palpable tension filled the air as the reality of actually fighting a war hit them. In the past, they could beg for more resources and make confident assertions about their capabilities; now, they would have to produce results with unproven forces and little battle experience. Soon, all their political skills wouldn't save them as Jin released the dogs of war.

Jin surveyed his commanders, looking for weakness. He saw no evidence of it and asked, “What are our loss projections?”

Youxia exhaled. “Our original simulation indicated 50% losses across fighter, bomber, and surface naval platforms within the first month. Personnel casualties totaled 500,000. However, with a two-week delay in the U.S. response, we cut our losses in half.”

Jin nodded slowly. “These are acceptable losses.”

General Leu, the youngest at the table and commander of the South Theater, leaned forward. “Mr. President, we’re prepared to execute a blow that will ensure China’s regional dominance for the next fifty years—and inspire our allies to join us in rejecting Western hegemony.”

Jin sat back and let the silence settle. Behind his inscrutable expression, calculations churned. The American era in the Pacific was coming to a close. Taiwan was the first stepping stone, followed by Japan, South Korea, and the Philippines. With Carpathian’s help, America would soon fall from her lauded position as the most powerful nation in history, and China would only have India to contend with.

“Very well,” he said. “Begin final staging operations.”

Around the table, the room fell into execution mode. Orders were relayed through encrypted networks. Target packages finalized.

The dragon was rising in the East.

U.S. NEWS

Susie Legman appeared on screen from her sleek, glass-walled New York studio. Her expression was grave, her voice steady, though the undercurrent of national anxiety was unmistakable.

“We have breaking reports from the White House that President Tilden has been taken to Walter Reed Medical Center,” she said. “In a brief statement, White House Press Secretary Amanda Pigeon described the admission as purely ‘precautionary.’ We now go live to White House correspondent Hugh Duffer for more details. Hugh, what have you learned?”

The scene cut to Hugh Duffer standing outside the north gate of the White House. Behind him, dark clouds gathered over the executive mansion. Winds from an approaching nor’easter swept through the trees, rustling leaves and tugging at the lapels of Duffer’s trench coat. His usually polished hair whipped in the wind, adding texture to the gravity of the moment.

"Susie," he began, his voice low, "sources inside the White House confirm that President Tilden was airlifted to Walter Reed approximately thirty-five minutes ago. I'm told he appeared extremely pale and was wearing an oxygen mask when Secret Service agents loaded him onto the Marine One helicopter—on a stretcher."

Susie's expression darkened. "Hugh, is there any indication that the President may have contracted COVID-23?"

Duffer gave a slow, deliberate nod. "While Amanda Pigeon insists the President is simply suffering from a cold, the timing and urgency of the evacuation—combined with the ongoing outbreak—have many here at the White House skeptical. I can tell you that aides were visibly shaken, and security protocols were tightened almost immediately."

Susie looked directly into the camera, channeling the unease of millions watching. "Polls indicate that eighty percent of Americans believe House Speaker Kevin Novak is more prepared to assume the presidency than Vice President Conja Sterns."

"Indeed," Duffer replied. "Sterns, who was selected as a symbolic nod to the progressive wing of the Democratic Party, is seen by many in the national security and business communities as too radical and untested to lead in a crisis. There's already murmuring on the Hill that if power is transferred, resistance could form—both behind closed doors and in the streets."

Susie leaned forward. "What's the constitutional process for transferring presidential authority—should it come to that?"

Hugh nodded, slipping into analyst mode. "After the assassination of President John F. Kennedy, Lyndon Johnson pushed for clarity on presidential succession. This led to the 25th Amendment, ratified in 1967. Since then, power has only been temporarily transferred—typically for routine procedures like colonoscopies or surgeries—usually without a formal invocation."

He coughed then continued, "However, in 2019, Speaker Linda Pagosa and a bipartisan committee revised the practical protocols for invoking the 25th Amendment. Under the new rules, if the President is hospitalized and unable to perform their duties, the Vice President automatically assumes the presidency. Alternatively, a majority of the Cabinet or a joint Congressional Committee can declare the President unfit."

Susie's tone turned sharp. "So, in the middle of a global crisis—with China threatening Taiwan and American cities already seeing spikes in unrest—the United States could be thrown into constitutional limbo?"

Duffer hesitated just long enough to make the pause count. "You'd hope cooler heads prevail and follow the rule of law. However, in today's hyper-partisan climate, this may escalate into a lengthy legal and political battle. And in that window, China could make its move on Taiwan. Domestic instability could escalate. And, we need to remember, our enemies are watching."

Back in the studio, Susie's lips tightened as she glanced at the scrolling chyron:

BREAKING: PRESIDENT TILDEN HOSPITALIZED — QUESTIONS LOOM OVER SUCCESSION

"Let's hope, for all our sakes, someone in Washington remembers what leadership looks like."

But in the backrooms of Beijing, and the war rooms of Moscow, the headlines weren't just news. They were an opportunity.

Landing Zone One

Carved into the volcanic cliffs that faced the Taiwan Strait, the base was almost invisible from the water. From a distance, it looked like nothing more than jagged rock and scrub vegetation battered by salt spray. But tucked into the stone, concealed behind armored blast doors painted to blend with the cliff face, lay one of Taiwan's hardened coastal redoubts—designed to survive missile strikes and keep men fighting even if the skies above turned to fire.

Once inside, a narrow, reinforced corridor descended into the cliff's heart. The walls bore the raw texture of blasted basalt, sheathed in steel mesh and lined with rebar-laced concrete. Every chamber had been poured with dense aggregate and layered with shock-absorbing insulation—capable of withstanding the pounding of Chinese cruise missiles and heavy artillery.

Near the entrance, a compact field hospital contained two treatment rooms, a surgical bay with basic life-support equipment, and a triage ward with fold-down steel cots. Medical lockers held IV fluids, antibiotics, and blood plasma substitutes, enough to treat dozens of wounded after an amphibious assault.

Deeper inside, the crew quarters consisted of triple-stacked bunks bolted directly to the walls, each with curtains, red reading lights, and lockers welded in place. The air smelled faintly of metal, detergent, and oil.

A stainless-steel galley connected to a cafeteria with long, bolted-down tables. Here, troops could cycle through in shifts, eating rehydrated rice packets, soups, and canned rations. The kitchen's ventilation system was routed through rock-lined shafts to disperse heat signatures and avoid detection from infrared drones.

The heart of the base was storage—reinforced concrete vaults holding ammunition, spare weapons, and crates of shoulder-fired anti-tank and anti-air missiles. Each vault was separated by heavy blast doors so that an accident in one wouldn't compromise the others. Supplies of food, water, fuel cells, and batteries were stacked floor to ceiling in climate-controlled rooms, enough to keep the garrison operational for weeks cut off from the outside world.

Everything was designed for endurance and concealment. Air filtration systems recycled the stale underground air, while desalination units tapped seawater drawn in through pipes disguised among rocks at the tide line. Communications ran through buried fiber and hardened antenna shafts that emerged high on the cliff, camouflaged as rocky outcroppings.

To an invader, the beach seemed bare and exposed. But hidden in the cliff face was a fortress: a self-sustaining, hardened warren of concrete and steel, manned by soldiers who could fight long after the first salvos had fallen.

Jake followed Gunny Stillwell through the dimly lit tunnels, the concrete walls humming with the low vibration of distant generators. The deeper they went, the cooler it became—a stark contrast to the humid surface heat baking Taiwan's coast.

The two men stopped at the quartermaster's room. "This reporter needs a basic combat load: vest, helmet, weapon, spare magazines, and comms." Stillwell barked.

The rotund quartermaster, Sergeant Donald Penn, efficiently piled Jake's combat load onto the counter, then retrieved an M-27 weapon. The M-27 Infantry Automatic Rifle was a modern U.S. Marine Corps weapon system, derived from the Heckler & Koch HK416 platform.

Jake looked over the weapon and worked its action. Trying not to reveal his CIA training, he pretended not to know how to insert a magazine.

"Sir, the mag is inserted here, then you pull back the bolt to load it." Penn offered helpfully.

Stillwell shook his head.

"Well, Mr. Hendel, let's familiarize you with your new friend."

Jake slipped on his body armor vest, put on his helmet, and followed the Gunnery Sergeant down the tunnel.

They stopped at a reinforced blast door marked "LIVE FIRE TRAINING AREA – CLEARANCE REQUIRED." Stillwell punched in a code, the door hissed open, and Jake stepped into a cavernous underground firing range. Steel targets lined the far wall. Spotlights and ventilation systems whirred overhead. The entire complex had been dug into the hillside like a modern Maginot Line.

"Set your selector to semi-auto," Stillwell ordered, his voice even but firm. "We'll start at fifty meters."

Jake dropped to a kneeling position and brought the M-27 to his shoulder. It felt natural. Despite being a war correspondent, Jake had spent enough time embedded with Tier-1 units to learn the mechanics of war—and more importantly, how to shoot straight when the bullets flew both ways.

He centered the reticle over the steel silhouette and squeezed the trigger. Crack. The first round rang out. The target clanged. Jake adjusted his aim and fired again. Another hit. Then three more in quick succession.

Stillwell nodded. "Good sight picture. Tight group. Try controlled bursts."

Jake flipped the selector to automatic, exhaled slowly, and let the rifle walk through a short volley. The muzzle rose with each firing, but the rounds stayed on target.

Stillwell raised his eyebrows. "Not your first rodeo, is it?"

Jake knew it was a high compliment from the proven veteran. Those weren't desk jockey years; they were tours carved deep into the man's weathered face, each line a story etched by shrapnel and scorching sun. Despite the forty-eight years life had stamped on him, Stillwell still moved with the cat-like efficiency of a predator ready to pounce.

"Where did you learn to shoot?" Stillwell asked, noting Jake's body mechanics and effectiveness.

Jake stood, reloaded a fresh magazine to buy time to think up a story. "I did a stint with a Navy SEAL unit for a documentary."

Jake had told the truth, just not the whole truth.

The Gunny chuckled. "Figures."

Jake looked back at the range, then at the aging NCO. "Do you think we can hold this beach, Gunny?"

Stillwell's jaw tightened. "We'll slow them down. Maybe kill a thousand or more. But if the PLA gets armor on the beach, the real fight will be inland." He pointed toward Taipei, barely 30 kilometers away. "Our job is to buy time for Admiral Flint to bring in the cavalry."

Jake nodded solemnly. "Then I'm in the right place."

Stillwell clapped a hand on Jake's shoulder. "We'll see how you feel when the beach turns red. Come on. Let's get you a bunk before it starts raining dragons. Hank has already picked his."

Pacific Command, Hawaii

Chief of Fleet Intelligence, Captain Abraham Newsome, a Jewish man who stood five feet eight inches tall, held an Engineering degree from Annapolis and a Ph.D. in International and Global Affairs from Harvard. Newsome spoke fluent Chinese and Russian. Flint considered Newsome the ideal G-2: intelligent, well-educated, and able to get into the mind of his enemy.

"Sir, Chinese troops are massing at over a dozen embarkation ports. We've observed a significant increase in trucks on major highways, and transport ships are moving massive quantities of munitions and supplies to their forward bases in the Spratly Islands," Newsome reported as he flipped through digital images. "This morning, we confirmed they're shipping blood products forward."

"When they ship blood, they're going to war," observed Admiral Flint, "the question is when?"

"Best guess, within 48 hours."

Newsome supported his team's analysis with photographs of PLA positions, "This image is of Subi Reef. The man-made island has been transformed into an airbase, featuring a double runway, hangars, and multi-story administrative buildings. Their base on Mischief Reef supports Chinese Type 022 Houbei-class fast-attack boats armed with

YJ-83 anti-ship missiles, along with other ships. The island also houses a sea-facing angled cruise missile launcher," Newsome observed, then pulled up a series of reconnaissance images, "This photo shows a Chinese KJ-500 airborne early warning aircraft on the runway of Fiery Cross Reef. Satellite recon shows that the PLA has deployed two paratrooper battalions to the island. The presence of KJ-500 planes shows the runways are long enough to accommodate H-6 bombers. Since the KJ-500 plays a significant role in China's ability to use long-range air-to-air and air-to-sea missiles, I think they will use them on our carriers."

"Naval build-up?"

"They have fifty-two vessels of different types anchored near Fiery Cross. Forty attack submarines were put to sea over the last three days. We believe they intend to seize control of the vital chokepoint between the Indian and Pacific Oceans, where 80% of global shipping passes. They have also fueled and loaded over three hundred merchant marine vessels. For now, they're keeping their carriers close to home, probably to deploy aircraft against Taiwan," Newsome observed.

A low rumble of agreement passed through the briefing room like distant thunder. Men and women in crisp Navy and Marine uniforms exchanged glances—some nodding, others silently reassessing what was about to unfold.

The commander of Carrier Strike Group Seven leaned forward. "Sir, with all due respect, this puts us a hair trigger away from full-scale war."

Flint's eyes locked onto his, unblinking. "We're already there. The Chinese have massed three carrier groups east of Taiwan, moved hypersonic missiles into Fujian, and initiated electronic jamming of our satellites and early warning systems. Don't kid yourself. We're not waiting for a declaration. We're waiting for the first funeral."

Flint turned to the operations display. The digital map displayed the Pacific theater, a hive of red Chinese military units advancing eastward from the mainland, with blue U.S. and allied forces clustered around Taiwan, Okinawa, and Guam. Yellow warning zones blinked where satellite intel showed new missile batteries and drone swarms mobilizing. "The President's rules of engagement don't allow us to fire unless fired upon. This makes us vulnerable to their first punch. Since this war will unravel quickly, I want command authority pushed down to the lowest possible level, even if that means a Lance Corporal. We don't have time to waste on the chain of command. If a fighter from a Chinese carrier fires on us, we take out the plane, the squadron, and the carrier. If they fire a missile, we will destroy the base from which it launches. I don't want escalation—I want obliteration. Clear?"

Every head in the room nodded. There would be no misunderstanding.

Flint stepped back and crossed his arms. "Washington will scream. State will whine. The President may even demand my resignation. But if it means saving our sailors, our Marines, and this nation's credibility, I'll walk into the fire first."

A murmur of respect passed through the ranks.

"Now, start distributing wartime Rules of Engagement to your XOs. By the time we finish this briefing, every sailor and every Marine under our command will know the mission: defend forward, strike hard, and never wait to bleed."

CIA Headquarters

When Oxley entered the subterranean command center known as the Crisis Room, the tension was as thick as the recycled air. Seated around the long table were CIA Deputy Director Raymond Jones, FBI Director Baker, National Security Advisor Jack Reagan, and over a dozen agency leads from Langley, NSA, and Cyber Command. The President's chair sat conspicuously empty.

"Let's begin," Oxley ordered, taking the seat at the head of the table.

Raymond Jones tapped his tablet, and the central screen lit up with a pulsing red digital map across the globe.

"Starting at midnight EST," James said, "a synchronized wave of cyberattacks targeted U.S. and allied military and civilian systems. We've attributed the breaches to coordinated state-sponsored actors from China, Russia, and North Korea."

Oxley leaned forward. "What have they hit?"

James didn't flinch. "Municipal water systems in Los Angeles, Dallas, and Norfolk. Regional power grids in Florida, Texas, and the Pacific Northwest. Telecommunications nodes across the Midwest. Civilian systems that support or neighbor military installations."

"And the military?"

"Our critical defense systems are still online, thanks to hardened subnets and quantum encryption," James replied. "But we've lost primary logistics support. Seventy percent of our domestic military bases are on backup generators. Pacific Command is running dark at ninety percent."

Jack Reagan added, "Civilian contractors like FedEx Military Logistics, Evergreen Air Cargo, and MCS Fuels have been compromised. The planes and trucks are fine—the command chains aren't."

Oxley asked, "What's their next move?"

James said, "We anticipate massive missile strikes against our airfields in Japan, Guam, and the Philippines. Their cyber ops are softening the terrain. They'll follow up with cruise missiles, hypersonics, and, perhaps, carrier-based air sorties."

Oxley's eyes narrowed. "Will they invade Taiwan—or just blockade it?"

"If they can blind and deafen our Pacific presence in the next forty-eight hours," James observed grimly, "they'll go for a land invasion. The PLA needs to seize control of beaches west of Taichung and airports north of Taipei. Seaports at Kaohsiung and Keelung will also be high-value targets."

Oxley's voice was low. "How long can Taiwan hold out?"

James glanced at his notes, then passed the question to Reagan with a subtle nod. The silence was deafening.

"Best case," Reagan said, "with full U.S. air and naval support? Three months. In the worst case, without intervention, it would take six weeks. The Chinese know they can't drag this out and will push hard and fast."

Oxley turned to Baker. "Domestic?"

The FBI Director opened a folder thick with classified reports. "We've identified ninety separate terror cells. Some are Chinese nationals posing as students or asylum seekers. Others are proxies—Middle Eastern, African, even American-born radicals funded by Chinese shell companies. Over the past week, we've foiled attempts to contaminate water supplies, derail trains, bomb substations, and target fuel depots." He paused, considering his words carefully. "These are coordinated asymmetric attacks."

Oxley shifted his attention to Reagan. "Jack, thoughts?"

Reagan, steely-eyed and composed, said, "Immigration records show over twenty-five thousand military-age men crossed the southern and northern borders in the past two years—most under asylum or amnesty. They're on public assistance, scattered across major urban centers, and living under the radar. The PLA has used the Cartels and Chinese Companies to build a multi-layered network of sleeper cells. These attacks are only the first wave."

Oxley sighed, then asked, "What's next?"

"Infrastructure, mass transit, fuel, cyber nodes, and symbolic targets—Capitol buildings, police HQs, schools. Biological or chemical agents in HVAC systems. Urban riots will be the accelerant—funded and fueled by PLA-backed agitators using online channels and crypto."

FBI Director Baker leaned in. "Ignite the powder kegs China's been setting up for years."

"Exactly," Reagan replied. "This war didn't start tonight. It's been a long game."

Oxley tapped the table. "Get all this to Admiral Flint. I want PACCOM ready for full kinetic engagement by 0600 hours. No half-measures. And alert JSOC—if we're going to win this war, we'll need to cut off the snake's head before it strikes our heart."

Everyone around the table nodded.

U.S. Space Force, Orbital Battle Station

The U.S. Space Force Astronauts had been stationed in geosynchronous orbit over Midway Island for two months. Their relief crew would arrive in four weeks. The three-month tours of duty allowed them to return to Earth for reunification with their families and additional training. At first, life in space had been fantastic, but over the weeks, the sixteen-hour days began to take their toll.

Colonel Nadia Rashid admired the stars, uncontaminated by manmade light. Astronomer by education, she relished the unobstructed view of the heavens and all the vivid colors obscured by Earth's atmosphere. Despite the wonder of the heavens, the blue orb she called home grew increasingly more alluring with each passing day.

The voice of AEGIS, the station's onboard AI, said, "Chinese rocket launch detected from Yunan Rocket Base II, China. Satellite confirmation received; this is no drill!"

Rashid gripped the armrests of her command console, eyes glued to the holographic display flickering in front of her. The display looked like something ripped from a sci-fi thriller – a Chinese YJ-21 hypersonic missile, a needle of white-hot death streaking toward U.S. soil!

"Projected target, Honolulu, Hawaii, ETA to detonation, twenty minutes," droned the machine voice of AEGIS.

Rashid's pulse quickened. This was why she and her crew were stationed aboard the orbital battle platform OBP – one of four stations that served as the linchpin in the U.S. Space Force's counter-missile defense network.

"Prepare Hyperion interceptor," she barked into the command channel. Her team, a mix of seasoned veterans and fresh-faced recruits, responded with a chorus of acknowledgments. They were the invisible guardians who protected the Western U.S. and Pacific Theater Command from nuclear attack.

Hyperion was a marvel of kinetic-energy weaponry, a sleek tungsten rod launched by a powerful electromagnetic railgun. Without an explosive payload, the sheer force of the impact at orbital velocity could obliterate an enemy missile on contact. The projectile also saved thousands of pounds of payload and billions in launch costs. Unfortunately, the payload priorities had only provided eight rods.

The colonel's years of training combined with fear and a sense of excitement as she wondered how well her command would perform. Twenty billion dollars of assets were under her control; she'd trained her crew well, but Hyperion had never been tested in battle. Success required millions of sub-second calculations to ensure the rod collided with the enemy missile. The margin of error was less than six feet. If she missed, hundreds of thousands of people could be incinerated.

"The wait is the hardest part," Rashid told her crew.

Watching the sinister rocket carrying up to five multiple reentry warheads streak across the heavens at 7,400 miles per hour was like watching the angel of death.

"Ten seconds to launch; planned impact at the height of rocket apogee," intoned AEGIS after the long wait. Rashid held her breath. The tension in the control room was thick enough to cut with a knife.

"Five, four, three..." The crew counted down in unison, their voices tight with concentration.

"Two, one, FIRE!"

A surge of energy pulsed through the OBP as the electromagnetic railgun launched the interceptor. On the holographic display, a tungsten bullet rocketed toward the incoming missile. Time seemed to slow as the two objects hurtled through space.

"Impact confirmed," announced AEGIS calmly, the tension bleeding from Rashid's shoulders. The crew looked down and saw a bright flash as the enemy missile disintegrated, a testament to the raw power of human ingenuity. Cheers erupted in the control room while generals and defense contractors celebrated on the ground.

But Rashid had a sneaking suspicion the celebration would be short-lived.

Alarms blared, and a cacophony of shrill shrieks tore through the sterile environment of the OBP. Rashid slammed her fist on the table, the tremor causing the holographic map to quiver as eight thick, pulsing red lines arced across the vast expanse of blue.

"Oh God, no!"

AEGIS alarms toned as the cyber-voice warned, "Eight Chinese DF-41 ICBMs launched from their Yunnan Nuclear Base! Calculating multiple trajectories. Auto rearming of Hyperion complete."

Missile launches confirmed," rasped a technician, her voice tight with barely suppressed panic. "This is not a cyber fake!" The air crackled with a tension thicker than the powdered coffee they drank. Faces were etched with grim determination to stop the missiles before they unleashed their unholy fire.

"Launch all remaining Hyperion interceptors."

A young captain blurted, his voice betraying his concern, "Space Force Recon indicates the Chinese are preparing ten additional YJ-21 hypersonic missiles for launch. We now have two bogeys on a direct path to the continental U.S.!"

A collective gasp filled the room. Thirty minutes to California. A lifetime, yet a mere blink of an eye in the face of nuclear annihilation. Options dwindled faster than the precious seconds ticking down on the clock. Every strategy, every defense plan, crumbled under the weight of a single, horrifying truth – there were not enough interceptors!

Amidst the despair, a flicker of hope emerged. A lone scientist, eyes gleaming with a desperate resolve, leaned forward. "Colonel Rashid, there's an experimental system. Unproven, high-risk, but…" he trailed off, his words hanging heavy in the silence.

"But what?" Rashid demanded, her voice a rasp.

The scientist met her gaze, steel answering steel.

"It may be our only shot."

Colonel Rashid didn't respond. She didn't need to. Every soul in the command module understood what was at stake—multiple nuclear warheads inbound, their trajectories arcing toward the hearts of nearly two dozen American cities. Millions of lives balanced on seconds.

AEGIS cut through the silence. "Contact with enemy bogey in three… two… one. Missile destroyed."

A blinding flash ignited across the curvature of the Earth. The Chinese rocket disintegrated into incandescent debris, scattering harmlessly into space.

No one cheered.

"Calculating trajectories for Bogeys Three through Ten," AEGIS continued, emotionless.

Then, a sudden flare erupted over the western Pacific.

"To our surprise," one of the analysts whispered, "Bogey Three just detonated… over Taiwan."

Rashid snapped her head toward the tactical display. "Say that again."

Lieutenant Sharma's fingers flew across his console. His face drained of color.

"The Chinese self-detonated it."

Seconds stretched.

Then another alert. Then another. Ten minutes later, six Chinese ICBMs had detonated at space altitude.

Captain O'Neil broke the silence. "Sensors indicate extreme electromagnetic output. Comparable to a Class Five solar storm. Analysis pending. It's within the range that our surge protectors should be effective."

AEGIS' alarms screamed.

"Warning. Bogey Nine detonated at orbital altitude over Guam."

Rashid felt the words land like a physical blow.

Rashid spoke quietly. "We just crossed a line." Lieutenant Rashid didn't look away from the screen. "These are the first nuclear detonations in combat since 1945."

She turned slowly toward the payload specialist, a fit, tall man whose genial facade hid his high intellect and, perhaps, his nation's secrets. Giles was a wild card, the only crew member she'd not trained with on earth. A civilian contractor, a last-minute addition to the team.

"Specialist Giles," she said. "We're in a nuclear war. We can't let millions of Americans die. What do you recommend?"

Giles hesitated—just long enough to betray the weight of what he was about to reveal. After years of keeping secrets, it was difficult to actually reveal ultra-top-secret information.

"I brought a controller aboard," he said carefully. "For our… latest weapons systems."

Rashid's eyes narrowed. "Go on."

"I have a Partial Beam Weapon (PBW). It has never been used in combat, but proved effective in the lab and in upper atmospheric tests."

Giles worked the controller keyboard and pointed toward the viewport. Outside the viewport, new modules glinted against the black—sleek, silent, ominous.

Untested technology in the middle of a nuclear war. Rashid needed to know the weapon's capabilities. "Brief me?"

"We have twenty PBW platforms in geosynchronous orbit, covering 80% of the Earth's surface. To our enemies, they look like large communications satellites. Depending on their setting, their beams can either disrupt enemy electronics or cause radiation-like damage. The weapon is precise and nearly undetectable."

Rashid's face showed her disdain at being kept in the dark, but this wasn't the time to show emotion. It was time to act.

"Coverage?"

"Roughly 80% of the globe. I have control of our PBW network in the Pacific theater." Giles said as he held up his controller.

"And you're here to test Space Force's newest toy?" Rashid asked cynically.

A thin smile crossed Giles' face. "If the opportunity presents itself."

Rashid nodded once. "Congratulations, Specialist. It just did."

Giles lifted a finger. "There's more."

Rashid exhaled. "Do tell."

"I also operate a network of SM-4 interceptors. It's older tech, but each orbital garage holds six missiles with conventional warheads. Similar to the ship-based SM-3, but faster, more maneuverable, and not limited by atmosphere."

"How long to bring them online?"

"SM-4s—under thirty seconds. The PBW requires five minutes to charge."

Rashid stared at him. "What is the capacity of the beam weapon?"

"Effectively unlimited. Power and cooling are the only constraints."

"Accuracy?"

"Less than one foot at five thousand miles," Giles said. "It has been tested only against space targets—but it should neutralize missiles in silos, aircraft formations, armor columns, and naval groups. Anything in line of sight."

Silence. Rashid knew the government had experimented with Particle Beam Weapons as far back as the Reagan Administration, but thought it was more of a bluff than reality.

"Very well, Specialist. I'm going to have to trust your toys."

A voice cut in over comms.

"Colonel Rashid, Space Command. General Archer on Channel Two."

Rashid keyed her mic. "Rashid here."

"What's your status? Any damage?"

"One hundred percent operational. The countermeasures worked perfectly."

Archer didn't waste words. "China used older warheads to trigger a wide-area EMP. We're seeing massive losses across civilian communications and legacy satellite networks. Beta and Charlie platforms are gone."

Rashid stiffened. "And our birds?"

"Delta tactical assets were EMP-hardened. They're still flying."

"That keeps Admiral Flint in the fight," Rashid observed.

"Exactly. The Integrated Combat System is live. He's not blind."

Rashid allowed herself half a breath.

Then Archer continued, voice dropping. "Intel indicates Russia may initiate anti-satellite strikes against you. Prep escape pods as a contingency—but stay in the fight as long as you can. You're critical to homeland defense."

"Wilco," replied Rashid.

"Has Giles briefed you on our PBW and SM-4 tech?"

Goosebumps rippled across Rashid's arms as the realization that her command and this whiz kid's gadgets were likely the only protection for 200 million Americans.

"Roger," she said.

"Excellent. He's your best option. Good luck."

The channel went dead.

Rashid turned back toward the viewport—toward Earth, glowing blue and impossibly fragile. This was a nightmare.

"Specialist Giles," she ordered, voice steady. "Bring all your systems online."

The war had reached space. And it wasn't done escalating.

Taiwan, Landing Zone One

At 00:00, Jake stood outside the Command Post with Lieutenant Seacrest and Gunny Stillwell. As the three men talked, the lights in a nearby town went out. Then, power lines sparked and fell to the ground, and transformers exploded. In the clear night skies, they saw an aurora borealis effect.

Stillwell asked Seacrest, "Should we go to battle stations, sir?"

Seacrest surveyed his position, then checked his communicator. It was down. The young Lieutenant looked confident as he ordered, "Gunny, have O'Reilly run a com check. Tell Sergeant Murphy to run the line. Calm the troops and tell them to stay undercover. I expect massive missile and artillery fire, combined with air attacks, before they try to come ashore at dawn."

Stillwell replied, "Yes, sir," and jogged to the nearest position.

Jake thought young Seacrest looked like George Patton as he raised his ever-present field glasses and scanned the horizon. Seacrest's command presence and quick decision-making were rare in a junior officer. It was why he'd been placed in command of this critical landing zone. In most organizations, the best get the most desirable assignments; in the U.S. Marine Corps, they often receive the most challenging ones.

Jake walked to the Lieutenant and asked, "Did they hit us with an EMP?"

"I've never seen one, but it sure looks like it," Seacrest replied, never lowering his field glasses.

"Lieutenant, how can I help?"

Seacrest's first thought was that the war correspondent might have access to valuable intelligence. He turned to Jake and said, "Find out what's happening. The more we know, the better."

Jake fired up his CIA satellite phone. Fortunately, Director Oxley had almost all of their equipment EMP-proofed. After going outside, he dialed Asian Director Jones.

"Asian Fox, over."

"What's the situation report?"

Jones considered how much to say. Finally, he went with complete honesty, "A worldwide misinformation campaign is confusing everyone. We're experiencing unprecedented cyberattacks on U.S. infrastructure, causing everything from cellular and internet outages to financial transactions to shut down. In many parts of the U.S., people are unable to make purchases. Ten minutes ago, the Chinese detonated multiple nuclear warheads at space altitudes to create a regional EMP. Hawaii, the Philippines, Japan, South Korea, and Taiwan have been the most impacted. We're in unprecedented territory. Right now, I don't know the impact of force readiness."

"This makes December 7th look like child's play," Jake noted.

"It gets worse. We've tracked over a thousand tactical missiles, striking every major U.S. installation in Japan, Hawaii, the Philippines, and many Taiwanese bases and civilian centers. We're receiving reports from major U.S. cities that riots have broken out in the streets. Seattle, Los Angeles, San Francisco, Chicago, much of DC, and Detroit are in anarchy. Sleeper cells are attacking schools, power stations, and media outlets. President Tilden is in a coma at Walter Reid, and the cabinet refuses to give the reins to Novak. Chinese logistics indicate as many as one million PLA troops are heading your way."

Jake digested the bad news and asked, "So, China's following their plan?"

"To the letter."

"What's the damage assessment?" Jake asked.

"We've lost dozens of ships, hundreds of planes, and most of our vehicles. Casualty estimates are in the thousands. Pearl Harbor and fifty U.S. military installations in the Pacific are currently under fire. At the same time, Chinese cyberattacks have caused power, communication, and public utility outages across the U.S., Japan, the Philippines, South Korea, and Malaysia. The impact on the military and civilian supply chain will be severe," Jones observed.

"What's next?" Jake asked.

"We expect heavy bombardment by PLA missile and air assets, followed by airborne and ground attacks in your sector. Once they soften us up, they'll try to establish beachheads and capture key air and sea ports." Jones hesitated, then delivered the worst news: "Right now, an armada of over five hundred ships carrying a million troops is heading your way."

Jake processed the information, then requested, "Keep me posted. World Traveler, out."

***

Jake located Lieutenant Seacrest as he was meeting with his non-commissioned officers.

Seacrest saw Jake approach and ordered, "Dismissed."

When the other non-comms jogged back to their posts, Gunny Stillwell remained. The young lieutenant looked at Jake and asked, "Any news?"

"I confirmed a theater-wide EMP. Per Chinese doctrine, they used the EMP combined with cyber-attacks and massive missile strikes on U.S. allied bases. We also have lawlessness in many U.S. cities. U.S. Coalition losses are well into the thousands. Of greatest concern is that 500 Chinese ships and hundreds of planes are headed our way," Jake replied.

Seacrest looked at Jake calmly as he digested the information. Finally, he shared what he'd learned through military channels, "That's helpful. Early military reports indicate that Taiwanese bases on their outer islands have incurred substantial losses. Brave troops are dug in and sacrificing themselves to buy time. About 70% of Taiwan is without power. The Chinese are targeting population centers with missile strikes. If they continue this tactic, the civilian death toll could be in the hundreds of thousands."

"How is Taiwanese military readiness?" Jake asked.

"Their weapons and modern comm circuits were EMP-proofed, unlike ours. They should still work, but many of their cities are without power. So far, Taiwan has lost over three dozen fighters, twelve patrol vessels, a destroyer, and 2,100 combatants. While we can mount a stiff defense over the main island, the survival of Taiwan comes down to the speed and effectiveness of the U.S. response."

"I need to let the world know the Chinese fired a nuclear punch. Not only is it news, but it will shift world opinion against China," Jake replied.

"Go for it!" Seacrest responded, then leaned in and whispered, "When the shooting starts, I want you to stick to me like glue. Your intel is vital, and we need you to report as long as possible. The world needs to know the truth," Seacrest said. It was the closest to an expression of emotion Jake had seen from the young lieutenant.

U.S. News

"We interrupt this program to bring you an emerging story. Just minutes ago, Chinese State Television reported that the region has experienced a massive naturally occurring electromagnetic pulse. While many military sources allege the EMP was a Chinese first-strike weapon, Chinese Chief

Science Minister Sun Mateso said that today's event was caused by solar emissions," Susie Legman reported.

As computer animation showed solar emissions on the screen, Susie said, "We have Dr. Samuel Johnson from the California Institute of Technology with us. Dr. Johnson, can you explain Dr. Mateso's statements?"

The camera shifted to Dr. Johnson in his faculty office. The sixty-year-old, grey-bearded professor and world-renowned astrophysicist wore a blue Oxford shirt and a tweed blazer. Behind him were bookcases and mementos.

Susie said, "Thank you for joining us today."

The diminutive professor responded, "Glad to be with you."

"Dr. Mateso told us that an intense geomagnetic storm occurred, damaging electronics across several million square miles of the Pacific and Indian Oceans. Skeptics dismiss his statements as propaganda, and many people are asking if an EMP can occur naturally."

Dr. Johnson replied, "Susie, an EMP can be caused by natural solar emissions or a nuclear detonation."

"Can you explain how EMP destroys electronics?"

"Imagine thousands of lightning strikes projected at one time. When they strike conductive metals such as silver, gold, copper, iron, or steel, they cause significant damage."

Susie asked, "Have we ever experienced a naturally occurring EMP that caused this much damage over such a wide area?"

Johnson replied, "On September 1, 1859, the Earth was hit by a coronal mass ejection from our Sun, creating strong auroral displays in the night sky across the globe. These solar emissions caused fires in telegraph stations. The newly laid transatlantic telephone cable was also damaged. We call this the Carrington Effect. Given the world's limited access to electronics at the time, the damage was minimal. If it had happened today, it would be an existential threat."

Can you provide viewers with an example of an EMP produced by nuclear weapons?"

Johnson nodded professorially and told her, "On July 9, 1962, high above Johnston Atoll in the Pacific Ocean, the U.S. detonated a 1.4 megaton nuclear bomb, 400 kilometers above the Earth to study the effects of a high-altitude nuclear explosion on communications, satellites, and the Earth's magnetosphere."

Susie looked surprised and asked, “What happened?”

“Even though Hawaii was nearly 900 miles away, the explosion caused streetlight failures, telephone outages, alarm system malfunctions, and disruptions in the power grid while creating an artificial radiation belt that damaged or destroyed several satellites. The long-lasting artificial radiation belt persisted for months, putting space missions at risk,” Johnson noted.

“Why do you think military analysts accuse China of using an EMP weapon?” Susie asked.

Dr. Johnson said, “Because Chinese and Russian military doctrine designates EMP as a first-strike weapon and solar activity at the time was nowhere near the magnitude needed to produce this widespread damage.”

“What is the advantage of using an EMP in a first strike?” Susie pursued.

“An EMP strike renders unprotected planes, tanks, trucks, ships, radar, drones, and missiles inoperable.”

“How does EMP affect our troops?”

“Human tissue is unaffected, so troops would live, but without modern weapons, they’d be limited to kinetic weapons, be forced to live off the land, and have to walk rather than ride. It’s a logistical nightmare.”

“How would we confirm a Chinese nuclear detonation caused this EMP?”

“When a nuclear device is detonated at space altitudes, it leaves particles in the atmosphere for weeks. We also know that NASA and military equipment tracked Chinese missiles into the blast areas and registered the event. We have undisputable evidence that this EMP was an act of war.”

Susie asked, “What is the strategic fallout likely to be?”

Dr. Johnson responded, “A 2013 joint venture from researchers at Lloyd's of London and Atmospheric and Environmental Research in the U.S. used data from the Carrington Event to estimate the cost of a similar event in the U.S. to be 3.02 trillion dollars. Government studies indicate that a nationwide EMP would kill up to ninety percent of our population within a year. I expect similar effects in the region, unless they receive massive aid.”

Susie couldn't let that one pass: "How could a weapon that destroys electronics but doesn't harm people kill so many people?"

Dr. Johnson was one of many scientists who had warned U.S. officials about the dangers of EMP. This was his opportunity to get his concerns before U.S. NEWS's 100 million viewers. He said, "A widespread EMP shuts down all commerce, including food, drugs, transportation, medical care, and utilities. If you have a heart attack, no help will come. Your TV and cell phone won't work. Your car won't start. Unless you stored food and EMP-proofed a radio, you'll be hungry and cut off. At thirty days, deaths from starvation begin. Civil unrest and murders over resources become brutal in urban areas. When people are malnourished, disease runs rampant. Even an infected cut could become fatal. Survival becomes primeval as law enforcement and the military are out of commission, and people kill to survive."

The producer whispered in her earbud, "Susie, cut to breaking news!"

"Thank you for your appearance, Dr. Johnson; you've given us all a lot to consider."

Susie looked at the teleprompter and said, "We have reports of missile attacks on Taiwan and U.S. bases in the region."

The producer played images of smoldering cities and bases as Susie continued, "Taiwanese news outlets are reporting that Chinese troops are conducting amphibious attacks on Taiping Island, Taiwan's most far-flung outpost in the South China Sea."

The producer played images of over a hundred commercial and Chinese naval vessels moving toward the tiny island, as well as dozens of landing craft moving ashore. Chinese bombers could be seen bombing Taiwanese bases as hundreds of PLA missiles struck buildings.

Susie said, "We also have reports from tiny Pratas Island, 170 nautical miles southeast of Hong Kong, and Penghu in the Taiwan Strait coming under fire. Although our incoming information has not been confirmed, we've received reports that the Chinese have captured the Kinmen and Matsu islands. Casualties are high on both sides."

The producer included B-roll images of shore batteries and Taiwanese ships from the previous week.

The producer's voice sounded harrowed as he said, "We've got Jake online. Cut to Jake in three, two, one,"

"We now go to Jake Hendel, who is embedded with the Taiwanese Army. Jake, what are you seeing?"

The camera showed a haggard Jake Hendel, wearing body armor. His weapon was slung over his shoulder. From beneath his Kevlar helmet, Jake's unshaven face and the blood stains on his clothing horrified his audience. Susie gasped at his appearance.

Jake's penetrating hazel eyes pierced the camera as he said, "Susie, we endured missile attacks during the night. As you can see, the People's Liberation Army destroyed this artillery position and dozens of others along this section of beach, indicating the Chinese are intent on coming ashore."

Hank panned his camera across the beaches and hills above, showing the audience several smoldering positions and two mangled canons. Two stretcher bearers were seen carrying a wounded U.S. Marine in the predawn light. Then an explosion rocked Jake!

The screen flickered to black for a moment, then jumped to static. For the first time in her career, Susie Legman was at a loss for words. The network studio fell into a stunned silence. Producers froze behind the glass.

"We have dead air! Cut to anchor two," the director barked.

But Susie didn't move.

"Jake, come in. Jake… can you hear me? Please answer!" she whispered again, unaware that her mic was still hot.

Silence.

Finally, the backup anchor's voice filled the void. "We are experiencing technical difficulties. We'll return to our coverage as soon as possible."

The screen split—one half with a live Pentagon briefing already underway, the other stuck on a frozen frame of Jake running toward a shelter, rifle slung over his shoulder, the flash of incoming fire just beginning to glow behind him.

Off air, Susie tore off her earpiece. "Did we lose him?" she asked, voice trembling.

Her producer, Dean Meston, stood behind the control desk, jaw tight. "I don't know. The satellite feed went out. The last ping came from east of Taichung. Could be a direct hit, or the uplink was fried by residual EMP."

Susie closed her eyes and clenched her fists. Jake Hendel wasn't just a field reporter. He was her Jake. Her fiancée. And now, he was gone—or worse, left to face a wave of Chinese Marines with nothing but grit and a borrowed rifle.

Landing Zone One

Smoke and debris filled the air like a choking fog. Concrete shattered. Sandbags ignited. Somewhere above, Chinese jets thundered past in a second wave.

Jake lay flat on his back, ears ringing. Blood trickled from a cut above his brow, and dust coated his clothes like war paint. His flak vest had taken the brunt of the blast.

"Jake! Jake, you okay?" Hank's voice cut through the mental fog.

Jake coughed hard, pushed up on one elbow, and nodded. "I'm good," he rasped with more assurance than he felt. "Gear?"

Hank held up the shattered remains of his shoulder rig and camera.

Jake grinned, dazed but defiant. "You got your Emmy moment."

"Maybe," Hank muttered, helping Jake up. Around them, Marines scrambled from cover, assessing damage and casualties.

Gunnery Sergeant Stillwell stormed out of a nearby shelter, his face a mask of fury. "Next time, get your asses underground before the sky falls! You want to die with a headline or live to report the war?"

Jake looked sheepish, but remained silent.

Stillwell turned, barking orders. "Check for survivors! Watch for follow-up strikes!"

As Jake adjusted his vest and checked his rifle, a radio crackled nearby. A young corporal passed a headset to Stillwell.

"It's for you," Stillwell said, holding out the radio handset to Jake. Press Corps. Some dame named Susie."

Jake grabbed it. "Susie?"

A sob of relief came through the line. "You're alive. Thank God!"

Jake exhaled slowly. "I'm fine."

"You went dark. I thought—Jake, I thought I lost you," Susie said with a mixture of fear and gratitude.

"Sorry for the scare. We lost the camera. Tell the technicians that I'll try to get a link on my SAT phone and call in," he said softly, then glanced around at the battered Marines rising from the rubble. "We're still in the fight."

Pacific Ocean

Vice Admiral Connor, a tall, austere ring-knocker from Annapolis, had been a roommate of Admiral Flint and a groomsman at his wedding. The two men trusted one another implicitly.

Connor glanced at the battle map projected above the command table of the USS Nimitz. It depicted the jagged maw of the East China Sea, a familiar theater of tension. But this time, the red blips representing potential threats were unlike anything he'd encountered. Hypersonic missiles, their trajectories marked in ominous crimson streaks, arced towards a designated point – the heart of Carrier Strike Group Three, led by the indomitable USS Nimitz.

Captain Ramirez was an Annapolis graduate and one of the first female naval aviators to fly the F-18 Super Hornet. She served twelve years in a fleet squadron, then was promoted to head of flight operations. Her impeccable flight record and penchant for mentoring junior aviators led to her promotion to Executive Officer (XO) and, finally, to Commanding Officer (CO) of a flying squadron. After completing Nuclear Power and Surface Warfare Training, Ramirez was given command of an amphibious assault ship. From there, Flint and Connor selected her to serve as XO and, eventually, as Captain of the USS Nimitz.

While some criticized her for being promoted due to DEI politics, Connor knew she'd earned her stripes and was glad to have her in command of his carrier. The fact that Ramirez had flown twice as many combat sorties as the next-most-experienced pilot on the Nimitz and had earned their respect gave her confidence that she was prepared for what lay ahead.

"ETA to impact, two minutes," Captain Ramirez announced, her voice taut with suppressed urgency. The bridge crackled with nervous energy, a stark contrast to the steely calm of the Vice Admiral.

"Deploy Missile Defenses," he ordered, his voice resonating with quiet authority.

A collective breath hitched in the room as a faint hum filled the air. A previously unseen grid materialized on the monitor, pulsing with an ethereal blue light around the carrier group. This was the Guardian System, the U.S. Navy's most classified project – a layered network of high-powered lasers, electromagnetic pulse generators, and cutting-edge radar for early detection and missile negation.

A wave of tension washed over the bridge as the first hypersonic missile breached the atmosphere. Its fiery contrail streaked across the sky, a harbinger of destruction. But just as it entered the Guardian's perimeter, a precisely targeted laser beam struck the missile, vaporizing it into a cloud of incandescent debris.

Ramirez quickly quelled cheers on the bridge when she announced, "Three missiles incoming, sir!"

The Guardian System whirred back to life, three more laser beams lancing out with pinpoint accuracy. Two PLA missiles met the same fiery end as the first. The third, however, swerved erratically, its trajectory thrown off by a well-timed electromagnetic pulse. With its guidance system and targeting computer fried, it careened wildly before detonating harmlessly in the ocean.

Relief washed over the bridge, tinged with a sliver of unease. The hypersonic barrage had been neutralized, but the threat was far from over.

"Sir, we have detected one hundred missiles incoming!" Ramirez said, wondering how many fire-breathing threats her system could counter.

"Activate point defense systems," Connor commanded. A hail of counter-missiles erupted from the decks of the surrounding destroyers, forming a metallic storm against the incoming threat. Soon, a dazzling display of defensive fireworks exploded in the sky. While a few missiles slipped through the net, their warheads were detonated by precisely timed bursts from the Guardian System's high-powered lasers.

The battle raged for a breathless ten minutes as missiles rained down, met by a relentless counteroffensive of lasers, countermissiles, and electronic warfare measures.

"Status report," Connor ordered.

Reports trickled in – minor damage to a destroyer from a near miss, but no casualties. The USS Nimitz remained unscathed, a testament to the effectiveness of the Guardian System.

"Two of our Hornets engaged a flight of Chinese fighters," Rameriz added.

"Keep a watchful eye; we're not out of the woods yet," Admiral Connor urged.

***

Ten minutes later, Captain Ramirez slammed her fist against the bridge console, the dull thud barely registering over the cacophony of alarms. The USS Nimitz, the pride of the Pacific fleet, had gone dark. Gone were the familiar whir of turbines and the rhythmic hum of electronics. A deathly silence hung heavy in the air, broken only by the frantic shouts of sailors.

"All systems down!" the comms officer yelled, his voice strained. "Navigation, communications, weapons systems – everything's fried!"

As he watched Ramirez and the crew's reaction, Connor's ordinarily stoic face was etched with confusion and dawning horror, "What the hell is going on?"

The answer came in a crackle of static from the emergency radio band. A frantic voice, barely recognizable over the channel, sputtered, "Mayday, …everything's down…Chinese fighters…attacking…we've been spoofed… navigation system compromised…under attack…mayday..mayday..we're taking fire…"

The message from the Roosevelt Carrier explained the sudden crippling of all electronic systems. It was a silent, devastating first strike, a technological sucker punch.

On the battle systems, the familiar icons representing allied ships – the sleek Japanese destroyers, the hulking Australian cruiser – flickered and faded, replaced by a blank screen. Connor could only imagine the chaos on those vessels, the crews fighting blindly against an unseen enemy.

A klaxon blared, red emergency lights bathing the bridge in an ominous glow. "Incoming!" the Yeoman shrieked, pointing at a blip on the backup satellite system.

A Chinese destroyer, its sleek, menacing silhouette emerging from the electronic fog. The ship looked like a predatory shark circling a crippled fish.

Connor's voice held a steely resolve. "Man, the backup guns! Ramirez, take evasive maneuvers! Launch fighters and sub hunters."

Ramirez and her crew shifted to backup systems, a relic of a bygone era. With a groan of protest, the mighty Nimitz strained to respond, turning sluggishly to avoid the incoming missile as her remaining countermeasures amped up.

On the radar screen, the Pacific suddenly teemed with activity. Chinese warships and submarines, cloaked in the electronic silence, materialized like phantoms. Their sleek forms targeted not only the American fleet but also the scattered ships of their allies. The Chinese had anticipated the chaos an EMP would cause and had their boats prepositioned.

Connor could see the fear flickering in the crew's eyes. But noted something more: a steely determination. They wouldn't go down without a fight. The roar of the backup guns filled the air, spitting defiance into the darkness.

Ramirez watched the scene unfold with grim acceptance. The Pacific, once a symbol of Allied dominance, now echoed with the clash of steel and fire. The battle for supremacy in the region had begun, plunging the Americans into a technological dark age, where they were outnumbered and fighting for survival. The PLA had changed the game!

Without warning, a Chinese hypersonic missile released five independent warheads that began a rapid descent on the USS Nimitz. Seconds later, Ramirez and the crew were thrown to the floor as the weapons impacted the carrier's deck.

Alarms beckoned firefighters to their stations as fully fueled aircraft and munitions detonated on the flight deck, generating a burning inferno whose tenacles reached the lower decks, where planes, fuel, and ammo lockers became a ticking time bomb. On the flight deck, shrapnel from dozens of explosions killed most of the deck crew while fingers of burning fuel crept into the lower decks.

Minutes later, ammunition lockers and aviation fuel tanks exploded. At the same time, three torpedoes struck below the waterline, opening the hull as the cold water pulled the mighty carrier down to her eternal rest.

Seven officers and ninety-eight sailors made it into the water before the ship slipped into the depths of the Pacific, where 5,000 of their mates would forever be interned. At home, the news of her loss dominated military channels as the world's greatest military was humbled.

General Drummond and his cronies on the Joint Chiefs of Staff met to discuss how best to spin the loss of an entire carrier group to the Press. In the end, they decided to blame Admiral Flint's lack of preparation and his G-2's intelligence failure.

Chapter 8

Hawaiian KHON-2 news reporter Tua Malaka stood atop the observation tower at Kadena Air Base, the Keystone of the Pacific. Kadena was home to the U.S. Air Force's largest combat air wing. In addition to the sizable 18th Air Wing, the United States Army, Marine Corps, Navy, and 40 additional tenant units were based there.

With Jake Hendel trapped in Taiwan and all commercial flights canceled into the region, U.S. News had cut a deal with Hawaii's KHON-2 News to get a reporter 'into the zone' the day before the war started.

Eager to make international news, Tua volunteered and flew to Okinawa via a private jet. The assignment was so rushed that he only had time to pack a quick bag and head to the airport. As fate would have it, Tua arrived just hours before a massive Chinese missile barrage struck. Without time to change from his travel clothes, the twenty-eight-year-old Hawaiian native stood wearing a nylon fishing shirt, jeans, and black running shoes.

His cameraman held his hand in the shape of eyeglasses, letting Tua know he needed to remove his sunglasses. Tua complied, then looked eagerly into the camera. This was the break his career needed.

"Three, two, one, live," said the cameraman.

"Today, China launched massive unprovoked missile attacks on U.S. Allied bases in the region. Designating Chinese aggression as an existential threat, Japanese F-35s and warships launched retaliatory strikes. Behind me, you can see the results of three separate Chinese attacks on Kadena Air Base here in Okinawa," Tau said stoically as he gestured with his free hand.

The camera focused on several burned-out vehicles, runway craters, and smoldering buildings. The scene eerily reminded viewers of Pearl Harbor after the surprise Japanese attack on December 7, 1941.

"China's navy and hundreds of transport ships have created a vast armada pointed at Taiwan. With the invasion imminent and China opening hostilities against U.S. coalition forces, Admiral Flint requested broader authority to conduct strikes against Chinese bases. Flint's request was denied by the Secretary of Defense, stating, *'The president wants better intel before committing U.S. forces to a conflict that could quickly escalate into nuclear war.'* That decision limits our commanders to defensive operations in an age where the Chinese missile forces can pick us off from thousands of miles away."

The studio played a video of Chinese missiles, fighters, and landers in the background as Tau continued, "The recent loss of the *Nimitz* carrier group has many wondering if the U.S. coalition can hold the line in the Pacific."

The camera cut to a tight shot of Air Force General Robert Taylor, the Pacific Base Commander. His uniform was crisp, but the fatigue lines etched into his face told another story.

"Thanks for joining us, General."

Taylor gave a curt nod. He disliked these press appearances, but he knew public sentiment could shift Washington faster than military dispatches ever could. If the American people pushed hard enough, maybe President Tilden would finally let his commanders take off the gloves.

"How did hostilities start?" Tua asked.

Taylor exhaled through his nose, jaw muscles tightening. China launched a series of coordinated missile attacks on our land and sea assets and detonated multiple nuclear warheads at space altitudes. The resulting EMP crippled our satellites and electronics, rendering many of our aircraft, vehicles, and communications systems useless. In allied host nations, power grids collapsed. Their militaries were caught blind and deaf before the first Chinese bomber crossed the strait."

The anchor's expression darkened. "What about China's numerical superiority?"

"They outnumber us in every category," Taylor said bluntly. "Ships, planes, tanks, artillery. They've built for mass. Our edge is in technology, training, and combat experience—but make no mistake, the numbers matter."

"And our losses?"

Taylor's eyes, usually a hard steel gray, betrayed a flicker of grief. "We've confirmed 4,800 U.S. and 5,280 Japanese personnel killed. Roughly ninety percent of our planes, trucks, tanks, and missile units are destroyed or disabled."

The anchor swallowed hard. "And naval losses?"

Taylor's voice dropped half a register. "The USS *Nimitz* went down to a Chinese missile swarm. With her, eighty-eight aircraft, 8,500 personnel, and six support ships. The Pacific hasn't seen a loss like that since Midway. Only this time, we were on the wrong side of the ledger."

For a moment, the studio was silent but for the faint hum of the lights.

"What has been the U.S. response so far?" Tua asked, regaining composure.

Taylor stiffened. "Our orders are clear: defensive fire only. We're holding back while the Chinese unleash hypersonics, cyber weapons, and long-range salvos. At Kadena, our missile defenses intercepted eighty-six of a hundred incoming warheads. Our F-35s splashed six of their new H-2 stealth bombers—after they'd already delivered their payloads. We've sunk six destroyers and a submarine. But under the current rules of engagement, we cannot strike their missile launchers, bases, or staging areas preemptively. We wait for them to fire first."

The words hung in the air like the echo of a gunshot.

Tua leaned in. "That's suicide in modern war. General, people are wondering if, with so many losses and the PLA's sheer mass, can China take Taiwan?"

Taylor didn't blink. "It's possible—but far from certain. Amphibious invasions of this scale are unforgiving. They need hundreds of ships to carry men, armor, and fuel across the strait. They need to seize airfields, suppress defenses, and land armor through mined beaches and kill zones. Taiwanese defenders are dug in behind every hillside and in every city street. They'll make Beijing pay for every meter. So, no—it's not a given."

Pacific Command

Newsome put up several slides and imagery detailing the widespread Chinese assault on Coalition Forces and said, "The sheer number of Chinese missiles overwhelmed our defenses and were much more accurate than previously thought. In Okinawa, over seventy percent of buildings and most of our aircraft have been destroyed. Our combined death toll has risen to 15,000 Americans. Currently, elements of the U.S. Army Corps of Engineers and Air Force Contingency Air Command are working to reopen air operations at ten of our larger bases. We're also using highways to provide auxiliary airfields."

Flint's eyes revealed the anger burning within.

Newsome continued, “Your orders that all ships move in erratic patterns helped send the older Chinese missiles off course and saved many boats and crews. While our electronic countermeasures and fleet missile defenses performed as designed, China flooded the zone, cutting down about half our cruisers and two dozen destroyers.”

Flint asked, “What impact did the EMP have on Fleet defense?”

“Sir, it took out about half our targeting radars and other vulnerable components. Then we experienced issues with systems affected by the cyberattack. It also appears that the Chinese deployed a cloaking system that hid their missiles until they were on top of us. Sea-based missile launches, most likely from Chinese Type 094 Jin-class submarines that were prepositioned, participated in the sinking of the Nimitz and two dozen other ships.”

Flint ordered his XO, “Get a call with Space Command. We need more Overwatch. What’s their next move?”

Newsome continued, “The PLA will continue to use DF 27 and DF 26 missiles to destroy our fleet and keep us at bay while they capture ports, airfields, and landing zones on Taiwan. I believe they will continue to flood the zone with massive numbers of missiles while their cyber forces play havoc on our electronics.”

An aide brought Flint an urgent message. Flint read it and said, “We just lost the USS Frank E Peterson and USS Hopper. We can’t keep losing critical ships.”

By the end of the first day, China had expended one-quarter of its 4,000 long and mid-range missiles, causing devastation to coalition bases in Japan, South Korea, and the Philippines. While the opening strikes weren’t a knockout punch, Flint knew the success of the PLA’s opening salvo would cause their generals to push the attack on Taiwan before the U.S. could regroup. He had to find a way to stop the bleeding and counterattack!

Taiwan, Landing Zone One

Hank picked up a backup camera while a local TV Station’s electronics technician repaired his unit.

Jake and Hank heard the air raid warning and scrambled into a slit trench. Hearing the incoming rockets, Hank poked his camera above the soil and pressed the start button. Jake and Hank watched the scene unfold on the digital display as flaming streaks emerged from the ocean. While many detonated in the sand, others struck vehicles, bunkers, and critical infrastructure.

The barrage was short-lived, and Jake poked his head above the ground to gain a better view. As he scanned the scene with his compact binoculars, he saw that many pillboxes, mortar trenches, and artillery positions had been hit. The accuracy of the Chinese fire made him wonder if there was a traitor among them.

"You, okay?" shouted Gunny Stillwell.

"Yes, how are your men?" Jake asked as he stood.

"The bastards took out six machine gun positions, two mortar platoons, and an artillery emplacement," Stillwell barked as he jogged off to check his remaining men.

Hank nodded and checked his equipment as Jake selected a backdrop for his report.

"Three, two, one, Mark!" Hank said.

Jake stood ten feet from Hank, near an air raid trench.

In the background, smoke rose from dozens of positions along the cratered beach as stretcher-bearers carried away the wounded. Since there was no morgue, the fallen heroes were tagged and placed in body bags. Should evacuation prove impossible, a mass grave would be dug.

Jake looked at Hank as he lifted his hand in salute to the dead American, British, Taiwanese, Australian, and South Korean troops.

***

Seacrest considered how best to defend his position with his dwindling forces. Fortunately, he'd received one hundred additional Taiwanese militia, men and women modestly trained to fire weapons, differentiate between allied and enemy uniforms, render first aid, and accept orders. While the lieutenant admired their patriotism, he wondered if he could count on them once the Chinese Regulars stormed the beaches.

"Sir!" Gunny Stillwell shouted as he and Jake walked into the Command Post.

Seacrest put down his map when Stillwell arrived with a dozen Taiwanese militia. Each combatant carried a modern sniper rifle and wore a sidearm. The men and women looked fit, wore their uniforms properly, and their faces bore out their determination.

Stillwell complied with standard orders that barred him from saluting an officer in combat. A habit that had gotten hundreds of American officers shot by enemy snipers in prior wars.

"Sir, we have been assigned a platoon of militia snipers," Stillwell reported.

Seacrest walked down the line as if inspecting a platoon. Not only was he curious, but it would reinforce his leadership. After reviewing the line, he asked, "Do any of you speak English?"

The first man in line stepped forward, stomping his heels and responding, "I'm Sergeant Matseu. Here are my orders."

Seacrest looked Matseu in the eye as he accepted the paperwork. The orders were from Unified Command.

Seacrest extended his hand, "May I see your weapon?"

Matseu unslung his weapon from his shoulder, held it before him, and opened the bolt of his T-93 rifle."

Stillwell and Seacrest glanced at each other. Their unvoiced reaction was that Matseu was the 'real thing.'

Seacrest took the rifle, turned to the side, and lifted it to see into the chamber. He then inserted his pinky into the breach and inspected it for dirt. The weapon was clean. Seacrest pointed the muzzle in a safe direction and closed the bolt. After letting off the safety, he slowly squeezed the trigger. Plink.

Seacrest looked at Stillwell and nodded his approval.

"Sergeant Matseu, your weapon is immaculate, and your trigger has been set at what, a pound and a half?" Seacrest asked.

"Yes, sir. We upgrade all our triggers and followers and bed the actions for maximum accuracy. All my troops shoot Expert," Matseu said proudly.

Seacrest stared at Matseu, then back at the line of Taiwanese militia. Finally, he extended his hand and said, "Sergeant, I'm glad to have you."

Sergeant Matseu almost saluted Seacrest, then stopped himself, "Sorry, sir, old habit. It won't happen again."

"No harm, no foul, Sergeant. Gunny Stillwell will show you your sleeping quarters and ensure you get fed. Once you're squared away, come see me. I'd like your thoughts on how best to deploy your team," Seacrest said.

"Yes, sir," Matseu replied.

Stillwell nodded and barked, "Platoon, attention. Follow me,"

After the snipers departed, Jake asked Seacrest, "What do you think of them?"

Seacrest replied, "As badly as I need personnel, I'd take a deer-hunting grandma with her thirty, thirty right now."

Coastal Command Headquarters, Taiwan

Seacrest attended a meeting of the commanders in his sector. A U.S. Marine Major, Tomson, and a Taiwanese Major, Seng, led the briefing.

Major Tomson stood before a large map and used a pointer as he began his briefing, "Many of Taiwan's outer islands bristle with missiles, rockets, and artillery guns. These islands will try to inflict as much havoc as possible to slow the PLA's advance."

Seven of the twenty officers present were U.S. Marines who had just arrived. For their benefit, Tomson said, "The main island is 394 kilometers long and 144 kilometers across at its widest point. It has 258 peaks over 3,000 meters in elevation. The tallest, Yushan, is just under 4,000 meters. The coastal terrain consists of only 14 small invasion beaches bordered by cliffs. Structures of steel-reinforced concrete blanket all coastal positions and the surrounding valleys and are honeycombed with tunnels and bunker systems."

Tomson looked to his colleague to continue.

Major Seng said, "All our beachheads are garrisoned. We have mobilized a counter-invasion force, comprising our standing military of 86,000 regulars, our reserve force of 260,000, and a growing number of Coalition forces. We are activating over two million young Taiwanese men in the military's reserve system, along with police officers, firefighters, airline personnel, bulldozer operators, construction workers, truck drivers, bus drivers, fishing boat crews, doctors, and nurses. Anyone with wartime skills will be pressed into service, bringing our numbers to 1.2 million."

Major Tomson picked up the briefing on cue: "Admiral Flint has dispatched five thousand additional Marines and two assault ships bristling with attack assets to supplement Taiwanese forces."

Tomson and Seng turned to a regional map.

Using a laser pointer, Seng said, "We're engaged in heavy air-to-air operations against Chinese forces at our offshore islands, Kinmen and Matsu. Nearly 200 U.S. Coalition bases have been struck by Chinese missiles. We believe the PLA will use long-range missiles to attack Guam and targets closer to the United States while holding their intercontinental hypersonic missiles in reserve."

Tomson looked at the audience and said, "Chinese cyber-attacks combined with terrorist attacks have left the United States scrambling. Over 3,500 municipal water and sewer systems are offline, gas pipelines are shut down, and fifty percent of the U.S. is without power. While these attacks will negatively impact resupply and reinforcement, they have not shut down the country's missile defense systems."

Seacrest raised his hand. Tomson nodded for him to proceed. "Sir, do we have an estimate of our remaining forces?"

Major Tomson replied, "No."

Seacrest nodded. Thank you.

"Let's move to zone defense," said Tomson, wanting to shift the dialogue to something they could control.

Major Seng said, "Due to high cliffs on the Eastern side of the main island, we expect the Chinese to focus their attacks on ports and beaches on our Western side. Landing Zone One will be a PLA priority since it is closest to Taipei. We also expect China's huge Airborne force to assault major airports like they did at Matsu Begianour, Matsu Negan, and the Kenman islands."

Major Tomson said, "Since force preservation is critical, we will use the turtle and shell approach to move troops to safety during missile and artillery attacks, then move them out to meet invaders."

Tomson used a balled fist to illustrate the turtle in its shell, then an open hand to portray men moving to their battle stations.

"We've installed additional anti-aircraft and anti-ship missiles and are prepared to lay waste to Chinese forces once they cross the fifty-kilometer line. We've also deployed most of our sea mines. Given China's numerical advantage in aircraft and ships, we will keep our air and naval forces close to home, where they can be most effective. Are there any questions?" Seng asked.

Seacrest looked around. He wanted to know if Tilden's standing orders had changed, but thought it best not to ask. He was also anxious to return to his men and didn't want to extend the briefing.

"That covers it for today. Good luck and good hunting!" Major Tomson said.

Pacific Command, Hawaii

Admiral Flint asked, "Since Chinese ships were used in the opening salvo, I'm ordering our submarines to sink all Chinese ships within a two-hundred-fifty-mile radius of Taiwan. What boats do we have in the vicinity?"

Vice Admiral Kirkland replied, "We have twenty submarines within 500 miles of Taiwan and five more en route."

Admiral Flint did the math, "That's not nearly enough."

Kirkland replied, "Not to win, but enough to send a message to President Jin that the U.S. isn't backing down. If we can sink their missile boats, submarines, and carriers, it will go a long way toward shifting the balance of power in our favor."

Flint smiled and said, "Agreed. With two carriers, dozens of cruisers, and even more destroyers out of the fight, I can't afford to bring more ships into Chinese missile range. For now, our subs will have to be the point of the spear, and Coalition forces in country will have to hold out until we can gain air and sea superiority."

Kirkland saluted and left the room.

Flint noticed Newsome's concerned look and motioned for him to speak.

Newsome said, "Sir, even if we sink their ships, their land-based missiles can still destroy targets up to 5,500 km away. Under the current rules of engagement, over half their forces are beyond our reach. If we're to have any chance at all, we have to take out their inland missiles, air and naval bases, and command and control."

"While I plan to follow orders, like Guderian, I'm interpreting my orders to our advantage," Flint offered, hoping Novak would soon become Commander in Chief.

Every man in the room piled on with a stream of positive comments.

Flint ordered, "Draw up plans to destroy their missile and nuclear forces, sink their ships, and take down their air forces."

Landing Zone One

Seacrest looked over the jagged ridgeline again, the faint glint of morning light revealing where the surf had carved out low spots in the beachhead. Every inch of terrain mattered now.

"Sergeant, I'm placing you under direct orders: hold this cliff line as long as possible. Drive a high body count. Then, be ready to delay their advance so we can move our forces inland. Can you do that?"

Matseu's dark eyes showed no fear, only the intensity of a soldier who understood the stakes. "Wilco, sir."

"Good," Seacrest said. "Target their commanders first, their radio men second, and then their heavy guns, and it'll throw their assault into chaos."

"Yes, sir."

Seacrest placed a hand on the young NCO's shoulder. "You're going to write your chapter in history today, Sergeant. The kind of chapter that defines a nation's future."

As Seacrest walked away, the first rumble of distant artillery echoed from the horizon. Matseu turned back to his troops, who crouched behind rocks and sandbags, rifles aimed at the enemy approach lanes. A few of them were drawing diagrams of the beach battlefield and ranging distance, as their training had taught them. Seacrest nodded his approval as a stiff breeze carried the scent of the sea—and the smell of war across his face.

Secret Call with the Order

Through a back-channel satellite network that paralleled CIA and NSA technology, Oxley had built a secret channel for the men of the Order. At the time he funded the project, he wondered if the $250 million he'd spent would have been better spent on other projects. Now, he was grateful he'd done it.

"How long can Taiwan hold out?" Oxley pressed.

Admiral Flint remained stoic, saying, "Under the current rules of engagement, two weeks."

Oxley asked, "Why only two weeks?"

"Our ammo lockers are nearly empty. Without missiles and torpedoes, our naval forces cannot gain control of the sea lanes around Taiwan. Without more fighters and anti-aircraft missiles, we can't achieve air superiority. They have a short supply chain; ours is elongated. This means China can move enough troops and heavy equipment onto Taiwan to overwhelm U.S. Coalition Forces. Then, there's the loss of vehicles. We were already grossly outnumbered in tanks, planes, artillery, and ships before the EMP. Now we've lost most of what we had."

Flint's haunting words sent a chill through the attendees. How could the world's most powerful military be losing so badly?

"What's the solution?" Oxley asked.

"I've requested all available planes, subs, and autonomous weapons systems from the U.S. The Air Force is deploying an additional 2,500 planes and helicopters. They can operate from repaired and improvised airfields within twelve hours. I'm using my subs to full advantage. At this point, defending Taiwan comes down to technology and tactics. I have to use autonomous weapons and space tech to kill on a scale we've never seen before, and be allowed to strike Chinese air, naval, and missile bases inland. While our autonomous weapons have never been tested in battle, they're our best option at the moment," Flint said stoically.

Oxley considered Flint's words. The Admiral was doing everything he could without directly violating his orders, but he was fighting with one arm tied behind his back.

"Once Tilden leaves office, Vice President Novak will shift strategy. So far, Peddlergate has led to the removal of 250 Tilden-aligned New World Order congressmen and senators through resignations, defections, and removal procedures. The operation has shifted the balance of power in the Senate to a 60/40, Republican and Independent mix as Governors have appointed replacements. The House makeup is 301/435, comprising conservative and moderate Republicans and Independents. This means we have a real chance of restoring a constitutional government in the near term," Oxley offered.

A long, uncomfortable silence ensued as each man wrestled with what was coming. Oxley's Christian values and patriotism fought for control as he considered the next steps. This was the most critical decision of his life, a mirror moment that would forever determine the course of nations.

Oxley's shoulders rose as a new sense of purpose filled him. He looked directly into the camera and said, "Gentlemen, God has placed us at this crossroads in human history. The next few months will determine whether or not the New World Order emerges with China at its center. While none of us can say whether we are in the 'end times,' I assure you that our action or inaction now will determine the future of mankind. Either we save the United States, or the Axis of Evil takes control."

Admiral Flint said, "The time has come."

"We'll reconvene at 19:00 tomorrow. Use this time to plan for your family's safety. As of now, many will label us enemies of the state. Like our forefathers, Jefferson, Washington, and Franklin, we are not traitors; we are patriots who must overthrow tyranny at home and abroad!" Oxley observed.

U.S. News

Susie Legman said, "Just in from White House Press Secretary Amanda Pigeon. President Tilden has been moved to the Medical ICU at Walter Reid. We now go to White House Correspondent Ned Divine. Ned, what can you tell us?"

Ned stood before Walter Reed Medical Center as healthcare workers passed behind him, "Susie, sources inside the hospital tell me that the President was placed on a ventilator. I've also learned that his family is returning from their trip to China."

"Has anyone offered a prognosis?"

"No, the hospital staff have been reminded of their HIPAA requirements, and Pigeon and the White House staff have purposely kept the seriousness of the President's condition hidden," Ned replied.

"Does this mean that Vice President Novak is in charge?"

Ned looked concerned and said, "Power is transferred to the Vice President immediately upon the death of the President. However, while the President is alive and conscious, the President must relinquish power, or no transfer occurs. Since Tilden failed to relinquish control, VP Novak sent a declaration to the House and Senate Leaders requesting the transfer."

"So, who's running the country?"

"The country is run by thousands of bureaucrats who only look to the President on strategic or emergent issues. However, many are concerned that White House staffers may be using the autopen to approve executive orders, pardons, and similar documents without the President's involvement. If this is the case, it's fraud on steroids," Divine observed.

Susie added, "Indeed. Many conservatives are also outraged at the recent gun confiscations by Police Chiefs in major U.S. cities under E.O.

666. Just this morning, the National Sheriff's Association said that E.O. 666 violated the Second Amendment and refused to implement it."

Ned nodded on camera. "It has become a dichotomy of constitutional interpretation in which those outside major cities have rights, and those inside don't. Of greater concern is that some specially trained military units are going house to house, confiscating firearms. They're using tactics like they used in Afghanistan and Iraq against U.S. citizens, kicking doors in and sweeping houses."

"Thank you, Ned. Please keep us posted."

Landing Zone One, Taiwan

Seacrest walked into the command post. As always, the lieutenant looked as if he were prepared for a close-order drill. His uniform was neat, gear immaculate, bearing that of a true leader.

"What's the latest intel?" Gunnery Sergeant Stillwell asked.

"The bottom line is that we've got to hold out at least two weeks to give Admiral Flint time to bring help. Right now, we're sinking their ships and shooting down their planes in high numbers, but eventually, their numerical superiority will win out. We're fighting a delaying action to buy time."

Stillwell grunted, granite in his voice, "Then we stack 'em up like cordwood."

Seacrest smiled. He always found Stillwell's grit reassuring. If he ordered a water gun attack on hell, Stillwell would lead the charge. He wished he had another 100 men like him.

Seacrest surveyed his beach positions and said, "We've put out all our antipersonnel and antitank mines, the propane canisters are in place, and all our concertina wire has been deployed; what else can we do?"

"I found some explosives in the cave," Stillwell noted with the calm of a thirty-year veteran, "We've got plenty of scrap metal from burned-out vehicles, so I have our demolition team turning them into improvised explosives. We learned a few things from Al Qaeda in Afghanistan. We'll make 'em pay for every inch of ground."

Seacrest loved the Gunny's ingenuity.

***

Just before sunrise, Jake popped into the Command Post. Seacrest was taking a call from Command. When the call ended, he motioned for Jake to come outside.

When the two men were alone, the Lieutenant said, "Paratroopers from the PLA's 15th Airborne Corps just overran Hsinchu Airport. They're landing cargo planes brimming with men and vehicles. A captured Chinese pilot told us they plan to capture Taipei, Taichung, Tainan, Hsinchu, and Kaohsiung within days. Capturing these cities will provide a major port, industrial center, agricultural hub, and key military bases – everything needed for sustaining a long-term invasion."

Stillwell held his officer's gaze, then said, "Let's make them pay a high price for our real estate."

Chinese Flight

A dozen Chinese J-20 stealth fighters flew ahead of a flight of twenty J-16 multirole fighter aircraft, ten Su-30MKK multirole fighters, and twenty H-6K bombers. A single KJ-500 airborne early warning and control aircraft coordinated efforts. Ten miles offshore, an armada of amphibious transport ships, destroyers, and landers raced toward LZ-1. The invasion force was supported by indirect rocket and missile units from Chinese frigates and land bases.

The ground trembled beneath Jake's feet as another impact from the barrage overhead reverberated through the Command Post. A fine layer of dust drifted down from the ceiling, and the dim emergency lights flickered with each blast. Jake glanced at the soldiers around him. Their faces, smeared with dirt and sweat, reflected the same thing his gut felt: fear.

Hank, who stood beside him, blew a low whistle as another thundering boom rolled through. "Tough way to start the day, huh?"

Jake didn't respond. His eyes were locked on the surveillance feeds. Frame after frame showed explosions blossoming around them, plumes of smoke and debris choking the camera's view. It was chaos, a relentless storm of steel and fire. The CP felt like a concrete casket as they waited for their turn to fight back.

With a crackle, static overtook the monitors. One after another, the feeds blinked out, the cameras obliterated. Jake clenched his jaw as the last live feed flickered, showing a smoking ruin where their forward observation post had been.

Seacrest stood like a statue, unaffected by the tremors. His bunker, encased in five feet of steel-reinforced concrete, was designed to withstand anything short of a direct hit, and so far, it had held. As the shelling slowed to a sudden, eerie silence, Seacrest approached the narrow steel window and pulled it open. Scanning the horizon, he saw nothing but the pale light of dawn breaking through the haze.

He lowered the glasses. "We need eyes on the prize," he muttered.

"Sir?" Gunny Stillwell stepped forward.

Seacrest turned sharply. "Launch a drone and prepare to move our men to their posts."

"Yes, sir!" The order was relayed within moments.

***

In a hill behind their position, the dull whirring of a drone's engines filled the small cave as a six-foot-long quadcopter rose and headed out to sea. The Marines hunched over their screens; their faces bathed in the blue glow as the drone cut through the thick air.

“Five minutes to contact,” the drone operator called out. The seconds ticked away, and the report came: “Sir, we have ten landers coming in from 270 degrees West.”

The enemy position was radioed to Seacrest, whose binoculars snapped up in search of the threat. He squinted into the distance until the silhouettes of the enemy craft began to take form, the faint outlines just visible against the haze. The enemy had come.

The wall clock read 07:12.

"Men, get to your positions!" Seacrest barked, his voice crackling through the comms.

Jake was already moving, Hank behind him, as the klaxon blared. Marines and Taiwanese soldiers scrambled from cover to their positions, some carrying heavy machine guns and antitank weapons, others ammo boxes and grenades. They dove into pill boxes and craters left by the earlier shelling, using the jagged edges of debris for cover. Others hacked at the earth with entrenching tools, carving new positions into the churned-up sand and rubble.

The roar of weapons being readied along the front filled the air—rifles locked and loaded, mortars prepped, artillery aimed. Anti-aircraft and anti-ship teams adjusted their units, each squad waiting, trigger fingers itching.

Back at the command post, Seacrest checked his wristwatch. The hands ticked in perfect rhythm, measuring not just time but the readiness of his men. He allowed a thin smile to cross his face.

Two minutes. A new record. They're ready.

Seacrest saw the first landing craft appear two kilometers from shore and radioed the information to Command while Stillwell updated his personnel.

"Missile Team leeward, fire! Mortar platoons prepare to fire. Shore batteries, fire on the landers when they reach one kilometer," Seacrest ordered.

Seacrest looked up as two dozen Tien Chi short-range ballistic missiles streaked from their nearby silos, locked onto their targets, and delivered a death blow. As the closest two landers caught fire, Seacrest saw Chinese Marines dive into the icy water. It was carnal and awe-inspiring!

Task Force Sea Serpent

Captain Taongas watched the fiery missiles emerge from the clouds and descend on his small fleet. Seconds later, two Tien Chi missiles struck his ship. The first projectile destroyed the bridge and superstructure. The second missile entered forward just above the water line, igniting the ship's magazine. Taonga's last memory was of a loud explosion followed by a blinding flash!

In less than ten seconds, two more Chinese tank landers, three assault ships, six frigates, and five troop carriers sank. The lucky few survivors entered lifeboats.

Chinese High Command

General Leu and General Chan sat with the other members of China's Central Military Commission as reports arrived from the front. After digesting the shocking loss of Commander Taongas' assault force, General Chan ordered, "Send in our reserve force and increase aerial bombardment and missile strikes on LZ-1! We must take that position within twenty-four hours if our timeline is to hold."

President Jin joined Generals Leu and Chan in a private conversation during the break.

Jin asked, "Do you think the next assault force will fare better than the first?"

General Chan chose his words carefully. While ritual disendowment was no longer in fashion, a few senior officers had been executed for failing Jin.

Chan said, "Yes. Our next assault will overwhelm enemy resistance. Once we get forces ashore, I anticipate rapid movement inland."

President Jin intently focused on his General, looking for the slightest hint of weakness, then asked, "What is your plan?"

Chan replied, "We will attack multiple positions simultaneously, capturing key ports, airfields, and landing zones where we can flood the country with up to five hundred thousand troops. Once we have a foothold, we will capture key cities and bases on our way to Taipei."

Jin nodded reasonably, then added, "President Tilden has been hospitalized and could pass away at any time. If that happens, the Vice President could throw the full might of the U.S. military at us. You must win the war while we hold the advantage!"

General Chan said, "If Novak becomes President, are you prepared to use tactical nukes?"

Jin realized Chan had turned the tables on him. If he said no, then he would lose their respect. He had to save face while remaining opaque.

"I'm not taking anything off the table. Your orders are to take Taipei within three days," Jin replied.

Walter Reed Medical Center

The harsh fluorescent lights cast an unforgiving glare on the sterile white walls of the ICU as Mrs. Tilden, clad in a bulky hazmat suit, stood alone beside the President's bed. Her gloved hand rested on his. The President's skin was pallid and clammy. Despite the layers separating them, a tremor ran through her at the thought of losing him.

His face flushed and dotted with sores, the President struggled to meet her gaze. His labored breathing rasped through the ventilator tube, snaking down his throat. He tried to speak, but only a wet gurgle escaped his lips.

Her practiced smile faltered as pity flickered in her eyes.

A sudden slackness in his hand pulled her attention back. Panic clawed at her throat. The rhythmic beeping of the heart monitor stuttered, then faded into a flat line.

A piercing alarm screamed for attention, shattering the sterile silence! Immediately, the door burst open as Captain Prince, MSRN, ran into the room, a whirlwind of efficiency. Her voice cut through the shrill alarm as she spoke into the handset, “Code Red, Code Red, MICU-352!”

Prince moved with practiced ease, checking for a pulse in his wrist, then his ankle. Nothing! Her eyes flicked to the monitor.

Mrs. Tilden stumbled back, her gloved hand flying to her mouth. The sterile room blurred. “This can't be happening. He can't be...”

Captain Prince barked orders, her voice a lifeline in the storm as the room filled with a flurry of white coats. Dr. Turner, the President's attending physician, and two other doctors entered without time to suit up. They swarmed the President, their movements urgent.

Dr. Turner threw Mrs. Tilden a grim look.

She shook her head, her voice cracked, “Oh God, no.”

Dr. Turner's face was etched with concern, but his voice was firm, “Ma'am, please. It won't help.” He ushered the First Lady to the door, never taking his eyes off the frantic activity around the bed.

While Turner removed the First Lady, Prince ripped the President’s pajama top open and cycled the defibrillator. The rhythmic thrum of the device charging added drama as it reached its peak.

Prince grabbed the paddles, “Clear!”

The team moved back as Prince placed the paddles on either side of the heart and pressed the button. An electrical shock immediately caused the President’s body to arch violently.

Turner watched the monitor, still flat, and ordered, “No response, hit him again.”

The defibrillator cycled with sterile efficiency, “Ready, clear…”

Tilden’s body jumped! Turner looked at the monitor, willing it to show a heartbeat. “No response, one more time!” Turner ordered.

A tense silence followed the electric jolt that racked the President's body.

Captain Prince leaned over him, checking the leads, hoping it was a misread. Everything was in order, no mistake. She felt for a pulse at his neck, wrist, and ankle. Nothing! All hope faded as the elder stateman’s soul slipped into a dark eternity.

Mrs. Tilden watched through the window, her body a statue encased in glass. The image of the President, his once-powerful body reduced to a canvas of illness, burned into her memory. How had this happened?

Why now? Dozens of questions assailed her mind as emotions raged through her. She fell back, but was caught by her secret service agent. “Ma'am, I’ve got you.” His words sounded hollow.

Finally, Dr. Turner placed the disc-shaped resonator against the President’s chest and listened to the stethoscope intently. Nothing! He repositioned the resonator on the other side of the chest. Nothing! The President’s heart had stopped, and there was no sign of body function. Turner’s shoulders slumped as if drawn down by the overwhelming feeling of failure.

In a voice void of emotion, he pronounced, “There's nothing more we can do. Time of Death, 16:24.”

The harsh pronouncement hung in the air, a death knell to an era. Mrs. Tilden, supported by her trusted agent, stared at the still form on the bed, a kaleidoscope of emotions swirling within her. Grief, yes, but something else too. A cold calculation, a sense of a future rewritten. The world outside this sterile room may be falling apart, but for Mrs. Tilden, a new chapter was about to begin. She had to get back to Solar Valley, to her future, but there was a State Funeral to plan. The timing could not be worse.

U.S. News

“We interrupt this programming for an important announcement. As of 4:24 PM Eastern Standard Time, President Tilden died of complications associated with a rare upper respiratory infection. For more on this emerging story, we now go to Ned Divine. Ned, what have you learned?”

Standing with the ambulance entrance as a backdrop, Ned said, “Susie, I’ve learned that President Tilden died of a rare form of Respiratory Syncytial Virus, commonly known as RSV. RSV hospitalizes 177,000 people annually, killing approximately 14,000, mostly over sixty-five.”

“Have they said how the President contracted the infection?”

“No, just that the President had caught a cold, and his symptoms worsened.”

“Do you know anything about the swearing-in ceremony for President Novak?”

“Right now, I don’t think he cares much about ceremonies. Constitutionally, he became President at 4:24 PM Eastern, the time of the death of President Tilden.” Ned responded, then added, “So, I imagine the ceremony will be a simple affair similar to when Johnson was sworn in at the death of JFK."

"I can't imagine any VP stepping into a greater challenge," Susie observed.

White House

Chief Justice Schuler stood in his black robe before Kevin Novak in the White House Press Room. Novak's wife, Margie, held the Bible as her husband repeated the Presidential Oath of Office. A hastily gathered assembly of generals, elected officials, key members of the Press, and the Novak family watched the historic event.

Afterward, the Chief Justice and the First Lady were seated, and President Novak took the podium, a President determined to pull the world back from the abyss.

Novak wore a navy-blue suit with a red and blue rep tie, and he said, "This is a time to weep with those who weep, pray for those in harm's way, and join hands in the cause of liberty."

At the death of FDR, Vice President Truman's words were uttered less than one hundred feet from where he stood. Novak could hear the ghost of Truman as he spoke to Eleanor Roosevelt, "I feel like the moon, the stars, and all the planets have fallen on me."

Unlike Truman, who succeeded a beloved President who led America out of the Great Depression, Novak replaced a globalist President who betrayed the American People. In assuming the presidency, Novak carried the daunting burden of saving the free world from a new dark age.

Novak's salt-and-pepper grey hair, fit physique, and confident air starkly contrasted with his predecessor's tight-rope steps and mental gaffes. Many Americans found comfort in having the fifty-two-year-old conservative take control of the nuclear keys. Several reporters observed that it was refreshing to have youth and energy return to the Oval Office. Around the world, five billion people watched in anticipation as his words were translated into forty-eight languages.

Novak looked at his audience of fifty people and said, "My fellow Americans, I will honor my oath to protect the Constitution against all enemies, foreign and domestic. I will seek to pull our world back from the grip of subversive forces, dead set on destroying the greatest nation of freedom and prosperity the world has ever known."

A standing ovation occurred as everyone stood, a unity rare in Washington.

"If America fails, the free world will descend into a dark age of tyranny in which elite billionaires and communist leaders rule with an iron hand, crushing liberty forever," Novak warned.

Novak paused to let his words sink in.

"My first initiatives will be to restore law and order in our streets, win the Chinese War of Aggression, secure our borders, and move the U.S. to a sustainable fiscal policy. These tasks require all of us to unite and fight our common enemies. There's no room for people to sit idly by; it's time for all Americans to come to the aid of their country!"

Novak's words and demeanor caused a spontaneous eruption of applause as everyone stood in solidarity. Around the country, people began to cheer, while in China, President Jin cringed.

Landing Zone One

First Lieutenant Seacrest received word that he'd received a battlefield promotion to Captain. After a brief cheer from his radio man and command staff, Gunnery Sergeant Stillwell offered him a cigar. Seacrest held the stogie in his teeth while Stillwell lit it. Ever vigilant, the captain's eyes remained focused on the sea as the aroma of the fine tobacco gave a brief relief to battlefield stench.

"What's their next move, sir?" Stillwell asked.

Captain Seacrest took a few puffs of the cigar, then turned to his senior NCO and told him, "Intelligence intercepts indicate the PLA intends to take our position by nightfall. I expect them to hit us with everything they've got, then land tanks and troops."

Stillwell didn't flinch as he asked, "Any reinforcements?"

Seacrest said, "Five hundred Taiwanese Regulars, six mortar companies, and replacements for the artillery we lost. While there's a chance of close air support, we can't count on it."

Stillwell nodded agreement, then asked, "Sir, do you think President Novak will let Flint take the war to the enemy?"

"I sure hope so, Gunny. If we can't get control of the skies and sea lanes, we're..." Seacrest stopped mid-sentence. They all knew the score; no point in adding more fear.

Wanting to say something positive to buck up his Captain, Stillwell said, “Those Taiwanese missiles sure put the last invaders on the bottom. Their bodies are washing up everywhere.”

Seacrest nodded agreement, “Keep our men under cover as much as possible. Force preservation is critical.”

A tense silence fell over the command post, broken only by the rhythmic cough of the generator and the distant boom of outgoing artillery. Seacrest scanned the faces of his men – grim determination etched beneath smears of camouflage paint. They were outnumbered and outgunned, but their eyes held a patriot’s fire.

He met Seacrest’s gaze, a silent exchange passing between them. They had held this landing zone against overwhelming odds and couldn’t give up blood-bought land now.

White House Situation Room

The presentation screen flickered to life, bathing the Situation Room in a harsh blue light. General Drummond stepped forward, his pointer tapping a red bar that dwarfed its blue counterpart.

"Sir," he began, his voice grave, "as you can see, the PLA currently boasts a significant advantage in troop strength in the Pacific Theater. Their opening attacks crippled our bases in Guam, South Korea, and Japan. Frankly, Admiral Flint and his G-2 were caught with their pants down."

He gestured to another slide, a pie chart divided between blue and red slices. "Compounding this issue is the near-complete decimation of our naval presence in the South China Sea. The recent loss of the carrier group Roosevelt and the carrier Nimitz has left us scrambling to redeploy assets from the Atlantic, a process that will take weeks. While the British and Australians are sending destroyers and submarines, the PLA controls the sea and sky for 2,500 miles around Taiwan. The only good news is that Admiral Flint has fifty submarines in firing position."

A collective sigh rippled through the room. National Security Advisor Patel leaned forward, his brow furrowed. "Can Taiwan hold the line long enough for us to get reinforcements to them?"

Drummond pulled up a slide showing current strength estimates of the U.S. Coalition and China.

Drummond said, “The Chinese outnumber our forces by two to one globally and up to nine to one in the battle zone. While we have combat experience, better training, and more advanced technology, China can focus ninety percent of its forces in the theater.”

Novak digested the grim news, then asked, “How many of our forces can we send?”

“We must keep at least 50% of our assets deployed outside the theater to keep our global commitments. We also need 100,000 Army infantry and Marines to implement Executive Order 666 at home.”

“I’m resending E.O. 666. If there was ever a time when civilians needed firearms, it’s now. Proceed.”

Drummond nodded grimly. "As you can see, the EMP dropped our number of assets in several categories. The loss of two carriers and most of our aircraft in the region has limited our ability to gain air superiority. While we’ve repaired over 75% of our damaged runways and operate improvised airfields in Taiwan, Japan, and the Philippines, we’re at less than 20% readiness. Add the tyranny of distance to the equation, and China holds a significant advantage. Right now, there’s simply no way to save Taiwan!”

Novak felt the need to put some optimism in the room and said, “The Taiwanese forces have fought valiantly, inflicting heavy casualties on the PLA. Jake Hendel’s coverage at LZ One has generated worldwide support. So, I’m not counting them out just yet.”

Echoes of agreement arose across the room.

“What we need are major victories that show the world Americans love to fight, fight to win, and would rather die than lose,” Novak continued.

Drummond tapped the screen once more, and a map of the Pacific Ocean pulsing with red and blue icons representing forces appeared. It was the General’s way of shutting down the President: "The PLA has amassed amphibious forces off the coast of Taiwan. They are also deploying paratroopers to key air bases and bridge heads. Their objective is clear: a full-scale invasion.”

Drummond, a Tilden loyalist, paused to let his words sink in, now to discredit his Commander-in-Chief.

“Mr. President, the fact is that we lack the forces needed to defend Taiwan and maintain our global and national commitments. The smart play is to cut Taiwan loose and prioritize America's interests. For God’s sake, Taiwan isn't even a NATO member. We can't afford to give up the Indo-Pacific over one island nation."

Not missing Drummond's jab, President Novak gripped the arms of his chair, knuckles turning white. The weight of the situation, the hopes of a nation resting on his shoulders, pressed down on him. He looked around the room, meeting the grim expressions of his advisors. He thought, if these Pentagon politicos don't have balls, I'll turn to my theater commander!

"Admiral Flint," he finally spoke, his voice firm, "tell me... what options we have for victory?"

Drummond straightened at the unmistakable haymaker throw by the President. Novak's jaw muscles flexed over his intense anger toward the previous Administration and the Joint Chiefs who'd become politicians. Tilden had virtually given away Taiwan and possibly South Korea and Japan to the Chinese. He wanted to bash his predecessor, but reminded himself that everyone needed him to be 'presidential.'

Flint's image showed on the hologram in the center of the table as he spoke, "Mr. President, to win, we have to change the game."

Drummond protested, "Admiral, it's irresponsible to waste more assets than you've already lost. The Chinese caught you with your pants down!"

Flint ignored the jab and calmly said, "Mr. President, to defeat the Chinese, we must conduct preemptive strikes on all PLA forces, including those on the Chinese mainland, with the mission of interdicting their supply lines, disrupting their communications, regaining control of air and sea lanes, and removing their cyber and nuclear capabilities."

Drummond leaped from his chair, "That's a proposal for nuclear holocaust!"

"I'm interested; don't hold anything back," Novak ordered, the glare in his eyes forcing Drummond to sit.

"Mr. President, would you define victory for us?" Flint asked the prearranged question.

Novak said, "I want you to stop the invasion of Taiwan and render China incapable of taking territory in the Pacific for a decade or more. I want you to destroy ninety percent of their navy, air force, and missile forces while we have the opportunity."

A few Joint Chiefs recoiled at the new President's hawkish words. Others found his clarity refreshing.

Admiral Flint's lips formed a slight smile as he responded, "In that case, Mr. President, we'll take the war to them. No holds barred!"

Drummond objected vigorously, "Admiral, the fact is that our support for Ukraine and Israel has rendered us critically low on artillery shells, all categories of missiles, torpedoes, missile defense, and small arms ammunition. Then, there's the retention and recruitment crisis. We're experiencing shortages in key NCOs, technical specialists, and officers. This means we're limited in the number of resources we can send to the Pacific. And don't forget, we'll need a lot of those troops to restore order at home and buck up NATO against Russian aggression."

Novak ignored Drummond and asked, "Admiral, how does your operation work?"

Flint calmly replied, "Star Wars is a battle plan that utilizes our strengths in advanced technology. Specifically, autonomous and space-based weapons systems combined with the firepower of our submarines to gain the upper hand."

Novak bit his lip. The thought of fielding an army of autonomous weapons conjured up images of Terminator movies with robots killing humans. After a brief pause, he realized he had a choice to make. In an act of bravery, Novak said, "Send in machines in place of personnel. Walk me through the details."

"Star Wars uses a coordinated cyberattack to destroy unprotected electronics in China and North Korea, followed by submarine and autonomous weapons systems to destroy Chinese naval and air forces and their commercial ships carrying troops and supplies. To have the best chance of success, we must take out the Chinese air and missile bases. Once we establish sea and air superiority, we'll use Army and Marine forces to capture the Chinese reef bases and reinforce Taiwan. Allied forces will then implement a no-fly / no-shipping zone to protect Taiwan, Japan, and the Philippines from Chinese aggression."

"How many of these AWS Units do we have?" Novak asked.

Flint said, "Mr. President, we have 3,500 aircraft, 5,000 seacraft, and 10,000 land units. When you add in our remotely controlled vehicles, we have over 21,000 units available. In addition, we have highly classified space-based assets that General Archer assures me can do what we need."

Novak was pleased. He asked, "When can we start?"

"Mr. President, we can launch cyberattacks within one hour of your orders."

Novak stared at the Board, deep in thought. When he came out of his analysis, he ordered, "Initiate operations."

The room grew eerily quiet. Knowing there could be no turning back. Novak removed a card from his pocket and provided the code to the USAF Colonel in charge of the nuclear sequence.

"Verify the code, but don't initiate the launch sequence," Novak commanded.

A USAF Colonel keyed in the commands and asked for Novak's code.

Novak read the alphanumeric code and waited.

"The code was authenticated. All systems are operational. Mr. President."

Novak nodded as he stared at Drummond. The only question in his mind was when and how to remove the Chairman of the Joint Chiefs. If heads had to fall, Drummond was at the top of his list.

Chapter 9

Admiral Flint stepped into the Command Center and let the doors seal behind him. The room hummed—screens stacked floor to ceiling, keyboards clattering, data flowing nonstop through the Integrated Combat System. The war was everywhere at once: missile tracks arcing across the Pacific, naval engagements blinking red and blue, air battles flickering in real time.

Flint planted his hands on his hips and absorbed it all. Land. Sea. Air. Then the summary map—friendly and enemy troop dispositions layered in unforgiving clarity. His forces were committed. No gaps. No reserves hiding offstage. Good.

He turned to his G-2. “How are we doing?”

The officer didn’t sugarcoat it. “Admiral, Patriot batteries have intercepted approximately seven hundred PLA missiles. Okinawa, Taiwan, the Philippines, and Japan are now out of interceptors. From this point forward, missile defense rests almost entirely on the fleet.”

Flint’s jaw tightened. “And our counterpunch?”

“We currently have thirty submarines inside effective firing range of the Chinese coast. That gives us a fighting chance against their flood-the-zone strategy.”

Flint cut him off. “What about our beachheads, ports, and airfields?”

The answer came fast—and grim. “Chinese casualties are high, but so are ours. Anti-ship cruise missiles are limiting our ability to reinforce by sea. PLA amphibious landings are underway at multiple critical beachheads, and airborne units are massing.”

Flint studied the map again, then nodded once. Decision time.

“Here’s the plan,” he said. “Ohio and Michigan—both converted Ohio-class boats—are ordered into the South China Sea. One hundred fifty-four Tomahawks per hull. We’re going to hammer ships, airbases, and missile sites.”

He tapped the display.

Twenty Los Angeles and Seawolf-class attack submarines will interdict shipping lanes and strike strategic targets. Accounting for losses, we should be able to eliminate eighty percent of the Chinese Navy within seventy-two hours."

A murmur rippled through the room.

"For air superiority," Flint continued, "the Air Force is committing over fifty percent of our remaining fighters and bombers. All available AWS units are deploying to the theater."

He paused, letting the weight settle.

"Our objective is clear: sea and air dominance within seven days while we move sixty thousand additional troops and equipment into the fight."

Everyone in the room knew the truth. It wasn't enough. AWS was unproven. Chinese missiles and nuclear weapons still loomed. And the numbers favored Beijing.

Flint changed the subject before doubt could take root. "Status on the main island."

Brigadier General Mike Boyce, USMC, stepped forward. "Admiral, expeditionary forces retain four thousand two hundred Marines from an initial five thousand, plus twenty-five hundred Army Airborne. Three SEAL Teams are protecting Taiwanese leadership."

He continued, "Yesterday, we inserted elements of the 621st Contingency Response Group from McGuire to open improvised runways. Taiwan's underground fuel depots remain intact. Their defense industry is producing hundreds of missiles per day."

Boyce pointed to the map. "Our kill ratio at LZ-1, LZ-2, and LZ-3 is running twenty to one. Despite limited ships and aircraft, anti-ship and anti-aircraft fire has slowed the invasion. We're doing the same with handheld anti-armor."

Flint looked at him. "What do you need?"

"Air superiority over ports, airfields, and landing zones," Boyce replied. "And we need to destroy their invasion forces at sea. Right now, the mines have slowed the PLA down, but not taken them out."

"You'll have priority," Flint replied. "How are the improvised airfields holding up?"

"They're functional—but fragile," Boyce observed. "Fuel and comms are good. Ground crews and spare parts are not. We're losing aircraft to parts faster than we can keep them flying."

Flint folded his arms. "How long can you hold?"

Boyce didn't hesitate. "The beaches are nearing collapse. I've ordered withdrawals when positions become untenable."

"To the hills?" Flint asked.

"Yes, sir. Then the passes. We can hold those for weeks—with air and logistics support. Without it…" Boyce shrugged grimly. "If the PLA secures a major port and a couple of airports, the odds turn ugly fast."

Flint stared at the map. Time was being purchased with blood. American blood!

Distance, attrition, and the Chinese EMP had backed him into a corner—but a wounded boxer could still kill you. He straightened.

Flint ordered, "Initiate Operation Terminator."

The war entered its next phase. A new type of warfare in which conventional forces faced autonomous machines and space-based weapons for the first time. The rules of war were changing in a hundred different ways all at the same time. Limited nuclear strikes. EMP and cyber. Submarine warfare on a scale exceeding anything a Carrier Group could muster. All of it was happening at light speed.

Beijing, China

General Leu looked at President Jin and said, "Mr. President, our strikes have prepared the landing zones for amphibious invasion and their key airbases for occupation. Our submarines are currently lying in wait to sink Allied ships coming from the U.S., and we control air and sea lanes around Taiwan. At this point, we can either starve the Taiwanese or capture their island."

President Jin asked, "What about the U.S. Carriers?"

General Leu said, "We plan to lure their remaining carriers into our trap, then use our hypersonic missiles and pre-positioned submarines to destroy them. Our cloaking technology will allow us to get into striking distance before they know we are there, and our EMP attacks have taken out much of their early warning system."

President Jin asked, "Should we strike their bases on the West Coast and Alaska?"

General Chan said, "It would be ideal, but doing so could catalyze the will of the Allied nations and the UN against us, like it catalyzed the Americans against Japan in World War II. Public opinion in support of Taiwan has increased significantly, largely due to the efforts of Jake Hendel, an embedded reporter for U.S. News. For these reasons, I recommend that we concentrate on capturing Taiwan while we hold the advantage. Once we've done so, we can let our broader attacks in the U.S. bring the once-great nation to its knees."

President Jin leaned back in his chair, allowing silence to heighten his generals' anxiety. When Chan and Leu looked nervously at each other, Jin said, "America is not what it once was. In World War II, Americans had nuclear families, trusted their government, and were united. Today, they're divided and have anarchy in their streets."

The generals nodded dutiful agreement.

"America fought a stalemate in Korea and then lost in Vietnam and Afghanistan. The only recent wars they've won have been against third-class tyrants like Saddam Hussein or Nicolás Maduro. Their decline on the world stage is imminent. All we have to do is stay the course," Jin said, growing confidence reflecting in his voice.

Taiwanese Coastal Highway

Master Sergeant David Smith from the 621st Contingency Response Unit demonstrated to his Taiwanese allies how to operate the MWS-M625 Weather Data instrument, while Sergeant Peter Sand operated the backpack-sized air traffic control system.

"Make sure you observe real-time differential correction of the Global Positioning System signal, augmented with a local area correction. That EMP screwed with the satellites. Don't trust it," Smith barked.

"Will do, Master Sergeant."

"Where's that fuel truck?" Smith shouted.

Corporal Bob Simmons replied, "They're keeping them in the tunnel to protect them from enemy fire, but they're ready."

The Master Sergeant surveyed the area. Conditions were crude, but then they always were. He ordered, "Are we clear on wet bulb temperature readings and weather?"

"Yes, Sergeant."

Master Sergeant Smith announced, "This field's open for business."

***

Five minutes later, the remaining fighters from Squadron 22 passed over the makeshift field and came back around for landing.

"Here goes nothing," Smith said as Simmons joined him.

The first fighter landed hard but soon rolled to a stop 100 meters from the tunnel entrance. Thirty seconds later, the other fighters taxied in.

As the pilots climbed down, the fuel truck arrived, and American and Taiwanese crews swarmed over the planes, replacing missiles, ammo, fuel, and oxygen as the Master Sergeant kept time on his stopwatch.

While green, the Taiwanese crews were thorough and worked fast. When the pilots climbed back inside the planes and closed the cockpit, Smith saw they'd made the turnaround in under twenty minutes.

"Not bad!" Smith said to Simmons.

Landing Zone One

The shrill wail of the air raid siren sliced through the humid air, shattering the fragile calm. "Incoming!" Seacrest roared into the microphone, hoping his men would hear the warning.

Seacrest watched, a knot of dread tightening in his gut, as his men disappeared into the network of fortified positions. Seconds later, missiles, streaks of white fury against the darkening sky, slammed into Seacrest's position, shaking the ground with each detonation. A symphony of destruction that threatened to tear the world apart. The air filled with the acrid tang of cordite and the sickeningly sweet smell of burnt flesh.

When the rain of hellfire ended, a heavy weight of despair settled on Seacrest's shoulders. He steeled himself and pushed open the reinforced steel shutters protecting his command post. The sight greeting him was a scene ripped straight from Dante's Inferno. Three machine gun nests were reduced to smoldering craters, mortar emplacements lay in ruins, and the beach was littered with the twisted remains of what were once hardened positions. Bodies, whole and in pieces, were strewn across the sand.

Seacrest ventured out as he fought down the rising bile in his throat. This wasn't the first time he'd seen the aftermath of the battle, but it never got easier. Looking back inside the CP, he shouted, "Damage report!"

"Most of the hard-wired lines are down, sir. Thankfully, eighty percent of the radios are still functioning. The clinic's full, and we've lost thirty men along with most of our artillery and missile units. The recon drone spotted a sizeable Chinese armada approaching. Taiwanese air support is marginal, and our reinforcements are taking heavy losses as they try to reach us. We'll be lucky if half of them arrive," replied Sparks O'Reilly, his red face etched with determination. "Looks like we're in for a real party, sir."

Despite the overwhelming odds, Seacrest felt a surge of defiance. He wouldn't let his men break. "Gunny, you've seen more combat than anyone here. What's our best course of action?"

A hint of a smile played on Stillwell's lips, "Reinforce the defenses and focus our heavy weapons on the landers. Those snipers will be able to earn their pay once Chinese Marines disembark. We've got the firepower to blunt their first wave, then we'll have to fall back, sir."

Seacrest met Stillwell's gaze, a silent acknowledgment of respect passing between warriors. "Make it a living hell for them."

Stillwell saluted and disappeared into the smoke.

***

At 0930, naval artillery and missiles rained down on LZ-1. As Seacrest watched helplessly, position after position was destroyed. Five minutes later, two squadrons of attack aircraft destroyed half his remaining artillery pieces and his anti-aircraft battery. The bodies were strewn all around. It was a slaughter.

At 0959, Seacrest emerged from his bunker and scanned the horizon. A lump formed in his throat as multiple landers emerged from the haze. Based upon their wakes, the landers were coming in at full speed.

Seacrest moved inside and ordered his men, "Prepare to defend yourselves!"

O'Reilly turned to him and said, "Sir, fighter strike group inbound."

"ETA on the fast movers?"

O'Reilly made an inquiry. After a long pause, he said, "We should hear them soon."

Seacrest walked outside in time to see missiles streaking from beneath six fighters. Seconds later, plumes of smoke rose from several landers.

"Good shooting!" Seacrest cheered.

The fighters turned, then made low strafing runs, emptying their guns into the landers. Several landers were aflame, but several were still coming in fast! While the air attack had been effective, there were too many targets for the small squadron.

As Seacrest peered seaward, dozens of land-based missiles flew overhead. Seconds later, the fire-breathing ordnance disappeared over the horizon, seeking vengeance.

At 1005, three Chinese Type 72A Landers stopped in the shallow water, their 37 mm deck guns and machine guns wreaking havoc on his position. Then smoke canisters landed inside his perimeter, and Seacrest realized the Chinese were establishing a smoke screen behind which they would disembark tanks and armored personnel carriers.

Gunny Stillwell emerged from the smoke with a report, “Sir, we’ve lost another twenty men and another machine gun. I issued all our handheld missiles; maybe they’ll be enough to blunt the first wave.”

“How many mines remain operational?” Seacrest asked.

“Hard to say. Everything’s been through a meat grinder.”

Seacrest lifted his radio handset and ordered, “Artillery, fire on the enemy at the water line. Missile teams one and two concentrate fire on those landers. Machine gun squads open fire on their troops when they disembark. Mortar platoons one, two, and three fire on the APCs and tanks. Sniper team, fire at will and be prepared to use grenades.”

As the two men watched, mortars and missiles streaked through the air, and explosions erupted inside the smoke screen. Rising smoke plumes confirmed hits on enemy vehicles as Seacrest’s personnel continued to fight.

“We’re giving 'em hell,” Seacrest told Stillwell.

“Yes, sir,” Stilwell said in a low growl.

“Let’s see how many vehicles break through.”

Stillwell nodded and said, “We need to get those tanks on the beach as soon as they arrive.”

Seacrest ran into his Command Post. Once inside, he asked O’Reilly, “What’s the ETA on armor?”

O’Reilly said, “They’re coming over the hill now. We also have an inbound squadron of three attack aircraft. The forward air observer requested they put all their ordnance on the water line, then strafe disembarking troops.”

Seacrest nodded in the affirmative.

Chinese Amphibious Force One

Commander Okida slammed his fist down in defiance as reports came in from his commanders. From the drone footage and the frantic reports crackling over the speaker, it was clear that the second assault was failing.

"They're taking a beating, sir," Executive Officer Ossolo observed, his voice laced with a concern that mirrored Okida's own. "Heavy losses. Should we hold back the remaining landers?"

Okida ran a hand through his already ruffled hair. The pressure from the generals had created a constant thrumming in his skull. Their orders to 'take Landing Zone One at all costs!' flashed through his mind. The brass didn't care about his losses; they only cared about results.

He met Ossolo's gaze, a silent struggle between duty and conscience. "No," he finally said, the word heavy on his tongue. "We need to capitalize on the chaos and take the beachhead before they can reinforce!"

Okida straightened, his voice regaining its edge as he issued orders. "Saturation fire. I want those beaches softened up for our troops. Then, launch all remaining landing craft. We must hit them in an overwhelming wave!"

Ossolo gave a curt nod, the worry in his eyes replaced by a steely resolve. Relaying the orders, his voice boomed across the command deck, galvanizing his crew into action. The tension crackled in the air, thick enough to choke on.

Suddenly, a klaxon shrieked, red lights strobing in a frantic rhythm. "Sir," the communications officer barked, his voice tight with urgency, "enemy aircraft inbound!"

Okida's heart pounded in an ever-increasing vibrato. Intel told him they held complete air superiority, and Taiwan was out of anti-ship missiles. A curse ripped through his teeth. "Call for fighter support! Activate surface-to-air missiles!"

A flurry of activity erupted on the decks of the surrounding vessels. Turrets whirred, seeking the incoming threat. Launchers hissed as missiles streaked skyward, fiery serpents chasing unseen enemies.

Landing Zone One

The roar of the jets shattered the tense silence. Captain Seacrest squinted through the smoke, a flicker of hope sparking in his eyes. The sleek silhouettes screaming in from the east were Taiwanese AT-3 attack jets. Each plane's underwing and wing tip weapon mounts were loaded for bear!

Seacrest saw his dead air controller and grabbed his mike, his voice laced with a newfound urgency, "Target the landing craft!"

His words crackled through the airwaves, a desperate plea answered by a chorus of acknowledgments. Below, Marines scrambled for cover, seeking protection from the deadly ballet about to unfold.

Leading the air attack was Major Cai, his face grim beneath his helmet. These were the last reserves, a dozen left out of sixty, the final gamble to hold the line. He glanced at his wingmen: a mix of veteran pilots and fresh-faced rookies thrust into the inferno.

"Remember your training," Cai barked over the roar of his jet. "Target the landers! Once your primary ordnance is gone, strafe the troops and vehicles. We need to buy these Marines some breathing room!"

His words were barely finished when an alarm shrieked, and a crimson warning light flashed on his heads-up display. Chinese missiles! He cursed under his breath.

Banking sharply, Cai led his formation in a breathtaking display of aerial acrobatics. Eleven Bravos weaved through the incoming missiles, a hail of flares and chaff blooming like fiery flowers against the darkening sky. Two young pilots, overwhelmed by the chaos, faltered – their screams cut short as their planes plunged into the churning sea. Another plane, with a veteran pilot, took a direct hit, his aircraft breaking apart in a fiery explosion.

There was no time for mourning. Every pilot, every plane lost, was a devastating blow to Taiwan's dwindling air force.

With a growl of defiance, Cai released his payload, and five anti-ship missiles streaked toward the Chinese armada. He then pulled hard, G-forces pressing him into his seat as he dodged another SAM, the roar of its explosion rattling his fighter.

Below, a chaotic symphony of fire and steel played out as anti-ship missiles slammed into their targets, sending plumes of smoke and fire skyward. Taiwanese cannons strafed the beaches, painting the sand red with the blood of Chinese soldiers. But the enemy pressed forward, relentless and seemingly inexhaustible in numbers.

Tears welled in Cai's eyes, not just for his fallen comrades but for the future of his nation. Could they hold? Could they win against such overwhelming odds? Pushing his fighter to the deck, Cai skimmed the coastline, following the highway as he prepared for another strafing run.

Every attack, every soldier killed, brought hope. He would keep fighting, keep flying, even if it was his last act. For Taiwan, for his fallen brothers, for a sliver of hope in a seemingly hopeless war.

Seacrest cursed under his breath as a dozen Type 99 tanks lumbered onto the beach, their massive cannons swiveling toward his men. They looked like mechanized behemoths, their advanced design starkly contrasting the Marines' cobbled-together defenses. These weren't the rickety T-72s they were used to seeing – the extended chassis and the distinctive smoothbore gun of the Type 99 spoke volumes about the firepower they possessed. It was China's best tank against his fragmented defenses.

"Forty-two rounds per minute," Seacrest muttered, the knowledge a cold weight in his stomach. Enough to turn their fortifications to dust.

"Tanks on the beach, sir!" a harried voice crackled over the radio, "They're followed by APCs!"

"Target the tanks!" Seacrest roared into the handset, his voice a beacon of defiance amid the chaos. "Put everything we've got on them!"

Seacrest scrambled to his feet, scanning the sky. There! The sleek silhouettes of the remaining attack aircraft streaked in from the east, their engines screaming a battle cry. Major Cai, bless him, was making good on his promise.

Below, the Marines scrambled for cover as the first wave of tank shells slammed into the beach. Sand and debris erupted into a choking cloud, punctuated by the sickening screams of the wounded. But the Marines fought back, their anti-tank weapons spitting fire.

A TOW missile found its mark, a fireball erupting on the side of a Type 99 tank, which ground to a halt. Then, a dozen more hand-held missiles flew into the steel onslaught, destroying six more tanks and the same number of APCs.

Seacrest watched with awe as the fighter's white-hot tracers arced through the air, spitting death toward the enemy armor. Incendiary rounds slammed into the red-hot engine cylinders of the tanks, igniting fuel and ammunition with spectacular explosions. Within moments, eight supposedly invincible Type 99s were burning hulks, spewing black smoke that stained the already murky sky.

"Thank heavens for close air support," Seacrest muttered to Stillwell.

Stillwell, a wry smile playing on his lips, replied, "Looks like we owe Major Cai a drink."

Seacrest allowed himself a chuckle. The respite was welcome, but he knew it wouldn't last. The remaining APCs were disgorging soldiers onto the beach. The battle was far from over. Seacrest grabbed his weapon and headed outside the bunker. Leadership Principle #1: Never ask your men to do something you won't. Time to face the music.

Squadron 22

"If you're out, return to the contingent field and rearm and refuel. If you've got ordnance, form up on me," Major Cai ordered.

Immediately, his four youngest pilots broke from the formation. Cai wasn't surprised that the inexperienced men had used up all their ammo in one pass. At least they'd made a dent.

As the squadron flew back over land, two more fighters were destroyed by SAM fire. Cai knew he couldn't afford to keep losing fighters and pilots at this rate, but there wasn't anything more he could do.

"Make every shot count, and remember we've got friendlies down there," Cai ordered, leading his remaining fighters back for a strafing run.

Chinese Amphibious Invasion Force

Commander Okida received the report that his men had made it ashore but were suffering heavy casualties. Worse, several of his troops lay motionless, afraid to advance. The Taiwanese and their American advisors were better prepared than Beijing had predicted. Nevertheless, his superiors would blame any failure on him.

"Commander, the shore commander requests permission to withdraw," Executive Officer Ossolo reported.

"There'll be no retreat. What units remain?"

Ossolo looked down at his pad and replied, "Sir, we have four more tank landers at sea and one disembarking tanks and APCs as we speak. Our missile batteries and deck guns are out of ammunition."

Okida decided it was now or never and ordered, "Order our remaining landers ashore. Request fighter cover and call for reinforcements. We must establish a beachhead before the enemy can reinforce!"

Squadron 22

Major Cai slowed to attack speed and dove on the enemy. As he dropped below 1,000 meters, he lined up his sights and fired controlled bursts, exploding four tanks and two personnel carriers. Suddenly, his missile alarm sounded. Cai banked toward land, pushed the throttles forward, pumped flares and chaff, and dove for the deck.

To his horror, his flare dispenser was jammed, and he was out of chaff! Major Cai's evasive maneuvers were all that was left to save his plane. He banked hard to starboard and pushed the throttles to full military power. As he flew over the hill, the SAM seemed to accelerate! Major Cai immediately dove into the small valley, and the enemy missile crashed into the hillside!

Out of immediate danger, Major Cai remembered images of U.S. Marines and Taiwanese Army soldiers firing artillery and machine guns at the enemy in a desperate attempt to hold their position.

A sinking feeling came over him at the realization that the brave troops wouldn't live another day. They were being used as cannon fodder to slow the Chinese advance until the full strength of the U.S. military could arrive. Until then, defending Taiwan against the numerically superior PLA was like trying to extinguish a forest fire with a water gun.

Landing Zone One

Jake Hendel stood on the crest of a rocky hillside overlooking a stretch of sand that, until days ago, hadn't warranted a name on most maps. Now it held the world's breath.

"Three—two—one—live!" Hank shouted, raising his voice above the thunder of artillery.

Jake wore body armor streaked with dust and soot, an M-4 slung across his chest more for survival than symbolism. His clothes were stiff with grime. A blood-stained bandage wrapped his left hand. He gripped the microphone with his right, knuckles white. Several days of beard growth etched exhaustion into his face.

In a New York studio thousands of miles away, Susie Legman stared at the monitor, horrified. This wasn't the man she knew. This was someone forged by fire. A wounded man in a horrific battle in a land half a world away.

“Just one hour ago,” Jake said, forcing calm into his voice, “Chinese landing craft came ashore directly below me, offloading tanks, armored personnel carriers, and hundreds of troops.”

The camera panned across the beach—burning vehicles, craters filled with seawater, Marines and Taiwanese soldiers firing from shattered revetments.

“U.S. Marines and Taiwanese forces are engaged in desperate close-quarters fighting, attempting to repel Chinese regulars while the Taiwanese Air Force provides intermittent close air support. What you’re seeing is a modern-day Alamo in the Pacific—coalition forces holding a narrow strip of ground against overwhelming odds.”

The earth convulsed! An artillery round detonated less than fifty meters away.

Hank stumbled as the shockwave slammed into them. The camera lurched wildly as debris rained down. The explosion's roar punched through the broadcast, sending viewers around the world flinching in their seats.

“MOVE—MOVE!” Hank yelled.

They sprinted downslope, boots skidding on loose rock, and dove into a crude fighting position carved directly into the granite hillside.

Moments later, Jake was live again—breathing hard, dust streaked across his face, eyes locked on the lens.

“For the past twelve hours,” he shouted over the din, “coalition positions have been subjected to an unrelenting barrage of missiles and naval gunfire. Entire defensive lines have been erased. Tens of thousands of coalition personnel and civilians are believed dead or wounded.”

The background was a wall of sound—machine guns, explosions, jets screaming overhead.

“Chinese forces are deliberately targeting civilian population centers using massed missile and bomber attacks,” Jake continued. “The United Nations has begun referring to these actions as potential war crimes.”

Another blast rattled the hillside. Jake flinched but held position.

“As I report this,” he said, voice steady but tight, “the question echoing across the world is simple: How long can Taiwan hold?”

He paused, glancing toward the beach where Marines fought and fell in the smoke.

"The answer," Jake said quietly, "will be written in blood. And time is running out. Like the Alamo of old, these brave troops, men and women, will fight to the bitter end."

The camera held on his face as the sounds of war swallowed the signal. Susie Legmann's hand rose to her face as an uncontrolled cry rose from her heart. "Take care, my Jake. Come back to me, darling!"

Millions of viewers fell silent in their homes, offices, and on their phones as they looked at the last image of Jake Hendel at the Alamo in the Pacific.

Pacific Naval Command, Honolulu, Hawaii

Hundreds of red icons pulsed across the big board, overwhelming the scattered blue markers of U.S. Coalition forces. The imbalance was impossible to ignore. Taiwan was being swallowed by a rising red tide, and with every passing minute, the blue contracted.

Occupation was no longer a theoretical outcome—it was imminent.

And if Taiwan fell, Flint knew the dominoes wouldn't stop there. The Philippines. Okinawa. Half a dozen smaller nations caught between ambition and geography. China was executing its 2050 Indo-Pacific strategy ahead of schedule. So far, it was working.

The question was no longer why they had moved.

It was how to stop them.

Flint turned to his Chief Intelligence Officer. "What's the latest?"

Newsome didn't hesitate. "PLA forces are projected to overrun Landing Zones One through Four within the next few hours. Chinese airborne units, supported by ground-attack aircraft, seized Hengchun Airbase ten minutes ago."

A ripple moved through the room.

"Taichung and Tainan airbases have taken heavy damage and are barely operational. The Port of Kaohsiung is under sustained naval assault and could fall at any moment. We're also receiving confirmed reports of Chinese air commandos securing major highways linking LZs One through Four to Taiwan's primary urban centers."

They weren't just landing. They were locking the island down. Flint clenched his jaw, working his cheek muscles as he stared at the map. Red lines tightened like a noose.

Finally, he spoke. "It's time to change the game."

Newsome straightened, encouraged—but wisely remained silent.

Flint turned to his executive officer. "Get Jake Hendel on the line. I want eyes over the beach—now."

The XO nodded and moved fast.

Flint returned his gaze to the board. The enemy had momentum. It was time to take it away.

Landing Zone One

Jake's CIA satellite phone vibrated, and he answered, "World Traveler."

"Jake, this is Admiral Flint. How are you faring?"

Jake shook his head and said, "The men are exhausted, low on ammo, and readiness is below thirty percent. Close air support and infantry-level missiles are all that's keeping us alive."

Flint could hear Jake's concern and asked, "How long can Seacrest hold?"

Jake thought aloud, "About ten minutes after the air force stops coming. He needs tanks on the beach, indirect fire units in the hills, and attack aircraft urgently."

Flint paused to think it over, then said, "Have Seacrest declare a broken arrow."

Jake knew a broken arrow meant that a U.S. unit was in immediate danger of being overrun and called in all available resources. It provided some hope. Maybe some help.

Flint continued, "Once he declares it, convince the world that we must hit them with everything we've got or lose our Alamo in the Pacific."

Jake's tired mind processed Flint's words. Was the Admiral really willing to take the gloves off? Were there enough units left that could arrive in time to change the outcome?

"Will do," Jake responded.

Knowing his friend could soon be killed, Flint said, "Jake, keep your head down. We need you. Tell Seacrest I'll send the cavalry once he sends the message. Out"

Jake smiled, wondering what Flint had in mind. While the situation was desperate in Taiwan, thousands were dying from anarchy in U.S. cities. Jake wondered how the 1,000 men of the Order could hope to prevail against the present evil, a force that vastly outnumbered them. Then an inner voice reminded him, "With God all things are possible."

***

Jake caught up with Hank and told him, “I’m going to the CP. Why don’t you grab some sleep?”

Exhausted, Hank nodded and headed to the bunker without a word.

Five minutes later, he arrived at the CP and was allowed in by the Marine guards. Scanning the cramped room, he located Seacrest and Stillwell bent over a map table. The newly promoted Captain looked at him and asked, “How is the press fairing?”

Jake smiled, “Can we speak privately?”

Seacrest examined Jake’s face, then said, “Men take five.”

After the radioman, Stillwell, and the small staff vacated the post, Seacrest asked, “What’s up?”

Jake cut to the chase, “I’m CIA, and Admiral Flint uses me to provide local color.”

Seacrest didn’t look surprised.

“He wants you to declare a broken arrow.”

The young captain nodded and called his leadership team back inside. While the order didn’t come through official military channels, Seacrest knew it was likely to be his last chance at survival.

No sooner was the blast door closed than Chinese naval artillery landed on their position, knocking them off their feet.

The artillery barrage lasted for two minutes, followed by six Chinese attack aircraft that mercilessly assaulted their position.

“Launch our remaining anti-ship missiles and SAMs. Have the quartermaster issue our remaining ammunition,” Seacrest ordered.

Through the fog of war, Seacrest could see that most of his fixed beach positions lay in ruins. His men looked like a swarm of ants as they dug new firing trenches among the rubble.

“Sir, that last attack took out the minefield. All we’ve got left is the Voo gas, steel cutters, and concertina wire. None of it will stop armor. We’re down to 12,000 rounds of 5.56 and 10,000 of belted ammo. The only bright spot is that those replacements gave us twelve more artillery guns on the hill, and we have six tanks on the beach,” Stillwell observed.

His radioman added, “Sir, Central Command informed us that twelve landers are ten clicks out and heading directly for us!”

Every eye was on the young Captain. This was his moment of truth.

“Broken arrow! Send it over both comms!” Seacrest ordered.

In his heart, he knew he and his men were about to make the ultimate sacrifice. Faced with imminent death, Seacrest was surprised he felt no fear. He was resolute in doing his duty to the last breath. It's what Marines do.

For a moment, his mind traveled back to the Normandy Coast and the American Cemetery, where rows of perfectly positioned crosses marked those Americans who'd died to save a people not their own in a faraway land. Would he and his men receive a similar honor?

Seacrest shook off the imagery and looked at Stillwell, "Send 'em to hell!"

Stillwell's leathery face held a stoic resolve as he responded, "Yes, sir."

Seacrest admired his gunnery sergeant's grit. Stillwell was a good Marine, and that's the highest compliment a man can receive.

Seacrest watched as O'Reilly typed *Broken Arrow, LZ 1. Repeat Broken Arrow, LZ1. Seacrest, out*. Seacrest looked to his radioman and nodded.

O'Reilly tuned the radio, then said over the airways, "Broken Arrow! Broken Arrow! LZ-1. Repeat, Broken Arrow! LZ-1!"

Pacific Command

Admiral Flint gripped the edge of the display. The faces of his team shimmered before him, their expressions grim. The daring strike against China had been a success. Tomahawk missiles, unleashed from his hidden ballistic submarines, had carved a path of destruction across the Chinese mainland. Vital missile bases, airfields, and fuel depots lay smoldering ruins.

But euphoria was a luxury he couldn't afford. Taiwan still lay in the Dragon's talons.

Seacrest's declaration sent chills throughout the Pacific Command as the reality of the Chinese capturing their first landing zone reverberated across the Integrated Combat System (ICS). Because the ICS allowed the surface action group, strike groups, and all ICS-equipped assets to operate as a single system, within seconds of receiving Seacrest's message, all available units began responding.

Flint told his commanders, "We're not letting U.S. Marines get overrun. Initiate Operations Gut Cutter and Star Wars."

Several of his direct reports looked concerned at Flint's escalation, but immediately complied.

All across the theater, ships, submarines, and aviation units moved into action for a massive counterattack. Space Command repositioned celestial assets to optimize their effectiveness. A separate communication was sent to the Taiwanese military for reinforcements and air support at LZ 1.

Flint stepped out of the Command Center and dialed his satellite phone.

President Novak pulled his phone from his coat pocket and said, "Novak."

"Mr. President, we have a Marine Unit in danger of being overrun at LZ 1," Flint muttered.

"Jake's words, the Alamo in the Pacific, are ringing hauntingly true, aren't they?"

"Yes, sir," Flint replied evenly.

"Do all you can for them. Keep me posted." President Novak replied.

Northern Desert, China

The stealthy bat-winged RQ-180 Avenger descended to 20,000 feet as it approached the remote missile silos in China's northwestern desert. The base was one of over one hundred nuclear launch points in the communist country. At a cruising speed of 400 mph, the Avenger had 12,240 miles of range remaining, more than enough to complete her mission and return to base.

The Avenger was flown by a ground control crew of two from a remote site in Germany. The Avenger's turbofan engine and stealth features reduced infrared and radar signatures, allowing her to slip in and out of China undetected.

Lieutenant Herb Cousens picked up the phone, "Sir, they're preparing to launch."

Colonel Rick Jennings frowned at the news and ordered, "Bring her home."

Cousens turned the unmanned aerial vehicle around and set the autopilot for the most efficient flight path.

"Get the data to Command," Jennings ordered his communications officer.

***

Flint saw the report and immediately called his Commander-in-Chief.

When the President answered, he said, "Novak."

"Mr. President, China has initiated pre-launch procedures on its Intercontinental Ballistic Missiles."

Novak responded, "Take them out. Keep me posted."

Novak terminated the call and peered at the Joint Chiefs. He knew there were traitors among them. These were mainly paper generals, incompetent in war but skilled manipulators who played the Beltway game effectively. Thank God for the back-channel Oxley established.

USS Ohio (SSGN-726)

Captain Steve Morrison stood on the submarine's bridge reading his orders. As curious officers and enlisted men looked on, Morrison ordered, "Prepare to launch Tomahawks. Ready torpedoes. This is not a drill."

The USS Ohio and four older models had been converted into cruise missile submarines (SSGNs). Each submarine carried 154 Tomahawk cruise missiles, giving each vessel the equivalent firepower of an entire Surface Battle Group. Morrison knew Flint was holding his ballistic missile submarines, a.k.a. boomers, in reserve in case nuclear ordinance was needed.

The USS Ohio, USS Michigan, USS Florida, and USS Georgia had vertical launching systems in a configuration dubbed "multiple all-up-round canisters" installed in twenty-two of their twenty-four missile tubes, replacing one large ballistic missile with seven smaller Tomahawk missiles. The two remaining tubes were converted to lockout chambers for special forces personnel.

"Take us to launch depth!"

Two minutes later, Morrison's Executive officer reported, "Firing solutions are loaded, all systems are operational."

Captain Morrison ordered, "Fire!"

Within seconds, the first Tomahawk was launched, followed every few seconds by another missile until all 154 birds were in the air. An hour later, the four submarines had launched a spread of 616 Tomahawks.

"Make our depth 300 feet and assume a heading of 270 degrees, all ahead two-thirds. Ready countermeasures. We must assume the PLA knows our launch position and will be hunting us," Morrison said.

While the submarines disappeared into the depths, the long-range Tomahawks took out Chinese ships, airports, and naval bases within a range of 1,500 miles. Traveling at 550 miles per hour, the weapons took up to three hours to reach their targets.

Spratly Islands

Admiral Chong examined his digital map of Chinese outposts, which included three airfields. His reverie was interrupted as red images began popping up on Mischief Reef, his furthest base.

"Get me imagery on Mischief!"

Soon, camera images were shown on the big screen. To his horror, Chong saw missiles streaking from the sky.

"Sir, they're U.S. Tomahawks," Captain Yangon replied.

The Admiral ordered, "What's the status of our attack submarines?"

"Sir, twenty submarines have missed their reporting times and are presumed to be lost to enemy action," Yangon replied.

As the two men watched, fuel depots ignited, planes and ships blew up, and buildings exploded. A minute later, all closed-circuit cameras went black.

"Get me a damage report!" Chong ordered.

USS Henry M. Jackson (SSBN 730)

Admiral Flint had ordered the submarine to sea two weeks earlier in preparation for war. Since then, the stealthy submarine had taken up a position 1,500 miles east of Taiwan and was in an ideal location to launch enough nuclear ordinance to destroy ninety percent of China.

Her skipper, Captain Joshua Harris, accepted an urgent message from SUBPAC Command and read it twice before handing it to his Executive Officer.

Harris looked at his XO and said, "This is a first."

The XO replied, "Guess we'll get to use our nuclear keys after all."

"I verified the message; it's legit," Harris confirmed.

Captain Harris picked up the handset for the PA system and made an announcement, "This is your captain speaking. We've been ordered to prepare one Trident 2 D5 missile for launch."

Officers and crew across the submarine went to their combat stations, a moment they would remember for the rest of their lives. It was the first time they'd be ordered to fire a nuclear missile.

"Once we've fired, take us to 300 feet and a heading of 90 degrees. Our launch will light up Chinese and Russian radars like a Christmas Tree, so be prepared to run silent and deep," Harris ordered.

Chinese Carrier Liaoning

The South China Sea was deceptively calm. Beneath its glassy surface, the USS Colorado, a Virginia-class attack submarine, glided silently at 400 feet. Commander Claude Dwyer stared at the sonar display, his jaw tight. The Chinese carrier Liaoning was 22 nautical miles northeast, flanked by two destroyers and a frigate—an iron phalanx slicing through contested waters.

"Passive sonar confirms target profile," whispered Petty Officer Langston. "Carrier signature matches Liaoning. She's moving at 18 knots. Escort pattern is tight."

Dwyer nodded. "Bring AWS online. Set for coordinated launch."

Above them, the Liaoning was a floating fortress—aircraft stacked on deck, radar arrays sweeping the horizon. But it was vulnerable. The U.S. Navy's Advanced Weapons System had been designed for this moment: a networked strike package combining AI-guided torpedoes and stealth drones. No warning. No escape.

"Activate Manta."

The Weapons officer watched as Seaman First Class O'Brien typed in the code and hit enter. "Manta activated. All systems are go."

The U.S. Navy Manta Ray was an unmanned underwater vehicle, a silent predator beneath the waves. Built for long-duration, autonomous missions without human oversight, the Manta Ray deployed efficient hydrodynamics that made it graceful, stealthy, and powerful. Designed to operate in contested maritime environments, it used buoyancy-driven gliding, allowing it to travel vast distances with minimal energy. It could also rest on the seafloor to conserve power, then reawaken for mission continuation. With a wingspan of forty-five feet, a length of thirty-three feet, and armed to the teeth, the vehicle punched well above its weight class. Space consumed by human life support in manned vehicles was filled with weapons.

"Authorization code confirmed," XO Martinez acknowledged. "Strike package green."

Dwyer keyed the final command. "Execute."

From the depths, the Manta Ray awakened, moved into position, and fired two Mark 48 ADCAP torpedoes. The weapons surged forward, their guidance systems linked to a constellation of underwater drones feeding real-time telemetry. The AWS algorithm adjusted mid-course, threading the torpedoes between the escort vessels with surgical precision.

On the Liaoning, alarms blared. The captain barked orders in Mandarin, scrambling fighters and deploying countermeasures. But it was too late.

The first torpedo struck portside, just below the waterline. A thunderous crack split the hull, sending shockwaves through the carrier's superstructure. The second hit amidships, igniting fuel reserves and rupturing the engine compartment. Fireballs erupted skyward. The deck buckled. Aircraft tumbled into the sea like toys.

From Colorado, the crew watched the sonar bloom with chaos.

"Multiple explosions, she's breaking up," Langston said.

A minute later, "The Liaoning disappeared from the surface."

Dwyer exhaled. "Message to COMSUBPAC: Liaoning, sunk. Commencing exfil."

As the submarine turned west, the South China Sea swallowed the wreckage. Above, satellites recorded the aftermath. Below, the ocean returned to silence as the Manta Ray returned to sleep mode and waited for her next victim.

East China Sea, Aircraft Carrier Shandong

China's first domestically produced aircraft carrier, the Shandong, entered service in 2019 with a grand celebration. The carrier was conventionally powered by steam turbines with diesel generators, making it inferior in range and speed to U.S. nuclear-powered carriers. Despite being outmatched in head-to-head battles, Shandong had proven effective in ground attacks and in air superiority.

As her Captain Matuso Ling watched from the bridge, a Shandong J-15 fighter was catapulted up the carrier's twelve-degree ski jump ramp. The jet seemed to drop before finally gaining altitude.

Ling was pleased that his pilots had flown over 200 sorties, helping China capture the Penghu Islands and establishing air superiority from the Chinese Coast to their Spratly Island bases. Unfortunately, Ling lamented, he'd lost six fighters to the inexperienced crews of Chinese antiaircraft batteries and six more to friendly fire from Chinese Ships. Two additional planes had crashed on takeoff. Ling rationalized his losses as the cost of gaining battle experience.

"Sir, incoming missiles from the East!" said the nervous radar operator.

Ling ordered, "Cease air operations, initiate anti-missile defense, notify command."

Two Maritime Strike Tomahawk missiles rose from the water with a fiery blast. The twin merchants of death followed their inertial guidance systems to the Shandong. When they reached a range of ten miles, their Digital Scene Matching Area Correlation systems took over, providing terminal guidance.

Flying in just above the waves, the Tomahawks proved challenging targets for the carrier's missile defenses, and maritime haze blocked them from the gunner's view.

As Captain Ling stood on the bridge issuing orders, the first American missile struck the carrier amidships at the water line. The blast's force and hydrostatic shock ripped a twenty-foot hole in the carrier's hull, knocking sailors to the deck.

The second Tomahawk arched up, striking the Shandong's hangar bay. The explosion of over 1,000 pounds of high explosives immediately ignited the ship's aviation fuel stores and dozens of aircraft. Seconds later, bombs and missiles detonated, forcing the landing deck upward, rendering the ship incapable of flight operations. As fires spread and additional munitions ignited, the Shandong began listing to port. The firefighters' inexperience, combined with the loss of water pressure and the burning of aviation fuel, condemned the Shandong.

Captain Ling decided to save his remaining pilots and crew and ordered, "Abandon ship!"

Ten minutes later, Ling and two hundred of his surviving crew watched as the Shendong rolled over and slipped beneath the waves. As the once proud carrier sank, burning oil and gas covered the surface, complicating rescue operations.

John Warner (SSN-785)

The nuclear-powered Virginia-class attack submarine slipped silently through the dark waters like a silent shark stalking its prey. The black boat's lethal payload included torpedoes and missiles along with special operations forces, unmanned undersea vehicles, and the Advanced SEAL Delivery System, making it one of the most potent and versatile weapons in the world.

Commander Dan Caldwell and his crew had stealthfully positioned themselves in the South China Sea without detection. Now, he hoped the moonless night and fog would buy enough cover for them to fire their package and simultaneously destroy the last enemy carrier. While usually an ice-cold operator, the loss of thirty-one Annapolis classmates to enemy fire had made the war very personal.

As fate would have it, he was in the right place, at the right time, with the right weapon to change the course of the war. It was everything a submariner could hope for. Then, as he considered his next move, his exuberance was tempered by the fact that he was about to attempt something that had never been done before: sinking surface ships with torpedoes while simultaneously launching missiles. It wasn't the safe play; it was the long ball. If he succeeded, his boat could save hundreds of thousands of lives and possibly change the tide of the war. If he failed, he and 134 souls would join his classmates in a watery grave.

The burden of command required that he weigh his mission against loss of life. It was the age-old conflict that made command burdensome. Caldwell ran through his options one last time. He could break off from the surface ships and launch his missiles from a less risky location, but this would leave a carrier loaded with eighty aircraft and two Renhai-Class Destroyers as a threat to Taiwan and any U.S. ships coming in from the States.

Caldwell also knew his men would perform better if they bought in.

Looking to his XO, he said, "The carrier has eighty aircraft. Those destroyers have 112 Vertical Launch System cells, capable of firing long-range surface-to-air, anti-ship, and land-attack cruise missiles, plus rocket-assisted torpedoes. That's more firepower than almost any ship afloat. They must be destroyed if we are to save Taiwan."

His XO looked concerned, and Caldwell could see the fear in his crew's eyes.

"The sooner we launch our missiles, the sooner Chinese missiles and radar will be offline, and Admiral Flint can move in additional carrier groups. Right now, we have Marines, Americans, dying to slow the Chinese horde. Let's help even the odds."

He remembered the advice of his first skipper, now Admiral Flint, who'd told him, "Dan, if you are ever in a position to change the outcome of the battle, it's always worth the risk. We're paid to take it to the enemy, and you can't do that by being timid."

The XO's bearing betrayed his fear as he came over to Caldwell and said, "Sir, there's no way to avoid drawing attention. When we launch, the Chinese will pounce with everything they've got."

Every eye in the command center was watching the exchange as Caldwell looked directly and sternly at his XO and said, "That's right. I figure we have two minutes to sink the carrier, two Destroyers, and a few of the escorts while we launch missiles. That's why we must fire efficiently, then slip away quickly."

Caldwell saw the doubt in the eyes of some of his crew and added, "We sank a dozen Iranian cruisers and took out a dozen missile sites on our last tour. So, we know how to fight this boat. Currently, we have the element of surprise and the opportunity to alter the war's outcome. It's a ballsy move, but the home team needs a touchdown, right now, or the game could be over."

Caldwell's command presence masked his concerns. Theoretically, a sand pan with a depth charge could sink his billion-dollar boat, and the U.S. had just lost whole carrier groups to the Chinese. The Russians were another potential threat. Then there was the possibility that some lucky destroyer skipper would score with a torpedo or depth charge. Nevertheless, Caldwell, a prior Annapolis quarterback, knew it was time to throw the long ball.

Caldwell picked up the mike and flipped on the boat's public address system. "This is your captain speaking. Right now, God has placed us in the right place at the right time with the right weapon to change the outcome of the war."

Throughout the submarine, crew members listened intently.

"The home team needs a win. And, yes, the odds are against us. But we have to try. When I was playing football at the Academy, the Army-Navy game was all-important. The score was 21-17 in the Army's favor. We were driving on the Army 35-yard line with three seconds left on the clock. So, I called a Hail Mary and asked my line and backs to block like hell. The Army Defense swarmed us like flies on a picnic pie, and I was running for my life. Then, hope against hope, Nate Burson, my star receiver, broke double coverage, made the corner of the end zone, and I threw with all my might. I took a vicious hit, and as I lay there, I heard the crowd cheer! When I made my way to my feet, I saw Nate standing in the end zone, ball in hand. The scoreboard read Navy 23, Army 21." Caldwell paused for effect. "Team, it's time to throw the Hail Mary. I know it's asking a lot. But it's no more than you're capable of doing if you give it your best. Block like hell, we're throwing the long ball."

Their skipper's inspiring speech resonated, each crew member committing their all to the cause.

"Mr. Wallace," Calwell looked directly into the eyes of his XO and ordered, "Take us to launch depth."

Bringing the Virginia-class submarine to launch depth involved a precise and coordinated set of commands and procedures governed by the Officer of the Deck, the Diving Officer of the Watch, and the Submarine Control Party. Caldwell watched the controls to ensure his crew had brought the boat to a stable launch depth.

Caldwell ordered, "Raise the attack periscope."

The Quartermaster of the Watch complied and responded, "Aye, raise the attack periscope."

The Virginia-class boat used a photonics mast rather than a traditional optical periscope. The unit was operated via a joystick and console rather than a manual handle.

A moment later, the Quartermaster replied, "Attack periscope is raised."

Caldwell ordered, "Sweep."

The operator immediately rotated the periscope mast 360° to visually scan for contacts.

The non-penetrating photonics mast sent surface images to high-resolution displays in the control room as the crew looked on. As predicted by weather reports, a broken fog shrouded the surface, but the periscope operator was able to obtain visual identification of the carrier and its four escorts. They had the Fujian, pride of the Chinese fleet, in their sights!

"Mark that carrier. Designate it Sierra One. Develop a torpedo-firing solution. Prepare all missiles for launch. Make it snappy, we're vulnerable up here."

Seconds later, the Fire Control Technician responded, "Sir, the torpedo firing solution is complete."

Caldwell looked at the battle screen, rechecked the location of the Chinese ships, and ordered, “Fire tubes one through four at Sierra One.”

In a series of swooshes, four Mark 48 torpedoes began their 2,500-yard journey.

“Reload tubes one, two, three, and four with Mark-48 ADCAP torpedoes, set speed to 55 knots, autonomous mode,” Caldwell barked.

Looking at the combat display, Caldwell saw a dozen other Chinese ships.

“Mark that destroyer, Sierra Two, the missile ship, Sierra Three, the distant destroyer, Sierra Four, and the missile cruiser, Sierra Five. Prepare firing solutions, one fish per target.”

“Ay, targeting,” responded the weapons officer.

“Sir, torpedoes are running straight and true; carrier impact in eighty seconds,” sonar reported.

The tension was high as Caldwell wiped sweat from his brow with his sleeve, knowing they’d just alerted the whole Chinese Navy! He hoped he’d called the right play, or they’d pay a high price.

The Weapons Officer replied, “All tubes are loaded, one torpedo for each designated target. Targeting solutions are loaded. Ready to Fire.”

“Fire tubes one, two, three, and four, then reload tubes one, two, and three with Mark-48 ADCAP torpedoes, set speed to 55 knots, autonomous mode. Load the Mobile Submarine Simulator in tube four,” Caldwell ordered.

Four successive swooshes could be heard. Seconds later, the autonomous torpedoes were streaking toward the enemy ships.

The missile officer added, “Sir, launch orientation achieved. Tubes are flooded, and the outer doors are open. Awaiting Authorization to Launch Missiles.”

“Sir, second set of torpedoes running straight and true,” noted the Sonarman.

Caldwell removed the launch key from around his neck while his XO did the same. Both men walked to the console, inserted their keys, and turned them to provide launch authorization.

"Authorization is confirmed. Weapons are ready to fire on your command,” reported the Weapons Officer.

The control room of the John Warner buzzed with quiet intensity. The crew, bathed in red tactical lighting, watched their instruments with icy focus. Captain Caldwell stood behind the fire control console, arms crossed, his voice low and deliberate.

"Confirm target package Lima-Seven-Two," he ordered.

"Confirmed, Sir," replied Fire Control Technician First Class Mendoza. "Coordinates match. Targets are confirmed."

Caldwell gave a single nod. "Weapons free. Launch all missiles in sequence."

Mendoza's fingers danced across the console. "Firing in 5… 4… 3… 2… 1…"

The sub shuddered, a resounding metallic thump reverberating through the hull like the beat of a distant war drum. Even in the belly of the ocean, the crew could feel each of the twelve Tomahawks leave — not violently, but like something massive shifting in the depths.

On the sonar screen, a telltale acoustic void indicated that the missiles had launched cleanly and silently. This meant that all Tomahawks cleared the surface — their booster rockets igniting as they clawed into the sky like harbingers of fire.

The Tomahawks, flying at 550 miles per hour, soon dropped to 100 feet, hugging the deck with machine precision. Each missile carried a 1,000-pound warhead and flew a course designed to weave between radar gaps. Within three hours, each weapon would strike its target.

Sonar reported, "Sir, we have registered four hits on the carrier!"

The crew cheered!

Chinese Carrier Fujian

The Fujian was an entirely different design from the Shandong and the largest of China's fleet, being only slightly smaller than the U.S. Navy's Ford-class ships. U.S. intelligence had learned that the Fujian was equipped with an electromagnetic and steam-powered catapult, indicating a significant step up in Chinese carrier technology and the capability to launch heavier aircraft.

The Fujian turned to recover a squadron of Su-33s returning from air-to-ground attacks on U.S. Allied positions. The Russian jet had proven its versatility early in the war by covering a range of combat scenarios, from air-to-air dogfights to ground strikes. The presence of Russian pilots with recent combat experience in Ukraine had helped his younger pilots learn combat tactics.

Captain Sumoto Changli told his Air Group Commander, "I'm pleased with your pilot's strike effectiveness. With the American air and naval forces temporarily out of the fight, your less experienced pilots have the opportunity to gain valuable combat experience. That will all change when the Americans use their vast air and sea transport capabilities to rearm their Pacific Command. All the more reason to do maximum damage now, while China owns the skies."

The Air Group Commander nodded in agreement.

A strange foreboding struck Changli as he gazed out the window, cursing the fog rolling across the East China Sea. The haze distorted radar returns, cut visibility, and left him blind at the worst possible moment. The heavy rains had forced his air group commander to cease most air operations.

He scanned the bridge crew. "Where's our sonarman?"

The XO stiffened. "Sick bay, Captain. Replacement en route."

Changli almost barked a reprimand but stopped himself. A public scolding would weaken confidence. There would be time later.

The first torpedo struck amidships, followed by three more torpedoes striking the stern and bow. As fate would have it, a minute later, a Tomahawk cruise missile fired from the USS Ohio tore through the forward aircraft elevator, igniting fuel stores and ammunition lockers. Primary and secondary explosions blew away most of the flight deck and superstructure. Fires raged like demons, following seeping fuel deep into her lower decks, killing everyone in their path.

Beneath the water, the carrier shuddered violently, her screws silenced, her spine broken. Seawater surged into compartments before sailors could dog the bulkheads, drowning men where they stood.

"Evasive action! Fire control active! Seal those compartments!" Changli roared, gripping the railing as the ship listed under him.

Damage-control teams fought desperately—pumps whining, hoses spraying, sailors hammering at watertight doors. It was a losing fight. Within minutes, the engine room was flooded. Auxiliary power failed, plunging the cavernous interior into blood-red emergency lighting.

The XO turned to him, face pale. "Captain, we're listing hard to starboard. Engines are gone. Fires are out of control. We can't contain them. Sir… It's hopeless."

The words struck harder than any missile. Changli felt hollow, gutted. Not only had he lost the pride of China's Navy, but he had also condemned most of his crew to death. His name would be cursed in Beijing, etched forever into the roll of failure.

Still, duty demanded clarity. His voice was steady when he spoke. "Abandon ship."

Chaos erupted as the ship's remaining sailors scrambled for lifeboats. Only a quarter of the crew escaped the listing hulk before warheads detonated in a chain reaction and turned the night sky white-hot.

Those who survived looked back in horror and awe. Their last sight was Captain Changli, standing rigid on the bridge catwalk, cap tucked beneath his arm, saluting as the explosions engulfed his ship.

Moments later, the Fujian—once the jewel of the People's Liberation Navy—slipped beneath the cold, gray waves of the East China Sea.

John Warner (SSN-785)

The submarine waited at periscope depth to send and receive communications and attempt to gain visual confirmation of strikes.

"See if you can get visual, record images," Caldwell ordered to the Quartermaster.

"Aye, sir. Bringing up images now. Camera recording," replied the quartermaster.

The amplified image showed the Chinese Carrier Fujian listing to starboard. Fires and massive smoke stacks were now visible. They also saw that two cruisers were altering course, most likely to help with rescue operations. Seconds later, fuel stores and ammunition detonated, creating a massive fireball. Then the carrier split in half. Moments later, the ship's remains began their slow descent to the bottom.

John Warner's crew cheered!

Under his breath, Caldwell murmured, "That's for my shipmates."

Medoza responded, "All Birds away!"

Caldwell looked at the missile launch clock, ninety-one seconds. A new record.

"Torpedoes, ready to fire, sir."

"Fire tubes one, two, and three. Reload tubes one, two, and three," Caldwell barked.

"Sir, we have active pinging coming from Sierra two; she's confirmed as a Luyang III-class Destroyer. Range 12,000 yards, speed thirty-five knots, she's headed straight for us," Sonar reported.

"Sir, we have two aircraft heading our way, distance to the lead bogey is 11,500 yards, speed ninety knots!" the radarman reported.

Caldwell knew the destroyers carried sonar-equipped helicopters armed with torpedoes and depth charges. The airborne threat would be on them in less than four minutes. He also knew that his torpedoes were homing in on their host ships. His gut told him he'd scored a major victory; it was time to evade and escape.

He ordered, "All stations, rig for ultra-quiet! Conn, Sonar, designate contact Sierra Six: possible helo. Sierra Seven: helo. Helm, all ahead flank. Come right to course 185. Dive the boat. Make your depth 700 feet."

Immediately, the crew secured all loose objects, the kitchen stopped preparing food, and all unnecessary conversation ceased as the boat began a rapid descent. The eerie quiet added to the crew's anxiety. This was no maneuver; real enemies were hunting them.

"Sonar, confirm layer depth." Caldwell's order sought to confirm they had dropped below a thermal layer that would disrupt enemy sonar.

"Sonar confirms we just dropped below the thermocline, sir."

"Helm, level off below the layer. Steady as she goes. Launch Mobile Submarine Simulator (MSS)," Caldwell ordered, hoping that the unit's fake sub noise would draw away any enemy torpedoes that dove this deep.

He knew that reducing the noise from his propellers would further reduce his acoustic profile. He also had three remaining tubes loaded with torpedoes, if needed. Loading tube four would make too much noise. He considered deploying bold canisters, bubble-producing noisemakers, but decided the single simulator would create a better deception.

"Let's change course and try to slip away undetected while the Chinese target the Simulator. Come left to the new course 090. Dive to 1000 feet. Helm, make turns for five knots. Run silent."

The crew remained silent, each sailor and officer knowing that depth charges or torpedo blasts at this depth would leverage water pressure to maximize their lethality.

"Sir, we have depth charges in the water! Distance twelve hundred yards." Sonar reported.

"Stay on them," Caldwell urged.

Seconds later, the crew heard a metallic echo, similar to distant thunder, and felt slight vibrations in the hull.

"Deploy towed array sonar. Dive to 1200 feet!" Caldwell ordered.

Two minutes passed in silence as the captain and crew heard depth charges as close as eight hundred yards.

Once fully deployed, the towed array TB-34 trailed 200 yards behind the sub in quieter water layers, providing better detection of surface contacts.

"Sir, I have one hit on Sierra Two," Sonar reported.

Caldwell looked at his crew in the command center and smiled. It was a silent but well-received message: good job.

A minute later, sonar reported, "I have a hit on Sierra Four. Sierra Two is breaking up!"

Caldwell and his crew heard two more depth charges at a distance of 1,400 yards.

The XO leaned toward Caldwell and whispered, "Must be from those helos."

Caldwell nodded.

Sonar reported, "Sierra Four is breaking up."

A minute later, Sonar reported, "I have hits on Sierra Three and Five!"

Caldwell wanted to give the crew an "atta-boy" over the PA system, but decided that maintaining stealth was the first priority.

Two minutes later, Sonar reported, "We have depth charge detonations at 800 yards."

The weapons officer announced, "Sub-simulator has gone silent."

"Make a course for Guam – Polaris Point / Ordnance Annex. We need to replenish torpedoes and missiles. Check with SEAL Commander Marsh and see if he needs anything."

"Aye, Captain, making course for Guam," replied the XO.

The John Warner slipped away silently as her towed array sonar monitored the surface. It was time to reload and get back in the fight as soon as possible.

Pacific Command

Admiral Flint and his command monitored the track of their missiles as they destroyed Chinese ships, air bases, and land fortifications. Three hours later, Newsome reported, "Sir, two hundred thirty-five PLA Naval vessels, including all three Chinese carriers, and three hundred and seven merchant ships providing troop and supply mobility have been sunk."

Admiral Flint looked pleased. "Excellent, what about land targets?"

"Sir, eighty percent of China's offensive missile capability and twenty key airfields have been destroyed."

"What's the ETA on the high-altitude detonation?" Flint asked.

"Ten seconds, sir," replied his XO.

The Command Center was quiet as they waited for the first detonation of a U.S. nuclear weapon in battle since 1945.

The violent burst of electromagnetic energy from the rapid acceleration of charged particles in the high-altitude detonation interacted with gamma rays and atmospheric molecules, disturbing or permanently damaging exposed electrical systems. Ground observers witnessed an auroral display of reds, greens, oranges, and yellows in the night sky, as the violent energy wreaked havoc on the ground.

Satellite imagery revealed a large circular region captured within the EMP's arch. On the ground, China's network of surveillance cameras captured images of power lines sparking and falling, transformers blowing, and planes crashing over a 2,500-mile radius. Surveillance cameras in Beijing and the port of Shanghai captured images of trucks and cars coming to a stop, street lamps exploding, and buildings going dark as frightened citizens emerged to see what had happened. Newsome found it interesting that the Chinese had protected their surveillance cameras from EMP, but failed to protect civilian infrastructure.

"That should shut down most of their supply chain," Flint observed. "What's the after-action report?"

"Most Chinese commercial satellites are non-responsive. Space Force jammers have shut down the remaining command-and-control satellites, rendering them cyber-blind. Our space-based pulse weapons are targeting nuclear silos in China and North Korea as we speak."

Flint's jaws worked at the realization that the next few hours could start a nuclear Armageddon, followed by a nuclear winter that would kill ninety percent of the human race. No theater commander or President had ever been this close to the end of the world as we know it.

U.S. Space Force, Orbital Battle Station

The voice of AEGIS said, "Pulse Weapon energized and ready to fire!"

Colonel Rashid looked at Payload Specialist Giles and said, "You have control; the planet's fate is in your hands."

Military psychologists had carefully vetted Giles to ensure he would perform his duty regardless of the stress or moral dilemma. Rashid realized that the good-natured scientist, turned space warrior, was much more than he appeared to be. She'd grow up with civilian whiz kids, but Giles was different.

"I've moved two additional pulse weapons platforms into range, giving us ten in the zone. Target coordinates are loaded. I'm engaging in Autonomous Attack Profile Alpha. The firing sequence begins in three, two, one, fire."

Colonel Rashid held her breath while trying to look calm.

As the orbital crew peered through their observation windows, packets of energy flew to their earth-based targets with pinpoint accuracy.

"Sir, I've activated the SM-4 network as a precaution. If the Chinese or Russians fire on us, I can destroy them quickly," Giles noted.

Rashid replied, "Keep your guard up."

Pacific Command, Hawaii

Sir, Space Command just notified us that they're implementing phase one of Star Wars," the XO said.

Satellites and drones allowed Flint and his team to observe images of domelike missile doors atop underground Chinese silos as they began to smoke.

"Sir, that's the initial pulse wave," Newsome narrated.

A second later, Flint's team watched as rocket fuel exploded, blowing debris high into the air across Chinese missile bases. Then, he watched as dozens of mobile launchers cooked off.

A loud cheer arose across the Command Center.

Within ten minutes, all known Chinese silos had been destroyed.

Flint said, "Space Command, good shooting. What's the damage assessment?"

Space Command General Archer replied, "All known silos are out of commission, along with fifty percent of Chinese mobile launchers. We can remove additional ground assets for you if you can designate them on the ICS."

Flint was shocked at the surgical precision of the strikes. The ability to remove the enemy from a space base out of harm's way made his mind race with battlefield possibilities.

"We're tracking them down. Keep tight overwatch on the region. You may need to counter their mobile launchers if we can't locate them. And keep a close eye on North Korea and Russia."

Archer said, "Affirmative, overwatch is active."

"Well done, General," Flint said, then ended the transmission.

Cape Kennedy, Florida

A Falcon Heavy rocket lifted the Boeing X-37 reusable robotic spacecraft into the heavens. The Falcon consisted of a center core with two F-9 boosters attached and a second stage on top of the center core. It possessed the fourth-highest capacity of any rocket to reach orbit, trailing behind the SLS, Energia, and the Saturn V.

Amidst the sounds of grasshoppers and native birds, the Falcon Heavy blasted through the early morning haze with a flame that could be seen up and down the coast. The unmanned spacecraft was designed to land like the retired space shuttle and was operated by the Department of the Air Force Rapid Capabilities Office in collaboration with the United States Space Force.

After reaching its elliptical high Earth orbit, the mysterious X-37B, code-named Omega-6, deployed several small satellites not listed in the U.S. military's official catalog.

Three hours after launch, the mission commander informed them that, "Omega-6 has deployed the last Lighting-3 Pulse weapon and assumed her planned orbit. All weapons systems are live. Switching control to AEGIS now."

Pacific Command, Honolulu

Newsome looked at his boss and knew what he was thinking. He said, "Sir, Operation Star Wars was a complete success. All known Chinese nuclear launch silos and fixed position launchers have been destroyed."

"What's the update on Operation Gut Cutter?" Flint asked.

Newsome put a tally on the screen, saying, "The operation destroyed sixty percent of their remaining supply and troop ships and seventy percent of their warships. We're still working to locate thirty-two Chinese submarines."

Flint asked, "Chinese Air Forces?"

"The PLA retains 500 fighters, 200 attack aircraft, and 250 helicopters. Most of their cargo planes remain operative. The net-net is that the PLA could still capture Taipei within the week."

"Major challenges?" Flint asked.

"We're down to 150 Tomahawk missiles, and small-arms ammo is critically low. With China retaining a significant conventional missile force and air superiority, we cannot deploy the 190,000 available Coalition troops to Taiwan. While over four million Taiwanese civilians have volunteered for military service, they lack training and weapons."

Flint's XO asked, "What if we move in our amphibious assault ships?"

Flint thought it over and replied, "Issue the order, but remind them that China still has plenty of missiles. Use that new cloaking technology."

"While we've greatly reduced the risk of China striking the U.S. mainland, Taiwan remains at risk," Newsome replied skeptically.

Flint said, "Let's hope our Joint Forces can hold the line long enough for us to bring in the cavalry. Air Commander, it's time to test our sixth-gen fighters."

Colonel Mark Larson, AirForce Liaison, smiled and replied, "Yes, sir."

Night Skies, Chinese Air Space

The newly formed and highly classified squadron launched from Andersen Air Force Base under a moonless Pacific sky, the kind of night aviators remembered long after wars were over. There were no afterburner flares, no radio chatter, no signatures to betray their presence—only twelve fighters and a host of "loyal wingman" drones lifting smoothly into the darkness and vanishing from every known sensor domain. They were Boeing F-47s, the first operational embodiment of the United States' Next Generation Air Dominance vision, and they were about to change the geometry of air warfare forever.

Across thousands of miles of contested airspace, a massive Chinese air package was already airborne—fighters, bombers, escorts, and command-and-control aircraft moving with confidence born of numbers and proximity. Nearly two hundred aircraft surged westward in disciplined formations, supported by ground radar, airborne early warning platforms, and space-based sensors. By every model that had governed air combat for decades, such a force should have been impossible to surprise.

They never saw it coming.

The F-47s did not penetrate hostile airspace in the traditional sense. They existed outside the battlespace as it had been understood, operating beyond visual range, beyond radar coherence, beyond the enemy's ability to detect or interpret what was happening. Their stealth was not merely about reduced signatures—it was about information denial. Enemy sensors did not fail; they simply received nothing meaningful to process. Targets simply never appeared.

First, one formation lost contact. Then another. Chinese pilots reported system anomalies, vanishing datalinks, and radar returns that dissolved into noise. Bombers went silent mid-mission. Escorts found themselves flying through empty sky where friendly icons had been moments before. There were no dogfights, no flares, no warning shots—only the growing realization that aircraft were being removed from the airspace without ever knowing they were under attack.

The engagement lasted less than an hour.

When it was over, more than two hundred Chinese fighters and bombers were gone—neutralized at range, never having detected a single adversary, never having fired a shot in return. No wreckage fell near the F-47s. No radar ever painted them. No pilot on the opposing side could later describe what had happened, only that the sky itself had turned hostile.

The squadron returned to Andersen before dawn, landing as quietly as it had departed. Maintenance crews waited in silence. No victory music played. No announcements were made. In the hangars, the pilots removed their helmets, their expressions subdued, men and women who understood what they had just witnessed—not a battle, but a demonstration.

Air superiority had crossed a threshold.

The lesson was unmistakable: wars would no longer be decided by who could see the enemy first, but by who could remain unseen entirely while shaping the fight from beyond perception. The age of massed formations and mutual detection had ended. In its place stood a new reality—one in which dominance belonged to those who controlled information, signature, and time itself.

For the first time in modern history, an air force had destroyed an opposing air arm without detection at any level. And every nation watching understood the implication: the balance of power had just shifted, quietly, irrevocably, in the dark skies over the Pacific.

Pacific Command

Colonel Mark Larson stood in front of Admiral Flint's Leadership Team and said, "Our little experiment was a complete success. Our flight of 12 F-47s was accompanied by 72 loyal wingmen, unmanned airships under the F-47s' control. For this operation, we used six YFQ-44A Fury collaborative combat aircraft to provide total enemy sensory denial. The remaining Collaborative Combat Aircraft (CCA) were YFQ-42As, aka missile trucks."

Flint nodded his head.

"After-action reports indicate that we shot down over 200 Chinese aircraft without a single US loss."

The room applauded.

"Well done, Air Force, well done," Flint replied.

Chapter 10

The venerable B-52 lumbered down the runway with Captain Connor at the controls. Connor was the third generation of pilots to fly the old warhorse. Unlike his grandfather, who carried nuclear weapons that could annihilate a million people as part of Curtis Lamay's nuclear deterrence, or his father, whose B-52 killed thousands during Desert Storm and Operation Iraqi Freedom, Connor carried a weapon that destroys enemy command, control, and communications without harming a fly.

While EMP research had previously focused on nuclear detonations, the Air Force had recently developed the High-Powered Joint Electromagnetic Non-Kinetic Strike Weapon (HiJINKS) to deliver an electromagnetic pulse capable of knocking out all enemy electronics, including those protected by circuitry.

As his plane neared the drop point, Connor ordered, "Bombardier, prepare to launch four HiJINKS."

The Bombardier flipped the arming switch, ran a systems check, then started the launch procedure."

A minute later, the first HiJINKS drone dropped from its wing attachment point, plunged 2,500 feet, activated its motors, and flew away under its own power. Three additional HiJINKS followed.

"HiJINKS away, returning to base, over and out," Connor reported.

Chinese Central Command, Beijing

The HiJINKS weapon penetrated enemy territory and unleashed an electromagnetic pulse in the heart of China's Command and Control Center, knocking out all enemy electronics that had survived space-based weapons or were outside the range of the high-altitude EMP.

General Chan and Leu watched their Combat Command System monitors go black.

Chan yelled, "What's happened?"

Colonel Soto Jieng replied, "Sir, readings indicate we've been hit by a high-energy pulse strong enough to destroy even our protected circuits."

General Leu countered, "But we've not received any indication of an American nuclear detonation. How can that be?"

Jeung replied, "They must have a new weapon."

General Chan fell back into his chair. While ritual disembowelment was no longer practiced, President Jin could make him and his family disappear. Chen looked at his long-term colleague and ordered, "Initiate Operation Cobra."

The People's Liberation Army Rocket Force received the orders and tasked their remaining mobile nuclear missile launchers to fire on U.S. Bases.

Landing Zone One

Seacrest watched as two Chinese Type 72 landing ships emerged from the haze, firing their 37 mm cannons onto his position. Each lander could hold up to 10 vehicles and 250 troops. Things were about to get busy.

"What's the count, Gunny?" Seacrest asked.

Stillwell responded, "With reinforcements, we have 129 healthy, 35 walking wounded, twelve machine guns, two SAM units, twelve working artillery pieces, and a dozen anti-tank weapons. None of our tanks survived. We're critically low on ammunition."

Seacrest digested the bleak assessment, then said, "Have the artillery deploy their canon-launched mines at the waterline. Prepare to ignite the Voo gas and IEDs. If they get tanks on the beach, hit 'em with all we've got, then fall back."

"Yes, sir," Stillwell replied.

"Pass the order to fire at will," Seacrest commented.

O'Reilly said, "Sir, Command reports six harriers inbound. Chinese bogeys sighted!"

Seacrest looked out and saw four Chinese Z-10 Attack Helicopters, choppers resembling the U.S. Cobra gunship, fly in from the sea and begin firing on his position. The landers were coming in fast!

"Time to earn our pay," Seacrest observed calmly as he lowered the steel window shutter.

Stillwell admired his officer's courage, "Yes, sir."

Harrier Squadron

USMC Major John Deluca said over the radio, "Airedale and I'll take those gunships; the rest of you put your missiles on the landers. Remember, we've got marines on the beach, Cobra out."

The six planes broke off as ordered.

Deluca and wingman Andy "Airedale" Ivey dove on the attack choppers, firing two AIM-9 sidewinder missiles.

While the inexperienced Chinese pilots tried to evade, the sidewinders found all four targets, disintegrating the helicopters in mid-air.

The reverie was short-lived as two Chinese landers made it ashore. After dropping their ramps, the beach defenders watched in horror as a dozen tanks, followed by six APCs, quickly poured into their position. Once clear of the lander, tank cannons and machine guns began targeting what was left of the allied forces.

***

Jake and Hank watched from their hilltop position as the Harrier twos flew back around for another run. As the fast movers closed on the enemy, rockets streaked from beneath their wings, detonating on the decks and superstructures of the landers, killing sailors.

Then, to their horror, two surface-to-air missiles rose from the farthest lander. A second later, they saw a brief flash of red and black as a Harrier exploded, showering debris across the ocean. Then, the lead plane and his wingman dropped low and pumped chaff and flares, causing the second SAM to explode harmlessly above the waves. The remaining jets formed up on the lead planes and began strafing the enemy with their guns and rockets.

Moments later, smoke streamed from two additional landers as they lowered their ramps and disembarked ten tanks and four hundred Chinese Marines. The enemy's war cry could be heard above the battle noise. Jake and Hank felt goose bumps as they watched the enemy move in mass toward the ragtag defenders.

Hank zoomed in on the Chinese horde. The brutal digital images showed allied positions being overrun as Chinese marines swarmed them like ants on picnic pie. With most of the concrete defenses and the wire destroyed, the Chinese established a beachhead.

"If the enemy gains access to the roads, they could be in Taipei within a day!" Hank shouted above the noise.

Jake said, “Let’s hope Seacrest and Stillwell have something up their sleeve.”

Landing Zone One

Seacrest watched as hilltop snipers cut down dozens of advancing Chinese. While his men managed to destroy four tanks, hundreds of determined Chinese troops threatened to overrun his remaining forces!

When another lander dropped its ramp, two hundred more PLA Marines disembarked, and Seacrest ordered, “Hit the Voo gas!”

A few seconds later, 100,000 gallons of propane were released from dozens of tanks beneath the shallow water, turning the sea into a flaming inferno. Seacrest could see troops diving underwater to extinguish the flames on their burning flesh. A few tanks and APCs also caught fire in the surf as dozens of Chinese Marines ran from the water.

“Sir, those tanks are a real problem,” Stillwell observed.

Seacrest never lowered his field glasses as he said, “Let’s hope Baker can blunt their thrust.”

***

“Fire your last missiles—now!” Sergeant Ian Baker didn’t wait for acknowledgment. His platoon had already exhausted every option except the final one.

Javelin teams fired their remaining rounds as the machine-gun squad poured relentless fire into the advancing mass. All along the beach, U.S. Marines and Taiwanese soldiers were firing everything they had—rifles overheating, barrels glowing red, men screaming commands through smoke and sand.

The beach had become a slaughterhouse.

The lead Chinese tank, first in a column of four, surged forward through drifting smoke. A Javelin streaked out with a sharp whoosh, arced, then plunged straight into the seam between turret and hull. The tank vanished in a white-orange bloom. The turret lifted skyward, spinning end over end before crashing back into the surf.

Captain Seacrest watched through his binoculars as three more tanks erupted in sequence, followed by six APCs engulfed in flame. Baker’s teams were performing miracles—but miracles burned ammunition fast.

Then the infantry came.

Wave after wave of Chinese Marines poured ashore, boots pounding wet sand, voices raised in raw, chilling war cries. As they crossed the high-water mark, artillery-seeded mines detonated beneath them. Bodies and gear were thrown into the air, limbs cartwheeled through curtains of smoke. White plumes erupted along the shoreline like violent surf, only these splashes were blood and bone. With nowhere left to go, the invaders surged inland.

Seacrest nodded once at Gunny Stillwell. No words were needed. Stillwell triggered the claymores.

The first volley fired in a perfect sixty-degree arc, each charge hurling hundreds of steel balls into the advancing troops. Men dropped instantly, cut down in vast swaths. Seacrest waited—counted breaths—then Stillwell fired the second line.

More bodies fell. Screams rose.

The water along the beach darkened, red foam swirling around broken forms dragged back by the tide.

Third volley.

Fourth.

Entire sections of the assault collapsed, but still they came—stepping over the wounded, over the dead. Some fell screaming, impaled on Taiwanese gut cutters buried beneath the sand, traps laid in the hours before dawn.

It wasn't stopping them.

Seacrest lowered his binoculars.

Up front, the fighting had turned savage—rifles discarded, men grappling in the smoke, bayonets and knives flashing. Hand-to-hand. No quarter.

"Gunny," Seacrest snapped, "we're done here. Fall back. Preserve what's left."

He grabbed the handset. "Sergeant Matseu, I need fire now—cover our withdrawal."

"Wilco," Matseu replied instantly. "We've got you."

From the hills, Matseu's co-ed sniper platoon opened up, firing with brutal precision. Through Seacrest's optics, PLA troops dropped in ones and twos, then clusters—heads snapping back, bodies folding mid-stride. The snipers were invisible, perfectly camouflaged into the rock. Only brief muzzle flashes betrayed them.

"They're keeping us alive," Seacrest muttered.

The radioman leaned in. "Sir—ammo's critical across all positions."

Seacrest didn't answer. Two more Chinese landers slammed their ramps down offshore. Tanks rolled out. APCs followed. Hundreds more troops spilled onto the beach.

Stillwell met his eyes. "Recommend we blow the road and seal the cave. That'll buy us time to fall back to the valley positions—maybe get resupply."

Seacrest didn't hesitate. "Do it."

As the withdrawal began, Seacrest saw new movement along the cliffs—Newly arrived Taiwanese reservists firing RPGs and handhelds from elevated positions. One APC erupted in flame. Another slewed sideways, tracks torn apart.

Reinforcements. Finally.

With sniper cover and fifty newly arrived Taiwanese fighters, Baker led the remaining thirty-six Marines and allied troops toward the cave entrance.

Wounded were dragged by their vests. Those who could walk did. Those who couldn't were carried—or left with a nod and a clasped hand. The fighting fit provided what fire they could to slow the enemy horde.

Once the last living defender crossed the threshold, Quartermaster Petersen slammed the blast doors shut.

Steel locked into place with finality. The beach was lost. A few had lived to fight another day.

Minutes later, Seacrest's command element climbed ladders and narrow stairways to prepared hilltop positions. Stillwell nodded to the demolition sergeant.

The charges fired. The road from the beach disappeared in a thunderous collapse, rock and fire sealing the route under tons of debris.

Seacrest watched the CCTV feed as smoke rolled through the shattered cut.

"That'll buy us time," he said quietly. But not much.

U.S. News, Hilltop Position, LZ 1

Jake and Hank came out next to the newly arrived reservists and surveyed the battlefield as the stench of burned flesh and the acrid tang of smoke filled their nostrils.

"You get that?" Jake asked.

Hank smiled, "Absolutely."

"Let's help Flint win hearts and minds."

Hank moved to a position where he could film Jake with the battle in the background and counted down, "Live in three, two, one!"

"I'm embedded with the U.S. Marines and Taiwanese Troops at a critical beachhead here in Taiwan."

Jake gestured with his left hand as he held the microphone in his right.

"As you can see, fighting is heavy as Coalition troops fend off another wave of numerically superior Chinese forces. In preparation for landing, the Chinese have mercilessly pounded our position for days. Despite heavy losses, these brave men and women have proven resilient against twenty-to-one odds. Many of them have made the ultimate sacrifice."

Susie Legman forced down her emotions and asked, "Jake, does Taiwan have enough resources to fend off the invasion?"

Jake knew this was likely his last chance to garner support for Taiwan and plowed ahead, "Susie, we should never count out the Patriots. In 1776, no one gave our colonists a chance against England, the world's largest military power. Back then, armed citizens armed with hunting rifles subdued a superior English force. So, I'm pulling for Taiwan's patriots."

Four Chinese attack aircraft came in low and strafed the positions behind Jake, forcing him to take cover. While Hank was filming, a Harrier destroyed one of the Chinese planes. Good, Jake thought, we need to show a win on camera.

After the planes passed, Jake continued, "Two weeks ago, I was taken to some abandoned buildings near Taipei, where men and women in full combat gear conducted military drills in preparation for a Chinese attack. These civilian militias are trained to integrate into the Taiwanese military. While their training is limited, military heuristics state that an attacking enemy will need at least a nine-to-one numerical advantage to take a prepared position. If this holds true, China would need sixteen million troops to capture Taiwan."

"That's inspiring, but Taiwan is cut off. How long can they hold out?" Susie asked, her voice breaking with emotion.

Jake shook his head and said, "Most Taiwanese will die before they bow to Chinese rule. Weigh this against China's conscript Army and troops facing heavy odds of being killed, and you can see why many Chinese troops lack motivation. While we're low on ammo and have lost most of our planes, trucks, and tanks early in the battle, we retain a vast submarine, drone, and missile force. Commanders tell me that U.S. advanced technology is the game changer on the modern battlefield, and we have it in spades."

Susie asked, "Can you explain that?"

"A forty-thousand-dollar missile, fired by an infantryman, can destroy a fifty-million-dollar jet and kill a pilot that takes four years to train. It's the reason Taiwan has developed its own missile factories."

Susie asked, "What are the keys to Taiwanese victory?"

"First, they must stop China from capturing airbases, ports, and landing zones. They also must retake captured airports. Then, they must gain sea and air superiority. Once these objectives are accomplished, the Allies will need to thwart China's expansion into the Indo-Pacific," Jake said as a Chinese missile exploded nearby!

The worldwide audience gasped as they saw Jake knocked to the ground, and the video feed died.

Susie screamed, "Jake, Jake, can you hear me?"

The producer shouted, "Cut to commercial! Try to get him back."

The chief technician worked feverishly to retrieve Jake and his breaking news report, but to no avail. "He's gone," reported the chief tech.

The producer asked, "What do you mean, gone?"

"The satellite uplink was destroyed, and Jake and Hank's biosensors have flatlined," the young geek said, his voice breaking. A palpable fear sucked the air from the room as the news desk fell silent.

China

While satellite imagery showed that 300 ICBM silos in three different missile fields had been reduced to smoldering embers. The PLA's three dozen mobile launchers remained intact. Worse, only eighteen could be located. Of great concern was that China still possessed seven ballistic missile submarines and a formidable bomber force, leaving them with enough nuclear ordinance to destroy several U.S. cities.

"Sir, we've detected twelve missiles launched from Mainland China," Newman announced.

"Get Space Force on the line and implement countermeasures," Flint ordered as he watched the missiles move quickly across his battlefield monitor. Had he pushed China to the point of nuclear desperation? It was the moment every U.S. commander feared.

"General Archer, over."

"Take out all Chinese bogeys?" Flint ordered.

"We're targeting them now. Space Command, over and out."

U.S. Space Force, Orbital Battle Station

Colonel Rashid reread her orders, then turned to Payload Specialist Giles and ordered, "Target all Chinese ICBMs, fire at will."

Giles had anticipated her orders and had already prepared firing solutions. His greatest fear was that the rapid-fire scenario would cause his weapon to overheat and fail.

"Sir, we have CSS-20 Chinese missiles inbound. If they exceed the release point, we could have up to fifty-four independent warheads to target. I recommend using the SM-4s to prevent as many bogeys as possible from releasing their warheads while the HPW is charging," Giles said, his tone stone cold.

Colonel Rashid checked her display and pressed the button to activate AEGIS, which fired its last six SM-4s.

Six SM-4s are running straight and true. Intercept to first ICBM is thirty seconds," the voice of AEGIS announced.

Colonel Rashid remained silent as the green images on the holographic display showed the race of death unfolding. Being so far removed from the battlefield, Rashid had to force herself to remember that they were no longer playing a computer simulation.

Her lips held a slight smile in admiration of her Payload Specialist, who'd arrived with new weapons in the nick of time. Not believing in happenstance, Rashid wondered what more Archer had withheld.

Giles heard the tone; his weapon was fully charged. He glanced at the hologram, then moved his cursor to the bogey closest to apogee, clicked his mouse, and pressed the fire button.

Instantly, an energy pulse streaked through the heavens and struck the first missile. Less than a second later, a bright yellow flash erupted as the weapon detonated. Giles selected another bogey and pressed fire. The second rocket's fuel cells exploded. As the temperature gauge rose on his gun, Giles fired, and the third ICBM blew up.

The payload specialist's face registered no emotion as the green images of the hologram reflected off his eyes. His batteries were down to twenty-five percent, and the software had shut down the firing mechanism to prevent the weapon's pulsars from overheating. Even in the extreme cold of space, the weapon generated an incredible amount of heat and needed time to cool.

The color drained from Colonel Rashid's face when she noticed the HPW had gone offline. "What's happening?"

Giles's fingers worked the keyboard as he replied, "The system is programmed to protect the weapon from thermal overload. I'm trying to override the lockouts now."

Aegis toned on with its cyber accent, "Tracking fifteen enemy missiles. The highest bogey will reach apogee in ten seconds!"

Giles worked the keyboard feverishly, trying to countermand the HPW's self-protection features.

"Bogey One has released three multiple reentry warheads (MRW). Tracking now," Aegis announced.

"Can you target those MRWs?" Rashid asked.

"The weapon has a shotgun setting; while we've never tested it, it's our best hope."

As the crew watched three independently targeted warheads descend to Earth, Giles overrode the lockout and instantly fired a wide-angle energy pulse. The cone-shaped energy packet spread like a shotgun blast, allowing one emission to strike multiple targets.

As three weapons detonated simultaneously, the auroras over the Hawaii night sky were unlike any since the U.S. Starfish nuclear space tests in 1962. Across a wide swath of the Pacific, sky gazers saw a startling flash as bright as daylight, slowly fading from green to yellow to orange before settling into a vivid, unsettling red.

The blasts generated an EMP over the Pacific Ocean, knocking out streetlights on many islands and destroying or damaging approximately one-third of the satellites in orbit.

"All three multiple reentry warheads detonated at 250 miles above Earth's surface, 500 miles due East of Honolulu," Aegis responded as it projected plots on the remaining bogeys.

Rashid cringed.

"HPW overheating! Temperature is critical!" Aegis clamored.

Giles placed his cursor on the furthest two bogeys and pressed the fire button. The pulse weapon launched an energy cone to counter the looming threat.

To Colonel Rashid's amazement, two more bogeys detonated before they could release their warheads.

"Good shooting. Fire as soon as you can. We can replace the system, but not lives on the ground," Rashid ordered.

Aegis interrupted, "SM-4-1 has struck its target! SM-4-2 has struck its target. SM-4-3, SM-4-4, SM-4-5, and SM-4-6 have destroyed their targets."

Giles looked at his monitors. The HPW was in the red! Worse still, the damaged pulse generators could deliver only 50% of their rated power. He held the cursor in the middle of a cluster of two rockets and fired.

The weapon's energy flashed through space, a deadly cone of electromagnetic pulse striking two missiles. Due to the suboptimal energy charge, the rockets did not explode!

Rashid anxiously asked, "Aegis, status report."

"Enemy bogeys remain on course. They'll reach apogee in three, two, one."

Rashid and the crew held their breath! Giles felt his heart miss a beat.

After agonizing seconds passed, the hologram showed the two ICBMs flying past their release point without deploying their warheads!

"What happened?". Rashid asked Giles.

"We must have hit them with enough energy to scramble their computers."

"What happens now?"

"The rockets will continue on their last course until they run out of fuel. After that, they'll proceed harmlessly into space until gravity acts on them."

"What about the remaining bogeys?" Rashid asked.

"HPW's out of the fight. I'll try the rail gun, but it's a long shot," Giles said as he selected 'RG' on his weapons panel and noted it was loaded and charged. He then selected the ICBM closest to its launch point and fired.

The rail gun used electromagnetic forces to fire a tungsten rod at the Aegis-calculated point of impact at 7,800 miles per hour. The absence of explosive propellants or heavy warheads to launch into space made the rail gun an attractive weapon for the Orbital Battle Station. The fact that it was not nuclear prevented the U.S. from violating space treaties.

"Target intercept in one second," Aegis announced.

As the crew watched, the tungsten rod struck the Chinese ICBM's engine. The bright, conventional explosion generated a tallow flash of light.

Giles already had the next Chinese weapon targeted and pressed the trigger as soon as the gun reloaded. Less than two seconds later, the ICBM exploded. Giles was down to two rods. The recently installed weapon's magazine held ten rods, but the remaining projectiles had not been delivered. He had to score four for four, or it'd be up to the Navy.

Giles fired at the farthest ICBM. Two seconds later, the interceptor missed! Giles fired again, and his last projectile flew wide, missing again.

Aegis announced, "Bogey 12 deployed three MRVs. Will estimate track."

Giles looked dejected.

Colonel Rashid verified that General Archer and Space Command Control were aware of the incoming warheads, then looked to Giles and said, "Great shooting! Now it's up to the Navy's missile defense."

The payload specialist nodded, 'Thank you,' as he and the crew watched six nuclear weapons descend on U.S. Forces.

Space Command

The command bunker at Peterson Space Force Base vibrated faintly as generators spun up to full capacity. Every screen lit with the burn arcs of maneuvering satellites. Orbital Battle Station Two had already slewed its nose forty-three degrees starboard, dumping reaction mass to swing into attack posture. OBS-3 followed, slower, clawing its way into position like a heavyweight turning to face a new opponent. The celestial drama marked a new era in warfare.

"Telemetry lock confirmed," a technician reported, voice tense. "OBS-2 has Chinese launch signatures in range. Booster ejections confirm anti-satellite payloads. Flight time to target: fourteen minutes."

Archer leaned forward on the rail above the pit. "Weapons free when in envelope."

"Copy, General. Arming railgun capacitors now."

A low, rising hum filled the ops center, more felt than heard, as superconducting rails bled energy from the station's reactor into massive storage banks. On a wall display, OBS-2's targeting reticle danced, locking onto the ascending Chinese ASAT booster—an orange line carving upward from Jiuquan Spaceport.

"Enemy countermeasure activation detected," Colborne said sharply. "They're dumping noise into the spectrum. Multiple jamming nodes are active. Possible spoofing attempt—GPS constellation feed corrupted on bands Delta through Foxtrot."

"Kill the feed," Archer snapped. "Switch all dependent systems to inertial and alt PNT. I want spoof-resistant mode across the theater."

"Yes, sir."

At that instant, the wall screen flared. A hypersonic streak rose from Vladivostok, then another. Russian heavy-lift boosters, their contrails slicing eastward. Four icons marked in crimson.

Hamilton checked his chrono. "OBS-3 is still forty minutes out of range, sir. OBS-2 has one shot window in eleven minutes."

Archer's hand curled around the railing. Minutes. This war could be over in a matter of minutes. "Authorize shot when stable. If we miss, we don't get a second try."

The order rippled outward. In high Earth orbit, banks of liquid helium-chilled superconducting rails were brought to zero resistance as a 15-kilogram tungsten penetrator projectile slid into the chamber.

"Capacitors at eighty percent… ninety… full charge."

"Target locked," the weapons officer confirmed.

"Fire."

The screen shuddered as the railgun spat its first round across space. No muzzle flash, no roar, just a needle of tungsten accelerating to Mach 23 in a silent arc. The display tracked its trajectory with clinical precision. Eleven minutes later, 400 kilometers above the Gobi Desert, the tungsten slug tore through the Chinese booster's fuel tank. A blossom of debris, vapor, and shattered metal scattered into the void.

"Splash one," Colborne murmured, half in awe.

"Three more birds in the air," Hamilton reminded.

Archer's expression never shifted. "Then we keep shooting."

Across the Pacific, nervous commanders listened to the same feed while Strategic Air Command brought nuclear bombers to their alert points. The first round of the orbital war had been fired, and Archer knew it was only a matter of time before the communists fired back—not at satellites, but at cities.

He glanced at the operations clock. Forty minutes until OBS-3 had its shot. Forty minutes that could decide the survival of a dozen major U.S. cities and tens of millions of souls.

Pacific Command, Hawaii

Admiral Flint and his staff watched the ICS as enemy missile after missile detonated at space altitudes.

"Space Force is doing an amazing job, but this isn't over by a long shot. Activate fleet missile defenses for imminent attack," Flint ordered.

Across his command, targeting radars with direct data links to the ICS, downloaded missile tracks to weapons systems, and calculated firing solutions, utilizing a combination of energy weapons and missile interceptors.

Flint looked at Newman and said what everyone was thinking, "The next few minutes will determine the outcome of the war. If the Chinese destroy our remaining carrier groups and a few more air bases, they'll own the Pacific all the way to Midway."

Newman nodded stoically and said, "Or, leave several American cities in ashes."

Flint's jaw ground as the tension he felt deep inside surfaced.

"MRV-1 will impact in two minutes. MRV-2 through MRV-6 will impact starting in three minutes. The projected targets are two Carrier Groups, plus Honolulu, Seattle, San Diego, and Tokyo," replied the duty officer.

"Situation report?" Flint asked.

"We have all bogeys targeted. Interceptors are launching. Space Force is repositioning Orbital Battle Stations as we speak, but they won't be able to help us in time," the duty officer replied.

Flint felt helpless as he watched six nuclear warheads descend on his Command. He could lose seventy-five percent of his remaining forces if the Chinese were successful.

"Release all Autonomous Weapons," Flint ordered, knowing he needed to deploy them before they were destroyed. Now that he'd done all he could, he looked for one more thing that could be done to change the outcome.

As Flint and his team watched the holographic display and checked the computer screens, a U.S. Standard Missile-6 (SM-6) successfully intercepted the Chinese MRV targeting the Philippines. Ten seconds later, another SM-6 took out the MRV, targeting San Diego. Two seconds afterward, SM-5 destroyed the MRV, targeting Seattle.

Cheers arose in the Command Center!

"Sir, U.S. Missile Defense indicates that their tracking systems have been spoofed, and their remaining anti-missile missiles are compromised! Chinese MRVs targeting Carrier Groups Nine and Ten remain on target. Impact, one minute."

"Warn all ships!" Flint ordered reflexively, knowing his commanders were already acutely aware.

"Sir, we have multiple sea-launched missiles, apparently from Chinese submarines; targets appear to be Carrier Groups Nine and Ten," announced the XO.

Off the coast of the Pacific Missile Range Facility in Kauai, Hawaii, Aegis Weapon System-32 intercepted the MRV targeting Honolulu. The latest U.S. sea-based missile interceptor performed flawlessly.

Flint and his team breathed a sigh of relief.

Sir, Carrier Group Ten reports problems with their antimissile defense. Possibly related to recent nuclear detonations or the effects of the Chinese cyber-attack."

Pacific Ocean

The USS George H.W. Bush (CVN-77) was the beating heart of Carrier Strike Group Two, her decks crowded with the aircraft of Carrier Air Wing Seven, all primed for war. Flanking her were the Leyte Gulf, a Ticonderoga-class cruiser bristling with Aegis radar arrays, and four Arleigh Burke destroyers of Squadron 26. Together, they were a moving city of steel and firepower that had flown over ten thousand sorties in Iraq and Afghanistan, crushed piracy in the Gulf of Aden, and patrolled every contested waterway in the world.

Now they faced annihilation.

Rear Admiral Robert D. Westen stood on the flag bridge, watching the ICS display as the countdown ticked mercilessly downward. His multi-object kill vehicles had already lofted skyward, streaks of light clawing toward the heavens. Designed to destroy multiple incoming warheads with sheer kinetic energy, they were the last shield between the carrier group and extinction.

The first SM-4 interceptor winked out on the screen, telemetry severed. It vanished into the void, never arming. The second broke lock, wandering off course. The third simply died—no detonation, no impact. Westen felt a cold line of sweat cut across his temple – Americans weren't supposed to lose to the Chinese.

"Twenty seconds to impact," the ICS voice intoned with machine calm.

"Activate all countermeasures!" Westen snapped. His voice was harsher than he intended, but it galvanized the crew.

The cruisers and destroyers hurled their last defensive salvos into the night sky. Sea Sparrow missiles clawed upward. CIWS Phalanx cannons spun to life, vomiting tungsten at invisible hypersonic ghosts. Electronic warfare pods shrieked bursts of white noise.

"Ten seconds to impact!"

Chinese spoofing attacks flooded their sensors, injecting raw falsehoods into targeting radars. Interceptors swerved wildly, chasing phantom signatures. Westen's stomach turned as icons winked red—missile after missile failing in the digital fog.

Then, at the edge of desperation, the shipboard pulse weapon fired. A blinding lance of directed energy seared into the darkness, cutting through guidance packages, frying seeker heads on enemy bogeys. On the tactical display, three inbound tracks blinked and disappeared. A heartbeat of relief swept the CIC, but it only lasted a second as the last enemy warhead rode through the chaos. Plunging from space, unimpeded, until at 5,000 feet above the ocean, it blossomed into white fire.

The 300-kiloton detonation ripped the sky apart.

A column of plasma vaporized the upper atmosphere. Electronics died in a searing electromagnetic scream. Radar screens went black.

The blast wave rolled across the formation like the fist of God. At five thousand feet, the 300-kiloton detonation had maximized its lethality, coupling its energy directly into the atmosphere and sea.

On the George H.W. Bush, everything not welded down became a projectile. Aircraft chained to the flight deck were ripped loose, tumbling into fireballs as jet fuel ignited. Radar masts bent like straw. Compartments along the starboard bow collapsed under pressure differentials, sucking men and machinery into the void.

In the Combat Information Center, half the consoles went dark in an instant. The electromagnetic pulse had fried circuit boards even through hardened shielding. Westen, thrown hard against the bulkhead, hauled himself upright in time to see sparks shower from the main ICS screen. The ship shuddered with a sound no carrier captain ever wanted to hear—the unmistakable roar of uncontrolled fire in the hangar deck.

"Damage control!" he shouted, though his voice was hoarse, nearly drowned out by klaxons. "All hands, fight the ship!"

On the Leyte Gulf, the cruiser's Aegis array glowed cherry-red before tearing loose entirely, the 6,000-pound slab of radar crashing across the deck in a shriek of metal. Her crew scrambled, smoke filling compartments faster than the ventilation systems could clear it.

The destroyers fared no better. One, USS Mason, took the brunt of the shockwave; her superstructure was fractured, and power was lost. She drifted dark, fires unchecked, men overboard in the boiling sea.

Space Force Command

Back in the U.S., Space Force registered the detonation in a dozen ways—satellite feeds cutting out, seismic stations spiking, radio traffic collapsing into static. The ops floor froze for a fraction of a second.

General Archer broke the silence. "Confirm yield."

"Three hundred kilotons, sir. Mid-air burst. EMP saturation confirmed across the battle group."

Archer's expression hardened, though his chest tightened with the realization. The first nuclear strike against a U.S. carrier group since Pearl Harbor—only this was no surprise attack, no sneak raid. This was deliberate escalation, a shot across the bow of the entire world order.

"Get me Admiral Flint," Archer ordered. "Now. I want Strategic Command at DEFCON One. And tell Arnold—this isn't a drill. They've crossed the line."

A colonel nearby whispered what no one else wanted to say. "Sir… that was just one warhead."

Archer didn't answer immediately. He let the weight of the words hang, the reality sinking across every face in the room. Then, slowly, he said, "Then we prevent the next."

Pacific Command

A grave silence could be felt as Flint and his team watched images of the nuclear detonation. One second, they saw ships at sea; the next, surveillance cameras went blank. While satellite images showed their ships remained afloat, smoke began to stream. The loss of redundant imaging and surveillance systems was unnerving.

As the image cleared, the planes on the flight deck could be seen exploding as aircraft ordnance and fuel cooked off. The carrier deck was an inferno! While the rugged carrier remained afloat, Flint knew she was out of the fight. With luck and skilled firefighting, the best he could hope for was to get the G.W. back to port for repairs.

"See if you can raise them. Initiate rescue operations," Flint ordered, a deep feeling of nausea striking him like a boxer's sucker punch. His heart grieved for the thousands of men and women who were dead or would die a horrible death in the months and years to come.

"Let this strengthen our resolve," Flint said aloud, surprising himself.

Over the ICS, Space Force announced, "The last bogey fired at CSG-10 has been destroyed."

"Sir, Carrier Strike Group One is on the horn," the Communications officer announced.

Flint picked up the handset, "Flint."

"Sir, this is Rear Admiral Walsh."

"It's good to hear your voice, Mike. How are you?"

Walsh replied, "Better than CSG-10. Any word on their condition?"

"Negative. We've initiated rescue operations. CSG 2 should reach its location in twelve hours. We also have six Coast Guard Cruisers en route from Hawaii," Flint replied as unemotionally as possible.

"I request permission to engage Chinese targets?"

Flint considered his options. If he allowed CSG-1 to go within range of China's mid-range missiles, he could lose another carrier strike group, planes, and ships that would undoubtedly be needed down the road. With every fiber in his being, he wanted to fight! But Admirals weren't supposed to make decisions with their balls; they were supposed to use their brains.

"I've got the submarine force pounding their navy and merchant marine. Operation Terminator has commenced, and Space Force is retasking two Orbital Battle Stations to the Pacific. Move into position to support rescue operations, but be ready to strike at a moment's notice."

Walsh bit his lip but knew Flint was right, "Aye, aye, sir. Wilco, over and out."

Oval Office

President Novak sat with Oxley, Jones, and General Lawrey in his newly acquired Oval Office.

"Admiral Flint has kept me up-to-date on the battle in the Pacific. While we lost Carrier Strike Group Ten, we still hold Taiwan and maintain a high kill-to-death ratio against the Chinese. Right now, I need to know more about the globalist threat," Novak said.

Oxley replied, "Ethan Carpathian remains in Solar Valley with his twelve disciples and several key U.S. officials and bureaucrats. We believe they will remain a clear and present danger even after we destroy China's war machine."

Novak met Oxley's eyes and asked, "I've read your reports. Walk me through the threat."

"We believe that they plan to kill six billion people, including all followers of the world's three great religions, people like us, and then build a Carpathian Utopia. It's master race theory on steroids, but without a war machine," Oxley replied.

Novak digested Oxley's profound but straightforward assessment and asked, "How?"

Oxley replied, "Carpathian will attempt to force Communist nations aligned with China and the U.S. Coalition into a large-scale nuclear confrontation, thereby killing billions and destroying the threat either camp poses. Recent events bear this out."

"What is his motivation?"

"Carpathian believes in building a green world that remains within what they consider the world's carrying capacity of two billion people. He says he wants to build a new world order in which the common man owns nothing but is happy – essentially a new form of communism where he and his tyrants rule."

"Is he just a powerful, but misguided idealist trying to save Mother Earth, or the man of lawlessness, the son of destruction, prophesied in Revelation?" Noval asked.

"I believe he's the latter," Oxley said as he looked directly at the President.

Novak held the CIA Director's gaze for several seconds, then protested, "Many thought Hitler was the Anti-Christ, but he failed. What gives Carpathian the edge?"

"He operates from a well-developed and comprehensive plan that is being implemented by the world's most powerful economic leaders. His team has thought of everything. For example, he plans on uniting the planet under a one-world religion called Dregodarit. It's a deep fake, an anti-Christ play that provides a mixture of secular hedonism and eastern enlightenment. It's now the fastest-growing religion in the world. Then there's Helmut Scheid, who has prepared a one-world cyber currency. Installing this currency will enable them to control the global economy without needing military might. Scheid's first step in the takeover was to use his Red Rock Funds to engineer our market collapse. Soon, he will introduce Dragon Coin, and governments and citizens will rapidly transition from fiat currencies to it. As you saw in Peddlergate, Carpathian and his allies exercise significant influence over world leaders. So, unlike Hitler and his thugs, Carpathian has 12 of the world's brightest minds in each of the 12 economic sectors, operating as one. Their sophisticated plan is currently playing flags against each other while manipulating public opinion, global economics, and world health. Mr. President, Carpathian is the most dangerous tyrant that the world has ever seen, silky smooth and popular, with the heart of Satan himself. Never before has any enemy been better positioned to take over the world," Oxley offered.

Novak looked surprised and asked, "So how do you think they'll murder six billion people?"

Oxley said, "The four horsemen."

"You refer to the Book of Revelation?"

"Yes, the four horsemen of the apocalypse appear with the opening of the first four of the seven seals that bring forth the cataclysm of the apocalypse. The first horseman, a conqueror with a bow and crown, rides a white horse. The second horseman is given a great sword and rides a red horse, symbolizing war and bloodshed. The third horseman, who rides a black horse, carries a balanced scale, symbolizing famine and starvation. The fourth horseman rides a pale horse identified as Death. The short answer is that they plan to use a combination of war, civil unrest, starvation, and plagues."

Novak asked, "But six billion people? How is that possible?"

"Our studies show a ninety percent death rate for Americans, just one year after the destruction of our infrastructure by an EMP, war, or economic disaster. Since the average American only has three days of food on hand, they will starve within a month. Since few know how to farm or forage, there's minimal opportunity for survival in a grid-down scenario. Add population density that demands commercial farming, and the U.S. and many other nations will experience mass starvation. Starving people get diseases. Then, we will have a growing number of civilians killing over food and weapons. Our once-powerful military could collapse within ninety days. Unless we act decisively right now, it's the end of the world as we know it," Oxley observed.

"The end of the world as we know it, TEOTWAWKI," Novak said, quoting the prepper acronym, then continued, "What shocks me is how effectively the globalists manipulated the masses and remained undetected. How do you fight an enemy with this level of sophistication?"

Oxley said resolutely and without emotion, "We use the Joshua Protocol. No holds barred; no quarter given."

Novak was alarmed. The Joshua Protocol was a never-before-tried Hail Mary. A desperate attempt to save the world from descending into the abyss. In his heart, he knew Ox was right; it was now or never.

"Give me the battle plan, Ox."

Oxley said, "Secure the military by taking out the treasonous generals. Target and destroy the globalists. Close the border, take out the Cartels who run Mexico, and hunt down enemy agents who used our broken immigration system against us. Cordon off our banking and financial systems while keeping the markets closed to protect remaining wealth. Use Space Force to destroy all of the nuclear assets of Russia, North Korea, Iran, and China. Destroy China's military might and that of all her allies. We must be prepared to do the same for India if it tries to seize this opportunity. Restore our infrastructure and the food and medical supply chain. We don't have time to be timid; success depends on taking decisive action while we still have the assets." Oxley hesitated, then continued, "The longer we wait, the worse our odds become."

"Agreed. How do you plan to take out Carpathian?" Novak asked.

Oxley said, "Jake left some nano-technology in his home. The bigger problem is getting the twelve disciples and other globalist billionaires who are part of the New World Order, along with Faccini, Wilhite, Rapier, and the other American traitors."

"Cutting out the cancer to save the patient?"

"That's an apt analogy."

Novak's face contorted with a mixture of concern and strength of will. "Can the CIA handle it?"

Oxley responded, “No, but the men of the Order can. You’ll recall the men of the Order overthrew King George just two hundred fifty years ago. It was the men of the Order who captured the Promised Land. It was the men of the Order who overcame Nazi Germany. Only the Order has the divine authority and clandestine ability to pull it off.”

Novak looked at Oxley for a long time. It was one thing to be a member of the Order; it was another to be the quarterback in a game called Armageddon. It was faith versus logic. Novak said, “The thought of turning over the free world to these tyrants is unthinkable. I’ll order the military strikes while you target the globalists, subversives, and traitors.”

Chapter 11

The sea was unnaturally calm, a deceptive mirror that masked the chaos beneath its surface. High above, the azure sky stretched uninterrupted, betraying no hint of the violence that would soon unfold. It was the day ancient mariners might have considered the calm before the storm. But today, the storm was not of nature's making.

In the deep waters of the South China Sea, the Chinese Navy's flagship destroyer, Changzheng, cut through the waves with a menacing grace. The vessel was bristling with missile launchers, radar arrays, and anti-aircraft guns—a fortress on water. The ship's captain and crew were supremely confident after their many successful attacks on U.S. Coalition bases and warships.

Silent and undetectable, an AWS submarine, sleek as a barracuda, glided through the depths. It was an autonomous warship designed for stealth and lethality, with no crew to keep alive and no fear of dying. Its sensors locked onto the Changzheng, calculating the optimal strike.

The submarine released a barrage of autonomous torpedoes—silent predators that left no trail, no signature for the destroyer's sonar to pick up as they sped through the water, adjusting course in real time like robot kamikazes.

The Changzheng's crew had no time to react before the first explosion tore through the hull, followed by two more in rapid succession. The ship lurched violently, alarms blaring as sailors scrambled to battle stations.

But the damage was already catastrophic—compartments flooded, systems failed, and the destroyer listed heavily to port within minutes. Another set of torpedoes struck, this time aiming for the munitions hold. The explosion that followed was deafening, a plume of fire and smoke erupting from the ship's midsection.

Minutes later, the Changzheng rolled over, the stern lifting out of the water just before the boat disappeared beneath the waves.

All across the Pacific, AWS surface ships and submarines sank Chinese military vessels, then turned on their sizeable commercial fleet. Back home, the President and a host of military contractors cheered.

Guangdong Province, China

The largest of China's mid and long-range missile bases was humming with activity as hundreds of soldiers went about their duties, unaware that death was coming from above! Since the commencement of hostilities, the base had been a beehive of activity as launchers were prepared, solutions loaded, and missiles fired on Coalition targets.

The U.S. Air Force's Expendable Hypersonic Multi-mission ISR (intelligence, surveillance, and reconnaissance) and Strike Weapon had been developed as part of the USAF Project Mayhem. Designated EB-5, aka Dark Horse, the plane's black fuselage borrowed lines from the SR-71 but had been widened and lengthened significantly to improve velocity, high-altitude handling, and payload. The Dark Horse streaked toward the base at five times the speed of sound. Unburdened by life support systems, the bomber could carry twice the payload of a B-52.

Dark Horse's AI Brain ran a million calculations per minute. On the final approach, the weapon verified the enemy's position and loaded flight solutions. Once released, the autonomous drones would deliver advanced bunker-busting bombs, each capable of penetrating ten meters of reinforced concrete.

***

There'd been no warning! No radar signature of an enemy plane or missile! The scene was sudden destruction as the first launcher disappeared in a fiery explosion. Immediately, anti-aircraft guns spun to life, and missiles launched desperately to intercept the incoming threat. As the Chinese activated decoy flares and electronic jammers, the weapons struck the heart of the missile base, each explosion resonating deep underground.

Silos collapsed, command centers disintegrated, and ammunition depots erupted in fireballs that sent shockwaves across the landscape. The missile base was reduced to smoldering rubble in a matter of seconds! Dozens of similar attacks occurred at Chinese missile bases all across the war zone.

Fiery Cross Reef

The reef base was Beijing's crown jewel in the disputed South China Sea. This fortified hub served not only as a military outpost but also as a symbol of China's territorial ambitions. Two hundred troops garrisoned the island, living beneath radar towers and surface-to-air batteries, protected by layered bunkers, retractable missile shelters, and hardened hangars capable of housing twenty-four J-11 fighters and four nuclear-capable Xian H-6N bombers. The Chinese considered it to be impregnable.

From the belly of a submersible mothership, twenty-six Anduril Ghost-X rotary drones slipped into the night, their carbon-fiber frames designed to evade radar cross-section returns. They skimmed barely meters above the waves, nap-of-the-earth profiles hugging every swell and trough. At a kilometer from shore, they climbed to 250 meters, vanishing into cloud cover. One scout drone pulsed data through low-probability-of-intercept comms, feeding navigational cues to the others.

In a coordinated attack, submersible landers disgorged AWS ground units which emerged onto the reef like predators from a deep lair: hybrid machines of steel and polymer, some tracked like miniature tanks, others wheeled for speed, all bristling with grenade launchers, chain guns, and antitank missiles. With GPS compromised in this sector, the AI-driven mesh network used terrain-mapping sensors, each unit feeding position data into the swarm. These units were silent, coordinated, and killed without hesitation.

At 0200 hours, the algorithms executed, and the AWS line surged forward. The first Chinese sentries barely had time to register the movement before being cut down by 7.62mm bullets that stitched through their torsos. Grenade pods thumped in mechanical rhythm, airburst rounds shredding sandbagged positions and turning bunkers into smoking craters.

From above, reconnaissance drones loitered unseen, transmitting the assault in real time to the Coalition's ICS interface. Commanders watched the feeds—infrared signatures flaring as soldiers fell, comm arrays sparking under directed fire, missile launchers erupting in sympathetic detonations.

Perimeter defenses neutralized, the barracks were next. Antipersonnel missiles punched through corrugated walls, followed by cascading grenades. Entire platoons died in their bunks. Those who stumbled out with rifles met automated fire with merciless precision. Within minutes, resistance had collapsed into isolated pockets of panicked defenders, each swiftly silenced.

The terminators spared nothing. Anti-aircraft guns, too slow to traverse, were gutted by shaped charges. Vehicle parks burned, fuel depots erupted in secondary explosions that painted the night sky orange. Communications towers toppled, and aircraft exploded where they were parked.

When the killing was over, the machines did not celebrate. They paused, their sensors sweeping for residual heat signatures or signs of weapons activity. Finding none, they transitioned seamlessly to Phase Two: systematic eradication of infrastructure. Fuel lines were set alight, hardened shelters collapsed with thermobaric charges, and weapons caches were destroyed.

By dawn, the reef base was nothing but scorched concrete, twisted rebar, and silence.

Half the AWS units re-embarked aboard their assault submarines, vanishing beneath the waves en route to the next target. The remainder stayed behind, deploying perimeter drones and automated gun turrets, establishing a machine occupation force on soil China had once claimed.

Pacific Command

Admiral Flint watched as the last images of battle were shown. He shook his head at the carnage the AWS units had caused.

"This is a historic moment. An autonomous military unit has taken an enemy position without human involvement," Flint said, his tone a mixture of triumph and fear.

Newsome replied, "AWS and Space Force have proven their value. The frightening part is that China and other nations could soon have similar technology."

Flint nodded, then ordered, "Implement Phase Two."

Chinese Naval Command

Admiral Lin Fong stared at the combat display; his pale face etched with the strain of seeing imminent victory snatched from his grip. The screen showed the South China Sea, usually a scene of bustling Chinese dominance, now a graveyard. Hundreds of ships, even the pride of the People's Liberation Army Navy, the Fujian carrier, all lay on the bottom.

President Jin stated that the U.S. President would grant China two weeks of autonomy. Then Tilden died. Intelligence told us the U.S.

lacked enough autonomous weapons to have any measurable impact and that Taiwan would fold like a paper tiger. “What is it they say? Military intelligence is an oxymoron that makes morons of us all,” Admiral Fong said under his breath as he shook off the surreal images of destruction and ordered, “Report!” his voice hoarse and unsteady.

"It was an attack of unknown origin, sir," came the strained reply of his Executive Officer, "No human intervention detected, nothing on radar. One second, nothing, the next they destroyed hundreds of assets." He swallowed hard. "Then, this."

The officer gestured to the display where sleek, robotic drones patrolled the wreckage, their designs a chilling mix of shark and manta ray. Lin recognized the American unmanned, autonomous weapons code-named Navajo.

“The world’s first fully autonomous weapons were supposed to be an experiment, a technological marvel not yet in mass production, sir.”

"Where are the Americans now?" Fong demanded, a flicker of hope sparking in his chest.

"No American radar signatures within 2,000 kilometers, sir. It seems that the Navajos acted independently. It also appears the Americans used cyber-attacks to shut down our radar and targeting systems, and somehow ‘cloaked’ their ships and planes. One minute, they were on radar; the next, they were gone."

Fong felt a cold dread creep in. The world had been wary of autonomous weapons, fearing an arms race where machines made the decisions to kill humans, the so-called Terminator Syndrome. Now, that nightmare was a reality.

“What naval assets remain?” Fong asked.

“Sir, we retain 239 merchant ships. Enough to move our invasion force onto Taiwan while we retain air superiority. While all three carriers and seventy percent of our cruisers, frigates, landers, and destroyers are gone, we’ve caused enough damage to occupy Taiwan,” the XO replied.

Admiral Fong stood watching the monitors. His XO was right. China retained a powerful force. Maybe enough to complete his mission. Politically, he had told Jin that the invasion could take up to seventy percent of their assets, and it appeared he’d been correct. Nevertheless, he knew what happened to Admirals and Generals who became scapegoats for their leaders' failures. The only way for him and his family to survive was victory.

"Execute Operation Rapid Dragon!" Fong ordered.

Beijing

Across the Taiwan Strait, President Jin watched the holographic display in his bunker with a mix of awe and terror. The Navajos and American submarine missiles had decimated the Chinese fleet, and U.S. technology had been far more effective than predicted.

With the hawkish Novak in the Oval Office, how had the calculus of war changed? Novak was an unknown, dangerous leader who'd shown he wouldn't hesitate to escalate. Clearly, the winds of battle had changed. What to do now?

General Youxia responded, "Great Leader, dozens of our missiles have been shot out of the sky near Hawaii. The enemy's missile defenses are effective, but they cannot provide complete coverage. Our flood-the-zone strategy this morning allowed us to sink the USS Frank E Peterson and USS Hopper Gene. Unfortunately, none of their submarines were in port."

Jin asked, "How do you assess our chances for victory?"

"Sir, we're down to five percent of our medium-range missiles. Our long-range missiles are at twenty percent. Conventional ground forces, including artillery, tanks, and APCs, are at ninety percent readiness, and we retain 1.6 million troops. We also retain two-thirds of our short-range missiles and most of our aircraft. Thus, we retain the resources needed to capture Taiwan," Youxia replied.

Jin looked at his direct report and gestured for him to continue.

Youxia added, "Our opening attacks wreaked devastation on the American bases but brought Japan, South Korea, and all NATO countries into the war. While American conventional forces in the region have been severely weakened, U.S. autonomous weapons, submarines, and space forces remain powerful. Our spies tell us that we've killed over half a million Taiwanese civilians and fifty thousand of their regular military. While the U.S. successfully landed F-16, F-18, and F-35 fighters and helicopters on the main island, many operate from improvised fields and lack proper support. These high-maintenance aircraft will not be able to operate for very long under these conditions."

"How are our assassination attempts on President Tsai He Wen proceeding?"

General Youxia had hoped to avoid the question but said, "Sir, the Americans sent special units of their SEAL Teams to form security details around the Taiwanese President and key civilian leaders. All six of our hit teams have perished."

Jin accepted the news without emotion, then asked, "When can you capture Taipei?"

General Youxia used a pointer and maps to reinforce his comments: "Currently, we're holding beachheads at Landing Zones 1, 2, 3, and 4 and offloading heavy equipment. Losses have been high, but we're slowly pushing inland. Our Airborne Units have captured airports at Hsinchu, Taoyuan, Kaohsiung, and Taichung, where we're rapidly using our air transport capabilities and those of our Russian allies to move thousands of troops and heavy equipment onto these bases. We've moved 45,000 troops, fifty tanks, 200 artillery units, and dozens of SAM and Rocket units onto these captured airfields, and will soon be operating fighters and attack aircraft from them."

"Good, what comes next?"

"We plan to use additional missile, air, and naval attacks to wipe away any resistance and pour thousands of assets onto the four captured landing zones, link up with our troops at captured airports, and push into Taipei. Once we capture Taipei, we will occupy four key ports and offload half a million soldiers and thousands of pieces of heavy equipment, thereby overwhelming our inferior enemy," General Youxia said.

Jin thought it over and saw the logic in his general's plan. "How long before the Americans and their allies can move in enough forces to stop you?"

General Youxia carefully worded his response, "Sir, it will take the U.S. weeks to reinforce in any significant numbers. Our destruction of their carriers to date will force the Americans to think twice about bringing ships within the range of our missiles. We also retain a significant submarine force and enough tactical nuclear weapons to deter them. The key is aggressively exploiting our numerical and proximity advantages."

"How do you plan to halt the U.S. counterattack?

"By flooding the zone with missile barrages that exceed their defensive capabilities, we will sink their ships. We also have three dozen submarines on station, waiting to pounce."

Jin remembered an old saying. '*When you release the dogs of war, they control you.*' The only honorable way forward was victory.

Jin ordered, "Put everything into the battle! I want you to take Taipei within the week!"

USAF Squadron 11

In 2021, the Pentagon had discreetly greenlit one of its more unorthodox programs: converting lumbering cargo aircraft into long-range strike platforms. The plan was simple—use cheap, plentiful transports to drop palletized missile packs out the back like so many humanitarian aid bundles. Only this time, the "aid" came in the form of precision-guided cruise missiles. It was cost-effective, scalable, and, most importantly, exportable to U.S. allies who could not afford bombers.

Colonel David Jones, U.S. Air Force, had been the man tapped to make the concept work in the Pacific theater. A former Air Force Academy standout, Jones carried himself with the square-jawed presence of a combat leader but the calculating mind of a logistician. His squadrons ran lean, efficient, and battle-ready, boasting an unheard-of eighty-five percent readiness rate. When senior staff balked at his insistence on retrofitting C-17s and C-130s with EMP surge protection—generally reserved for nuclear-capable bombers—Jones had pushed back. If you want me to haul nuclear or precision ordnance into a modern war zone, then my planes need to survive the EMP environment. His stubbornness had won the argument, and now his cargo fleet was the only one rated to deliver in a nuclear-contested battlespace.

Tonight, his gamble was about to pay off.

Three autonomous Ghost-X drones flew ahead of the formation, weaving a cloaking screen across the Pacific night. Enemy radar systems that should have lit up with a dozen American cargo aircraft instead saw nothing but static.

"G-2 confirms sixty-nine Chinese radar sites destroyed," Jones said, eyes on the digital overlay. "Four dozen SAM sites neutralized. We've got a clear corridor, but I'd rather not bet my career on it. Glad we've got the cloak running."

His co-pilot, Captain Marie Shilling, didn't take her eyes off the instruments. "I'm still worried about Russian and Chinese fighters. They're flying CAPs all up and down this sector."

The navigator broke in. "Thirty seconds to the drop zone."

In the cargo bay, Loadmaster Ken Lunsford gave a quick scan of the pallets. Each was rigged with precision timing, parachute deployment mechanisms, and safety interlocks. His team gave the ritual thumbs-up.

"Sir, payload secured and ready," Lunsford reported.

Jones checked the digital clock, then nodded once at Shilling. "Release Penetrators."

At his command, hydraulic rollers spat three pallets into the black sky. Cargo doors yawned as the packages tumbled free. A second later, parachutes snapped open, jerking the loads upright. Beneath each chute, six AGM-158 JASSM-ER "Penetrators" hung nose-down, sleek gray bodies bristling with folded wings and sealed turbofans.

The chutes stabilized the clusters just long enough for onboard computers to orient their trajectory. One after another, the missiles cut free, dropped, then ignited. Wings snapped open with mechanical precision, engines coughing before roaring to life.

Jones craned his neck back in time to watch thirty-six Penetrators peel away, each finding its own invisible flight path. The formation scattered across the battlespace like a swarm of hornets.

Every missile carried a thousand pounds of high-explosive warhead and the ability to strike within four feet of its aimpoint. At a range of eleven hundred miles, they didn't need the cargo birds to come close to enemy airspace. Tonight's drop—just 150 kilometers from the Chinese coast—put them in the sweet spot.

The targets: forward air bases, radar stations, hardened naval piers, coastal SAM batteries, and command-and-control nodes along the Fujian coastline. Within minutes, they would crater runways, shred hangars, and shatter communications hubs. Ships in port would die in their berths.

Jones exhaled slowly, tension ebbing from his shoulders. "Package is away," he said.

On the tactical display, a forest of green icons streaked toward the Chinese coastline. Dozens of warheads, each guided by GPS-inertial hybrid navigation, immune to jamming, too many to stop.

"Colonel," Shilling said, voice tight with both awe and fear, "we just turned a cargo plane into a bomber wing."

Jones's eyes never left the screen. "No," he corrected her. "We just rewrote the playbook. Congratulations, airmen, we just made history."

Fighter Escort, Taiwan Strait

The sun bled into the horizon as four F-15C Eagles knifed through the sky, their afterburners glowing like molten spears. Captain Daniel Scott, flight lead, scanned his AN/APG-63(V)3 AESA radar, eyes narrowing as ten contacts bloomed on his scope. J-20s—China's stealth fighters—sleek delta-canards closing fast. His fatigue evaporated in a surge of adrenaline.

Just yesterday, he and his men had scrambled out of Elmendorf, Alaska, burning across the Pacific with tanker support to reinforce Japan. Kadena Air Base was still smoldering when they landed. Charred hulks of F-35s and Eagles lined the taxiways, victims of precision missile strikes. Only buried fuel farms and tireless repair crews had kept the base alive. For many American pilots, the fight had ended before their wheels ever left the ground.

Now it was payback time.

"Ninety miles out," Scott muttered as they closed on Jones' flight of lumbering C-130s returning from their mission. The transports were fat, slow targets—chickens in a fox's den. On his scope, hostile fighters slid into intercept vectors, licking their chops.

"We've got company," he radioed, voice steady.

"Lock and load, gentlemen. Nobody touches the heavies on my watch." His gloved hand tightened on the stick.

The Eagles split into combat spread, radar locks snapping onto the J-20s. Digital symbology scrolled across Scott's HUD: range, closure rate, missile readiness.

"Fox Three! Engaging bandit, three o'clock!" one of his wingmen called. An AIM-120D AMRAAM peeled off the rail, its rocket flare burning against the twilight. Seconds later, a bright blossom flared on Scott's scope—kill confirmed. Debris and flame fell toward the East China Sea.

"Splash one," Scott growled. "Keep the pressure up."

A missile warning screamed in his headset. He broke hard right, pumping chaff and flares. Two PL-15s streaked past, seekers confused by the countermeasures. His G-suit squeezed as he yanked the Eagle through a high-G turn, the jet groaning but holding.

"Two bogeys on our six!" his wingman barked.

"I've got 'em!" another pilot cut in, rolling inverted and dropping in behind the pursuers. His Sidewinder lock tone shrieked. "Fox Two!" The AIM-9X darted off the rail, homing on heat. One J-20 disintegrated in fire; the other broke high, only to be finished by a radar-guided shot seconds later.

The sky became a kaleidoscope of missile trails, chaff clouds, and flares. Controlled chaos, lethal and precise. The Eagle drivers kept their comms clipped, professional—no wasted words, just targets, locks, kills.

Scott swung back into the fight, lined up another J-20, and fired. His AMRAAM found its mark, tearing the stealth fighter apart in a cascade of wreckage. The surviving Chinese pilots tried to disengage, but the Americans pressed the attack, forcing them to defend, herding them toward the sea.

One by one, the dragons fell, until the last bandit spiraled into the waves, its pilot ejecting into the fading light.

Scott leveled his Eagle, chest heaving. Around him, contrails and smoke trails marked the battle's end. Ten J-20s destroyed. Four Eagles are still airborne. Not a bad day's work.

"Good shooting, boys," he said, pride cutting through the fatigue. "We just wrote a new chapter in air combat history—third-gen metal against fourth-gen stealth. And we came out on top."

He glanced at the radar feed—C-130s lumbering homeward, safe.

"Mission accomplished. Let's get our chickens back to the barn. Drinks on me."

The Eagles wheeled west, orange afterburners carving the dusk sky, a trail of victory behind them.

Hilltop 463

Captain Seacrest's command had been bled out. One hundred and fifty-two U.S. Marines, two hundred and seven Taiwanese regulars, and two hundred and one reservists—gone.

The butcher's bill was staggering, yet G-2 estimated they'd taken more than 4,500 PLA troops with them on land and at sea. It was a grim calculus, but it had bought the Coalition precious hours to regroup.

Now Seacrest stood inside his new command post on Hill 463, a reinforced concrete bunker dug into the ridgeline east of LZ-1. The position overlooked a narrow valley that funneled Chinese infantry into a killing zone. Every approach had been zeroed in—mortars pre-sighted, machine guns interlocked, rockets and Javelins placed for crossfire. If the enemy pushed here, they would bleed for every meter. And if Hill 463 fell, Seacrest would order a fallback to Hill 507, where combat engineers were ready to collapse the roadway tunnel between Hill 463 and Hill 507, forcing the PLA to abandon its armor and slog infantry through the mountains.

It was a textbook defense—at least on paper. The reality was a lot harder. Ammunition had arrived, but not enough. The Marines would have to lean on their AWS units and pray for close air support.

Seacrest raised his field glasses, his bandaged hand trembling. His ears still rang from the last bombardment, and blood crusted along the side of his face. His leg ached, and the concussion left his thoughts drifting. He steadied himself. He couldn't afford weakness if he ever hoped to maintain command presence.

"Sir, you need to evacuate," the corpsman insisted. The young sailor's voice cracked under the weight of exhaustion. "You've lost too much blood. That head wound looks serious. We need to get you to a ship."

Seacrest lowered the glasses and met his eyes. His voice was calm, almost gentle, but steel lay beneath it. "Doc, I'm a U.S. Marine officer. You can tag me and bag me when my body assumes room temperature. Until then, I'm in this fight."

The corpsman straightened, snapped a salute, and managed a tired grin. "Send 'em to hell, sir."

Seacrest allowed himself the faintest smile, then turned to Jake Hendel. The war correspondent looked out of place in a bloodstained jacket, but he had pulled Seacrest from the rubble of his last command post. Seacrest knew he owed the man his life.

"Thanks again, Jake."

"You'd have done the same," Jake replied. His voice carried the flat tone of a man who'd seen too much blood and managed to keep going anyway.

"Any news?" Seacrest asked.

Jake exhaled. "Hundreds of terrorist cells are hitting U.S. infrastructure. Riots in major cities. Pacific bases devastated. Shortages everywhere. I won't sugarcoat it—we're in deep trouble."

Seacrest digested the news silently, then said, "Flint's communique confirms our subs and AWS drones counterattacked. Took down their carriers, most of their missile ships, destroyers, and frigates. Heavy losses on their transport fleet, too." His tone hardened. "Problem is, they still have most of their air force. Airborne troops have seized key airfields. If they can fly in enough troops and armor, Taipei could fall within days."

Jake nodded grimly. "How's resupply?"

"The improvised strips are working. Flint pushed in hundreds of AWS units, a batch of experimental laser weapons, and 5,000 Marines. Scuttlebutt says we'll get more assault ships once we control the skies. For now, the radar cloak is keeping our forward assault boats alive."

Outside, a convoy of trucks disgorged autonomous infantry. Jake marveled as four-foot-tall tracked machines rolled down ramps with unnerving precision. Each bristled with weapons: machine guns, missiles, mortar pods. Their optical sensors glowed like eyes. Nearby, ATV-sized gun platforms followed, packing heavier cannons, mini-rockets, and grenade launchers. Among them were mobile anti-aircraft units and ammo carriers, all networked into a seamless swarm.

Jake shook his head. "How effective are they?"

Seacrest's eyes were tired but steady. "Scuttlebutt is they took a fortified reef base. Without a single man stepping ashore."

Jake watched the machines trundle toward the enemy, their movements eerily precise. He had covered wars on every continent, but this was different. This was no longer a matter of man against man. This was something colder, something ruthless.

The battlefield had changed forever. Somehow, war had become less heroic and more commercial – bloodless steel beings killing men!

Deep down, the whole scene reminded Jake it was time to pull the ripcord.

Pacific Command

The command deck of the Pacific Joint Operations Center hummed with tension, every console alive with feeds from satellites, drones, and submarines prowling beneath the waves. Admiral Flint stood at the center table, hands clasped behind his back, his eyes fixed on the war map.

"What's the score?" he asked.

G-2 Officer Newsome stepped forward, tapping the remote. The first slide appeared—grainy satellite video of silos erupting into fireballs.

"Sir, Space Force strikes have eliminated all known Chinese silo-based nuclear assets and most of their mobile launchers. Iran and Pakistan's facilities are gone, and their production capacity has been neutralized. North Korean launchers are under attack now. Our biggest risks are submarine-based launches, mobile assets we haven't located, and any Russian escalation."

On the main screen, one silo after another blossomed into destruction, shockwaves rattling the speakers.

"Conventional posture?" Flint asked.

"Fighters are arriving from the mainland, the Middle East, and the Atlantic. We're strong in personnel, but weak in heavy equipment. Submarines have carried the fight so far, but missile stockpiles are running thin. Surface reinforcements are en route—days away. Until PLA missile and sub threats are reduced, moving carriers in closer is too risky."

Flint knew there wasn't much his carrier's 80 or fewer operational planes could do against thousands of China's land-based aircraft, anyway. So far, his submarines and US high-tech had been the game-changers. Perhaps the day of the carrier-centric navy was over.

He nodded grimly. "And on the ground?"

Newsome flipped to a map of Taiwan, red markers blooming at captured airports and beachheads.

"The PLA is pressing up coastal highways. Airborne units are expanding from captured airfields. Coalition defenders are inflicting heavy casualties—our kill ratios are favorable. Assault ships have been decisive, providing reinforcements, resupply, and close air support. But if we can't retake those airfields and hold the ports, the island will collapse."

Flint's eyes lingered on Taipei, now within striking distance of PLA armored thrusts. "It's a race against time," he said. "Where are NATO reinforcements?"

Newsome read from his slate. "Australia: twelve warships, four subs inbound. NATO can move four additional carriers into the Straits within ten days. HMS *Queen Elizabeth*, accompanied by Typhoon 4s and F-35Bs, is set to arrive in eight days. Canada: twelve frigates, three days. Japan has committed twenty destroyers. Token assets from most other allies. South Korea is providing intel, refueling, and logistics, but no combat ships."

"Understood," Flint responded.

He already knew the math. Sanctions would significantly impact China's economy within ninety days. But Jin didn't need ninety days. He needed one week, and if Taipei fell, the geopolitical map could be rewritten forever, with China having the first stepping stone in its land grab.

"Chinese losses?" Flint asked.

"Confirmed: three hundred thousand killed or wounded. Two-thirds of the PLA Navy has been destroyed. Half the merchant fleet was sunk. Eighty percent of the landing craft were destroyed at sea. But that still leaves 1.5 million combatants and more conventional forces than we field in our entire U.S. inventory."

Flint studied the red tide as it pressed inland. "They've taken ground at LZs One through Four, but we're dug in on the fallback lines. Our commanders are holding the valleys as long as possible, then blowing the tunnels and forcing the PLA into the hills. That'll slow armor and let AWS units attrit them from cover."

"AWS units," Newsome added, "are exceeding expectations. But their numbers are limited. We need mass deployment to turn this around."

Across the room, eyes locked on Flint. He could feel the weight of history pressing down.

"Jin can't afford to lose face," Flint observed. "He won't stop." Nods rippled around the table.

"Then neither will we. Effective immediately: every Space Force asset, every missile, every AWS unit goes into the fight. One big surge, one big massed attack. Continue interdiction of their shipping. Get every available fighter and strike aircraft forward-deployed. Ground and sea terminators—move them in. And prep the 82nd and 101st Airborne. The key to victory is interdiction, stiff defense, and destroying their command and control."

He stabbed a finger at the red airfield icons on the map and said, "We're going to retake those airports, and we're going to hold them. Because if we lose the skies, we lose the island. And if we lose the island…"

Flint let the thought hang, his piercing blue eyes finishing the sentence for him.

Hilltop 463

Dark, ominous clouds blew in from the sea as high winds turned raindrops into projectiles. The high surf mercifully slowed the flow of enemy troops onto the beach and shut down PLA air operations. A godsend that gave Seacrest time to reinforce his new position and resupply. During the night, a dozen C-130 transports and twenty-six helicopters flew supplies to the four landing zone defense forces. Apparently, U.S. pilots knew how to fly in bad weather. Thank God.

Jake rubbed the new beard growth on his face as the rain pelted the Command Post's steel battle curtains. It had been forty-eight hours since his communication link to his news network was destroyed, and Chinese cyber-attacks had crippled Taiwanese broadcasting. Yesterday, his CIA SAT phone had been destroyed by a stray round that might have killed him.

The storm moved on, revealing the afternoon sun. As he looked through his binoculars, Jake saw Chinese tanks, APCs, and thousands of Chinese marines moving slowly up the road toward their position. While Seacrest had blown the beach road, Chinese engineers had reopened it a day later.

As the battle emerged, Seacrest commanded 256 troops, ten Clouded Leopard Armored fighting vehicles, and a dozen hand-held anti-tank missiles. A surface-to-air missile battery was located two miles up the coast road, and two dozen artillery units had been moved into the valley just beyond the hillside. While the storm's end meant he could have air support, it also meant the Chinese would start flying sorties against him.

"Command is sending in more reservists and fighting vehicles, but I doubt they will make it here before the next attack," Seacrest said solemnly.

"Enemy contact at forward post-Alpha!" Stillwell barked.

Jake wondered if the young captain was about to pass out as he staggered toward him. How much more could anyone expect of the young officer, badly wounded, barely able to stand?

Jake placed his hands on Seacrest's shoulders, looked deeply into his soul, and said, "You can do this. This is the day! You are the man! Send them to hell!"

He could see that his words had penetrated, but sensed Seacrest needed more encouragement.

Jake closed his grip on Seacrest's shoulders, bowed his head, and prayed, "Lord, be with us as you were with Beniah; allow us to slay the lion in the pit with only a spear. In Jesus' name, I pray, Amen."

Buoyed by prayer, Seacrest's shoulders rose as he turned to face the enemy.

Seconds later, the first line of advancing PLA troops stepped on land mines while hundreds more fell to small-arms fire. The Taiwanese snipers had received thirty more troops and were dropping targets like flies. Still, the massive formations pushed forward like Iranian human wave attacks.

Seacrest focused his binoculars on Baker. To his alarm, it looked like an army of ants was swarming on a picnic pie as they rolled over Baker's position. His last image of Sergeant Baker was of the brave noncom fighting off the enemy with his entrenching tool!

Seacrest shook his head and said, "Broken arrow! Send in reserves and put all available missiles on those tanks!"

Dozens of smoke trails flew through the air as U.S. TOW 2B anti-tank missiles struck home. The initial blasts were followed by massive explosions as the tank's ammunition and fuel ignited.

When the Chinese commander wisely deployed smoke, Jake could no longer see troop movements but could still hear the sounds of battle interspersed with screams. All around him, Marines and Taiwanese troops fired into the fog of war, hoping to halt advancing troops.

Responding to Seacrest's urgent call, six Apache helicopters appeared overhead. Each aircraft carried a 30 mm M-230 chain gun under its forward fuselage. Four hardpoints on stub-wing pylons bristled with AGM-114 Hellfire missiles and Hydra 70 rocket pods. The helicopter's infrared targeting systems quickly located tanks and APCs through the smoke, dispensing death. Despite taking heavy fire, the aircraft's redundant systems allowed them to deliver their full payloads, blunting enemy progress.

Jake saw flashes of exploding vehicles through the smoke. Then, watched as the Apaches' chain guns swept back and forth, delivering withering fire on the Chinese troops.

Suddenly, in rapid succession, two helicopters blew up in midair while the others pumped chaff and dropped to counter Chinese surface-to-air missiles. To no avail, all choppers were soon destroyed.

Sparks O'Reilly announced, "Sir, we have six F-35s and a squadron of Harriers inbound. ETA, six minutes."

Seacrest acknowledged the report with a nod, then unholstered his sidearm and worked the action. Without a word, he'd sent the message: prepare for close combat.

Jake unslung his rifle and chambered a round. It was show time, perhaps his last. He looked back at Hank.

Hank grabbed his rifle, joining Jake at the firing slit of the Command Post. The post's high position above the battlefield would allow them to rain down fire until their ammo ran out. So many targets, so few cartridges.

Sparks said, "The last terminator unit is coming through the tunnel now."

As if commanded by a higher power, the wind shifted from the North, and the smoke cleared. Jake was shocked at the carnage. Hundreds of bodies and burning vehicle hulks lined the battlefield. Nevertheless, two hundred meters away, Chinese Marines supported by surviving tanks and APCs were pushing through the carnage!

"Send in the terminators," Seacrest barked, his orders relayed by his radio operator.

As Jake watched, a dozen terminators advanced from the tunnel, firing their missiles and machine guns, slaughtering everything in their path. Tanks, APCs, and troops fell to their heavy fire. With no conscience, the machines charged rapidly into the fray, leaving a path of death and destruction.

"Those terminators are keeping us alive," Seacrest observed.

Stillwell nodded, "Yes, sir."

Jake saw that the Chinese commander had turned his tank guns on the terminators, but scored few hits due to their mobility. Eventually, the machines ran out of ammunition, and all resupply drones had been destroyed. With no opportunity for resupply, several terminators rammed enemy vehicles and detonated their high-explosive charges. Other units drove deep into the human waves and exploded, showering lethal shrapnel into the dismounted infantry.

"Their killers until the end, aren't they?" Jake observed.

Hank nodded.

"Send in all remaining AWS units! Where's my artillery!" Seacrest barked.

Zhurihe Joint Training Base

Two hundred fifty miles from Beijing, General Leu stood rigid at the edge of the command center, fingers white against the railing as he stared into the emerging disaster. Once, the People's Liberation Army had seemed an immovable colossus, its fleets and armies a wall of steel across Asia. Now that illusion burned away before his eyes, torn apart by an enemy that possessed no blood, no fear, no hesitation.

The sky screamed with the whine of autonomous aircraft—everything from sleek, angular strike drones to nimble reconnaissance craft the size of a man. PLA fighters clawed upward in desperate sorties only to vanish in blossoms of fire, their wreckage spiraling earthward. Helicopters fared worse, shredded before they cleared the horizon.

In the harbor, the navy's proudest symbols died in succession. Type 055 destroyers, once the pride of Beijing's blue-water ambitions, erupted into pillars of flame. Amphibious assault ships cracked open, spilling fire and fuel into the sea until the very water seemed to boil. Merchant ships, requisitioned for the war effort, disintegrated in sudden, surgical strikes—unseen missiles turning hulls into shredded metal coffins.

Leu shifted his gaze to the mainland. Columns of black smoke poured skyward from what had been a central operations hub. Ammunition depots erupted in chain reactions, one thunderclap after another shaking the city. Tanks, armored carriers, trucks—all reduced to twisted skeletons by relentless bombardment. Power stations winked out. Water mains ruptured. Communications nodes blinked to black. The lifeblood of the base bled away in minutes.

On the ground, the machines advanced with a cold inevitability. Tracked and wheeled platforms moved in disciplined formations, their fire control algorithms selecting and killing with surgical precision. Infantry formations that had taken years to train and equip were scythed down in seconds. To his amazement, U.S. resupply drones followed methodically, feeding magazines and missile racks as though the entire battlefield were one enormous, living machine.

Then came the strikes from orbit. Invisible pulses of directed energy stabbed downward, detonating fuel depots, frying radars, turning command posts into lifeless bunkers. Communications went dead; entire sectors of the Chinese military vanished from the network. Leu's orders dissolved into nothingness. The command web that bound millions of men and machines unraveled in silence.

They had underestimated the Americans. All of them had. Beijing had expected a swift victory, supported by a fatal opening salvo of cyberattacks and an EMP, followed by massive missile and air attacks. President Jin had told them the U.S. President would delay counterattacks for two weeks. Instead, Washington had unleashed a fury of technology far beyond what Chinese planners had prepared for—autonomous, precise, and merciless. Years of preparation, of grand strategy and Party doctrine, were being obliterated in three days.

A trembling officer approached, pale as ash. "General Leu... President Jin requests your presence in Beijing."

Leu knew what awaited him: accusations, humiliation, a scapegoat for the Party's failure. And he knew who that scapegoat would be.

He turned and looked out one last time, absorbing the scene—the shattered windows rattling with concussions, the green glow of dead screens, the frantic officers still clinging to procedures as if paperwork could hold back the tide.

Without a word, Leu strode across the catwalk to the rear of the Command Center. Standing outside on the back of the building, he saw the distant mountains that loomed in pale blue haze, unscarred—for now. A faint, wry smile tugged at his mouth, the expression of a man who had already reckoned with fate.

He drew his pistol, its weight familiar, almost comforting. For a moment, he studied it, his mind unnaturally calm. Then he raised it to his temple, inhaled one final breath, and pulled the trigger.

The sound of his death was lost in the thunder of war.

Politburo, Beijing

Deep beneath Zhongnanhai, the Politburo chamber reverberated with the distant rumble of detonations. Even here, insulated by steel and concrete, the war pressed in like a storm at the door.

President Jin sat smoking a cigar at the head of the lacquered table, face carved in stone. Around him, senior Party officials and generals barked accusations, their voices rising over one another in a chaotic din.

"They've decapitated our southern fleet!" roared Admiral Wu, his uniform streaked with ash from a command post destroyed hours earlier. "Our ports are firestorms—our ships at anchor never had a chance. Autonomous drones bypassed our layered defenses entirely, while U.S. missiles killed with precision."

"They struck from orbit!" another general spat, slamming his fist on the table. "Our satellites are blind. Our anti-satellite missiles failed before they left the pads. Our intercontinental nuclear missiles detonated in their silos. We are down to only eight mobile nuclear launch vehicles. This is a slaughter, not a war!"

Jin raised a hand. Silence fell instantly. His eyes, dark and calculating, swept across the room. "Where is General Leu?"

No one answered. Then, an aide leaned in, whispering urgently into Jin's ear. The president's jaw twitched once. He sat back, his silence more damning than words. Everyone in the room knew what had happened. Leu had chosen the only honorable escape left.

"Then he has accepted his fate," Jin said coldly. "And left us to bear the burden. He died a coward, a man who could not see his mission through until the end. His name will be associated with shame for perpetuity."

The ministers shifted uneasily. Defense Minister Zhang finally spoke, his voice low and subdued. "Comrade President, we cannot match their machines. Our networks are compromised. Our command structure is fractured. If this continues another twenty-four hours, the nation will not withstand it."

Jin's gaze hardened. "So, we escalate. We take Taiwan and announce our victory to the world! This is not a time for cowardice; it's time to strike harder." The room stilled. "Invoke the Second Deterrent Protocol."

A sharp intake of breath circled the table. The Second Protocol was an unspoken Party doctrine: limited nuclear release against Coalition staging hubs—Japan, Guam, and Hawaii. Enough to halt the assault, to remind Washington that China's arsenal was not depleted.

Admiral Wu leaned forward, his voice almost trembling. "Mr. President, the U.S. has responded in a measured way to our nuclear attacks. Such escalation virtually ensures full-scale U.S. nuclear retaliation. We've seen their power. Do you want to risk the lives of a billion people over national pride?"

Jin's eyes narrowed. "The line was crossed the moment their soulless machines laid waste to our bases. If we do nothing, China could cease to exist. Better to burn the world than watch it collapse around us."

He looked around the table, daring any man to contradict him. None did. Fear hung heavy, thicker than the stale air.

"Prepare the launch orders for our nuclear bombers and submarines. Target the A-list bases in Japan, Guam, South Korea, and Hawaii," Jin commanded. "Soon, the world will remember why China cannot be challenged. Tomorrow, we lead our communist allies in taking over the world."

Admiral Wu, hiding his shaking hands beneath the table, mustered the courage to confront Jin. "There is a better alternative. One that is being lost in the fog of war."

Jin looked hatefully at Wu. "Go on."

"Supreme Leader, we have more powerful weapons in play. Carpathian and his team have the U.S. on the brink of collapse from within. As Sun Tzu said, 'To fight and conquer in all our battles is not supreme excellence; supreme excellence consists in breaking the enemy's resistance without fighting. One need not destroy one's enemy. One need only destroy his willingness to engage.'" Wu let the ancient words hang for a moment, having their full effect.

The anger in Jin's face lessened as he said, "Go on."

"The Americans are fighting in the streets, murdering one another over resources. Their power grid is failing. The plagues are killing millions. The American economy is on the edge of ruin. When they open their markets, their wealth will evaporate. NATO is a paper tiger without U.S. might and money. This means that despite regional battle losses, we're winning the global war."

Wu saw a faint glint, a sign of change in Jin's eyes. "Our enemies are mortally wounded and will soon fall. Better to allow them time to die than to taunt them into action."

Jin considered Admiral Wu's words. His General had used the words of his favorite philosopher against him. Well played, general.

"Perhaps you are correct, and we can win the war via non-military means. What do your simulations tell you?"

Admiral Wu, feeling more confident now, said, "The American death toll will be over 290 million people within one year. Our bioweapons and destruction of Western infrastructure will kill over 600 million people in Europe. The U.S. dollar is collapsing. The Euro will soon follow along with most currencies, ushering in Dragon Coin. The one world cybercurrency will allow us to control the global economy. With fortune on our side, Russia will take full advantage of the current situation. If we wait and preserve our forces, we can fulfill our 2050 Strategy of global domination without firing another shot."

Jin saw the wisdom in Admiral Wu's analysis but still wanted to eliminate the American and NATO threats once and for all. But China didn't have to be on point, did she?

"Your analysis is on point. We can simply allow our other weapons to have their full effect. But Russia…" He paused, letting the name hang in the room like the echo of an artillery shell. "…Russia is both proud and desperate. Pride blinds men, and desperation drives them."

Admiral Wu caught on quickly and nodded. "Their economy bleeds from sanctions. Their general's thirst for victory is driven by a desire to redeem their setbacks in Ukraine. If we give them resources—funds, technology, diplomatic cover—they may turn against NATO without ever realizing they fight our war."

Jin's eyes glinted. "Precisely. We need not command them; we only need to encourage their trajectory. Provide them energy deals at a discount, let our banks launder their gold, and whisper assurances through back channels. When Moscow smells opportunity, it will lash out."

He leaned forward, lowering his voice. "NATO's greatest weakness is not its weapons, but its will. Each nation is divided by its own fears. If Russia tests that alliance—cyber strikes on Poland, 'peacekeepers' in the Baltics, pressure on Germany's energy lifelines—the cracks will widen. The Americans grow weaker every day and cannot bail out the Europeans. And if NATO fractures…" He allowed himself a thin smile. "…then our path to world dominion lies wide open."

A hush fell over the chamber. The plan was not a traditional battle strategy—it was a campaign of patience, pressure, and manipulation. The generals recognized it for what it was: the art of winning without fighting, the spirit of Sun Tzu reborn in the twenty-first century.

Admiral Wu finally broke the silence. "So, Russia believes it is avenging its own grievances, while in truth, it is moving our pieces across the chessboard."

Jin stubbed out his cigar, the ember hissing as it died. "When the bear fights the Eagle, the dragon will rise."

The Kremlin, Secure Conference Line to Beijing

The ornate Kremlin office was dark, the heavy drapes drawn. Only the glow of secure screens lit the long table where President Vladmir Karamazov sat, his broad shoulders hunched forward, eyes locked on the encrypted video feed. Across the screen, President Jin of China appeared equally grim, framed by the crimson backdrop of the Zhongnanhai command chamber.

The line had been established on a hardened channel, routed through buried fiber and satellite relays. Both men knew that in speaking these words, they were stepping into history — and perhaps ending it.

Jin broke the silence first. His voice was calm, but the fatigue etched into his features betrayed him.

“Comrade Karamazov, our fleets are broken. The Americans have used autonomous systems in ways we never imagined. Their new Overmatch systems are more than theory. My generals whisper of defeat. That is unacceptable. China cannot be humiliated before the world. Our communist alliance cannot be allowed to fail at this critical juncture.”

Karamazov’s pale eyes narrowed. He understood the tone; it was not a complaint but an invitation.

“You propose escalation.”

“I propose survival,” Jin replied coldly. “The Americans and their NATO lackeys believe they can fight us both with impunity. They must learn the cost.”

Karamazov leaned back, fingers steepled. His intelligence staff had already gamed the scenario: U.S. carrier groups crippled, their submarines still lurking, NATO resolve fractured but dangerous. Russia’s own arsenal — vast, silent, waiting — was the counterweight.

“You would have me commit Russia to Armageddon.”

“Not Armageddon,” Jin said, eyes flashing. “Surgical fire. Limited nuclear release. We strike the U.S. submarine bastions in the Barents and Pacific, their NATO air bases in Europe, and their submarines and carriers at sea. Then, utilize high altitude detonations to rain down EMP on all NATO countries. One coordinated knockout punch. Then…”

For a long moment, the Russian leader said nothing. The room was so quiet that the hum of the encrypted line became audible. Inside, the Russian Leader’s heart leapt at the once-in-a-lifetime opportunity for total victory. Then Karamazov exhaled slowly.

“My admirals assure me we can target their boomers with Poseidon drone torpedoes and hypersonic warheads. NATO bases in Germany,

Poland, and Norway are already plotted. But understand this — once we cross this line, there is no retreat. The Americans will answer."

"No. They will hesitate due to the collapse of their economy. We've already destroyed the American way of life as they've known it. Soon, the U.S. will be a war zone with people killing over food." Jin countered. "Their democracy will fracture. Their leaders will argue while their forces burn. That is the difference between empires and republics."

Karamazov allowed himself the faintest of smiles. He admired the Chinese president's ruthless logic, even as he despised the necessity of their alliance. Still, with China taking the brunt of the U.S. Coalition's firepower, Russia had a rare opportunity to emerge as the world's superpower. Slowly, he nodded.

"Very well. Russia stands with China. We will bring the West to its knees."

Jin inclined his head. "Then it is agreed. We stand by for coordinated nuclear strikes and begin hunting their submarines and carriers immediately. The Americans will learn that the age of their supremacy is over."

Karamazov replied, "It is agreed."

The line went dead.

In the silence of the Kremlin office, Karamazov reached for the red folder beside him. Inside lay the preliminary nuclear strike orders — coded, sealed, waiting. He rested his hand on it for a long moment, then pressed the intercom.

"Summon the General Staff," he ordered.

Hilltop 463

Seacrest announced, "The air strike is coming in. They'll bust up more of those tanks and ACPs. We also have two more platoons of terminators coming through the tunnel."

Jake thought Seacrest's face held an astonishing serenity for a man about to die. It was an otherworldly peace that passed all understanding. He wondered if Davy Crockett held a similar resolve before his death at the Alamo. Then Jake realized the irony of having covered wars across the globe and finally dying in one.

Jake's moment of reflection was terminated as artillery rounds pummeled their position, and battle screens were hastily lowered. The shelling continued for two harrowing minutes while the men in the room sat with their backs resting against concrete walls.

When the barrage ended. Jake looked out and saw a large column of tanks surging forward. Behind them were heavily armed APCs, followed by dismounted infantry.

"They're one hundred meters out, sir," Stillwell reported.

Jake and Hank began firing alongside their comrades-in-arms, a mix of men and women from ten countries now engaged in a desperate battle.

Jake placed the reticle of his scope on the center mass of the closest Chinese Marine and fired. The 5.56 mm bullet quickly dropped the soldier, then a dozen more.

Shell casings from Hank's rifle bounced off Jake's helmet as he ducked down to reload.

"We're down to four magazines a piece. Make 'em count!" Stillwell barked, a slight glint in his eyes, knowing he would soon die with his boots on and join the eternal brotherhood of Marines!

***

Six F-35B Joint Strike Fighters flew in with abandon, striking Chinese vehicles in the nick of time. Behind them, ten AH-1Z Super Cobra helicopters moved in with blazing missiles and cannons. All across the battlefield, enemy vehicles exploded, and men fell.

"They're from the USS America," O'Reilly reported.

Seacrest smiled, "I guess our old crewmates decided we were worth saving. I hope their arrival means we control the sea lanes."

Jake knew the USS America and her fellow amphibious warships were designed to move Marines ashore and provide support. He'd written an article on them. Now, he would see how effective they really were.

O'Reilly said, "Sir, we have four MV-22 Ospreys and six CH-53E Sea Stallion helicopters inbound with ammunition and reinforcements. They want us to send back our wounded."

Seacrest said, "Have them land on the other side of the tunnel. We need to minimize their time on the ground. Tell Peterson to take a platoon and distribute the ammo. I want every remaining position reinforced. Let's hope that someone thought to bring antitank weapons."

Seacrest staggered, then fell. Hank caught him before he hit the ground.

Hank removed the captain's helmet and saw the discharge from his ears. He did a quick medical assessment and looked at Stillwell. "We've got to get him to a chopper, stat."

The squint in Stillwell's eyes showed a deep resolve to save his officer, "Corpsman!" he yelled, then said, "Hank, go with him. The command is mine until an officer shows up. I can't leave. You're his best chance."

Hank nodded. It was the only reasonable course of action. After all, he was a SEAL doc, a highly advanced medical technician.

Hank and Jake removed the stretcher from the wall and placed Seacrest on it. When the corpsman arrived, Jake announced, "I'm staying."

It was one of those life-altering, split-second decisions no one should have to make, a gut-induced revelation of a man's true character.

Stillwell heard Jake while he surveyed the battlefield. He turned and looked at Jake, then nodded his approval.

Hank hated leaving his friend, but he had to keep his patient alive. Hank nodded and said, "Good luck, Jake," as he took one end of the stretcher and the corpsman took the other.

Jake never heard his friend's goodbye as he returned to his firing position.

USS America

Captain Seacrest's heart had stopped mid-flight. The corpsman barked for paddles, Hank holding the IV line steady as the Black Hawk bucked through turbulence. The smell of ozone filled the cabin when the defibrillator discharged, Seacrest's body arching violently against the stretcher straps. After a long, terrifying pause, the monitor beeped—thin, erratic, but there. The fluids kept his veins open, but Hank knew the truth: with massive head trauma and sheer exhaustion, Seacrest had less than a 10% percent chance of surviving the night. Beyond that, there was assurance of a full recovery.

Through the open side door, Hank caught sight of the Wasp-class assault ship below. The flight deck was alive with organized chaos: Harriers and F-35Bs being refueled and armed, Ospreys lifting off in formation with squads of Marines bound for Taiwan, crew chiefs waving batons in the fading light. War at full tempo.

As the helicopter slammed onto the deck, a stretcher team sprinted forward. Seacrest was rushed into the ship's clinic, where Lieutenant Commander Robert Stevens, MD, USN—UCLA trauma surgeon and SEAL veteran— waited. He had requested activation the moment the war broke out, knowing the Navy would need hands trained for impossible cases.

Stevens bent over Seacrest, eyes narrowing as he checked vitals, pupils, and wounds. He didn't waste time asking what happened—every second mattered. "Prep him for surgery," he ordered. His tone was calm, clipped, the voice of a man who had seen too many men die and refused to let it shake him now.

On the way to the operating room, Stevens paused by another exam table. Hank sat slouched, blood crusted on his arms, uniform torn and blackened with soot.

"Looks like you chewed some tough bush," Stevens said, voice lower now, almost conversational. "What's your assessment?"

Hank swallowed, the weight of exhaustion in his eyes. "He coded on the flight. Pupils fixed. Raccoon sign… classic basilar skull fracture, multiple contusions. He's tanking—systolic pressure dropping, heart rate slowing, breathing patterns irregular. I know you'll do what you can, Doc."

Stevens's expression didn't change, but the set of his jaw betrayed the truth: the chances were near zero. Even at UCLA, with a neurosurgical team, the odds would be grim. Here, on a moving ship in wartime, with a single trauma surgeon, it was barbaric. But abandoning the fight was worse.

He shifted the subject. "How's Jake?"

Hank gave a tired, almost bitter laugh. "Too brave for his own good. He chose to stay in the fight."

Stevens studied him for a moment, then asked, "His odds?"

Hank shook his head once; the odds were grave.

The Navy doctor nodded slowly. It was the answer he expected, but the confirmation still landed like a stone. The Order was losing irreplaceable men.

Then a flashback raged through the portal of time, assaulting his consciousness. August 6, 2011. A brave attempt to rescue a SEAL Team under heavy fire on a mountain in Afghanistan. They'd gone in like the cavalry of old, valiant, heroic, but without proper air support.

As they prepared to fast rope into the battle below, a 13-year-old boy with an RPG fired into the helicopter bay, killing all aboard. The Pentagon identified the Americans as 17 members of the elite Navy SEALs, five Naval Special Warfare personnel who support the SEALs, three Air Force Special Operations personnel, and an Army helicopter crew of five. All but two of the SEALs were from SEAL Team 6, the unit that killed Osama bin Laden. Despite none of the actual members of the bin Laden raid being aboard, the symbolism could not be overcome.

Stevens shook off the memory. Time to be in the now. He put a hand on Hank's shoulder, firm, steady. "The corpsman will patch you up. Get some rack time. I'll find you when it's over."

Without waiting for an answer, Stevens turned and followed the stretcher team into the operating room, the heavy steel hatch clanging shut behind him like the lid of a coffin. For Hank, the sound was final, like the toll of a bell—one more brother in the hands of fate.

Damn, it was hard. A single tear ran down his face.

Hilltop 463

Major Thomson arrived just five minutes after Seacrest was evacuated. As he gazed skyward, the sun's warm rays shone through. Good weather was usually welcome, but he'd hoped for a monsoon today - anything to slow the enemy hordes.

Smoke hung low in the air, mingling with the smell of burnt metal and scorched earth. Major Thomson ran through the tunnel and entered the reinforced command bunker; his eyes fixed on the advancing wave of Chinese. His jaw clenched as he noted the distance to the enemy —a mere one hundred meters. He quickly assessed that he had too few men and conventional weapons left to stop the assault. It was now up to the Geek Squad.

Stillwell lowered Seacrest's binoculars and said, "Welcome to the Alamo, sir."

"They're closing rapidly," a voice crackled over the comms, urgent and strained amidst the chaos. The radio was suddenly filled with units reporting heavy casualties; many units were overrun.

Thomson knew he had fewer than 200 troops left and didn't hesitate. "Activate trojans for an all-out assault. Gunny, prepare to fall back," his voice cold and resolute.

The small valley seemed to come alive as dozens of small, tank-like robots, no bigger than a compact car, rolled out from the tunnel. Their metal hulls gleamed under the harsh sunlight, armed with an array of weaponry—from machine guns to anti-tank missiles. These lethal autonomous weapons had been programmed with a singular purpose: to engage and neutralize enemy forces. Unlike the more miniature infantry AWS units that had bought them time, these antitank weapons had greater lethality and survivability.

As the Chinese tanks and marines advanced, the robots moved swiftly, scanning the battlefield with precise sensors and identifying mechanical and human targets.

The chatter of machine guns filled the air as bullets tore through the ranks of advancing soldiers. Missiles launched, sending explosive rounds into enemy vehicles, turning them into twisted heaps of burning metal. Some combatants dove for cover, while others froze in their tracks, horrified at the sight of the killer machines.

Major Thomson watched through his binoculars, observing the unfolding carnage with a mix of awe and grim satisfaction. These machines culminated in years of military development—a force multiplier that could shift the balance of power on any battlefield. And today, they were proving their worth.

Thomson had brought a cadre of officers and specialists with him. Among these, AWS Commander Eric Skinner had graduated from the Georgia Institute of Technology with a degree in advanced robotics engineering. While there, he participated in the Naval Reserve Officers' Training Program.

Skinner operated a PC that monitored key battle statistics, allowing him to override the terminators as needed. If the machines didn't receive new orders, they simply kept firing until they ran out of ammo or targets.

Stillwell stared at the scene in disbelief. He had started his career thirty-five years ago when infantry battles were fought by men carrying rifles with fixed bayonets. The efficiency of these units was as mesmerizing as it was terrifying.

Stillwell muttered, his voice a mixture of admiration and unease. "They don't miss."

Across the battlefield, the AWS units continued their relentless assault as Chinese soldiers fell by the hundreds, mowed down by precise bursts of gunfire and airborne fragmentation grenades. Vehicles exploded in brilliant fireballs as the robots pinpointed their vulnerabilities. The metal beasts seemed unstoppable, their hardened exteriors shrugging off small arms fire and artillery like rain. Only the occasional direct hit put them down.

The whine of jet engines signaled the arrival of the aerial terminators—sleek, drone-like aircraft armed with missiles and laser-guided bombs. A dozen of them streaked across the sky, heading for the Chinese beachhead. Skinner followed their progress on his screen, watching as they descended on the landing zone. Moments later, the horizon erupted in plumes of smoke, marking the destruction of enemy landing craft and vehicles.

Thomson allowed himself a brief moment of hope. The tide of battle seemed to be turning. The Chinese assault was faltering, their forces decimated by the relentless onslaught of machines.

The ICS fed real-time data to Skinner's display, showing a clear and steady reduction in enemy numbers.

Stillwell exhaled slowly, shaking his head in disbelief. "I've never seen anything like that."

Thomson nodded, though his expression remained stoic. "War's changing," he said. "For better or worse, this is the future."

As the battle raged on, the major couldn't help but wonder what kind of world they were creating. But that was a question for another day.

Skinner stroked the keys with the precision of a surgeon as the machines seemed to halt in place.

"Keep pushing," Thomson ordered, his voice cutting through the comms static, "We're not done yet."

"They're reloading, sir. Behind smoke screens and with covering fire." Skinner assured him.

To Thomson and Stillwell's amazement, dozens of APC-sized vehicles made their way across the battlefield, rearming the robots. Once each unit was serviced, it continued forward.

Thirty minutes later, Skinner showed Thomson drone images of smoking vehicles and a battlefield covered in dead bodies. The soil and seas ran red with blood.

Jake rose from his firing position and said, "What happened here today will forever change war."

"How so?" Thomson asked.

"This is the first war in which Autonomous Weapons have been given permission to kill humans in mass."

Thomson studied the journalist's face for a long moment, then said, "The Admiral had to go high tech or give away the farm. It's that simple."

O'Reilly brought Thomson a note. The Major read it and looked at Jake.

"President Novak requests your presence at the White House. You're going home by the first available means. He told Flint to arrest you if necessary."

Jake continued firing, dropping enemy troops with abandon. At first, Thomson thought he was going to have to arrest Jake, then the reporter stood, out of ammo, handed him his weapon, and extended his hand.

"Aye, aye, Sir."

"Get the hell on that chopper, marine." Thomson laughed. It was a backhanded compliment. "It's been good serving with you."

Jake shook Thomson's hand, turned, and made his way through the tunnel, each rapid footfall bringing him closer to the light at the end.

Waiting outside was a Blackhawk helicopter.

"You're Jake Hendel, right?" the crew chief asked.

Jake nodded.

The crew chief gave the pilot a thumbs-up and escorted Jake to the chopper. Once strapped in, the helo lifted off, and fatigue quickly pulled Jake into a deep sleep.

New York City

On the flight home, Jake Hendel had stared at the clouds, trying to reconcile the last seventy-two hours. The smoke, the fire, the screams—men and machines torn apart in a valley half a world from home. Now the war correspondent was being flown home on a government jet, courtesy of President Novak himself. The contrast was disorienting.

The cabin was quiet, but Jake's head was not. Every detail replayed in his mind: the artillery shrieks, the acrid stench of burning fuel, the body bags zipped one after another. Ninety countries, five continents—his memories were a ledger of misery, each entry carved into his soul. Would he ever feel normal again?

The wheels touched down at Andrews Air Force Base with a bump that jolted him from his thoughts. The engines wound down. The hatch opened.

And there she was, an angel of light, piercing the darkness in his soul!

Susie Legman broke past the cordon, her heels clattering across the tarmac. She was running, hair whipping in the wind, eyes already wet. Before Jake could form a thought, she was in his arms—feet off the ground, arms locked around his neck, sobbing into his shoulder.

Something broke inside him then, not in pain, but in release. The tears came unbidden, years of grief and guilt pouring out. The hardened fortress he had built after Somalia cracked wide open under the simple force of love.

For five long minutes, they clung to each other, unmoving, the war suspended, the world forgotten.

Finally, Susie pulled back just enough to look at him, her silver-blue eyes reddened with emotion. She brushed his cheek, her hand trembling. "Welcome home, Jake."

He held her gaze, voice low, steady, but edged with a finality she had never heard before. "I'm home… for good."

And for the first time in decades, he believed it.

All those scars. All the filthy duty stations. The smell of death. The endless lonely nights. The bittersweet memories of Barbie and young love. All gone.

Pacific Command

Newsome opened his slide deck and reported, "The battle for Taiwan began with unprovoked acts of aggression by China and her allies 21 days ago. As you can see from the battle statistics, U.S. Coalition forces lost 129,000 personnel, 90% of our prepositioned vehicles and aircraft. Naval losses included six Coalition aircraft carriers and sixty ships. These staggering losses in such a short time highlight the speed at which modern wars are fought. In many ways, we underestimated China's missile capabilities and almost lost to their numerical advantages. Had it not been for our sub force, high-tech, and dogged marines, the outcome could have been very different."

Admiral Flint's face was lined with regret over the losses. Each lost life affected an entire social system of family, friends, and communities.

Each death cut off the potential of that person. He closed his eyes momentarily, the burden of command pressing his heart like a vice.

Behind closed eyelids, Flint's mind wandered across the white marble crosses in countless cemeteries. War costs too much! The thought echoed through his mind and fueled his nightmares. While his team had won a great victory, there would always be another enemy to vanquish.

Then a sobering thought hit him, a brutal epiphany, as he wondered if the republic he'd sacrificed so much to save would soon crumble from within.

Flint pulled himself out of the dark concerns within his mind and rejoined the present as Newsome continued, "Chinese Coalition losses are as shown. They've lost 483,000 personnel, 70% of their merchant marine, 90% of their naval ships, 95% of their nuclear missiles, 40% of their tanks and artillery, and 80% of their air force."

Cheers arose all across the room!

Newsome continued, "As you can see, Taiwanese military casualties are 250,000, including militia. Civilian losses are estimated to be over 1,000,000 due to the Chinese targeting civilian centers. Coalition civilian losses outside Taiwan, including those who died in Hawaii, are estimated at 75,000. The destruction of civilian and military infrastructure across the region is estimated to be five trillion dollars and will take a decade or more to restore. Our ammo lockers are below 20% for torpedoes, missiles, artillery, and small-arms ammunition, leaving us severely challenged to maintain global commitments. Right now, our AWS capabilities are below 50% of pre-war levels. Civil unrest in the U.S. has closed most of our military industrial complex."

The grim statistics were a testament to the rapidity with which modern wars unfold.

"50% of the Chinese power grid is down, and most major ports are inoperable. As a result of infrastructure damage, the World Health Organization estimates that over 150 million Chinese will perish due to starvation and disease in the next twelve months," Newsome said solemnly and seated without mentioning estimates of US loss of life.

Admiral Flint received a standing ovation as he took the podium. As a young officer, he'd dreamed of such glory; after three decades of war, the adulation left him unmoved. What kind of monster would celebrate this kind of carnage? Despite his repulsion for praise, he raised his hand and forced a smile.

It was their victory, and Flint knew he had been the same way when he was their age. Somehow, the burden of command had driven out youthful exuberance, replacing it with a more mature perspective. Yes, they were enemies, but most were just people caught up in a war they didn't want, pawns in a global chess match played by the rich and powerful.

Flint said, "As of 1200 EST, President Novak will officially end hostilities."

More applause arose!

"Take today and relish the victory," Flint finished without mentioning their other problems.

An eerie silence spread across the room as hearts turned homeward.

"While no foreign nation will ever defeat us in battle, we must never fail to recognize the enemy within. Those powerful manipulators who seek to control our hearts and minds, setting us on a course of destruction like nothing the world has ever seen. It is the globalists and their new world order that we must resist with all our might, lest our republic fall and never rise again."

Solar Valley

Ethan Carpathian stood four stories beneath the Dragon's Temple, deep inside an underground bunker carved from the bones of what had once been the most advanced civilization on Earth. The air was cool, sterile, and faintly metallic. Power hummed through hidden conduits in the walls.

Behind him, a massive digital world map pulsed with data—markets, troop movements, infection curves, energy flows. One metric drew the eye more than any other. World Population: Declining. The number ticked down again.

Carpathian didn't turn as he spoke. "How is Phase Two progressing?"

Helmut Scheid answered without hesitation. "On schedule."

Carpathian's silence was pointed.

Scheid felt it and continued. "The United States no longer has room to maneuver. They have no way out."

Carpathian turned slowly. "Could President Novak still interfere?"

Scheid's smile was thin and predatory. "The American economy is finished. If they reopen markets, equities collapse—trillions in paper wealth vaporized overnight. Their credit rating is already down to B-. They can't borrow enough to stabilize anything." He spread his hands slightly. "No economy means no revenue. No revenue means no government. The United States is—how do they say it?—a dead man walking."

Carpathian's lips curled faintly. "Desperate people accept any flag offered?"

"And more importantly," Scheid said, "they accept any currency we offer."

He gestured toward the map. "Our global cyber currency is already positioned as the only stable medium of exchange. As governments fail, people will trade land, factories, infrastructure—everything—for the digital coin they need to eat. Even today, a loaf of bread costs $500 US." His eyes gleamed. "It will be the greatest transfer of wealth in human history. And Washington's insatiable appetite for debt, money they used to buy the vote, kept the self-dealing politicians in power. Their lust for money and power paved the way."

Carpathian turned to Amy Rapier and Lawrence Wilhite. "When do you intend to launch Chimera?"

Wilhite swallowed. "We already have."

The room went still.

Carpathian's gaze snapped to him. "You proceeded without informing me?"

Wilhite raised his hands slightly, backing away. "We believed you had reviewed the report."

For a long moment, Carpathian held his stare—cold, assessing, calculating how easily Wilhite could be replaced. And Wilhite and Rapier's days were numbered. He would not tolerate manipulators or liars in his inner circle. Best to just use them, then toss them away.

Then he looked away. "Continue."

"The early data is conclusive," Wilhite responded quickly. "The virus is exceeding projections across multiple regions."

"Excellent," Carpathian replied. "The sooner we reach sustainability thresholds, the sooner equilibrium is restored."

Judy Isenberg broke the silence. "Is there any scenario in which the Order wins?"

Priest Longshen smiled serenely. "No."

All eyes turned to him.

“The destiny of the Chosen One cannot be altered,” Longshen said calmly. “We need only wait. The Four Horsemen will remove the undesirables from among us in their good time.”

Carpathian stepped forward, his reflection fracturing across the glowing map. His voice dropped, reverent and dangerous, as he recited the ancient Dregodarit prophecy: “A Dragon shall rise in the East, ridding the earth of the followers of the unseen God. He shall rule the world through his Chosen One. His High Priest shall uphold his right hand.”

As the population counter ticked down another 50,000 lives, Carpathian said, “Hail the Dragon, the power of the air. Hail the progeny of a fallen world.”

The bunker hummed on, indifferent—while the world above continued to die.

After the meeting, Scheid and Isenberg held a side bar conversation far out of earshot of the rest of the group.

“Helmut, does Ethan really believe in this dragon religion? I mean, I play along, even enjoy some of it, but it’s a bit far out there.”

Scheid considered how to answer. Then he remembered his grandfather teaching him, “Helmut, you will need a point man. Someone who is a charismatic leader. A man who can bring people together under a cause. He must be well admired and able to deceive the masses. In my day, that man was Adolph Hitler... Let’s hope you can do better.”

“Judy, I understand your concerns, but remember, Ethan is the man of the year, the talk in every boardroom, they’re writing favorable articles and books about him. No offense, but none of us has his charisma and charm. We need him on point if we are to fulfill our dreams.”

Isenberg considered Scheid’s practical words, then said, “Yes, you’re right. It doesn’t matter who he calls God, does it? It doesn’t matter as long as the people follow him into the new world order.”

Scheid smiled and said, “That’s correct. Besides, Carpathian is much brighter and more appealing than Hitler. We’re lucky to have him on point. Who else could have accomplished as much in such a short time?”

Isenberg’s eyes rose at the comparison. While uncomfortable with Scheid’s Nazi references and Carpathian’s eccentricities, the economist was right. Carpathian was the only man who could pull off the most significant transfer of wealth in human history and deceive billions into extinction. Right now, people were flocking to him like lost sheep to the

Shepard. Besides, Carpathian had made her a full member of the New World Order, one of the twelve picked to rule the world.

"You always have a way of making sense of things, Helmut. We could never have made the money we've made without him. Our futures are entwined."

Honolulu

The USS America eased into Pearl Harbor under a bruised gray sky, her decks scarred and crowded, her arrival watched in silence by sailors and Marines who knew the war was far from over. As the gangway dropped, corpsmen moved first, guiding stretchers toward waiting ambulances.

Hank watched as Captain Seacrest lay strapped down, pale but breathing, monitors blinking steadily as the team loaded him on a helicopter bound for the naval hospital. The smell of jet fuel and salt was heavy in the air.

Hank watched until Seacrest's chopper disappeared into the clouds, then let out a sigh. He hadn't realized how tightly he'd been holding himself together until the tension finally loosened.

Dr. Stevens stepped up beside him, "He's one tough Marine."

Placing his hand on Hank's shoulder, he continued, "He's made it this far. Men like Seacrest don't quit. He can make it back."

Hank nodded, swallowing. "I hope so." He stared out toward the harbor, toward the distant green hills. "I just hope Jake and Susie are safe. After everything we've seen… I don't know how much more the world can take."

Stevens rested a hand on Hank's shoulder. "That's why we can't stop. What's coming next won't look like the wars we've fought overseas. It's already here." He lowered his voice. "This is a global revolution—economic, ideological, spiritual. And America's going to need every good man and woman she has."

Hank turned to him. "What about you?"

Stevens exhaled. "I'm joining Jack Reagan. Oxley has him putting together a network—militias, veterans, local defenders. We'll push back against the cartels, sleeper cells, the criminal gangs, the chaos feeding off the collapse." His eyes hardened. "This is a fight for the soul of our country, our way of life. I intend to win or die trying."

The wind carried the sound of the harbor—engines, gulls, distant voices. Life going on, fragile and defiant.

"We don't get to sit this one out," Stevens said. "Not if we want something worth handing off to our kids."

Hank watched the ambulances disappear toward the hospital and nodded once.

"Then let's win it."

Stevens gave a grim smile. "We have to."

Brackettville, Texas

Jade hesitated at the edge of the hangar, the warm breeze tugging at her hair as if urging her forward. The place smelled of fuel, cedars, and sun-warmed steel. The dry air was burning away the humidity of her enslavement.

She'd lost a lifetime in captivity. Her head was spinning from the rapid transition from slavery to freedom. Her guards moved with quiet purpose around her, but she saw only one man. Uncle Herbstreet. He was decades older, heavier in the middle, but oh-so-real! He was her people!

The big sheriff stood rigid for half a second—then his composure broke. His shoulders shook, once, twice, and he crossed the distance in three long strides. When he pulled her into his arms, it was fierce and protective, like he was afraid she might vanish again.

"Oh God," he said, his voice breaking. "You're here. You're really here."

Jade buried her face in his chest. For the first time since the nightmare began, she felt safe. Then tears flowed. Not quietly. Not politely. She cried like a child who had been lost too long.

"I'm sorry," she whispered. "I tried to be strong."

"You were," Herbstreet said fiercely. "You survived. That's strength."

When she finally pulled back, her eyes were red—but clear. She turned to the others standing nearby.

Jake Hendel gave her a slight, respectful nod. The CIA officers stood a step behind him, faces unreadable. Two Navy SEALs—her rescuers—watched with quiet gravity. Jack Reagan wiped a tear from his eye.

"Thank you," Jade said, her voice steady now. "All of you. You didn't have to come for me."

Jake met her gaze. "Yes, we did. We're promise keepers."

Herbstreet placed himself subtly between her and the world, one hand resting on her shoulder. “No one will ever hurt you again,” he swore. Not a promise. A vow. “Not while I’m breathing.”

Jade looked up at him. “Then teach me.”

He frowned. “Teach you?”

“To fight,” she said. “To defend myself. To never be helpless again.”

Herbstreet searched her face, seeing something new there—something hard, unyielding. Not fear. Purpose.

“America has changed,” Jade continued quietly. “The world’s changed. But the men who did this to me—who did this to others—they’re still out there.”

Her eyes darkened, reflecting something more profound than anger.

“They can’t be allowed to keep breathing,” she said. “Not Carpathian. Not Scheid. Not any of them.”

Silence stretched.

Jake exhaled slowly. “What was taken from you… it doesn’t get erased. But what you choose to do now—that matters.”

Herbstreet nodded once. “I’ll train you,” he said. “Not to become what they are—but to make sure they never retake you.”

Jade straightened, standing taller than she had moments before. Her gaze was unwavering now—burning with a quiet, terrifying clarity. “I’ll train for me,” she said. “And for every woman who didn’t get out.”

The hangar doors stood open behind them, sunlight spilling in. The war for the world wasn’t over. And for Jade, it was personal.

Washington DC

President Novak sat with Oxley by his side in the White House Command Center. The room hummed with controlled chaos—generals hunched over digital maps, aides whispered in tight clusters, the muted thrum of a nation on life support. But in the corner, away from the noise, the two brothers of the Order spoke, the weight of history heavy on their shoulders.

“The whole country is coming apart,” Oxley observed, his voice low but edged with steel. “Now that we’ve dealt with Taiwan, we have war in our streets. The death toll from violence, pandemic, and enemy attacks by foreign operatives has already topped twenty million Americans.”

Novak bit his lip, the lines of exhaustion cutting deep into his face. Less than thirty days into his first term—an unelected president carried into office by crisis—he wondered if the odds were insurmountable. Could he ever restore order, prosperity, and prominence to the country he loved? Had America finally been destroyed?

"We've gotten rid of most of the corruption in Washington," Novak said bitterly. "Hundreds of them defected to China or their offshore havens. I've got a conservative bloc in the House and Senate; martial law grants me unprecedented power… but how do we restore law and order? How do we save what's left?"

Oxley leaned in, his glasses catching the glare from the overhead screens. "We start by admitting this isn't just a war of weapons—it's a war of faith, of culture, of survival. The Cartels are flooding our cities with enemy operatives. The billionaires in Solar Valley are pulling the strings. And Carpathian—" He paused, letting the name hang in the air like a curse. "Carpathian isn't finished. Taiwan was only Act One. The great equity grab is Act Two. Wilhite's plagues combined with war, famine, and the loss of U.S. farming will kill billions within the year."

Novak stared at the blinking red icons on the Situation Map—U.S. cities under siege, ports in flames, airports shut down. His gut clenched.

"Do you think Russia will move on Europe?"

Oxley nodded solemnly, "Karamazov will take full advantage of U.S. and NATO weakness. He's been manufacturing artillery shells, drones, missiles, and ammo around the clock the past year while building up his conscript army and recruiting regulars. Right now, Chinese, North Korean, and Pakistani soldiers are training with Russian forces. Most of his ballistic and attack submarines are at sea. And communications between Beijing and Moscow have increased tenfold. So, yes, he's going to try to take Europe."

Novak didn't react to Oxley's bleak assessment. He donned his eyeglasses, holding a copy of the Presidential Daily Briefing. After reading key sections, the President said, "Walk me through Carpathian's Four Horsemen."

Oxley met his eyes, and for a moment the Director's mask slipped, revealing the dread beneath. "He's referring to the Book of Revelation, The Four Horsemen come in four colors: White, Red, Black, and Pale. The White Horse symbolizes conquest, imperialism, and false peace. It's what was in place under your predecessor. The Red Horse symbolizes war, bloodshed, and conflict. This is the war against the Communist Coalition. This war has the potential to kill billions directly or indirectly. Nuclear war could be quick and devastating, while conventional war could last for years, like in Ukraine. The Black Horse symbolizes famine, economic hardship, and scarcity of essentials. While war always causes many of these ills, we believe Carpathian and his team will exacerbate supply chain shortages and barriers to commerce and exert a never-before-seen level of control over global economics. The Pale Horse, Death, represents mass mortality, the result of the other horsemen plus a global pandemic."

Novak shook his head, chills running down his spine. "Carpathian is apropos of nothing. Is he the antichrist or merely borrowing from scripture?"

A chill ran the length of Oxley's back, causing a slight tremor.

"I could make a compelling case that he is, but let me just give you what we know. We know Carpathian is building a new world order in which Dregodarit will replace all other religions. We know he brought about a miraculous peace in the Middle East. We know that peace is held together by economics and influence that he alone controls. We know Dragon Coin will become the one world currency. We've confirmed his plan and mechanisms for murdering six billion people to bring the earth down to the so-called sustainability level." Oxley said as he looked down sorrowfully. Then his chin rose. "Unless we stop him, the next battlefield won't be Taipei or D.C. It'll be Jerusalem."

The President sat back in his chair, the magnitude of the words crashing over him. "Armageddon. TEOTWAWKI, the end of the world as we know it."

Oxley looked straight into Novak's eyes, held his gaze, then nodded in confirmation.

Outside, dawn was breaking over a wounded capital. The sky bled crimson as if the world itself was bleeding.

Novak whispered, almost to himself, "God help us."

Epilogue

The Situation Room wasn't a single dramatic chamber like in movies. It was a secure suite of spaces located in the basement of the West Wing. The most recognizable component was a compact, windowless conference room with a large rectangular table surrounded by high-backed chairs.

The room had been designed for function over flash: neutral tones, tight spacing, and walls lined with screens showing live intelligence feeds, maps, video calls, and real-time updates from around the world. Lighting was subdued, and every element was engineered for secure, uninterrupted decision-making.

Beyond the conference room, the complex included an operations center staffed 24/7 that monitored global events, intelligence streams, and communications. There were also secure communications spaces that allowed the President and senior leaders to speak instantly with military commanders, embassies, or world leaders. The entire complex was hardened, highly controlled, and packed with redundant systems. It was a quiet, high-tech nerve center where critical decisions were made under pressure.

All but one chair at the table was occupied. Conversations died the instant the doors opened. Heads turned. Some faces were disciplined and unreadable; others were drawn tight, worn down by sleepless nights and a relentless stream of unwelcome news.

Across the far wall, a bank of screens flickered with a living map of collapse—satellite feeds, broken communications grids, troop formations moving with eerie precision. There was nothing random about it.

Africa was being methodically consolidated by Indian, Chinese, and regional military regimes. Eastern Europe burned as a full-scale battlefield. In South America, governments teetered or collapsed as Carpathian-backed factions ignited civil wars. Everywhere, the same pattern emerged: misinformation, manipulation, indoctrination, then control.

Globally, 100 million young people had been swept into the machinery of the New World Order, fed a steady diet of propaganda proclaiming Ethan Carpathian as the planet's savior. Carpathian youth militias swelled. Governments fell. Thirty-day training camps churned out recruits bound for Europe or other hot spots where they could "change the world" one country at a time.

The United States was no longer recognizable. In just sixty days, more than 35 million Americans were dead, not from a single cataclysm, but from a slow, grinding collapse. Disease spread unchecked. Food systems failed. Violence filled the vacuum where order once stood. Hospitals went dark. Supply chains disintegrated. Civilization hadn't shattered; it was eroding, piece by piece.

Even the military was breaking down. Desertion surged as soldiers faced an impossible choice: stand their post for an unraveling nation or go home to protect their families. Nearly a third chose the latter, not out of cowardice, but out of instinct. Blood over duty. Survival over structure.

The President entered, dressed in khaki slacks, a blue Oxford-cloth shirt, and a fleece bearing the presidential seal. President Novak didn't acknowledge anyone as he moved straight to his seat at the center of the table, eyes already locked on the largest screen. No ceremony. No delay.

"Mr. President," Director Oxley began the briefing, rising slightly from his chair. "We've prepared the forecast you requested. Admiral Flint will lead off."

"Let's hear it."

"Sir, the analyses from IISS have proven accurate. Without U.S. support, Europe's critical vulnerabilities have been exposed. These include Intelligence, Surveillance, and Reconnaissance (ISR) gaps, degraded air and missile defense, and insufficient combat mass. As projected, the Communist Coalition opened with a hybrid strike package: sabotage, cyber disruption, drone swarms, disinformation campaigns, and infrastructure attacks. They then made incursions into Estonia and the Baltic islands. NATO's initial response was fragmented and delayed, culminating in a breach along its northeastern flank," Admiral Flint reported.

Novak cut in, his voice sharp. "And the confusion fractured the alliance. Split them between immediate Article 5 action and those pushing for de-escalation?"

Admiral Flint leaned forward. "Yes. Mr. President. While Europe mobilized within 72 hours, without U.S. support, it was effectively blind to enemy movements. That, combined with infighting, slowed NATO decision-making and gave the enemy the freedom to implement a deep penetration maneuver."

Novak shook his head, "Go on."

Flint tapped his controller and brought up a map on the main screen. He continued. "Europe's delay allowed Russia to seize Narva, the Suwałki Gap, and key Baltic islands in a blitzkrieg-style attack. Narva sits on the eastern edge of Estonia, directly on the border with Russia, and is a strategic gateway. The Suwałki Gap is a narrow corridor between Poland and Lithuania, bordered by Kaliningrad (Russia) to the west and Belarus to the east. This is NATO's most vulnerable land link to the Baltic states. Now that it is cut off, Estonia, Latvia, and Lithuania are isolated."

Novak shook his head in disgust.

"Russia also seized two Estonian Islands, Saaremaa and Hiiumaa, and Sweden's Gotland Island, giving them control of naval access to the Gulf of Riga and dominance of the Baltic Sea's air and naval space. Together, these gains form a strategic triangle that allows the Russians to control the Baltic region."

Novak looked at Oxley and asked, "What's CIA's read?"

Oxley waded in, "Russia secured early leverage and shifted the conflict on their terms. Right now, they're positioned to move on Poland, perhaps Finland."

"Where are things now?" Novak asked Flint.

"At present, the war has evolved into an air-and-missile-dominated fight, but Russia and its allies are massing armor, mechanized divisions, and troops near the border. They've also operationalized 12 airfields and 3 ports in captured territory. Unlike Ukraine, Russian supply convoys have trucks with good tires and plenty of fuel to sustain their attack forces." Flint said.

"So, you don't think they'll stall as they did on the verge of taking Kiev?" Novak asked.

"No. They have a robust supply chain now." Flint replied.

"Do we know when they'll attack?" Novak asked.

"Our assets on the inside tell us that they plan to attack Poland within 3 days."

"What can NATO do to stop them?"

The question didn't hang; it dropped, heavy and final, like something already half-answered.

Director Oxley didn't look down at his notes. He didn't need them. "Right now, Europe retains significant ground capability, but NATO air defense networks aren't fully integrated. Munitions stockpiles are being burned faster than they can be replaced. Fuel reserves are critically low. And their aerial refueling capacity is limited without our tankers." He let out a slow breath. "The bottom line is that they can't sustain large-scale operations without U.S. support."

A flicker crossed one of the screens—interceptor tracks failing to meet inbound missiles in time. Red arcs punching through blue lines. Digital images of NATO bases being destroyed.

Admiral Flint leaned forward, forearms on the table. "And they're not fighting as one force. Not anymore." His voice was low, edged with frustration. "With the removal of Supreme Allied Commander Europe, General Christopher G. Gavolin, NATO's centralized command fractured. What used to be a unified response is now a patchwork of national decisions that cause critical delays."

He gestured toward the far end of the table. "I've brought General Gavolin onto our team."

President Novak turned slowly, his gaze locking onto the general like a targeting system acquiring a fix. "How long can they hold?"

General Gavolin didn't answer right away. He leaned forward, hands clasped, the weight of continents behind his eyes. When he spoke, his voice was steady, but it carried the unmistakable gravity of someone who had already run the numbers dozens of times.

"Mr. President… Europe can hold defensive lines for 6 months, assuming no major surprises. No systemic collapse. And no additional loss of fuel." A pause. No one moved. "But holding isn't winning."

His eyes lifted to meet Novak's. "Sustaining a high-intensity war without U.S. support will require roughly 300,000 additional troops, that's dozens of fully equipped brigades, thousands of additional armored vehicles, and a surge in drone and ammo production on a scale they are not currently capable of achieving. Even with all of that, a fuel shortage stops them in their tracks."

The screens shifted to factory outputs, supply lines, and red shortfalls cascading across graphs.

"That's about 250 billion euros annually in additional defense spending," Gavolin continued. "And even if they find the money…" He shook his head once. "Their supply chains aren't deep enough."

Silence settled over the room, thick and suffocating.

"They can delay defeat," he finished quietly. "But they cannot win. Not without us?"

President Novak shifted in his chair, lips pressed thin as the reality took hold behind his eyes; cold, mathematical, unavoidable. Most NATO countries had failed to meet their required investment in their militaries. While the U.S., UK, Poland, and Greece consistently met their commitments, Germany, Italy, and Spain were well below target. Now, Europe would pay dearly for its lack of preparation for war.

"Anything to add, Ox?" Novak asked.

Oxley nodded to Raymond Jones, who proceeded, remote in hand. "Sir, what we're seeing is no longer regional instability. This is coordinated activity across multiple domains, military, cyber, economic, and infrastructure."

The display shifted as Europe filled the screen. Red arcs marked missile paths and Russian advances. Key transport corridors blinked in and out as if the continent itself were struggling to live. One chart showed the sequence of events leading to the current state of affairs: cyber-attack, sleeper cell activation, targeting of infrastructure, including hospitals, commando raids to seize key bridges and air bases, rapidly moving mechanized columns and tank brigades supported by large-scale artillery and rocket attacks. While helicopter gunships were widely used along the front, the Russians had held back 80% of their fighters and bombers, using uncrewed aircraft instead. We think they're holding back their manned aircraft to support a deep penetration drive into the heart of Europe."

Several heads shook as foreheads creased.

"As General Gavolin stated, forward NATO units are holding, but they're operating under degraded conditions, limited ISR, constrained air support, and logistical strain. A fuel crisis is rapidly emerging in Europe, while Russia has up to 18 months of fuel in reserve. Russia is training 100,000 30-day wonders each month, volunteers marginally trained in weapons, squad tactics, communications, and first aid. With the Carpathian youth movement gaining ground, these numbers could double or triple in the next six months. Chinese troops and units from 12 countries are rapidly increasing their ranks. Not to mention the damage their sleeper cells and Islamic terrorist units are doing in Europe. 128 Churches and 35 Synagogues burned to the ground. 139 municipal water systems are contaminated. 156 municipal power stations bombed. 12 fuel depots destroyed. They're having a logistical and psychological impact well beyond their numbers."

Novak considered that sleeper cell attacks had effectively disrupted the US domestic supply chain and caused widespread power outages. He leaned back slightly, hands folded. "Air picture."

Admiral Flint said, "Mixed, Mr. President. While our allies have highly capable aircraft and pilots, they're flying blind. Limited air refueling capability restricts their range, reduced radar surveillance increases combat losses, and heavy missile saturation limits sorties. They're encountering a new generation of surface-to-air missiles with longer range and greater accuracy than anything we've seen before. Last week, the Poles lost four fighters to handheld surface-to-air missiles. They can't keep trading pilots who take years to train and planes that cost millions for cheap missiles."

A new image replaced the map. It showed airfields, some blackened, others smoldering.

"Key forward airbases were hit early. Aircraft losses on the ground were higher than anticipated due to commando raids and sabotage by sleeper cells. The Russians also used Iranian drones as hunter-killers, dropping grenades and incendiary devices."

Novak's jaw tightened. "Naval?"

"Degraded readiness across multiple fleets," Flint replied. "Maintenance cycles, delayed refits… we're seeing the consequences now of the European's underspending. Subsurface capability remains, but numbers are limited. Surface operations are increasingly contested. And the Baltic is lost."

Novak exhaled slowly. Should he try to save them?

Novak didn't look away. "How long?" he asked.

A long pause ensued as glances shot between Jones, Oxley, Flint, and Gavolin. Oxley and Flint looked to Gavolin to continue.

Gavolin chose his words carefully. "It's a logistics game that favors the Russians. At the current operational tempo, NATO ammunition will be depleted in 6 months. Fuel reserves could be exhausted sooner.

Without the US supplementing both, I give them 6 months. Then, they either turn Europe over to Ivan or go nuclear."

The prospect of nuclear war put a chill in the room. It has all happened so quickly. Six months ago, a Russian invasion of Europe was only a war game.

Novak asked, "What about Buck Rogers?"

Flint replied, "Mr. President, we took a look at what we could do with Space Force."

"Results?" Novak probed.

"Space Force could strike Russian nuclear silos with beam weapons, but we believe it would prompt Ivan to launch. Plus, we lost a lot of beam capability against China. I think it's best that we reserve our remaining unmanned platforms for homeland defense and bring our astronauts home while we retain capability."

"What about missile and drone attacks? AWS?" Novak asked.

"We used up 80% of our AWS capabilities against the Chinese. Our long and mid-range conventional missile systems are down to 30% of normal reserves. Our defense contractors can't shift to full-war production fast enough to provide what's needed in Europe, and we need what we have left for homeland defense," Flint offered.

Silence settled over the room, not shock, but confirmation.

Across the table, Jake Hendel hadn't spoken. He wasn't looking at the same things as everyone else. He was watching the pattern.

"Mr. President," Hendel said finally, his voice cutting through the room without raising in volume, "We need to think outside the box."

Novak turned. "Go on."

Hendel stood and stepped closer to the screens.

"Look at the sequencing," he said. "Economic and infrastructure disruption, first. A global propaganda campaign. A major war with China that drained our resources. Global pandemics that play like biological warfare. Coordinated attacks by sleeper cells targeting critical resources across Western countries. Then, ground warfare across the globe."

He pointed, not at a specific location, but across several zones.

"It's layered. Deliberate. Designed to blind, isolate, and overwhelm before a coordinated response can form. Carpathian and Sheid control 80% of Europe's fuel, raw materials, and supplies, knowing that NATO can't last more than 6 months without U.S. support. Carpathian has introduced autonomous weapons systems, advanced missiles, and drones into the European conflict on the side of Russia."

Flint, Oxley, and Jones nodded in agreement.

Jake continued, "Moving outward, Goebbels' social media campaigns and Carpathian's global satellite network, which controls 90% of global media, have led 83% of people under 30 to buy into the New World Order. They see Carpathian as the savior of the planet, and they have little to lose, no money, high unemployment, and desperation."

Flint, Gavolin, and Novak all nodded in agreement.

Novak said, "Go on."

"When Carpathian's electric AWS systems are in mass production, they won't need petroleum. This is perfect for Europe and oil-poor regions, while effective in all theaters. And those EVs are much faster and more economical to produce than those of the U.S. and our allies. Right now, he is manufacturing 250,000 military EVs a month. AWS drones, land attack platforms, and sea platforms." Jake paused reading the room, then continued, "Then, there are his youth zealots, 90-day wonders, who could number 20 million within the year. All this changes the calculus of war."

The National Security Advisor leaned forward. "You're saying this was planned end-to-end, one well-orchestrated operation on a global scale? That the countries are mere pawns on his chessboard?"

"I'm saying it was engineered to promote Carpathian's agenda. The Four Horsemen strategy is real, and the death count is rising by tens of millions daily. Right now, we have over 90 shooting wars and revolutions underway. Terrorist actions across the globe are up 1,000%. Broken supply chains are killing hundreds of millions. And biological weapons could increase deaths exponentially. Carpathian is bringing the world down to the so-called carrying capacity of 2 billion people while destroying any countries that don't bow at his altar," Hendel replied.

A long silence resulted from Jake's analysis. The CIA operative and world-class journalist had connected the dots. His conclusions were terrifying.

Finally, Novak asked, "What makes you think Carpathian has that kind of power?"

"He has the people on his side. Across all age groups globally, Carpathian commands an astonishing 73% favorable rating, according to respected firms such as Gallup, Pew Research Center, and Ipsos. Even traditionally skeptical audiences have shifted. These major pollsters report an unprecedented surge in trust and support for his vision of a green new world order."

Oxley added, "I agree with Jake, Carpathian is as slick as Satan himself. Worse, he and his team are executing on their plan at an unprecedented rate."

An uneasy silence fell. It was broken when Jack Reagan spoke up, "There's been a noticeable increase in financial transactions between Carpathian-aligned nations and the Communist Coalition. Currently, the Communists have access to petroleum at ten times the rate of our European allies. They also possess a more robust supply chain in all areas."

Novak studied him. "I understand the oil situation and Carpathian's youth movement, but where is he manufacturing weapons? We destroyed 90% of China's manufacturing capacity."

Reagan said, "While China was dealt a setback, American Military Industrialist Jermey Prime controls over 172 manufacturing plants across 60 countries. Prime is one of Carpathian's 12 disciples. More evidence that this was preplanned."

Hendel hesitated—not from uncertainty, but from the weight of the answer. "Mr. President, we're looking at more than a coalition of nations," he said. "We're looking at the coordinating intelligence behind them."

A quiet shift moved through the room. Everyone understood what that implied.

"You believe Carpathian is orchestrating everything, that he's the…?" Novak stopped short of stating what the ancient prophecies had said, then continued, "de facto leader of an emerging global superpower?"

Hendel didn't answer immediately. Instead, he nodded toward the screens.

"Ask a simpler question," he said. "Who benefits if global systems fracture and Carpathian's team controls world currency? Whose plan is fulfilled if 6 billion perish? Who comes out on top if Western countries fail and his party takes control of the 169 nations the polls indicate are shifting allegiance toward the new world order?"

No one spoke. They didn't need to.

Novak leaned forward again, elbows on the table now. "Walk me through it."

Hendel's voice remained steady. "Total collapse leads to chaos beyond control. However, controlled instability opens opportunities. Markets become unstable. Governments are weakened. Financial systems no longer function as they used to. Alliances break apart. Those who can influence these fractures and meet demand," he paused, "wield control over the world without declaring war. It's a form of domination through manipulation—pitting nations against each other, soldiers against soldiers, children against their parents. It's about ideological persuasion, convincing people to join him—the wealthy turn to him to protect what they have. The hope of betterment draws the less fortunate. And both Sheid and Carpathian have solutions for each."

Novak responded, "So, Carpathian sets the agenda, Sheid funds it, Goebbels sells it, and Prime makes the weapons for his global power grab?"

The room was still. Even the screens seemed quieter.

"Carpathian's four horsemen?" Novak observed as he stood. Not abruptly. Not dramatically. But with purpose. "It's brilliant. Diabolical. Biblical. And far too real. What are our options?" he asked.

The room shifted instantly.

Flint began, "Option one: escalate support to NATO partners—intelligence sharing, logistics coordination, force posture adjustments, parts and fuel, troops where possible."

"Risk?"

"We lose more capability at home. The current desertion rate is drawing us down every day, and we need our limited supply of high-tech ordnance and assets to defend the homeland."

Novak nodded. "Next."

"Option two: strategic restraint. Focus on domestic stabilization. Destroy the sleeper cells and terrorists here. Restore infrastructure at home, secure supply chains, and reinforce Homeland security. Get the economy working again. Recover so we can live to fight another day, then help our remaining allies."

"Risk?"

"We concede momentum abroad. Lose Europe." Flint said solemnly.

Novak nodded resolutely, "Next."

"Option three is a hybrid approach—limited external support while prioritizing resilience and war preparation at home."

Novak looked around the table. No perfect answers. Only trade-offs. He looked back at the screens, studying the fractured map of the world.

"Here's what I know," he said quietly. "If Jake is right, this isn't about winning a battle or even a continent." He turned back to them. "It's about determining who controls humanity's future."

No one disagreed.

"Then we respond accordingly," Novak continued. "We harden what we can, stabilize what we must, and put America First because if we fail to save America, the world slips into the abyss."

He looked directly at Hendel. "Jake, find a way to cut the head off the snake. I want you to take out Carpathian and his disciples before it's too late."

About the Author

Kent Giles writes military techno-thrillers rooted in real-world warfare, espionage tradecraft, and historical intelligence. His novels are built on verified research, operational logic, and the harsh realities faced by those who operate in the shadows.

Known for his detailed portrayal of military strategy, advanced technology, and global conflict, Giles novels have drawn favorable comparisons to Tom Clancy's Jack Ryan series, Vince Flynn's Mitch Rapp novels, and Brad Thor's Scot Harvath series.

His debut, Red Sky at Morning, earned a loyal following among military professionals, law enforcement, and preparedness communities for its tactical accuracy and disciplined storytelling. Operation Grey Wolf and Escape of the Grey Wolf, the second book in the Burke Eieger series, explore previously undisclosed World War II espionage, Nazi Germany's nuclear ambitions, and the rise of the Fourth Reich—not as a military power, but as a covert economic force. Dragon Rising delivers a fact-based, high-intensity march toward Armageddon, spanning the clash between Western and Communist powers, globalist economic warfare, media manipulation, and biblical prophecy.

Giles' deep background in global finance and geopolitics, gained from stints as a senior manager at four of the world's top consulting firms, brings an uncommon level of credibility. An expert marksman, martial artist, and outdoorsman, Kent writes combat and survival from personal experience—the way professionals recognize it: precise, brutal, and unforgiving. His vast network provides him with insights into the shadow world few know exists.

Kent Giles lives in the mountains of North Georgia with his wife, Ginger.

Other Books by Kent Giles

Operation Grey Wolf

Escape of the Grey Wolf

Red Sky at Morning

Protect this House

For more information and content, go to:

kentgiles.com

www.ingramcontent.com/pod-product-compliance
Lightning Source LLC
LaVergne TN
LVHW090550110826
845146LV00001B/91

* 9 7 9 8 9 9 4 5 0 3 8 0 5 *